A 747 WAS TRYING TO LAND ON MY BACK . . .

. . . anyhow, that was the way it sounded. I whirled—a long black hovercraft tore down the street, coming my way fast. Six feet above the ground, the monster covered blocks in seconds, sending a hideous roar ahead—and a shower of sparks as bullets sang around my ears.

I ran up the endless drive; bullet-shredded paving stung my ankles. I was almost to the door when ragged holes appeared in it, an erratic hem-stitch working in my direction.

My face slammed into the door as the bullets slammed into my body. The door opened and a man dragged me inside.

He had a very familiar face . . . **mine.**

THE
Probability Broach

L. Neil Smith

A Del Rey Book

BALLANTINE BOOKS • NEW YORK

TO CYNTHY, who will always be Clarissa to me—and to Robert Heinlein, whom I don't know, and Bob LeFevre, whom I do, with admiration, affection, and a deeper gratitude than I dare try to express.

I am also indebted to Ursula Le Guin, for her useful and (at least to me) very attractive term "propertarian." In return, may I commend to her attention the essays collected in Capitalism and the Historians, edited by F. A. Hayeck?

Contents

I:	The Noonday Gun	1
II:	Anarchy 'n' Order	9
III:	MacDonald's Farm	17
IV:	Second Prize, **Two** Weeks	25
V:	Over the Rainbow	36
VI:	Retaliatory Force	50
VII:	The Looking Glass	60
VIII:	Night of the Long Knife	70
IX:	The Constitution Conspiracy	79
X:	Shots in the Dark	90
XI:	The Eye in the Pyramid	105
XII:	Necktie Party	114
XIII:	The Meiss Connection	124
XIV:	Meeting With Madison	134
XV:	Breaking & Entering	146
XVI:	Balance of Madness	158
XVII:	Helium Heroics	170
XVIII:	Congress Shall Make No Law	183
XIX:	State of Emergency	199
XX:	A Matter of Honor	213
XXI:	Escape Velocity	225
XXII:	Surprise Party	233
XXIII:	Deadly Window	242
XXIV:	The Second of July	255
	Appendix: A Brief Historical Outline	265

My movement to the Chair of Government will be accompanied by feelings not unlike those of a criminal who is going to the place of his execution.

—George Washington
February 4, 1789

I: The Noonday Gun

Tuesday, July 7, 1987

Another sweltering Denver summer. A faded poster was stapled crookedly to the plywood door of an abandoned fast-food joint at the corner of Colfax and York:

CLOSED BY ORDER OF THE UNITED STATES GOVERNMENT
The Secretary of Energy Has Determined That This Unit Represents An Unjustifiable Expenditure of Our Nation's Precious And Dwindling Energy Reserves.   DOE 568-90-3041

Through its soot-grimy windows I could see them stirring sluggishly—panhandlers keeping out of the sun. Me, I was roasting in the parking lot, my battered department-issue Plymouth settling slowly to its hubcaps in the hot asphalt. Pushing a flavorless brown-bag lunch into my face, I wished vainly for a cigar and rehearsed my vast repertoire of excuses.

Things had started out rotten, breakfast interrupted by a call to a dilapidated Emerson Street garage. Somebody had strung up a corpse from the rafters, gutted and skinned it like a deer. The carcass had bled into a galvanized bucket on the floor and the skin was folded neatly over a straight-backed kitchen chair, the kind you usually find in garages, missing two rungs and held together with picture wire. The morning air had that breathless, anticipatory feel, promising a hundred degrees or more. It had made a fair start in

1

that garage, the usual cobwebs and motor oil were rapidly losing out to a cloying slaughterhouse odor.

This afternoon would be even more fun, explaining to the *News-Post* and assorted microphones—not to mention my division chief—why the patrolmen who had found the body during a routine curfew bust had puked all over the evidence. Shit, I'd almost done it myself.

I looked down at my sandwich and shuddered.

My stomach was giving me hell, anyway. Twenty-seven years on the force, and now the pain was creeping down my left arm into the wrist. Maybe it was the crummy hours, the awful food. Maybe it was worrying all the time: cancer; minipox; encountering an old friend in a packet of black-market lunchmeat. Maybe it was a depression they wouldn't call by its right name, or seeing old folks begging in the streets. Maybe I just watched too many doctor shows.

Forty-eight was the right age to worry, though, especially for a cop. Oh, I'd tried keeping in shape: diets, exercise, vitamins before they got too risky. But after Evelyn had split, it just seemed like a lot of trouble. I did manage to stay off coffee, quite a feat in a line of work that revolves around a station-house urn.

Nineteen years in homicide and the sight of human intestines piled on a gritty concrete floor could still turn me inside-out. Well, it's better than getting callous. Now as the sun baked my car top, fumes from a beat-up city bus were ruining what little appetite I had left. I missed my mealtime cigars, and couldn't quite tell whether the little carton of milk in my hand was starting to sour. Somehow it's worse, not knowing.

Most of all I longed to take off my sodden jacket, but the public's supposed to panic at the sight of a shoulder holster. I knew that sweat was eating at the worn, nonregulation Smith & Wesson .41 Magnum jammed into my left armpit. The leather harness was soaked, the dingy elastic cross-strap slowly rasping through the heat rash on the back of my neck.

If it were only—hell, make that *five* years ago. A man could enjoy a sanitary lunch in an air-conditioned booth. Now, CLOSED BY ORDER signs flapped on half the doors downtown; the other half, it seemed, had been shut by "economic readjustment." And unlicensed air conditioning was a stiffer rap than hoarding silver.

The bus at the corner gasped to a start, filling my car with blue smoke. Shouldn't have parked so near the street, damn it. I'd had my choice in the empty, litter-strewn lot. I gave up on lunch, wadding up the wrappers, when the radio, its jabber ignored until now, began talking about me:

"Five Charlie Nineteen, respond Code Three, possible homicide, southwest corner of Sixteenth and Gaylord." That's me, of course, better known to everybody but dispatchers as Lieutenant Edward W. Bear. The *W* is for William, but thanks to that son of a bitch A. A. Milne and a world full of funny-people, I settle for Win.

"Five Charlie Nineteen . . ." I threw the papers on the back seat and started the engine. It coughed asthmatically and a surge of adrenalin washed through me as it caught. Horn honking, I dipped and scraped into Colfax, spilling the half-empty milk carton on the floor. I cut across sparse traffic—squealing brakes and cursing bicyclists—roared an illegal hundred yards the wrong way up York, swerved left through a parking lot to Gaylord, and tore away in a wake of siren wail and swirling red light.

It was only another block. Four scuffed black-and-whites straddled the street, their lightbars blinking round and round by a littered curb fronting a crumbling neighborhood mosque that had seen previous duty as a Mexican Catholic church. Short of wind, I shrugged out of the car.

A body lay half-propped against the wall, blood streaming across cracked cement into the gutter. "What do we have here," I asked the patrol sergeant, "another VN-Arab rumble?" He shook his head and I remembered with embarrassment that he was an Arab himself. "Sorry, Moghrabi—just a bad day, today."

"Worse for *him*, Lieutenant." The victim—late twenties—lay clutching his middle, as if to keep his guts from falling out. He had good reason to try, stitched from hip to shoulder the way he was. A gap in the closely grouped pockmarks on the wall above said he had fallen where he'd been shot. In one outstretched hand was a stainless-steel snubbie. No punk's gun, anyway. A Bianchi holster identical to mine was exposed by his blood-soaked jacket.

I looked down at the curb. Sure enough, a brassy glittering in the wind-blown trash: two dozen spent cartridges. I levered one onto the end of a pencil: .380 Auto. That'd make it an Ingram machine pistol. Very fancy.

Lab people were arriving with evidence kits and VCR, uniforms herding up potential witnesses. I'd see their reports later, not that it would do much good: this wasn't as down-and-out as Denver neighborhoods get, but the stiff against the wall was Mr. Collegiate Affluence, despite the gun in his hand, and that meant silence from the citizens. Or lies.

Moghrabi had been keeping busy, supplying translations. He nodded at a patrolman and jogged over. "We've got something, a late-model white station wagon, Brazilian make. Want an APB?"

"Better wait. Probably dozens of station wagons still running in this town. Anything else?"

"The car's about the only thing they all agree on. You know witnesses. What about the victim?"

I shrugged. "They're still preserving everything for posterity over there. Let me know if you get anything else." He nodded, heading back where uniformed officers were trading broken Arabic for broken English. I got an okay from the video techs, bent over the body, and gently pried the revolver from its stiffening fingers. Ruger Security Six, like I'd figured. I opened the cylinder; dimples in four of the primers twinkled up at me. Four shots fired, Norma .357 hollowpoints. If any had connected, we'd be finding another corpse, possibly in worse shape than this one.

"Hey, Lieutenant?" A probationer hailed me from the middle of the street. On the other side, a meatwagon had joined the laboratory van. "Look what we found! We were measuring tire-marks and spotted all this *stuff* . . ." I rose stiffly, trying to ignore my knees. "Hey, Lieutenant, do you think—"

"Not when I can avoid it." It took an effort not to add "son." His fresh-scrubbed eager-beaver looks clashed with the patched and faded department-issue hand-me-downs. I bent forward, grunting under my breath. Why does evidence always fall *down?* Then I remembered this morning's ornament, hanging from a garage ceiling, and almost lost my spoiled-mayonnaise sandwich.

The sight in the street didn't help: scattered glass; blood all over the fragments, *splashed.* Those hollow-points had connected, all right. Might even be some brains scrambled into this mess if I looked hard enough. I resisted the urge. "Moghrabi!" I gestured that he should avoid walking through the evidence. "Sarge, you can have your APB, now. That station wagon'll be missing windows."

He nodded, heading for his radio. I went back to the body again, with a little more respect. His travel permit said he was one Meiss, Vaughn L., from Fort Collins, sixty miles to the north. His work assignment: Colorado State University. As a PH.D. on the Physics faculty, he rated his own wheels and the fuel to roll them. Car keys and parking lot receipt I handed to the sergeant, who would hand them to a patrolman, who would dig up the heap and hand it to the lab people. It's called "channels."

They'd find candy wrappers, Kleenex, an ashtray full of illicit butts or roaches, probably not much else. They always had hopes, of course: half a ton of Laetrile or Ever-Clear.

Presumably Meiss had parked nearby. There was never any shortage of space these days, and it was too damned hot to walk very far, especially for a small-town boy visiting the Big Heatsink. Which brought up a question: why does a cow-college professor end up soaking his B-negative or whatever into a Denver sidewalk, a roscoe in his fist that would stop a small locomotive?

The ambulance was ready to take our client to the taxidermists downtown. One of the techs passed by with a collection of plastic baggies containing personal effects. "Hold on. Let me see that." He handed over a bright golden disk, larger than the silver dollars I remembered from childhood, in deep relief a picture of a bald-headed old coot with ruffles at his throat:

ALBERT GALLATIN
1761 C.E.–A.L. 76
REVOLUTIONIST, PRESIDENT, SCHOLAR OF
LIBERTY

On the other side, an old-fashioned hillbilly whiskey jug, and forest-covered hills behind:

ONE METRIC OUNCE
GOLD 999 FINE
THE LAPORTE INDUSTRIAL BANK, LTD.

Was this what the shooting was about—a couple thousand neobucks? Maybe if there were more . . . It felt cool in my hand, a solid, comforting weight. Gold, legally kosher a few brief years ago, was presently hotter than vitamin C, and—

"Coin collecting, Bear?" I jumped despite myself, jerked back nearly thirty years to the Colorado Law Enforcement Training Academy. I turned resignedly to confront Oscar Burgess, several years my senior and small-arms instructor during my academy days. While I had slogged from rookie to patrolman, from investigator to homicide lieutenant, he'd left CLETA for Alcohol, Tobacco, and Firearms during its heyday in the early eighties, and now was Denver station chief for the Federal Security Police.

The years had only refined our mutual distaste. Where I was . . . let's say "heavy-set," he was gray and lean, cat-fast, with a frightening moon-map of a face, the hideous legacy of minipox. Behind him, his crew in fresh-creased jumpsuits brandished automatic shotguns. Their unit crest was emblazoned on the side of a black and scarlet van: a mailed fist grasping the naked edges of a dagger, blood creeping out between the fingers.

"I'll take that!" he said. I handed him the coin, trying not to make it meekly. "Got a smoke?" he asked. I started to reach for my shirt pocket, but recovered quickly. It was an old BATF trick, getting a citizen to betray himself out of generous reflex. He leered knowingly at my reddening face.

"What brings SecPol into a simple street killing, Burgess?"

He hooked a negligent thumb toward the grisly symbol on the van. "You ought to know better than to ask foolish questions. We're thinking about preempting this case—National Security. When the papers come through, you'll have to turn everything over to us and go back to busting jaywalkers." He grinned and watched his men confronting mine, knuckles white on holstered pistol grips all around.

"Didn't realize there was a full moon last night, Oscar," I said. He turned back, puzzled. I pointed to a tiny cut on his pock-marked forehead, dried blood at the edges. "Cut yourself shaving?"

He whitened. "Mind your own stinking business, Bear, or I'll have you back working curfew violations!"

"You and whose army, Fed?"

"I don't *need* an army, flatfoot!" I caught a glimpse of the ancient Luger he wore cross-draw at the waist. Then he let his jacket drop and flipped the coin at me as if tipping a bellboy. "Take good care of this. I'll be looking for it when we take over. Withholding precious metals is antisocial . . . and good for about forty in Leavenworth!" He laughed and stalked off to gather up his thugs.

The technician gave me an argument, but I signed six different forms and took the coin, to be surrendered at Properties tomorrow, on pain of pain. Eventually it would wind up in some bureaucrat's pocket, or melted down to feed a multiquadrillion neobuck federal deficit. Probably the former.

Shuffling through the wallet contents, I also took a small brown textured business card like one I'd seen somewhere before, if I could only remember . . . of course: one of the computer people downtown. That department number-fumbler and the late Dr. Meiss were both genuine, card-carrying crackpots:

> This card signifies that Vaughn L. Meiss is a Sustaining member of the COLORADO PROPERTA-RIAN PARTY, "The Party of Principle." Issue date: December 16, 1985. Issuing officer: Jenny Noble, State Director.

The address where Meiss had been going? State Propertarian Headquarters, by odd coincidence just catty-corner from the asphalt desert where I'd lunched on Swiss cheese and diesel fumes not an hour earlier.

II: Anarchy 'n' Order

I headed back for Colfax, easing over the worst of the chuckholes and weed-grown cracks, remembering predictions that if another Democrat were elected, there'd be grass growing in the streets within four years. They were a year ahead of schedule, but the Republicans could have done it cheaper.

In fame and influence, Propertarians stand somewhere between the Socialist Workers' Party and the Independent Americans. Politically they stand somewhere between H. L. Mencken and Alpha Centauri. Geographically they stand at the corner of Colfax and York, in a sleazy second-story office that would send Phil Marlowe bitching to the landlord. I parked in back and walked around to a grubby little five-by-five with pretensions of lobbyhood. The elevator, DOE Permit 86-5009, had a folding brass baby-gate and a control lever Joseph Conrad might have used to signal his engineer belowdecks.

It surged dizzily, then gasped to a halt, letting me into a narrow, bad-smelling hallway. Fossilized houseplants hung in a dirt-streaked front window, and the signs along the corridor—CITIZENS FOR COMMUNAL ENERGY and MIND-POWER OF THE COSMOS—promised I'd wind up either nationalized or *cleared*.

Finally I found COLORADO PROPERTARIAN PARTY. Underneath, the Bill of Rights was thumbtacked to the door, stamped diagonally in red: **Void Where Prohibited By Law.** I was a little puzzled. That computer-jockey had me believing that Propertarians practice a sort of hedonistic conservatism—or conservative hedonism—demanding, for example, that gun laws and drug laws *both* be repealed—and wouldn't *that* be exciting for a while? So why did they settle here, with every two-bit Love-A-Tree-And-Seize-The-Means-Of-Production nut-group in the state? Must be the rent.

The door swung in at a touch. I followed it, saying, "Knock-knock!" in a stage voice. A neatly bearded young man appeared from the back, looking me over. "Can I help you?"

"Lieutenant Win Bear," I said, doing a Jack Webb with my badge-holder. "Can I see whoever's in charge?"

He stiffened microscopically. "Er—I'm Jon Carpenter, and no one's in charge here—we're *Propertarians.*"

"Okay, who do I see about one of your people getting killed?" I found the card. "A Vaughn L. Meiss . . . ?"

He swallowed hard but came up game. "You'll want Jenny. Hold on a minute."

The place was freshly painted and didn't smell of piss like the rest of the building. It was brightly decorated with posters: "ILLEGITIMATE AUTHORITY" IS A REDUNDANCY and TAXATION IS THEFT! A small desk with a telephone and answering machine occupied one corner beside a rack of pamphlets. I could hear the illegal rumble of an air conditioner. First time I'd been comfortable all day.

A woman entered, tall and slender, thirtyish, lots of curly auburn hair and freckles. She wore the jacket to a woman's business suit and faded bluejeans, a lapel button declaring I Am Not a National Resource! "I'm Jennifer Noble. Vaughn is *dead?*"

"I'm afraid so."

Her color drained, she sat heavily on a corner of the desk, staring down at the floor. Presently she looked up again, composed. "What happened?"

"We found him at Sixteenth and Gaylord about an hour ago, shot to death." Ordinarily, I'm supposed to ask the questions, but I play a lot by ear. "I need some information. Maybe some of your people here . . ." I nodded toward the rear where faces were piling up in the doorway.

She brushed back a stray curl and squared her

shoulders. "I'll try to help. What can I tell you, Officer?"

"Lieutenant. Were you expecting Meiss at your headquarters today?"

She nodded. "Executive Committee Meeting. He's not on the Execom, but he called to say he had important news 'for the Party and all of us as individuals.' That's precisely the way he put it. He called me again last night to make sure the meeting was still on, and said exactly the same thing: something that would change everything 'for the Party and for all of us as individuals.' We'd almost given up on him by now—two hours is *late,* even by Anarchist Standard Time . . ." She trailed off, realizing all over again what had happened, visibly determined to hold back the tears.

"Tell me . . . Jenny, is it? I'm Win, Win Bear. Did he always carry a gun, or was something worrying him —maybe whatever he wanted to tell you?"

Jenny covered the two steps across the tiny room, got a chair, and put it beside the desk. "Would you like to sit down, Win? This might take a little while. Vaughn sounded, well, *conspiratorial,* but also enormously pleased about something. He did have one pretty constant worry, but that's an old story, and I'll get to it. And yes, he carried a gun. It was his philosophy, you see."

"Philosophy? I didn't know Propertarians were into violent revolution."

She smiled slightly and shook her head. "Not yet. Anyway, the government *gave* him that gun in the first place."

"How's that?"

"He'd worked on something, some government secret. After he stopped, I guess they forgot to collect it, or maybe he still had information to protect. But he *resented* getting a gun from them, because—"

"You folks don't like getting *anything* from the government?"

"Or *giving* them anything, either." She smiled, "but it wasn't that. Not this time. Look, can you stand a very brief lecture? It'll clear things up a little."

"When I get tired of it, I'll take a nap." I grinned. "It's nice and cool in here, and the first chance I've had all day to sit down."

She grinned back, which was enjoyable. "Would you like a drink? Coffee or Coke or something? Well then, I guess I'll start. You see, we Propertarians really try to live by our philosophy—*philosophies,* I should say. Oh, we all agree on fundamentals, but there are actually two main schools: the minarchists and the anarchocapitalists."

"Minarchists and ? . . ."

"Anarchocapitalists. I'll get to them. Anyway, Propertarians believe that all human rights are *property* rights, beginning with absolute ownership of your own life."

"The IRS might give you an argument." Actually, I'd heard this before. Surprising how much more interesting it was, coming from a pretty girl. "But it sounds reasonable for starters."

"It does? You'd be amazed how many people feel they belong to someone or something else: their families, jobs, God, the government. Anyway, every other individual right comes from that fundamental one: to own your own life. Since no one is entitled to interfere with it, just as you may not interfere with others', some Propertarians want a government whose only function is protecting everybody's rights—"

"I thought that's what we have now."

She laughed a little bitterly. "If that were only true! Even our limited governmentalists would reduce the state by 99 percent: no more taxes, no more conservation laws, no limits on the market. They call themselves 'minarchists' because that's what they want: a much smaller government, restricted to preventing interference with individual rights instead of being the chief interferer. This depression, the so-called energy crisis—they're *caused* by government interference!"

I nodded, wondering if any of these subversives had a smoke I could borrow.

"Anarchocapitalists"—she reached across to the literature rack, pulling out a paperback: *Toward A New Liberty,* by Mary Ross-Byrd—"don't want *any* government. 'That government is best which governs least; the goverment which governs least is *no government at all*.' "

"Which has what to do with Meiss?" I asked, trying to get back on track.

"It's why he carried a gun, and why he resented getting it from SecPol. A free, unregulated *laissez-faire* market should, and can, take care of everything government *claims* to do, only better, cheaper, and without wrecking individual lives in the process: national defense, adjudication, pollution control, fire protection, and police—no offense. Vaughn felt an ethical obligation to provide for his own physical security. Like Mary Ross-Byrd says, 'Take nothing from government; give nothing to government—the state does not exist!' I hope you won't start arresting Propertarians now—I mean for carrying weapons. Vaughn was just a little more consistent than most."

"Or a little more fanatic." I replied. "Jenny, *I* didn't pass the Confiscation Act, and I feel the same about dope and tobacco: just don't wave them around in public so I *have* to bust you. Hell, I even— Oh, for godsake, do you have a cigarette? I'm going into convulsions!"

She shuffled through a drawer, coming up with a pack of dried-out Players, hand-imported from north-of-the-border. I lit one gratefully and settled back to let the dizziness pass. "If you repeat this, I'll call you a liar. My hide's been saved at least twice by civilians—people who figured we might be on the same side. Totally forgot to arrest them for weapons possession afterward. Must be getting senile."

"Vaughn's gun didn't do him much good, though."

I shrugged. "Not against a machine pistol. Yes, that's what it was. The thing about gun laws, if you're gonna risk breaking them, it might as well be for something potent. The law only raises the ante. Look at how airport metal-detectors turned hijackers onto bombs. If it's any consolation, it looks like your professor managed to take at least one of his attackers with him."

"I'd rather he'd made it to the meeting," she said grimly.

"I was hoping you'd have some idea who did it. You people having any feuds?" I thumbed back toward a hallway full of very non-Propertarian organizations.

She smiled. "We're not that important. I sometimes wonder what'll happen when the government or organized crime begins to understand what we're getting at . . . But no, I don't know who did it, Win. I wish I did."

"Were you particularly close to Meiss?"

"We just went out a couple times, otherwise I didn't see him much except at Party meetings. Not at all the last few months. I was surprised when he called."

"You said he was worried about something?"

"That's one reason I thought he might have dropped out. He told me, when he first joined, that it wouldn't make certain people very happy. Security and all that. Later on, after he'd quit classified work, he implied that they might not let him wander around with all that secret information. It was kind of a sick joke: they'd given him a gun to defend himself, and . . ."

"He might have to use it on the people who gave it to him?"

"That kind of thing really does happen," she said.

I was thinking about Oscar Burgess, but nodded toward the literature rack. "You'd know more about it than I do." I fished around in my jacket, pulled out the Gallatin coin. "Ever see one of these?"

She smoothed the plastic wrapper and turned it over, raising her eyebrows. "Gold, isn't it? Feels heavy enough."

"You think Meiss was a hoarder . . . even a pusher? I've heard you people think a lot of gold and silver."

She shook her head. "I wouldn't know. Propertarians advocate hard money, but since the new currency laws were passed, they keep their mouths shut about what they have. I never heard Vaughn mention gold."

"You wouldn't know if he had more of these?"

"I don't know. I wish *I* had some."

"So do I. Any idea who this Gallatin was?"

"The name sounds vaguely familiar. Ask Jon—he might know . . ." She was starting to droop a little. Reaction was setting in. I stood up.

"Okay, Jenny, could I have a word with the others, one at a time? I'll get out of your way as soon as I can."

She smiled again. "Don't worry about it. They'll be anxious to help. You take your time." She turned for the door.

"Jenny—something else I'll deny saying if you repeat it: Meiss knew he was going to die, but he stayed cool enough to pull the trigger four times. I disagree with nearly everything you believe, but if you're all like that, there'll be Propertarians in the White House someday."

She looked at me as if for the first time, then grinned and patted me on the cheek. "We'll make an anarchocapitalist out of you yet, Lieutenant." She tucked the Mary Ross-Byrd paperback into my jacket pocket and walked out of the room.

Four of the directors didn't know Meiss except to see him at Party functions. Mary Lou Mulligan, a lady banker who'd quit after the '84 Currency Acts, had gone out with Meiss, but all he'd ever talk about was physics—and Jenny.

Jon Carpenter knew about Gallatin, though. In the 1790s, he'd talked a bunch of angry Pennsylvanians out of stringing up George Washington's revenuers, preventing a second revolution. Gallatin died in 1849, and Carpenter couldn't make heads or tails—mild chuckles all around—of "A.L. 76." Revolutionist? Gallatin hadn't come over from Switzerland until 1780. Scholar, certainly: Harvard professor, inventor of the science of ethnology, financial wizard, and Thomas Jefferson's Secretary of the Treasury.

But President? Of what?

I kept my eye peeled for anarchocapitalistic gun-toters, but detected no telltale bulges until I got to the Political Action director, a stocky, thirtyish ex-cop who confirmed what Jenny had said, adding, "I *warned* him to get an automatic! Now I can't even say, 'I told you so'!" He had quit the force to write a book on ethics. I think it was a .45.

On the way out, I passed a contributions jar, dug out five or six neobucks, and, shrugging, dropped them in—about the price of a good Canadian cigarette. Or the paperback in my pocket.

III: MacDonald's Farm

I didn't make it home until after they'd turned off the electricity. First, paperwork: the Meiss killing and the thing in the garage. Then I phoned downstairs to see how the lab reports were coming, and started blocking out investigation schedules. At five, I had a call to go see the division chief, Captain Roger MacDonald, the only man on Homicide shorter than me. But where I'm wide, he was round, with hair like a coat of wet paint and palms that were always damp. Naturally, he was the type who insisted on shaking hands.

"Want to see me, Mac?" I sat down, covertly wiping my hand on a pant leg. His office was the same peeling olive drab as mine, but lacked the homey comfort of other flatfeet sloshing coffee. His window was still broken, the masking tape beginning to get brittle.

"Yes, Win. I wanted to know how these two cases —the machine-gun murder and the, uh, skinning— are going."

"I've decided to hand the garage thing over to James," I said, wishing I had a cigar. "We always get a couple like this whenever they reduce the meat ration. I'll concentrate on Meiss—it has some interesting angles, and my desk is clear since we got that tax-assessor dismemberment straightened out—told you it was the sheriff's jurisdiction, just like the others . . ." He looked uncomfortable. I raised my eyebrows invitingly: "Come on, Mac, what's eating you? Sorry, make that 'What's on your mind?' "

"Well, I . . . it's stuffy in here. What do you say we take a walk?"

"You're the chief, Chief." I got out of the way as he waddled through the door and into the main office, where my colleagues were noisily generating red tape. My own typewriter had broken down again halfway into the investigation schedules. I'd have to wait until James was done with his.

Mac didn't say a word as we passed through little knots of clerks and stenos whom overcrowding had stacked up in the hall. He kept looking nervously over his shoulder, starting at every clatter, and turned right at the Men's. I stood outside, waiting.

The door swung open a crack. "Psst!" It was Mac-Donald, peeking out at me. "Win—come in here, will you?" I shrugged, and pushed the door into the usual haze of tobacco and marijuana smoke. Mac was down on his knees, peering under the stalls. He rose embarrassedly and strode to the sink, turning the water on full. He let it run.

"Water Board's gonna love you, Mac." I reached into my sock, extracted the two-inch butt I'd been thinking about all day, and lit up, exulting in my contribution to the nicotinic atmosphere.

He lit a cigarette, Mexican by the papers. "I know this seems ridiculous"—he puffed nervously—"but my office is *bugged!*"

I gasped, more from anoxia than surprise. "What?"

"You heard me. The telephone, too!"

"Mac, *we* do the bugging and tapping—we're the cops, remember?"

"Someone's doing it to us, Win. To me! And I think I know who!"

"And who will bug these selfsame buggers?" I misquoted, mainly to myself. "Turn off that stupid water. They've got filters that'll take it right off the tape, anyway."

He stood groping in the haze for something to dry his hands on, finally settled for his tie. "Win, I've got another problem, and I don't know what to do about it."

"Something else bugging you?"

He stubbed out his cigarette and lit another. Someday I'd do that, when I was making captain's pay. "Will you be serious? This isn't funny!"

"You need a vacation, Mac. Five days a year just isn't—"

"Win, listen! I've got to take you off the Meiss thing. I'm not supposed to tell you why, but I'll be damned if— What can they threaten me with? Losing my devalued pension?"

I nodded grimly. "Especially since you have to put in forty years, now. Times are tough all over. Go on."

"The word's been passed down the line, from god knows how high. There's more to this than I can tell you, more than I know myself . . . or want to! Anyway, you're off the case." He looked relieved.

I sat in the pollution, thinking. I'd had hints to lay off before, but seldom anything this arbitrary and senseless. I leaned against the grimy wall, arms folded across my chest, and said so, around my cigar.

"You've got to understand . . ." MacDonald pleaded. "There's something big—"

"Yeah," I said, thinking of the shiny golden coin in my pocket. "Who is it, Mac, the local Mafiosi—the government, maybe?"

Mac's piggish little eyes widened a fraction. "My God, Win, what makes you think there's a difference? Where have you been the last thirty years?"

I raised my eyebrows. "Well, you can't fight City Hall. Want me back on the garage killing?"

"*Thanks,* Win. I don't think that'll be necessary. One thing you can count on, tomorrow there'll be another dozen for you to work on. See you in the morning?"

"Bright and early. Let's get out of here and find some oxygen!" I flipped the last half-inch of my cigar into the urinal and swung out into the hall, a billow of smoke preceding me.

By 6:30, I was sitting in a coffee shop across from the City and County Building, waiting for my bus. The place was full of familiar faces, almost all of them city employees—one reason there wasn't a gray CLOSED BY ORDER sign on the door. I turned my face to the window, not wanting to talk, idly watching the street. Behind the counter a radio recited body counts from our latest victory in New Guinea. The Papuans should have run out of people three years ago.

Mac hadn't mentioned what seemed to me the first order of business: federal pre-emption. Burgess had been more than happy to mention it. Now I was black-balled without so much as a memo—much to my superior's relief—by vague pressure "from god knows how high." Mac's office was bugged, if you believed him, and his telephone tapped. An ex-security-cleared scientist who rated his own car and a government-issue handgun had been mortally afraid of the very agency he once worked for. The maraschino cherry on top was the fact that said professor had been gunned down with a .380 Ingram—a favorite item of hardware for covert SecPol operations.

So what was really going on? I'd probably never find out. Tomorrow morning I'd be back on ordinary Capitol Hill muggings.

Through the window I watched Mac emerge from the City and County Building, briefcase in hand. He paused to straighten his tie and stepped into the street. Suddenly there was a screech as a parked car accelerated violently. Mac turned, annoyance, incomprehension, sudden terror racing each other across his face. He ran, trying to make the median. Too late. The front bumper hit him at knee level—a sickening *whump* of hollow metal on solid flesh. His body flopped like a rag doll, head and arms draped over the hood, legs disappearing underneath. The car never slowed. I heard the engine race as the pedal was floored. Mac whipped to the pavement, his head smashing into the asphalt as the car devoured him, his outflung hand still visible, gripping the briefcase.

I was through the door, forty-one in hand, as the rear tires rolled over him and squealed away—a muddy white station wagon, road-dirt covering the license tag. I leveled the S & W, but they were gone. Others who'd followed me out or charged from the building opposite helped me get the body inside. A bus wheezed to a stop over the bloodstains and opened its doors. Nobody got on.

Procedural rituals took a writhing three hours, yet

somehow, not enough, not fitting. They stuffed him
into a steel drawer and shoved it in the wall, the
catch clanging shut on a friend of half my lifetime.
There was no record of Mac's decision to take me off
the case. I kept my mouth shut, and also failed to
mention what I thought were broken windows on the
station wagon. Maybe I'd just wanted them to be
there.

I made the last bus home. Mac had been a born ad-
ministrator, and I was just a gumshoe, but we'd
grunted and strained together through CLETA, gotten
bawled out over imaginary grime in our revolvers,
stood proud while his folks snapped us in our first real
uniforms. The bus stank of alcohol and human bodies.
It seemed odd to miss the traffic I used to curse—the
city was seamy, deserted, and Mac was dead.

"God knows who" had murdered Vaughn Meiss and
Roger MacDonald. I didn't relish finding out where I
stood. When the bus reached my stop, I stayed with
the group, managing half the eight blocks to my
apartment in the relative safety of numbers.

It's basically a place to hang my other suit: a high-
rise at Twelfth and Vine allocated to City and County
people and the odd Federal Finance worker. Lights
were still on in the lobby, but the power would be off
by now in the apartments. I didn't rate elevator service, but I was in no mood for good citizenship. I rode
the machine upstairs and let myself in.

For once I was ahead of the game: more room
than I really needed—but jealously accepted nevertheless. Two bedrooms, bath and a half when the
water was running, and a Coleman camp stove perched
atop the useless gas range. I drew the curtain and
switched on the lanterns.

The bedroom door was ajar!

A wave of fear went through me. It hadn't been
closed since Evelyn had decided she'd rather be a
cop's ex than a cop's widow. That's the way she'd
looked at it. When I finally picked up my one and
only slug, she served papers on me right in my hospital bed, and died five weeks later in a smashup on
I-70. I never figured out if I'm widowed or divorced,

and haven't been so much as scratched in the line
of duty since.

Now might be different. I stretched out on the
floor, feeling silly in my own apartment, and slowly
levered out the S & W. They should have hit me coming in. They were going to pay for that mistake. I
planned to punch several soft, custom-loaded 240-
grain slugs into whoever was behind that door.
Crawling painfully on knees and elbows, I tried to remember to keep my butt down.

A damned good thing I didn't pull the trigger. Creeping closer, I noticed a fine, shiny wire stretching from
the doorknob. I'd always cursed that streetlight shining in my window; now it had saved my life. I laid
the forty-one on the carpet and carefully traced the
wire to a menacing shape attached to the frame inside.
It looked vaguely like a striped whiskey bottle, but I
knew those "stripes" were cut deeply into the casing
to assure proper fragmentation. The wire led to a
ring, one of four clustered at the top. An easy pull
would raise and fire the striker.

A Belgian PRB-43: common in New Guinea, a
favorite with domestic terrorists, too. I felt grateful
they'd left something I was familiar with. Three or
four ounces of plastique—the neighbors would think
I was only moving furniture.

Pretty subtle, for SecPol.

Groping for my keychain, I reached around carefully and slid a key into the safety slot, blocking the
striker. I used nail clippers to cut the wire, and ran
nervous fingers up and down, feeling for others. Nothing. I eased the door open to face the mine, its little
stand hammered into the woodwork. Ruining my clippers forever, I removed all four tripwire rings and
retrieved my housekey. The neck unscrewed, sepa-
rating firing device from explosive container. I levered
the stand out of the wall and looked down inside—
enough bread-doughish explosive to make my pension even more academic than it was already.

I sat for a long time cradling the harmless bomb
in my lap.

Wednesday, July 8, 1987

I skipped breakfast, a little paranoid about what I might find in a cupboard or box of cereal. LSD? Spanish Fly? I ached all over from sleeping on the living room floor: there'd been a second antipersonnel mine under the bed and a thin copper lead running from a bathroom outlet to the shower stall. I slept well away from the furniture and didn't touch *anything*.

When I got up, I treated the place like the minefield it was, doing nothing casually. First, I called in sick—I'd try to get in later. Plausible, considering Mac and all. Next I hung a note out for the cleaning lady, hoping my pidgin Vietnamese was up to warning her away from the deathtrap my apartment had become. All that took forty-five minutes of carefully lifting things like telephone receivers with a bent coat-hanger, ducking and flinching.

I unwired the shower, then thought better of being caught there, naked and defenseless. Showers have never seemed the same to me since *Psycho,* anyway. I changed clothes and put on my flak-jacket, three pounds of multilayered Kevlar back-and-breast, guaranteed to stop a .44 Magnum. As usual, I skipped the crotchpiece. Even if it worked, I'd be screaming in a voice only dogs could hear. Six fresh rounds for the Smith & Wesson, and an eighteen-round case of spares. With twelve from the plastic speed-loaders in my jacket, I was prepared for a short war.

Department policy is against carrying extra guns since there are hardly enough to go around—one reason carrying your own is winked at—and they figure it's too easy to plant a weapon on someone you've blown away in a fit of grouchiness. This wasn't my day for regulations. My handmade one-shot derringer is also chambered in .41 Magnum—and practically certain to break at least two fingers going off. Under the circumstances, that might be a bargain.

Late for the bus, I decided to splurge on a cab. An hour later, I jammed myself in with five other passengers, and rode all the way to work with a hand on the firm rubber grip of my revolver. No one was taking me for any rides I hadn't planned.

At the office, I didn't mention the interesting way I'd spent the night; it just might lead to being taken off the Meiss case, now the *MacDonald* case as far as I was concerned. I ran into a snag at the motor pool—they wanted to know where I was going. I couldn't just say "here and there" as usual—they'd get upset when they couldn't reach me by radio. But I didn't want to end up being tailgated by a dirty white Brazilian station wagon, either.

I climbed back upstairs to think, and found the day's reports on my desk. Nothing I didn't expect—except that Meiss had a mother in Manitou Springs. It was longer than the journey I had in mind, but would cover my ass nicely: Manitou Springs is south on I-25.

Fort Collins, and Colorado State University, are north.

IV: Second Prize, **Two** Weeks

It was good to push my Plymouth out of that eternal curtain of brown smoke. Millions of Bike-induced coronaries won't put a dent in pollution, when the State House exempts its own "Public Service" gunk factories. With a cautious eye on the rear-view mirror, I settled back and let the miles peel off—ice-blue Rockies on my left, Kansas somewhere off to the right—and tried forgetting corpses, Burgess, maybe even poor old Mac a while. I couldn't forget the body-armor, though, even with the drop in temperature outside the inversion-bowl that makes Denver the second-stupidest place in America to build a city.

Once out of dispatcher range, I switched to the commercial band. There was a Jim Kweskin revival underway—beat hell out of what they'd been playing last year. Too soon, though, the real world horned in —what passed for news from New Guinea, Japan breaking relations, more ration reductions. I flipped over to CB for some amateur entertainment.

There was plenty: farmers swapping yarns along their lonely furrows; truckers seditiously exchanging tips. Suddenly the band exploded with obscenity: President Jackson is a ————, four or five unpopular federal agencies are ————. The diatribe began to repeat itself. I slowed, listened—yes, there it was again: a CB "bomb," a cheap, battery-operated tape-player with a seven-minute loop, and an equally expendable transmitter, buried by the roadside and simmering up through a ten-foot copper wire, waiting for FCC gunships to triangulate and blast it to pieces. Remote-control radicalism. The People's Committee for Free

25

Papua entertained me almost all the way to Fort Collins, then quacked suddenly and went off the air.

Spread across ten miles between I-25 and the foothills, to the south Fort Collins is a virtual ghost town of abandoned tract homes. The older section is a pleasant Edwardian-vintage hamlet with broad, tree-lined avenues. I'd been there before, and I liked it. Unfortunately, it takes federal permission to change a cop's location, and seniority—meaning pensions—isn't transferable. I stopped briefly for a Jaycee city map, then navigated my way to Colorado State University.

I wasn't going to like Dr. Otis Bealls or his little Errol Flynn mustache. A nicotine-stained yellow-gray, it was the only hair he had—except for a scraggly fringe around the back of his head—and appeared to be growing from his nostrils. Affecting baggy tweeds, cheap velveteen waistcoat, and rimless plastic spectacles he fiddled with continuously, he failed to convey the academic impression he aspired to. The whole ensemble reminded me of the proverbial dirty old man who "carved another notch in his gold-handled cane."

The bastard wouldn't see me for an hour and a half. My idea of hell is a waiting room, plastic and tubular steel, a busy-busy secretary pointedly oblivious as you riffle through six-year-old copies of *Today's Health* and *Wee Wisdom*. Only in this case it was journals filled with squiggles I wasn't even sure were numbers. The street map was more entertaining. All that time, the fancy telephone blinked on and off like a horror-movie computer, burning up the lines.

When he finally condescended, it was like being sent to the principal. He lounged behind an aircraft carrier of a desk, playing with his glasses and shuffling papers. Finally, glancing at his watch, he asked without looking up, "Well, what can the CSU Physics Department do for the Denver Police?"

"Then you haven't heard about Dr. Meiss?"

"Heard? What kind of trouble is he in, now?"

"The worst. He was killed yesterday. I understand he worked—"

"Officer, please! Ph.D.'s do not *work* here! Janitors,

stenographers, other menials *work* here. If I may optimistically exaggerate, undergraduates *work* here. *Professors* pass the Torch of Civilization, deliberate our Vast Body of Knowledge. They Labor in the Vineyards of Science, pushing back the Barriers of the Un—"

"Dr. Bealls," I interrupted. "One of your Laborers won't be hanging around the Vineyards anymore. He's lying on a sheet-steel table at the Denver City Morgue, so full of machine-gun bullets, he's gonna need a forklift for a—"

"Bullets? My dear fellow, certainly no one in *this* department—" He keyed the intercom, which was stupid—the office door was open, secretary sitting eight feet away. "Shirley, ascertain whether Dr. Meiss is in his office or in class. Have him come immediately if he's free."

She swiveled and looked right in the door. "Vaughn didn't meet his eight-o'clock, sir, and he hasn't called in. I mentioned it when you came in at eleven." Score three points for Shirley.

"Thank you, Mrs. Binh." He purpled. "That *will* be all." Rising abruptly and skirting the desk, he closed the door and hustled back. "I'm sure there's a more reasonable explanation for this. He's punctual, at least that can be said."

I made curiosity grimaces. "You feel he had some failings?"

"My good man, you simply don't *know!*" He leaned back, polishing his glasses with an edge of his jacket. "In a field already overcrowded with nitwits, mystics, and Bohemians, he is— Where can I possibly begin?"

"How about—"

"—His disgraceful activities! My deepest frustration, as head of this department, is to be obstructed from assuring the, um, *gratitude* of its employees. Variant opinions, particularly in these times of economic reappraisal, betray a certain *inhumility*. Nor have we room for contumacious individualism. Socially Responsible Science cannot proceed in such a manner."

And Mac had asked where *I* had been! "What form did his particular contumaciousness take?"

"He writes *letters*—wild, irresponsible things, absolutist, *subversive!* Do you know, he claims this institution would be more efficient run for profit? As if *efficiency* were a valid criterion in education!" He peered confidentially over the tops of his glasses. "Let me tell you—not even the department's Trotskyites and Birchers willingly associate with him."

I grinned. "He was a Propertarian. A book I'm reading says they think the whole right-left political spectrum is eyewash. That might rankle your garden-variety radicals a little."

"As may be. He was dangerous, antisocial . . . some sort of Bolshevist!"

"Bolshevist?" I hadn't missed the sudden change of tenses. "I wonder how Mary Ross-Byrd would like that?"

"Who? Oh, I see—just like all the others. Well, I warn you, I'm an old hand. Not a man on this faculty isn't anxious to pull me down. Daily I withstand ridicule, plot and counterplot. I'll cooperate fully with responsible authority—my happy duty as a grateful citizen—but I will *not* suffer abuse from a public servant, do you understand?"

"Sure, Doc, I understand—that's a mighty fine pair you've got."

"Pair? Pair of what?"

"Noids—skip it. What else was unconventional about Meiss?"

"Ahem . . . Well, he used to—*tends* to—confuse his proper role on the faculty. He's completely aloof from his colleagues."

"You mean the Trotskyites and Birchers who wouldn't associate with him?"

"I mean they frequently complain he goes out of his way to make his professional undertakings vague and esoteric. They—"

"Couldn't understand what he was doing."

"I would find other words. He has no right to set himself above his peers." He fumbled nervously through a desk drawer, glanced up at me, and thought better of it, regretfully shoved the drawer closed.

I laughed. "Go ahead. I'm a nicotine fiend, myself."

He colored. *"We were speaking of Dr. Meiss!"*

I considered lighting up, myself, decided not to push things. "So we were."

"Yes. He seems to be more candid with his students than his colleagues, mixing in a vulgar and undisciplined fashion—they call him by his first name! I've even heard it said he sees them socially, drinks with them in utter disregard for decency and the law."

"Prohibition's tough on everybody. Think any of these colleagues'd like him a bit less candid—via several dozen nasty little bullet holes?"

He sat up, really shocked, I think. "Officer, *please!*"

"Lieutenant, Dr. Bealls, Homicide lieutenant. I wouldn't want abuse from a public servant, either. What about Meiss's extracurricular activities?"

He assumed his frostiest expression. I gave it a B-minus. "I assure you, *Lieutenant,* I do not meddle in the personal lives of my subordinates."

This was getting me nowhere. "Listen, Bealls, I'm just doing my job, and it isn't very easy. Everybody I work for is dead, and it depresses me. What do you say we call a truce?"

He sat a moment, color returning to normal. Then he nodded microscopically. So I rushed him: "Okay, tell me what sort of physics Meiss was up to lately."

He surprised me: "May I see your identification again? I assure you, I've good reason." I handed my badge case over. He looked at the shield, weighing it in his hand—amazingly heavy; wouldn't feel like authority, otherwise—then flipped over the felt liner and spent more time on the plastic ID. "I don't suppose you'd mind if I called your department to confirm this?"

I recognize a National-Security reflex when I see one. I sat tight, practicing my poker face. If they told him no, Lieutenant Bear's in Manitou Springs, it'd take weeks to talk my way out. "Not at all. 226-2421—better get it from the operator, just in case. Ask for Lieutenant James J. James. The J stands for—"

"I don't think that will be necessary." He sneaked a peek at his watch. "You see, Dr. Meiss once pursued investigations of a . . . *sensitive* nature. He no longer does that sort of thing—of course, if he's really dead, I suppose that's the case anyway, ha ha. *Ethics,* he maintained, but you can see how They were just as happy. They were disturbed by the turn in his views."

"So I've been told. About when did all this happen?"

"Not all at once. I gather he made it final two, two and a half years ago."

I remembered the date on his Party card. "So why the panic now? That's a long time, as government secrets go."

Bealls went into his spectacle-scrubbing bit again. "Understand, sir, he was—considering his mediocre talent—quite far ahead in the field. The price of catering to reckless independence. I'm afraid no one else has been able—and if that weren't enough, walking around with all that information in his head—"

I couldn't help it. "Was he supposed to turn it in? His head, I mean. The usual practice is to do that *before* you start working for the—"

"—abandoned everything, charging off on some trivial commercial track, leaving nothing behind but—"

"What do you mean?"

"A series of lucrative grants from private industrial sources. Not general endowments, mind you, but personal *carte blanche.* Anything his whim desired! He was *bought,* simple as that, out of his proper field and service to his country. I dare say he had more resources available than the rest of this—"

He fumbled with his glasses, putting them on upside down. "Well, I can tell you, serious consideration was being given certain measures. There were those who could see he was denied tenure," Bealls added brightly. "They would have thanked me for that. It is not beyond consideration." He blinked and rearranged his spectacles.

Before he could open his mouth again, I said, "Would it be possible to examine his office, you know, for clues and things?" I expected resistance, but was prepared to argue.

An examinatory stare and thoughtful pause. Bealls probably intimidated a lot of undergrads. "It's quite irregular, Lieutenant. I ought to insist on a warrant or something, ha ha. But we don't want it said we failed to cooperate, do we?" He looked at his watch again.

"We most certainly don't," I chimed. "How about his lab—or is that from watching too many Franken-stein movies? Maybe he was one of those mathemati-cians who work it out with a—"

"No, Dr. Meiss did have facilities. I suppose you may examine them." He peeked again at his watch. "I can scarcely see any objection to that!"

Bealls led me through his outer office, stopping to tell his secretary where he'd be if anybody wanted to know. Anybody *important*. She looked at me as if to ask whether I knew what I was getting into, but when her boss removed his glasses once again, I winked and patted my coat lightly where the hammer of the forty-one wears out the lining.

I've been accused of lots of things, but never of stupidity. In a business lucky to solve one out of twenty, I get my man about half the time, and, un-like fictional detectives, I've never been clubbed from behind or slipped a Mickey Finn. Not yet, anyway. The one time I got burned, some puke was shooting through a tiny window in a fire door, and my miser-able .38 couldn't punch through. I bought the .41 Magnum the day I got out of the hospital.

Bealls was still watching his watch. With a ninety-minute stall, the busy phone, and his utter delight at getting me into another part of the building, I wasn't exactly without suspicions. I was the good guy, and couldn't shoot first, that being the Code of the West or something, but whenever Bealls's visitors showed up, they weren't gonna get a chance with that machine gun —not if Smith & Wesson, Inc. had anything to say.

Vaughn Meiss's office was a cinderblock cubicle in a nest of cinderblock cubicles along a cinderblock hall, all painted a depressingly familiar government gang-green. Bookcases teetered to the ceiling on all four walls, and a desk heaped with books and papers was

crammed into the middle somehow. On the ceiling,
over crumbling acoustic tile, he'd taped a Propertarian
poster: IRS—IT REALLY STEALS! A small blackboard
was covered with much-erased squiggles like those in
Bealls's magazines, plus, for a nice human touch, the
word "Shit!"

Bealls ushered me in like a hotel bellboy, turned
the keys over, then excused himself—which was honest, people like him need a lot of excusing—to hustle
off for "another appointment." I peeked around the
corner and watched him scurry away, staring at his
watch.

I mugged around, wondering if I'd recognize a clue
written in Meiss's academic Sanskrit if it jumped off
the board and started chewing on my tie. A quick
once-over of the bookcases: fairly predictable—lots
of math and physics, a couple of shelves of Propertarian stuff, a little science fiction. No secret panels,
mysterious codes, or hollowed-out volumes.

One strange datum: the desk was piled with *histories* covering the Revolution and two or three sub-
sequent decades. Bookmarks—campus parking tickets
going back to 1983—indicated special interest in
Alexander Hamilton, the Federalist Party, and, by
golly, Albert Gallatin.

Another curious thing: in an absolutely jam-
packed office, one drawer of the desk, the second on
the right, was conspicuously empty, or almost so—a
half-empty box of Norma .357 Magnum ammunition,
158-grain hollowpoints; a felt-tip pen bearing the odd
inscription LAPORTE PARATRONICS, LTD., LAPORTE,
N.A.C., TELECOM GRAY 4-3122; a singe pistol cartridge in an unfamiliar caliber marked D & A AUTO
.476; and—another coin! This one was about the size
of a quarter:

ONE HALF METRIC OUNCE
SILVER 999 FINE
THE LAPORTE INDUSTRIAL BANK, LTD

The other side was even weirder, a ferocious-looking
elder in a Karl Marx beard:

LYSANDER SPOONER
A.L. 32–110 ARCHITECT OF LIBERTY

These dubious clues in my pocket, I resolved to
stop by the city of Laporte after I finished here. If it
was the Laporte in Colorado, something definitely
funny was going on. Six or seven miles northwest of
Fort Collins, Laporte boasted fewer than five thousand inhabitants—an unlikely place for a bootleg
mint, industrial bank, or paratronics factory—whatever that was. It had once been considered—its sole
distinction—a potential capital of Colorado Territory,
back when Jack Slade ran the stage line and Denver
only had one of those new-fangled railroad things.

To the matter at hand: I found my way downstairs
(more green cinderblock), let myself in, and turned
on the lights—forty-watt or less by government decree.
The windows were heavily painted over—national security. There was also a stout up-slide-and-down bolt,
handmade from concrete reinforcing rod. Not a bad
idea, I thought, as I clanked it shut. It was good for a
few seconds' warning.

Vaughn Meiss's lab made all the stereotypes come
true: remember *The Fly?* It was just like that—strung
with wires and insulators, bulky pilot-lighted cabinets
looming in the twilight. Only the posters were out of
place. One on the back of the door read, GOVERN-
MENT SCIENCE IS A CONTRADICTION IN TERMS—AYN
RAND and, penciled in below: *Ayn Rand is a contradiction in terms.* Another, on the far wall, was a
still from some old Boris Karloff flick: THEY NEVER
UNDERSTOOD ME AT THE UNIVERSITY!

There was a dark, steel-framed cubbyhole on the
outside wall that might be a fire exit—I couldn't see
very well from where I stood, buried to the hips in
infernal machinery. All but one fluorescent tube had
been removed from the ceiling. Like everyone else
these days, I was developing a caveman's squint.

I worked my way to a console at the center,
seemingly the command post, covered with knobs and
dials. There were a couple of stained coffee cups and
a half-filled ashtray. I looked in vain for a pack of

cigarettes. In the center of the console was a big gray metal notebook. You never know where the next clue is coming from—I peeked: *nothing*. Very curious, and like that almost-empty drawer upstairs, a sort of clue by omission. Somebody around here was a klepto.

A scraping at the doorknob—Bealls, no doubt making sure I didn't arrest any electrons without reading them their rights—footsteps, and muffled conversation. I suppressed my original impulse to go undo the bolt, and stood still, shivering a little. *Then a crash!* The door bulged, glass shattering into paint-covered fragments. The forty-one flashed into my hand as I ducked behind the console. *Again!* The door jamb burst, splinters flying, a cataract of data cards fountained to the floor. A man stood framed in the doorway, tossed his fire-extinguisher battering-ram aside, and drew a weapon from his right hip.

Shifting gently to one end of the console, I lined the intruder's head atop my front sight like an apple on a post, and waited, heart pounding painfully. He scanned the dimly lit room, motioned to someone, left palm outward—stay back a moment—then moved in softly, head panning like a questing reptile. My hand was sweaty on the revolver grip.

As he drifted past, I swapped the Magnum to my left hand, laid the muzzle on the back of his neck, and rose. "Stand easy, asshole!" I whispered, trying to keep an eye on the door. He turned abruptly. I grabbed, jammed my thumb between the hammer of his automatic and the firing pin. The weapon pointed at my guts, the hammer fell. Pain lanced through my hand but the pistol failed to fire. I wrenched it away, smacked him backhand across the face with mine. Blood spurted, black in the dark, and he crumpled.

I kicked him hard, just to make sure, then lifted his unconscious bulk—something unpleasant twanged inside my lower torso—and propped him on the console. He mumbled something before I got a hand over his mouth, fell awkwardly against me, and slid. His jacket caught—there was a click, a whining rumble from across the room. More pilot lights winked on.

At the door, five million flashbulbs were going off at once. Someone crouched there, machine pistol spraying the room with death. Bullets whistled past me, shattering on the concrete wall, metal shards and paint chips raining down. "No! No!" Bealls screamed from the hallway.

My forty-one roared and bucked, roared again. The machine-gunner was blasted out the door, blood streaming in his wake like crepe-paper ribbons, and slammed into the wall behind. His head met the bricks like a ripe melon dropped on a concrete floor. I pocketed the captured automatic, shifted the revolver to my right. Four slugs left. More company through the door, guns blazing—Bealls was still yelling in the background. I fired—saw things shatter, people fall—and ran for the fire exit, plunging into darkness. Bullets buzzed and pinged behind me. I scrambled down a passageway, feeling dizzy, twisted. Instead of stairs, I found blue sky. I was at the bottom of a freshly excavated hole—like a grave.

Gunfire puffed the earth around me—a stinging slap numbed my right foot. Green grass and sunshine—I was out and running hard. Flopping prone, I leveled my forty-one on the hole in the ground, then remembered with a curse that the gun was empty. I rolled, groping for the automatic, crawling backward as I fumbled—

The earth rose with a deafening roar, heaved and buckled, ripped me from the ground. I landed hard but never let the Smith & Wesson go.

V: Over the Rainbow

After what seemed a long, long time, I sat up on the grass, my insides whirling crazily. I was never really unconscious, just preoccupied. Movie and TV people have the wrong idea about being "knocked out." Most times a heavy blow simply crushes your skull, and you're dead. I shook my head and was instantly *very* sorry. Some explosion! The whole building was gone without a trace.

I was sitting at the foot of a tall hedge. I tried to focus, but it was like driving tenpenny nails into my brain, so I gave up for a while. All around me through the fuzziness, lumpy green entities swayed gently in a warm breeze. Patches of sunlight, painfully bright, illuminated many gaudy-colored figures, their mouths dark *O's* of surprise or curiosity, but they were far too hazy, miles away down a dark tunnel of pain.

I simply sat, torn and bleeding, on the warm damp ground, surprised as hell at being alive. After a while, habit took over: I emptied the forty-one, found a speed-loader, restoked the revolver, and holstered it. The automatic went back heavy into my coat pocket. It seemed a pretty fair day's work.

I levered myself onto my hands and knees and stayed in that position, panting. Then I rose heavily, aching in every tormented muscle. Bolts of lightning stabbed through my eyeballs, each followed by a wave of nausea and the drumming of dull pain. I staggered, tripping once or twice but staying upright. By the time I reached the nearest park bench, passing out was an attractive prospect.

I risked another peek. Through my personal haze,

36

the scene was tranquil, bearing no relationship to the
meat grinder I'd just been through: a broad emerald
lawn and a five-foot hedge stretched endlessly in the
distance. On the other side, a corrugated metal shack
showed, robin's-egg blue The air was warm, heavy
with the scent of dark earth and growing things,
dappled with sunshine and shade amid small groves
of enormous trees; benches and sidewalks somehow
tinted tones of red, orange, or yellow. My own—not
concrete as I'd supposed—was a heavy, resilient rubber, pale lemon in color.

A hundred yards away, a silvery fountain feathered
high into the air. A band played lively unfamiliar
music, while children, dressed outlandishly, tossed an
ordinary frisbee. A dog barked, chasing the floating
disk from child to child. They might as well have
been the Seven Dwarves—my picture of their world
was dim and fuzzy. Shivering in sweat, I had only the
faintest interest in staying alive. My ears thrummed
mocking counterpoint to the cheerful music from the
bandstand.

Here and there, other people were dancing, talking
in small groups, lying in pairs under leafy canopies,
moving gently with the music. They wore a bewil-
dering variety of costumes: bright swirly cloaks, skirts
or kilts, trousers and tunics—riots of color strewn like
shining flowers across the forested lawn. Hunched and
feeble in my tattered suit, I clutched miserably at
some hostile stranger's pistol in my pocket. My knees
and elbows were caked with mud.

A hand on my shoulder—I started. A dark, pretty
girl in orange bellbottoms stood behind me. "Are you
all right?" she asked, almost apologetically. Before I
could reply, she slipped gracefully around the end of
the bench. A sheathed dagger, needle slim, hung from
a jeweled chain around her tanned and slender waist.

"Been hurt worse before," I managed to croak. All
this conversation was tiring. "Could you point me
back toward the Sciences Building?" I was beginning
to understand: the *Enquirer*'s headline would read,
POLICEMAN THROWN HUNDREDS OF FEET BY EXPLO-
SION, LIVES! with a thumbnail sketch of my service

record, duly exaggerated, and an account of how, while sailing through the air, I'd found Jesus.

The young lady looked dubious, but willing to let me pick my own handbasket. "You mean the university?" She pointed down a tinted pathway through the trees. I could see another sunlit space beyond, perhaps the slightest hint of moving traffic. Make that headline . . . HUNDREDS OF YARDS . . . ! "Across Confederation Boulevard, at the edge—why, you're bleeding!"

Just like a movie heroine. I didn't want to hear about it—you can do amazing things seriously injured, as long as you don't *know*. "I really think I'll be all right," I lied, and found a Kleenex, dabbing at the worst parts. The web of my thumb, where I'd kept the other guy's gun from going off, was split back half an inch. I wadded the bloody tissue into that fist and said, "Gotta get going. Police business."

"If you're sure," she said. "Please be careful."

"Thanks. I'll try." Stifling any further stoic repartee, I lurched painfully to my feet, plodded in the direction indicated. A hundred yards and a century later, I stopped at another bench, cheery pastel pink, and lowered myself wearily, wondering if I'd ever get up again.

I didn't seem seriously damaged, just sore, and incredibly tired. Pilots have fallen miles, *sans* parachute, and survived. Maybe I'd qualify for a Guinness record when this was all over—a brightening thought, somehow. I started humming an old railroad song and reached into my coat pocket. *"Last week a premature blast went off / And a mile in the air went Big Jim Goff / And DRILL, ye tarriers, DRILL!"*

The pistol I'd confiscated was a sweetheart:

THE BROWNING ARMS COMPANY
MORGAN, UTAH & MONTREAL P.Q.
MADE IN BELGIUM

"The next time payday comes around / Jim Goff a dollar short was found . . ." I've always admired the Browning P-35, despite its lack of authoritative stomp.

Impeccably designed and made to last for generations, it's no more powerful than an issue .38, but carries an impressive fourteen cartridges.

"*'What for?' says he, then this reply . . .*" On the other side, stamped in neat, tiny letters, was something that started me wondering exactly what I'd *do* when I found my way back to the university:

CALIBRE 9 m/m PARABELLUM
PROPERTY OF U.S. GOVERNMENT SECURITY
POLICE

"*'Yer docked fer the time you was up in the sky!' / And DRILL, ye tarriers, DRILL!*"

Wobbling the rest of the way across the park, I really wanted someplace to lie down and curl up, maybe suck my thumb a little. I wasn't really hurt: cuts and bruises—large bruises—and a grisly furrow in the heel of my right shoe where a passing slug had left splinters of copper and lead.

I labored along, people staring at me a little, and me staring right back. Whatever the local ordinances were, I saw more low-slung handguns, more dirks and daggers, than in a dozen B-westerns and swashbucklers spliced together reel to reel. I found myself grabbing convulsively at my left armpit more than once. Fort Collins sure had changed!

Maybe they were all dressed up for some kind of fair. I didn't recognize the costume period. Most people, including some cops I know, are frightened by weapons of all kinds, knives worse than guns, for some silly reason. These must all be toys, part of the celebration. I tried looking closer without being nosy —not my jurisdiction, after all—but the effort still brought tears. There hadn't been a hardware collection like this since the Crusades were catered. Women and children sporting arms right along with the men. But wait. *Were* they children, waddling like circus midgets, even brushing the ground with an occasional knuckle?

If only the fog of weariness and pain would—Can you have a migraine in a dream? Mud- and blood-

splattered from collar to ankles, amid all this re-
splendent sartorialism, I was about as attractive and
dignified as a Larimer Street wino. I'd even managed to
split a crotch seam.

At last I reached a low, meandering wall of multicolored brick, more bewildered than ever. The street
was a broad ribbon of sea-green crabgrass full of traffic, not a single vehicle even remotely familiar. There
wasn't a wheel in sight.

I'd once ridden an English hovercraft, admired the
same sort of ground effect machine on Puget Sound
before Ralph Nader shut it down. This wasn't the
same at all: these whispered along, quiet as an usher
in church. I was beginning to get an idea that I was
more than lost, I was profoundly misplaced.

Maybe I'd been hurt and was wandering around
with *amnesia.*

That old Greer Garson flick—*Random Harvest?*—
real people have spent years like that, building new
lives, families, then coming back in shock to their original personalities. This world around me was some
artist's conception of Tomorrowland. Had I spent the
last twenty years being someone else? It *would* explain the age I felt right now! Had *decades* passed
between the lab explosion and whatever happened in
the park, and now, after some second stress or injury,
was I myself again? *Random Harvest*—Ronald Col-
man was the guy.

Across the street, a three-story Edwardian building
had a low wall around it, too, and a large bronze sign:

LAPORTE CITY UNIVERSITY, LTD.
EST. A.L. 117

117 A.L.? They don't start a new calendar every
election year. What had happened here while I was
out to lunch? And where the hell was *here,* anyway?
All I wanted was to crawl off somewhere and lie down
for a couple of months. I was through detecting. Let
someone else do it.

I guess I came pretty close to flipping out at that
moment. That I didn't, I attribute not to any sterling

qualities, but simply to well-worn habits of mind and, perhaps, a dollop of shock-induced euphoria.

If I could just find someplace to start, some loose thread to pick until this whole mystery began to unravel—before I did. Do you just walk up and ask someone, "Excuse me, what *year* is this?"

I could always call the cops. They might want my badge and gun for their museum. Hell, they might want *me* for their—hold it! I was still *carrying* that badge, and the .41 caliber weight swinging against my ribs wasn't a grilled-cheese sandwich. I was still wearing my faithful old gray suit, my second-best tie, and everything else I'd put on in Denver this morning. However I'd gotten into this mess, it wasn't via any twenty-year amnesic vacation.

So much for the *Random Harvest* theory. A glance down the sidewalk, and there it was, my first sensible idea for the day—lower and wider than I was used to, with tinted panes in a wrought-iron latticework, and a fancy Kremlinesque spire pointing skyward:

TELECOM

Whatever that meant. Nothing orients you faster in strange territory than browsing through the phone book. There wasn't any door. I took two steps down into the booth and the street noises went away. It also seemed cooler inside, but I could tolerate an air-conditioned phone booth if the Secretary of Energy could.

No phone book. Just like back home. No *telephone*, either: just a simple, matte-finished panel like sandblasted Corningware. Underneath was a keyboard. I plunked myself down on the broad upholstered bench and abruptly the screen had letters on it:

—NEED ASSISTANCE?—
The Grand Combined Directory of Greater
Laporte!
Gray, Bell, & Acme Communications Systems

which changed in a few moments to:

INSTRUCTIONS: Please enter party you wish to 'com. Number will be indicated by a pulsing cursor dot. Enter *A* for Accept and remit payment. For information, please enter *O* for Operator. For free map displays, enter *Map* plus address desired. Thank you for choosing our services.

> Gray Telecom System, Ltd.
> Bell Telephone Co., Ltd.
> Acme Communications, Ltd.

Now *there* was something: a polite phone company! *Three* polite companies, and the service argued Messrs. Gray, Bell, and Acme might be bucking pretty lively competition.

I could have tried the local fuzz, but I figured I owed the thrill to my *alma mater*. The screen hadn't mentioned Long Distance, so I examined the keyboard. It wasn't laid out like a typewriter, but at this point, I felt lucky they were the same letters. It was back to hunt and peck after years of perfecting my own two-finger method. Finally, I decided on *O*.

So help me, an animated drawing answered, a pleasantly stereotypical old-timey operator, crisply pretty in a high-collared blouse and headset—like Betty Crocker's kid sister. "May I help you?"

I'd never talked to a cartoon before, but this seemed like the day for it. "Could you give me Long Distance? The Denver Police, two-six-six, two-four-two-one. And reverse the charges. This is Lieutenant Win Bear."

"One moment, please, Lieutenant Bear." The screen blanked, then she reappeared. "I'm sorry, we have no records for a Denver Police in either local or trunkline memories. Are you sure you're using the correct name?"

That stopped me. "What do you mean? Try 'Denver, City and County of.' "

Her face registered good-natured exasperation. "I'm *very* sorry, sir. I've accessed 36,904 listings: 'Denver, Aalain E.'. through 'Denver, Zucher W.'— but no 'Denver, City and County of'."

The 3-D display made it almost irresistible to try strangling her cute little cartoon neck. But *something* catastrophic had resulted in a brand-new calendar. Hell, Denver could be in a different *country* by now! "Hold on! How far away—if that's the way to put it —is your directory good for?" Back home you still can't dial lots of places—try calling Moscow for a little excitement at the FBI's expense.

She hesitated. "Sir, we list over seven billion individuals and organizations currently contracting with some twelve thousand telecommunications companies on this planet, the Moon, Mars, and Ceres Central. I am confident to sixteen decimals that there is no "Denver, City and County of" in the known solar system. May I be of further assistance, or would you prefer a *live* operator?"

There was a definite "asshole" at the end of that sentence. "No," I answered dizzily, "that's enough." The screen returned to NEED ASSISTANCE? I certainly did—oxygen and a saline drip. So much for The Next Best Thing to Being There.

Okay, Denver was obliterated. They'd finally Pushed the Button, and at least 117 years ago, judging by the university sign. Ragnarok's a pretty good reason to start a new calendar. Yet this society had pulled through it, recovered without a scar. Hey! People are on Mars!

But where did that leave me? All my friends must be dead. I was my folks' only kid. I had no close relatives or descendants I was *aware* of. Jesus, with Denver gone, did *anyone* I know have any descendants? Maybe the local cops could recommend a nice rubber room for my declining years.

Wait a minute! This was no way for Sergeant Billy Bear's son Winnie to be thinking! There must be *something* I could do, if only looking up Otis Bealls's great-grandson to punch him in the nose.

Maybe that *wasn't* such a screwy idea: Bealls might be long dead. That explosion might not have been in Meiss's lab, but IT—the opening remarks of World War III! On the other hand, he could have lived long enough to pinch the nurses in some postwar wrinkle-ranch. One way or another, my explosion would surely rate some footnote in his family history.

I typed out BEALLS, OTIS. The screen displayed something like a regular phone book page with a glowing orange cursor dot wiggling up and down the margin. *Beallses,* about sixty of them, but no Otis. I stared at the list, wondering how to ask someone, "Pardon me, did you have an ancestor named Otis, back before the End of the World?" The cursor dot slide-whistled up and down the page uncertainly.

Then, in the right-hand column across from the Beallses, it caught me, right between the eyes:

BEAR, EDWARD W., *Consulting Detective*
626 E. Genêt Pl. . . . . ACMe 9-4223

I wouldn't have taken a million "metric ounces" not to dial that number. Seeing your own distinctive name and more-or-less correct profession in a strange city's directory is interesting, but not that rare: five years after he was killed, my Dad was still getting mail for *another* Tech Sergeant Bill Bear. But on a Picturephone, possibly decades in the future?

Perhaps this wasn't the time for idle curiosity, sitting in a futuristic phone booth, torn and filthy, still disoriented and getting more that way every minute. I'm not sure *what* was called for. Catatonic schizophrenia, maybe.

PLEASE INSERT ONE TENTH COPPER OUNCE

I rummaged through my pockets: ball-point, notebook, badge-holder and wallet, empty cartridges, felt-tip, two dimes, a quarter, four pennies. How much is a tenth-ounce of copper? Those little watch-pockets they put in trousers are good for something: I pulled out the Lysander Spooner coin from Meiss's desk. Half an ounce of silver ought to do it. Do *polite* phone companies give change?

The coin! I hadn't associated the numbers—dates— with the university sign until now. To hell with it, time enough for going batty later. I inserted the silver coin,

the machine started hiccuping into its coin return. I
didn't have time to examine the result, because:

WE'RE SORRY, YOUR PARTY IS BUSY. IF YOU'D
LIKE TO WAIT, PLEASE ENTER *H* FOR HOLD. TO
CANCEL THE CALL, ENTER *C*—YOUR MONEY
WILL BE REFUNDED. THANK YOU.

I said, "You're welcome," and punched *H*, fidgeting
nervously. Is there another way to travel through time
besides starting at birth and plodding on to Social Security, collecting varicose veins along the way? Meiss
had to have gotten that coin from here. Was it *time
travel* he'd been working on? It wasn't any crazier an
idea than amnesia, and I could see how the government might be interested.

But who was this gink with my name? Let's see: if I
hadn't gone through Meiss's machine, I might have
survived World War III or whatever, eventually moving to Fort Collins. But I *did* go through, so I couldn't
have . . . anyway, I'd be at least 165 by now! Not that
I didn't feel it. Of course, I could have had a kid *after*
1987 . . . but no, the same objection applies: after
1987, I was—am—already *here.* This is where my
life line and Meiss's confounded gadgetry had carried
me, not through Armageddon to Father's Day.

Impatiently, I fiddled with the coin-return and
found a copper tenth-piece among the change: an
overweight penny with somebody named Albert Jay
Nock staring out of it. Damn it, still busy! Seething
now, I punched out MAP and 626 GENÊT PL. ACMe
was as good as its word: a city map materialized, two
pulsing amber dots explaining YOU ARE HERE and
ADDRESS REQUESTED. Pretty fancy. I'd have a few suggestion for Ma Bell if I ever got the chance—

Which I might! If Meiss had invented a time machine back in 1987, surely by now—I almost looked
up "Travel Agents, Time" in the *Grand Combined Directory,* but didn't want to risk getting a cartoon sore
at me twice in one day.

However, Genêt Place was only six blocks away,
and I was beginning to feel cocky—giddy if you prefer. Judging from the phone rates, I had a pocket full

of high-caliber change—including the gold slug I'd
never had a chance to turn in—and three freshly
loaded guns. I'd figured out, within certain sloppy
tolerances, what had happened to me. Thanks to my
almost Sherlockian genius, I even had a rough idea of
the history of this place—and a definite destination:
626 Genêt Place. Not bad, for only an hour in Future-
land!

Shock can be a pretty wonderful thing.

When I emerged, traffic was still heavy, and *fast*.
Looking for a break, I glanced back the way I'd come
only minutes ago. A flashing arrow at the curb spelled
out PEDESTRIANS and pointed to an escalator that
flowed down into a broad, well-lit area lined with
shops, then became a moving walkway. Halfway
through the trip, I passed a tunnel labeled, paradoxi-
cally, OVERLAND TRAIL. Here and there cheerful three-
dimensional posters advertised food, entertainment—
and tobacco. Prohibition was over! There seemed to
be a lot of ads for various intimidating firearms, and
something calling itself SECURITECH—WHILE YOU
SLEEP. Was that a burglar alarm or a sleeping pill?

I passed another TELECOM, decorated like a candy-
striped guardpost, an enterprise of CHEYENNE COMMU-
NICATIONS. At least Wyoming had made it through
Doomsday—but who'd know the difference? This
booth offered background music and scenic rear-
projections to convince 'em you were in Tahiti—or in
a phone booth with scenic rear-projections.

The escalator headed up again into the sunlight,
dumping me out on the other side of Confederation
Boulevard. Somewhere at the end of this day was a
mattress and a pillow. I wished I knew where. I was
weary, lightheaded, surrounded by the totally strange
and the strangely familiar. I started giggling a couple
times, mostly from hysteria rather than from the scenery.

Escalator tunnels and underground shopping centers
lay beneath every intersection, sometimes connected
with their neighbors up and down the block. I got a
lot of free rides that way, though once I rode too far
and had to double back. There was almost more city

below-ground than above, which made sense with a thermonuclear war in the recent past.

Forcibly reminded of certain biological facts, I stopped off at a door with appropriate markings, a model of understatement as it turned out. More than the usual monument to the ceramic arts, the rest room was an updated Roman bath: swimming pool, snack bar, even sleep cubicles for rent. I thought of Colfax Avenue hookers who'd love the setup, then noticed that such services—your choice, organic or mechanical —were available at a modest fee. To my taste, the whole arrangement looked too much like drawers in the city morgue.

Experimentally, I fed my shirt into another slot and got it back looking almost good as new. So I turned in my pants, jacket, shorts, and socks and stood around feeling silly in my Kevlar, shoes, and shoulder holster. I found an empty shower stall and afterward discovered that the laundry had fixed my pants. It all came to about an ounce of copper.

A few more blocks took me away from the energetic university district to a quieter residential area, elaborate in architectural extremes. Victorian and Edwardian gingerbread sat grandly between the baroque and a sort of Swiss-chalet style—ornate, almost rococo, but taken all together, neither garish nor intimidating. Just different. The homes were set back deeply from the road, on enormous lots with gracefully curving rubber driveways winding through gardens and wrought-iron fencery. If Edward W. Bear lived like this, being a P.I. must pay better here than it did in my jurisdiction.

Definitely feeling more like myself, whoever *that* was (another twinge of curiosity about this "Edward W. Bear"), I ambled along in the afternoon sun, absently aware that the almost-silent vehicles swooshing along beside me in the street produced no noticeable exhaust. Down in the curbing there wasn't a scrap of garbage. As my head cleared I began to notice other things—the streets might be Kentucky Blue, but there's a lot to be said for rubber sidewalks. Soon, except for where I'd kicked that SecPol agent, my feet were the only part that didn't hurt. I thought resentfully about

the million concrete miles I'd trod on downtown foot
patrol.

Here, the underground crossings ran to neighborhood groceries, stationery and candy stores—the kind
of mom-and-pop operation nearly killed off by city
zoning back home. I took another fling, stopping for
some cigarettes, my first decent ones in almost five
years. Two copper pennies for the most expensive in
the place.

Topside again, I did a little people-watching. It was
more than their weird colorful clothing and strangely
relaxed briskness. Something was missing—the barely
concealed hostility and fear that haunted *my* city
streets. These people never seemed to push or jostle,
never avoided looking at one another. They'd nod politely—even speak!—and they carried their heads
high, unafraid of the world around them. It sent shiv-
ers down my spine.

What I first took to be an extraordinary number of
children became even more confusing. Some of these
little people sported muttonchops and mustaches. I noticed gangly arms and clumsy gaits. Mutants—the city
was full of them. Even my bleary eyes could see the
effects of radiation-distorted genes: protruding jaws,
rubbery lips; some practically had muzzles.

Even more jarring were the weapons—men and
women alike, little people, *children*. I passed one obvious kindergartener carrying a pistol almost as big as
he was! Was there some danger here I wasn't seeing?
Or was the hardware merely a legacy of the brutal
time that must have followed an atomic war? Yet these
people seemed so full of cordiality. Could the source
of their pride and dignity be nothing more than the
mechanical means of dealing death they carried? Well,
the alternative, thousands of variations on the Sulli-
van Act, had been no shining success back home.

What the hell, it was a nice day, a fine day. Nothing
wrong that a long drink and a longer snooze wouldn't
cure. Maybe there was an opening on the local force
—would a century and a half's experience count for
anything?

At long last a fancy scrollwork signpost announced

PLACE d'EDMOND GENÊT. My stomach tightened, my mouth went dry. Who *was* this other Edward Bear?

All of a sudden a 747 was trying to land on my back! I whirled, a long black hovercraft tore down the street, coming my way *fast*. It bellowed, riding a tornado as other drivers bumped up over the sidewalk, swerved and slid to avoid being hit. Six feet above the ground, the monster covered blocks in seconds, sending a hideous roar ahead and a shower of parks. Bullets sang around my head.

I leaped a low hedge and rolled, thankful I'd reloaded the forty-one. Pain throbbed through my exhausted body; muscles screamed and cuts reopened. Crouching, I pumped six heavy slugs into the hovercraft, but on it flew, never hesitating. Dimly aware that my hand was bleeding again, I wrestled the automatic free from my coat and thumbed the hammer back, jerking the trigger again and again as the machine slid crazily around the corner. It was like a dream where nothing you do has any effect. Bullets whistled, tearing leaves and branches, plucking at my hair. The slide locked back on the Browning—empty.

Dipping and weaving more from fear and pain than strategy, I thrust both weapons into my coat and twisted, running, tearing at my hip for the derringer. A house rose huge before me, "626" embossed in foot-high characters on its broad garage door. I ran that endless curving drive as bullet-shredded paving stung my ankles. Halfway there, as if on cue, the door began to rise. Would I die, trapped in a garage like that miserable soul on Emerson Street—what?—only yesterday?

Ragged holes began appearing in the door, an erratic hemstitch working in my direction. I swam toward it in slow motion as the hovercraft, guns blazing, started up the drive.

My face slammed into the rising door as the bullets slammed into my body. Blood splashed the panel in *front* of me! The bottom edge rose past me as I fought to clear the derringer, bring it to bear for its one, pitiable shot. No strength to pull the hammer back . . . the pavement rose and smacked me in the face.

VI: Retaliatory Force

Ever wake up in a darkened room and a soft bed, with a headache clear down to your knees? My arms wouldn't move. When I inhaled, sharp pains skewered me from spine to sternum. I was alive, but leaking.

"Hold these," the first voice, softly feminine, said, "And feed them into the cutter. We'll have to remove it all, I'm afraid." Sounds of rasping, scraping. Whatever they were chopping off, I hoped I wouldn't sing falsetto afterward.

A fuzzy shadow loomed over me. "Great molten muskets! Look at *these!*"

"Don't jog my elbow, Lucy!" A masculine voice, and somehow familiar. "You're in Clarissa's light!"

"She's right, though," the first voice said. "Such crude dental prosthetics! And he's in advanced geriosis—see the swollen belly, the sagging tissue around the eyes? What little hair he has is turning *gray!*"

"Radiation or old age?"

"Neither, Ed." It was the first voice again, worried. "But you should see the scanner—poisonous congestion, ulceration. And the arteries! Even without these bullets in him"—*plink! plink!*—"he'd be gone in another ten years." *Plink!* I'd heard that sound before, watching buckshot pulled from a prisoner after a liquor-store holdup. I'd have resented the conversation that went with it this time, but the agony made everything else seem trivial. "Lucy! There's no response to somasthesia. Give it another notch!"

"Right . . . Any luck?"

"We're at redline already. The painkillers just aren't working."

"What painkillers?" I wheezed past the red-hot pokers in my chest.

"Take it easy, friend," the male voice said. "You'll be all right—won't he, Clarissa?" Even out of focus, he reminded me of somebody.

"Yes, yes, you will."

"Shucks, sonny, you're not missing any *important* parts!" It was an old lady. She leaned over me and winked.

"That's g-good news . . ." A whispery croak was all I could manage. "The pain . . ."

"I give up," the beautiful voice said. "Lucy, *electrosleep*—out in the van, a blue case under the regenerator."

"Sure thing, honey. Anything else?"

"Yes," the male voice said. "Check the 'com again. If that Frontenac comes back, I want a crack at it!"

"Have to beat *me* to the draw, kiddo! You see what *used* to be my front windows?" She gestured menacingly with a huge handgun. "Wish I'd thought to go for their boiler!" Her voice trailed off as she left, muttering to herself.

"So do I," he answered under his breath. "Clarissa, is it all right for him to talk . . . just take it slowly? Who are you? What's this all about?"

I tried to clear my vision. The guy looked enough like me to get drafted in my place. "Win Bear . . . Lieutenant, Denver—used to be a city, sixty miles south. Only it's *gone!* Blown to—" I stopped, breathing heavily against withering pain. "I'm, well, from the past—a time-traveler!"

He frowned perplexedly. Nothing was wrong with my vision. I could make out every hair in his bushy, very familiar eyebrows. "Friend, sixty miles south of *here,* there's only Saint Charles Town. Been there, oh, 125 years. Nothing but buffalo before that."

That queer cold chill I felt had nothing to do with bullet wounds. "But I was born there. That's where I Labor in the Vineyards, pushing back—" I started wretching, gasping, and sank back, too exhausted to finish.

This was it. I'd been booby-trapped, blown up,

machine-gunned, and on top of it all, run face-first
into a garage door. By some circumstance not bearing
close examination, I was alive. But evidently some of
my marbles hadn't made the trip with me. I knew this
guy: the other Edward Bear. If this wasn't the future,
where the hell was I?

Lucy came back, her horse pistol shrunken to
snubbie proportions. Clarissa gave her a nod. Before
I could protest, she shoved the little gun against my
neck—"This oughta do the job!"—and pulled the
trigger.

Thursday, July 9, 1987

The muzzle was still cool on the side of my neck. I
turned. "Lucy, how you've changed!" Standing over
me was a breathtaking peaches-and-cream blonde,
perhaps thirty, hazel eyes—when she smiled, the corners crinkled like she meant it—and an ever so
slightly upturned nose. She wore a bright-red coverall
with a circled white cross embroidered on the left
shoulder.

The wall seemed one huge window opening into a
honey-colored meadow and purple columbines. Maybe a mile away an evergreen forest fronted foothills
and the ghostly peaks of the Rockies. The illusion was
spoiled by a door through the wall and the railed top
of a staircase. Television? A beautiful job. I could almost smell the sage.

The rest of the room contained the bed I was in, a
wall-length bookcase beneath a pair of real windows
—sunshine, treetops—and one of the ten most gor-
geous women in whatever world this was. I took a
deep breath, found the pain completely gone, and
tried sitting up.

"Hold on, Lieutenant! You're not quite ready for
that!" The lady dimpled, pushing me back gently.
"How do you feel?"

"I guess I'll do, at that. Is this a hospital?"

"You want to get *really* sick? A *hospital*, indeed!
I almost believe you *are* a time-traveler as you claimed
last night."

"What else did I say? Hope I had enough sense to make an improper suggestion or two *your* way."

"You're a 'Man from the Past,' from a city that's never existed. Otherwise you were quite gentlemanly, all things considered."

"Too bad. So this is what the subtitles call 'The Next Morning.' And you—"

"Clarissa Olson, Certified Healer—*your* Healer, if you want." Dimples again. "Anything else we'll decide after you're up and around."

"In that case, I think I'll go on living for a while. When *will* I be up and around?"

"Well, you're healing pretty slowly. You were gradually dying of malnutrition: deficiencies in the nitrilosides, lecithin, ascorbic acid; a dozen degenerative diseases I've only *read* about. But as that clears up, your wounds will knit faster. Day after tomorrow—at least for a brief walkaround?"

"Where I come from, bullet holes take a lot longer than that to heal up! This has *gotta* be the future . . . or heaven, if you'll pardon my getting personal."

She smiled tolerantly. "Persist with this time-travel business and you'll need something stronger than what's in my bag over there!"

"I could do with something stronger, about eighty proof, in a tall glass. Forget time travel. Let's talk about bullet holes, and how come mine don't seem to be terminal."

She crossed the room; I enjoyed watching her do it. "Here's your explanation." Two plastic-covered masses, overflowing with shredded fiber. "That's why there was enough of you left for me to work on." I recognized the tattered remains of my Kevlar body armor. Someone had driven a tank over it while something red and squishy was inside. "Whatever this contraption is, it saved your life."

"That's what it's for. Sort of forgot I had it on. But it wasn't designed for machine guns. How many times was I hit?"

She frowned. "I removed—you really want to hear this?—okay, perhaps a dozen bullets, mostly fragments. And fiber. This vest was practically *stitched* into you. We had trouble cutting it off."

"That's a relief!" I risked a peek under the covers. "I thought you'd cut off something a little more valuable—at least to me."

She indicated the cast on my left arm. "You have a shattered wrist and fractured humerus. The shoulder blade itself and the collarbone are in bad shape, but they'll heal. Your right arm, I don't see how they managed to miss. You should see Ed's garage door!"

"And his mother's windows?"

"His what? No, Lucy—Lucy Kropotkin—is Ed's nextdoor neighbor. She'd be flattered, though. She thinks a lot of Ed."

"And so do you, apparently. I'm hurt to the quick."

I won't say she actually blushed. She's one of those naturally pink types you don't dare take home to Father. "Yes, I do. He's the real reason you're still alive. He drove off your attackers."

"I was elsewhere at the time. You want to tell me about it?"

"Well," she answered, "just about the time the shooting started, Ed was on the Telecom. He'd been at it all morning, clearing things for his first real vacation in years . . ."

One Freeman K. Bertram of Paratronics, Ltd, had a problem: someone had gotten away from a company warehouse, laden with a half-ton of valuable parts and equipment, despite a dozen of Securitech's best, plus an alarm system worth thousands of ounces.

Ed might not be the best-known consulting detective in the land, nor the most highly paid, but he was clearly headed in that direction at an age most North Americans considered young. There were more clients than he really had time for, and although he'd worked for Paratronics, Ltd. before, and this sounded interesting, plenty of schedule-juggling had gone into shaking three vacation weeks loose. With several hundred ounces already to his credit at Mulligan's Bank and Grill and a brand-new Neova convertible waiting in the garage, come law or high water, Ed was heading for Leadville's summer sun and man-made snow, business be hanged.

Could he recommend another operative, suggest security-tightening measures? Ordinarily, even this advice would cost plenty. Bertram's stereo image sulked until his lower lip threatened to fall right out of the screen. He wasn't used to taking no for an answer or having his gold turned down, but what could he do? Bertram made notes and promised to call back at the end of the month.

Connection finally broken, Ed started toward the garage, following his suitcases. Locking his skis on the squat little hull, he levered himself into the cockpit. The garage door ground slowly upward: for the twentieth time that week he—

Abruptly there was a hair-raising metallic chatter. Something else wrong with the door? Or the sportscraft? A glance at the instruments: no, wheels were down and locked under the flaring skirt, fans idling gently; thrusters waited silently in their nacelles for a take-off ramp somewhere along the Greenway.

He killed the engine and climbed out. Beneath the half-open door, a baggily clad form ran toward him, then slammed violently into the slowly rising panel. Spots of sunlight pierced the door as a brilliant dotted line raced toward Ed. The Neova's windows disintegrated as he dived, flinging back his sportcloak for the .375 on his hip. The shadow, faceless against outdoor light, slumped and fell in a pool of splattered blood.

A huge Frontenac steamer crabslipped up the driveway, bullets streaming. Ed pulled the trigger. Heavy slugs spat toward the steamer—five! six!—and silenced its machine gun. He thumbed the selector and ripped through the rest of his magazine, fountaining metal and glass from the black machine in three-shot bursts. It fishtailed clumsily across the lawn and limped away.

"Death and taxes! What was *that* about?" Enter a frail-looking elderly woman, .50 caliber Gabbet Fairfax smoking in her hand. She clutched her bathrobe together, shoving the monstrous weapon into a pocket, where it hung dangerously.

"I haven't the slightest idea, Lucy," Ed swapped magazines and holstered his gun, cautiously approaching the inert figure lying in the doorway. "Give me a hand. This fellow's badly hurt!" He gently rolled the body over and looked down. At *himself*.

"You were in nasty shape when I arrived," Clarissa finished, "blood loss, concussion, bruises all over. You also had a hairline fracture of the right large toe." First chance to show off my Tae Kwon Do, and I'd blown it. All at once, the whole of yesterday came trickling back, half-forgotten in my surprise at being alive.

Funny: you resign yourself to dying and it's almost annoying when it doesn't come off on schedule. I'd been through the process three times in the last twenty-four hours, and I knew. A Kevlar vest may keep your ticket from being punched, but it won't spare you the bullet's energy—just distributes it. I was lucky.

Which brought me up short. That guy in the laboratory corridor was cold meat. The one I'd pistol-whipped—where was my Smith & Wesson?—would have a broken cheekbone, possibly a punctured lung. Others, who can tell? There wasn't time for counting coup. One confirmed, uncounted possibles. Not my first time . . .

I'd run out of cigarettes about 2 A.M., pulled pants on over pajama bottoms, and strolled over to one of those little twenty-four-hour groceries with inflated prices and lonely teen-age clerks. Only this one wasn't lonely—not with a .25 automatic pressed against her temple. *He* stood well away, gun arm fully extended, prancing nervously as he watched her shove small bills into a wrinkled paper bag, preparing herself for death.

You're a cop around the clock. On my own time, I carried a beat-up .45 S & W sawed off to three inches. The door stood open, ten yards away—I didn't dare get closer. I knelt, braced my hands on the rear corner of his '57 Chevy, and pulled the trigger. She screamed for thirty minutes. When the coroner cut the stocking mask away, half the bandit's head came with it. But his gun had never gone off: he'd forgotten to shuck one into the chamber.

Stupidity is a capital offense.

When Evelyn and I were first married, we'd picnic up in the foothills, west of Denver—lushly green in springtime, yellow-gold in the high-country summer, and absolutely brim-full of rattlers. We never went without that old .45. Guess I wasted dozens of nasty things before I got too old and fat for hiking.

Many a cop sees thirty years without firing a shot in anger, others quit cold after their first. You'd be surprised how often. Some few start enjoying it, but we try to weed them out—too bad the feds don't follow the same policy. I was surprised how I felt: like shooting those rattlesnakes. The world was cleaner, safer. Not much, but a little. I hadn't liked doing it any more than, say, washing dishes, but I'd do it again. I'm not for capital punishment, a useless, stupid ritual, degrading to everyone involved—*except* at the scene and moment of the crime, preferably at the hands of the intended victim.

Rattlesnakes with machine guns. Wish I'd aimed for their goddamned boiler too.

Explaining to Clarissa how I'd ended up in her competent hands was difficult. I didn't really know. I was fairly confident I wasn't bananas: I could remember the first house I'd ever lived in, the name of my second-grade teacher, what I wore at my wedding—all the nuts and bolts. Somebody *was* persecuting me, but I had the persecution marks to prove it.

This *was* northern Colorado. Out my second-floor bedroom window, I could see Horsetooth Mountain, an unmistakable Fort Collins landmark. I could reel off everything that had happened, from the moment the investigation began at Sixteenth and Gaylord, to the moment the bad-guys done me dirt at the corner of Genêt and Tabor. But according to my shapely physician, today was Thursday, July 9, 211 A.L. After reflecting, she added that A.L. stands for *Anno Liberatis*.

"That's something, anyway. Mind if I ask what *happened* two hundred and eleven years ago?"

Clarissa shook her head in bewilderment. "But how can you *not* know? That's when the thirteen North American colonies declared their independence from the Kingdom of Britain. Every schoolchild knows—"

"Maybe I need to go back to school. Let's see . . . 1987, minus 211 . . . six, seven, seven, one—You're right! July Fourth, 1776! Obvious!"

She sadly shook her head again. "No, it was the *Second* of July—firecrackers, rockets, guns firing into the air . . . Lee and Adams—"

"July second—rings a bell somehow. Well, set it aside a minute. Now tell me *where* we are: this city of yours doesn't amount to a wide spot in the road, where I come from."

She shook her head a third time. It was becoming a habit. "Win, I'll be what help I can, even if it means playing silly games. Laporte is a *very* wide spot, indeed. One of the largest cities in the North American Confederacy. In—"

"Hold it! *Confederacy?* Let me think—who won the Civil War?"

"Civil War?" she blinked—at least it was a change from headshaking. "You can't mean this country, unless you count the Whiskey—"

"I mean the War Between the States—tariffs and slavery, Lee and Grant, Lincoln and Jefferson Davis? 1861 to 1865. Lincoln gets killed at the end—very sad."

Clarissa looked very sad, *systematic delusions* written all over her face. "Win, I don't know what you're talking about. In the first place, slavery was abolished in 44 A.L., very peaceably, thanks to Thomas Jefferson—"

"Thomas Jefferson?"

"And in the second place, I didn't recognize those names you rattled off. Except Jefferson Davis. He was President—no, it would have been the Old United States, back then—in, oh, I just can't remember! He wasn't very important."

"Is there a third place? I can't stand the suspense."

"Why, yes. There wasn't any 1865. The date that *would* have been 1865 was . . ." she looked up at the ceiling, "89 A.L."

I wouldn't give up. "Okay, who was President in '89? Wasn't it Abraham Lincoln—or maybe Andrew Jackson?"

"No, now you've asked an easy one: Lysander Spooner, one of the greatest philosophers who ever lived. I don't remember the dates, offhand, but he went on to be President for a long time after that. I guess the only President more important was Gallatin."

"Gallatin! *Albert* Gallatin?"

"Why, yes—second President of the old United States, and . . ." I felt dizzy. What had become of John Adams? Where were Andrew Johnson and the Civil War? What had happened to Lincoln, and who in hell's name was Lysander Spooner?

"Wait a minute, Clarissa, I didn't catch that last bit."

She sighed, giving in to the headshaking impulse again. "I *said*, Albert Gallatin was also the man who killed George Washington."

VII: The Looking Glass

Can time run edgewise? Or can a lifetime of memories turn out to be only a delusion? Those were about the only choices I had. There was a third: that I was hallucinating now. But, delusion though it might be, my life had taught me to trust my own judgment, and each time I'd questioned it, I'd been disastrously wrong. Every time someone urged me to doubt it for my "own good," there had been an ulterior motive. I wouldn't begin doubting myself now.

Which brought me back to the original fork in the road: either my whole life until now had been some kind of dope dream, or somehow history had shifted *sideways*. Correction: *I* had been shifted sideways in time.

Hold on, wasn't there some book . . . something about Grant's horse throwing him and— That's *right! If the South Had Won the Civil War,* by MacKinlay Kantor. If I'd been dropped into *that* world—two American States, one United and one Confederate; Cuba a southern state and Alaska still Russian—I'd be almost as confused as I was now! And it had all started with Grant getting killed before he'd won the war.

Okay, what was the *first* difference between this strangely revised history and the one I learned in school? According to Clarissa, there'd never been a Civil War, so something must have resolved the tariff and slavery issues. Whatever it was, there would be, in turn, some previous cause, and so on, right back to the Declaration of Independence. Could it be that the Fourth of July was on July second? Could two measly little days change the face of everthing I knew? It didn't seem possible, but I was *here!*

And where, oh, where, was the world I'd been born into, grown up in, loved and hated? Did it still exist? Had it ever existed?

That afternoon, Ed kept me company while Clarissa was calling on another patient. I caught myself hoping it was some fat old lady. Like every foreign traveler, I was discovering that I could brace myself for big differences like steam-powered hovercraft on grass-covered thoroughfares, but little differences—physicians who make housecalls—seemed almost too much.

Ed stifled a snicker as he came into the room. Everywhere Clarissa thought there was something wrong with me, whether inflicted in the last few hours or not, there were wires, coils, and antennae. She believed firmly I'd had one foot in the grave and the other on a vaudeville cliché for years. Some were connected to oddball hardware she'd left behind, or even to the phone—pardon me, *Telecom*. Some wasn't connected to anything at all—it just sprouted.

The major features of this ridiculous setup were large plastic pillows full of circuitry, placed as close as possible to every broken bone in my body. A miniature pair had even been attached to my big toe, like oversized Chiclets. Clarissa called them Basset coils —something about calcium ions—and claimed I'd be up and around in *days* instead of months.

I must have looked miserable, wired up like the Bride of Frankenstein, but a lot of the machinery was responsible for my dramatic lack of pain: *somasthesia* —some kind of electronic acupuncture.

But something else was on my mind. Once, years ago, I'd started having stomach trouble—heartburn cubed—flares of temper, and depression. Mother had gone that way: cancer. It took a long, long time. Rather than see a doctor and have my final doom pronounced, I put it off and the symptoms got worse and worse. I'd get along perfectly well, five, ten minutes at a time—then suddenly remember the sword hanging over my head. My life would turn to dull, flat pasteboard and I'd brood until something distracted me. Then the process would start all over again.

I finally got an appointment: that must have been one confused sawbones, as I danced him around the office, kissed him on both cheeks, and waltzed out with my brand-new shiny ulcer.

Now I was going through the same thing—suddenly remembering a particularly chilling aspect of the present situation, the world lurching out from under me, that pasteboard feeling again. Only this time I wasn't worrying about internal medicine but, you might say, metaphysics.

I shared my sideways time-travel notions with Ed, who surprised me by expressing simliar conclusions. "I'll have to admit, if it weren't for the physical evidence, I'd have written you off as some kind of lunatic."

"Evidence?" I was half-sitting now, draped in yards of cable, the cast on my arm beginning to be a nuisance.

Ed tipped his chair against a bookcase, serape trailing to the floor, and interlaced his fingers across his stomach—a gesture I recognized eerily as my own. "Well, besides your remarkably good looks, there are your guns. Manufacturing firearms requires heavy capital. It isn't exactly a cottage industry."

I smiled, remembering Eibar in Spain, and American cell-block zip guns. "I don't know. The Cao Dai used to turn out some beauties."

"I'll take your word for it—but any industry implies a lot about the culture behind it." He turned, picking up my guns from the top of the bookcase. "Now I'd never heard of this Smith & Wesson outfit, but I 'commed around and found out they went broke over a hundred years ago trying to sell a pistol called the Volcanic—appropriate, since it tended to blow itself to *Smith*-ereens."

"Turn up the painkillers!" I groaned. "What about the Browning?"

"Quite a different matter: made in Belgium, it says, for an American company headquartered someplace

called Morgan, Utah"—he pronounced it "Ootuh"—
"and Montreal . . . P.Q.?"

"Province of Quebec—used to be part of Canada.
Utah—'You-taw'—is, uh, west of here." I pointed my
good arm at the Rockies on the wall-size TV screen.

Ed raised an eyebrow. "That proves my point.
Canada's been part of our Confederacy since 117
A.L.—"

"Um . . . 1893? It's separate from the U.S., all right.
'People's Republic.' Go on about the guns."

"Well, look at mine. It's a Browning, too." He
hauled a .45-sized pistol from under his poncho,
popped the magazine, and shuffled the chamber round
onto the bed. It was beautiful, a soft dull gray with
slimmer, cleaner lines than an Army Colt.

J. M. BROWNING'S SONS', PERSONAL WEAPONS, LTD.
MFG. NAUVOO, N.A.C.

"Nauvoo—I've heard that somewhere before, but
what does it prove?"

"*Your* Browning," Ed said, "is made of steel,
smaller, but heavier than mine, which is almost entirely titanium. The last steel firearms were made in
this country over sixty years ago—I looked it up. Mine
was manufactured by molecular deposition, electron
discharge—processes that don't leave toolmarks.
Yours, though they've done a first-class job, was obviously cut from a solid slab, another method obsolete
for generations. No offense."

"None taken. You're way ahead of us technologi-
cally, that's obvious. Anyway, it's not really my gun. It
belonged to one of the people who attacked me."

Ed nodded. "I see. Well this morning while you
were sleeping, I 'commed Browning and took the
liberty of showing them this thing. Made by antiquated
methods, yet no antique. It caused quite a sensation. I
suspect they'd offer you a pretty tenth-piece for it."

I laughed. "Might need a grubstake at that. I can't
go on being a charity case forever. Kind of tickles me,
though. For once in my life, doing business with the
government turns out to be profitable!"

He smiled reassuringly. "Don't worry about charity. Just take it easy so your bones will knit straight."

"Thanks. Listen, Ed, that 'Nauvoo'—I remember now: John Moses Browning was brought up Mormon. Had two or three mothers, as I recall—"

"That's right." He nodded. "Lots of Mormons practice polygamy, although it's not too popular anywhere else, especially out west, here."

"Yeah? Well in *my* history, the Mormons *are* out west! Trekked out here after their settlement was burned—Nauvoo, Illinois. Illinois is a state, like the thirteen colonies—you know, Chicago?"

Ed grinned. "I'll say I do. It's the biggest city in the world! Nauvoo, though—let's take a look." He removed an object from the bookcase, fourteen inches long, maybe ten wide, half an inch thick. Sort of an overweight clipboard with a screen and keyboard. At the foot of my bed, the mountain glade disappeared, replaced by a map of North America.

"A bit southwest of Chicago," Ed confirmed. "I guess in my history, they never got—Win?"

"Hunh?" I blinked, a bit preoccupied. All of North America, from the Isthmus to the Arctic, seemed to be one country: the North American Confederacy—no state or provincial boundaries. Chicago was indeed the biggest apple, rivaled closely by Los Angeles and Mexico City. There wasn't any Washington, D.C., and Manhattan, in tiny, barely visible letters, seemed nothing more than a sleepy Indian village. Laporte was a major urban area half the size of Chicago, and Ed was right—*no Denver*. That sickening chill wrapped itself around my guts again. "—Sorry, Ed. This'll take some getting used to. Same history up through the Revolution, different afterward . . . or some strange mixture, anyhow."

Ed looked at me with concern. "Don't let a few little differences get to you. It's still the same old continent."

"Ed, I never *heard* of half the cities on that map! And in my world, Hollywood's in *California*. Something big is going on here. If I don't find out what, I'm gonna go stark raving batty!"

"I see." He reloaded his pistol and shucked it into his holster. "Win, my friend, something else is driving me . . . 'batty'?"

"Yeah." I returned his gaze. "Us."

"In a shell case—"

"Make that a nutshell and I'll second the motion."

"We look alike, have the same name, pursue much the same vocation. In some sense we might be the same person. Each of us is what the other *might* have been. We're twin brothers of some kind."

I looked away, uncomfortably aware of his dark shaggy hair, perfect teeth, unwrinkled face, and slim, youthful bearing. "I'm touched, Ed, but think again— *look* again. How old are you?"

"Forty-eight last May twelfth."

"Shit. Remind me to ask who does your hair! Okay, I got another one: I was born right *there.*" I pointed to the Denverless spot on the map. "How could we be twins if my hometown's nonexistent?"

He looked puzzled briefly. "I was born right about where you're pointing." He fiddled with the controls and zoomed in close. Laporte was now at the top, a little south of where Wyoming ought to be, and in the middle, in still-tiny print, the townships of Saint Charles and Auraria, the South Platte River winding between them. A sudden tension swept my body.

"Your parents. What were their names?"

"My parents are both living," he said firmly. "William and Edna Bear. They moved up to the northwest coast near Tlingit a few years ago, but they're both from this area originally."

I forged onward. "And they're both full-blooded Ute Indians—that's where the name Utah comes from."

"I hadn't made the connection. But you're right, they're from Indian stock. Doesn't mean very much, does it?"

"It never did to me," I said, "but to some . . ." I thought about Watts and of the Arab-Vietnamese gang-rumbles on my own beat. "Where I come from, people kill each other about it, sometimes."

"Another difference between our histories?"

"Or between our people. That makes you lucky on two counts, Ed. Dad got his in a B-17—a kind of military bomber—over Germany in 1943. Mom passed away in 1957, the day I graduated from high school. I wish I understood what all this means."

"So do I. It gives me a very strange, unwholesome feeling. How would you feel about meeting my folks?"

I shuddered and he saw it.

"Just take your time." He replaced the map with another scenic view, the Royal Gorge this time, then spent a long while looking out into the back garden. "Win, why should we . . . I mean, why should both our worlds, if they diverged so long ago, have produced—"

"A pair of identical gumshoes? I've been thinking about that. Maybe because we're both Indians."

"I don't understand."

"Well, I never set much store in being 'native American'—neolithically ignorant while the rest of the world was out inventing the wheel, gunpowder, carbon steel. Hell, if our esteemed ancestors had been able to get along with one another thirty days running, they could have thrown Pizarro and Cortez out on their hairy asses and developed a real civilization."

"So what's your point?"

"I don't know exactly where our histories diverged. I'd sleep better tonight if I did. But those histories are mostly *white people's* histories, right? I mean, George Washington got killed in the Whiskey Rebellion, that's what Clarissa tells me."

"And she's correct. Right between the eyes, like he deserved!"

"Splendid. Well in my history, old George—whom *we* think pretty highly of—died in bed from a bad case of the quacks. He had a head cold and they bled him to death for it."

"Seems only just; he was bleeding everybody else with Hamilton's taxes."

"All right, funny man, suppose he'd had a child *after* the Rebellion."

"In your history? But he was an old man."

"Never stopped Ben Franklin, did it?"

"Franklin? Oh, yes, the turncoat Federalist."

"Okay, okay. Now George couldn't have had another kid in *your* history, because he was dead, see? But my hypothetical kid—an extra one, from your vantage point—would have had kids of its own, right? And *they'd* have had kids. Pretty soon the whole population would be substantially different."

Ed saw some light. "By now there'd hardly be anyone like us, with close counterparts in each world. But that just makes it harder to explain our—"

"Not at all! Look—whatever the White-Eyes were up to back East, that wouldn't affect what *our* ancestors were doing!"

He nodded. "Not until much later, and by that time—"

"By that time our heredity—in each world—would be pretty much unaltered!" I was proud of that theory. For the first time I began to feel on top of things. The feeling was good, while it lasted.

Ed tipped the chair back again and relaxed. "That still leaves a number of things to figure out, though. For example, how you got here in the first place, and—"

"And who's trying to fill me full of bullet holes while I'm here. I thought I'd left the bad guys behind. You got any enemies?"

He shrugged. "You thinking that the Frontenac people mistook you for me? Anything is possible, otherwise you wouldn't be here. But couldn't your bad guys have arrived the same way you did?"

"That's a cheerful thought. Got any more?"

"Now that you mention it: I still don't understand one thing . . . I gather that, in your capacity as an investigator, you work for a government. Why that should be so, I—"

"That's right, the city government of Denver. What of it?"

"Cities with their own governments? Well, let it pass. Now the pistol you took in the laboratory is marked 'government property,' yet you find it perfectly reasonable to assume it was in the hands of its rightful owner, correct?"

"Sure, the *United States* Government—not the same thing at all. Look, I know it sounds strange—hell, it sounds pretty strange to *me*—but sometimes the interests of various government—local, state, national —*conflict*. That's—"

"A good indication," he said with a sour look, "that you have too many governments!"

"Let's skip politics. All I seem to run into lately is anarchists—and garage doors."

Ed got up and looked at my Browning again. "I wonder about your theory, Win. About us both being Indians. You figure we're here because changes in history reached our ancestors too late to prevent us being born?"

"That's right—setting aside the question of *whose* history is changed."

"Very well, but can you account for us both being detectives—or even for us having the same name? And something else: these firearms—the Utah and the Nauvoo Brownings—both invented, presumably, by John Moses Browning?"

"Yeah, what of it?"

"John Moses Browning wasn't an Indian."

"Damn you, Ed! Just when I'm getting things figured out, you have to confuse me with logic!"

"Not logic," he laughed, "just the Bear facts!"

"Ugh. Well, where does that put us now?"

He thought a moment. "If we knew how your bad guys got here—assuming they're not just local talent— that might tell us how to get you back to your own world."

There it was again, that stomach-wrenching thought. "Wrong," I said, unable to hold back my fears any longer. "Look, something caused this divergence, some event between the Revolution and the Whiskey Rebellion that wound up with Washington getting prematurely dead, I—"

"What are you driving at? I thought all of this was—"

"Critical! Suppose time travel is possible, Ed, not sideways time travel, but the good old-fashioned linear, back-and-forth kind. Suppose somebody went

back—maybe Vaughn Meiss, maybe the government —and killed the wrong dinosaur or his own grandfather! Suppose history has been fouled up for good!"

"What do you mean?"

"All along, I've been assuming that *I* traveled to get here. Suppose Meiss's machine just sort of held me in place while my own world was ripped out from under me and yours slipped in to take its place! Ed, I'm really scared! How do I know that whatever change in history *created* your world didn't *destroy* mine?"

VIII: Night of the Long Knife

I had a hard time sleeping that night. I was exhausted, and not only from exertion and gunshot wounds. Clarissa's wonderful machines were healing me at a rate that taxed my reserves and made me ravenous about every forty-five minutes. But sleepy I was not. Lying around in bed all day wired up like Donovan's Brain is not exactly conducive to a solid night's hibernation.

I'm not the warm-milk type, and booze has never helped me sleep. This anarchist's Disneyland apparently hadn't any prescription laws: Ed's medicine cabinets contained everything from aspirin to morphine. Ironically, the dozen plastic bottles Clarissa had left contained mostly vitamin E, bone meal, and ascorbic acid tabs the size of my badge. For inducing sleep, she preferred using a cross between voodoo and electronics she called electronarcosis. But it wasn't working very well for me.

Lying restlessly in the dark, I tried arguing Ed's terminal out of something to read. Then I heard it: a humming, soft but unmistakable. I might have slept through it. I turned. In the dim back-light of distant street lamps, I could make out a shadow against the windowpane.

My Smith & Wesson lay on the bureau, but I'd insisted on keeping the derringer under my pillow, and that made me mad. It was likely to ruin my hand, and all I needed now was another set of Basset coils. Nevertheless, I reached slowly behind my head, found the tiny, inadequate handle, and cocked the contraption under the pillow. One shot. I'd better make it a good close one.

The window, hinged at the top, opened outward.

A shadow silently threw its leg over the sill. One step across the floor, two, three. Starlight glinted on naked steel.

He was on me! A huge knife swung in a glittering arc and I twisted the gun to bear as his blade tangled in the wiring around me, skittered along the cast on my arm, and was deflected. The derringer went off in a blinding explosion, missing his face by a handspan. I dropped the gun from stinging fingers, grabbing at his wrist. He jerked it back—I let him, pushing the razor-sharp edge toward his face. It caught under his jaw, pivoting where it bit, slicing flesh and corded muscle, spraying us both with blood. He fought the blade as it trembled a quarter-inch from his carotid, both of us weakening fast in the deadlock. I heard bones breaking in his wrist.

Suddenly he let go, ripped himself from my failing grasp, and dived head-first out the window as— *Slap! Slap!* The glazing dissolved in a million crystalline shards.

The lights came on. Ed slumped against the doorframe, a spidery wisp of smoke drifting from the muzzle of his .375. I sagged back into the sweat-soaked bed, Clarissa's careful circuitry a dangling ruin. The bloody knife lay on the blanket, millimeters from my shaking, gun-bruised hand. Ed's glance traveled from my blood-streaked face to the foot-long blade. "Don't you know better than to try shaving in the dark?"

"The gore belongs to the other guy." I mopped my face with the sheet. There was dampness lower down, too—trust my bladder in a crisis. "Think you hit him?"

"I doubt it." He examined the empty window frame, leaning outward for a moment. "He left his ladder behind. Wait a minute . . . something here just below the sill." He held up a plastic box the size of a cigarette pack, hanging from a skein of wires. "A defeater. Damps the vibrations caused by forced entry. Complicated, and very expensive. Only the second one I've seen since—"

"If that thing makes a humming sound, he should demand his money back. That's what gave him away."

"Excess energy has to be given off somewhere—heat or sonics. Maybe it just wasn't his day."

I snorted, surveying the shambles. "You didn't see him lying on the ground out there?"

"No. Missed him by a mile. He probably picked up a fanny full of splinters, though." He nodded toward the shattered window.

I grinned. There was an odd, oily gleam around the edges of the frame. Maybe just an odd effect of the light. "How'd he survive the fall?" I looked again. The amoeboid glistening was still there.

"Simple, with ten-foot juniper bushes packed around the base of the house. Think you'll be all right if I look around a bit?"

I hesitated. "Before you go out . . . it's the sheets— I've kind of embarrassed myself, it seems."

He didn't laugh. "My fault, really. I considered putting on extra security, but decided the autodefenses would be enough. Now I've let you get attacked again, in my own home."

"It all worked out okay, didn't it?"

He shook his lowered head. "You don't understand," he said softly, "You're my guest, ill and gravely wounded—and not, as it appears, adequately—"

"You didn't invite me to bleed all over your driveway! You saved my life then, and showed up just in time tonight. The sheets will wash, but all this bullshit *won't!*"

He breathed deeply. "Nevertheless, I'll hear nothing more about charity. I've shown how much my charity is worth!" He started for the door, but the knife caught his eye and he paused, then reached for it.

"Fingerprints!" I hollered, "Don't screw up the evidence!" I flipped a corner of the blanket over and picked it up by the blade. The damned thing was almost a short sword, fully eighteen inches from pommel to point, razor-sharp to the hilt and halfway along the back. It must have weighed two pounds.

"Fingerprints?" Ed protested. "What kind of evidence is that?"

I sat, trying to take it in. "Look—our worlds may have differences, but this ain't one of 'em! No two fingerprints are—"

"I've heard that theory, but what good does it do? We still have to catch the culprit, and if he's already caught, what's the point?"

"Jesus Christ! Don't you people keep any kind of records, licenses, *anything* that uses fingerprints for identification?"

"People wouldn't stand for such a thing. I wouldn't."

Anarchy has its drawbacks, especially for cops. "Suppose we lift these prints—then we could prove we'd caught the right guy!"

Ed considered. "Provided individual fingerprints really are unique. Can you prove that?"

It was my turn to consider. I'd always taken it for granted: millions of prints on file with the FBI, no two sets alike. But if the feds ever ran across a set of ringers, they'd never tell. They might even rub out the poor slob with the duplicate digits! It's a sad world. "I never heard of anyone *dis*proving it. Get me some talcum powder and Scotch tape."

"What's Scotch tape?"

"Grr! Some sort of transparent sticky ribbon, like for wrapping packages. I hate to start giving lessons, but it looks like you could use this one."

"There's probably a thing or two we could teach you, as well," he said good-naturedly.

"I'm learning every minute. Don't forget the clean sheets." He left me wondering how we'd get all the wires back into place. Clarissa was going to be one upset cookie. I glanced at the window. Something definitely odd going on there. Seemed like more glass, now than Ed's autopistol had left.

Ed came back, a bundle under one arm and a satisfied look on his face. "I checked around a bit. The bushes under this window are pretty flat. Couldn't have been a comfortable landing. There's a faint trail of broken glass halfway to the street—quite invisible, I had to use instruments. No blood, though."

I laughed. "Don't feel too bad. I missed him at six inches!" I pointed to the derringer lying on the floor, realizing for the first time that my fingers weren't broken.

Ed picked up the little gun, looked it over with disbelief, and put it on the bookcase. "Window's coming along fine," he said, running a finger over the edges, "I've called Professional Protectives. They're sending a team over. Where do you want this stuff?"

I took the talcum powder. "Hope I haven't lost my touch since I saw this in *Crimestopper's Textbook*. This should stick where his hands left an oily residue. Then we'll pick the powder up with some tape, and—"

Ed held up a hand. "Sounds kind of messy. Wouldn't it be simpler to let the Telecom do it?" He picked up the clipboard and pulled loose a little knob that trailed a fine, retracting cable. He passed the knob over the surface of the knife handle. "Now we've got a permanent record. Want to see?"

I nodded dumbly. The wall lit up, showing the six-inch handle expanded to six feet, its entire surface visible on the screen.

"Now we'll try a little contrast enhancement." The image began to *unravel* a millimeter at a time, replaced, line by line, in sharper detail. Dust particles, minute scratches began to disappear. Most of the prints were smeared, except for a beauty at the back, near the guard. "More ultraviolet," Ed said to himself, and the smears began to fade. Along each pristine ridge, individual pore-prints could now be discerned.

"Okay, genius, I'm impressed. What about the overlapping ones?"

More adjustments. The prints moved and separated like an animated movie title, arraying themselves like an FBI reference card. This seemed to satisfy Ed. "Now let's do the alarm defeater." He picked it up by its wires and let the Telecom look it over. Images were duly refined and placed below those from the knife, each paired with its identical mate, proving, unnecessarily, that our intruder had handled both objects.

However, at the bottom of the screen was a third row. "Where somebody else handled the defeater.

Probably me." He scanned his fingers and let the camera snap back. The bottom row shifted and danced, identified Ed's thumb and forefinger marks, leaving four strange prints. Ed looked highly pleased. "You know what, Win? I'll bet whoever owns these prints hired our knife-wielding friend."

"Or sold him the defeater, Sherlock. Don't get ahead of yourself."

"No comment." Ed grinned. "You want your bed changed?" He reached for the bedclothes he'd brought with the useless powder and tape.

"Yes—and don't remind me there's another use for that talcum! What about all this gadgetry?"

"I think we can hook you back up again. Clarissa left instructions in the 'com. I'd hate to wake her at this hour. Slide into this chair while I straighten things out."

"Ed, is there anything that Telecom of yours won't do? Must be a hell of an expensive rig."

"It came with the house, like the plumbing and the autovalet. But it won't change this bed, worse luck." He opened a wall panel and chucked the damp bedding inside. I sat in the chair, wiping the toad-sticker with a pillowcase. The blood was dry and flaked off easily.

"At least," Ed said, tucking in the last corner, "you've won yourself a handsome Rezin." He levered me back into bed and began attaching wires.

"Resin? What are you talking about?"

"The blade. It's a Rezin.'"

"*Looks* like steel, but if it's some fancy Confederate epoxy—"

"Are we speaking the same language?" Ed looked exasperated. "R-E-Z-I-N. Named after the inventor, Rezin Bowie of Tennessee." He sorted cables, looping them back over their supports.

"Any relation to Jim Bowie?" I asked, examining the wicked "false" edge along the back of the knife.

He thought for a moment. "His brother, I believe—one of the Alamo victors, and later President of the Republic of Texas?"

I laughed. "The way I heard it, Bowie's side lost

at the Alamo. Although the delay cost Santa Anna the war."

"It cost Santa Anna his *life*. And any big knife sharpened halfway up the back, is called a Rezin. Quite a promoter, that Bowie fellow."

"So I've got myself a genuine Rezin. Spoils of war, and all that?"

"You think its former owner will come back and claim it? Besides, it's the custom."

I looked at the heavy brass guards projecting from the handle. "Guess I'll have somebody cut these off, though."

"For plague's sake, why?"

"Considering all I know about knife fighting, it'll make it easier to remove when somebody takes it away and shoves it up my ass."

Tomorrow we'd tackle our mysteries one by one. With two attacks catching me flat-footed (pardon the expression) in twenty-four hours, how I got here would have to wait until we found out who was putting the hit on me, and why. Maybe it was just a case of mistaken machine gun, and they were really after Ed. Somehow I doubted that. On the other hand, if it was me they were after, they might know how I'd gotten here, and by implication, how to get back. On the third hand (*third* hand?) I had a lot to learn about detecting in the North American Confederacy.

"Okay," I said, enmeshed again in therapeutic wiring, "fingerprints are out." Ed was having coffee and pie. I was sucking vitamin-sludge through a flex-straw, and not liking it. "What about the Frontenac? Anyone in the neighborhood—Lucy maybe—remember the license plates?"

"What's a license plate?" He finished up his pie as I watched jealously.

"Well, scratch *that* line of investigation. It's a large metal tag you screw to your bumper—skirt—which the state issues for a sizable fee. Funny thing—if you're caught without one, you just might end up *manufacturing* them!"

"How's that?" Ed lit up an enormous stogy, leaned back, and inhaled.

"They're made by convicts on big stamping machines. How about giving a pal one of those hawsers you're smoking?"

Ed looked puzzled. "Slaves make license plates, and if you don't . . . purchase? . . . one, you become a slave yourself? A convenient circularity for someone." He looked at his cigar. "And Clarissa said no smoking until your nitriloside reserves are built up."

I tried to explain how convict employment—along with conscription and jury duty—isn't considered slavery, but he just snorted. How could I explain that licenses are necessary to public safely, especially when his culture apparently found no use for such a concept? "Look here, Ed, how many people get killed on your roads every year?"

He puffed his cigar again, and I began to look at homicide from an entirely new angle. "No idea at all." He reached for the Telecom pad. "Last year, around five or six hundred if you discount probable suicides."

"What? Out of what population—and how many of them drive?"

More button-pushing. "Half a billion in North America, and maybe three vehicles for every person on the continent."

"Shuddup and give me a goddamned cigar!"

"Your funeral, Lieutenant."

I lit up ecstatically. Needles and dials began doing funny things, but I ignored them. Anyway, the final problem—how to get back to the good old U.S.A. if it still existed—was unresolvable at the moment. Which brought me back to the same old issue: how come history was different? Not an urgent matter, perhaps, but something I could pursue lying in bed, using the same Telecom mine host brandished so unfairly.

And perhaps there was a bit of urgency to the matter, at least for the sake of an old policeman's mental health. Ed hadn't stopped with the fingerprints on the knife handle, on the alarm defeater, nor with those on the tips of his own fingers. After the security team had arrived, he'd insisted on showing my poor bruised hand to his marvelous machine. After all, we still had four extra prints to account for.

So maybe it was important to figure out where our histories diverged, maybe the most important thing of all.

Ed and I have the same fingerprints.

IX: The Constitution
Conspiracy

Friday, July 10, 1987

By morning, the bedroom window had healed up nicely. My troubles were a different matter. Who can explain their own times and the past that created them? I don't remember enough from high school and a Junior College curriculum in Police Science. What little I can parrot is just a hodgepodge of other people's opinions.

Hell, they revise it every year. I never did figure out what caused World War I, and with each decade World War II seems more FDR's doing than Japan's. If I didn't understand my own world, how could I understand this one?

Ed and Clarissa didn't have quite the same problem. For them, there'd never been a World War II; no Roosevelt I could discover had ever scored higher than dogcatcher. Not that they were much more help than I might have been. I enjoyed Clarissa's frequent, only partially professional visits, and I don't know where I'd have been without Ed, but history was less important to them, and viewed from a radically different perspective. To most Americans it's a succession of battles, wars, Presidents, and Kings. To Confederates, history's Thomas Edisons mean a lot more than its Lyndon Johnsons. Inventions, ideas, philosophies, are central; invasions and elections are temporary aberrations.

Take the Westward Movement: France at war with England and the world; Jefferson's Louisiana Purchase; Lewis and Clark; the Homestead Act; cattle barons and squatters; gold in California; the U.S.

Cavalry and war with the Indians. But to Ed it meant
Sam Colt, whose repeating sidearm allowed *individuals,* rather than mobs, to make a place for themselves,
self-sufficient and free. And it meant renting or buying
land from Indians cannily eager to take gold, silver, or
attractive stock options.

It was more productive to talk to Lucy. She was
older, a lot more widely traveled, and tended to view
the past as something that had happened to her personally. She had axes of her own to grind, but at least
that gave me a context and detail I couldn't get elsewhere.

"Elsewhere" meant mostly maps, fiction, reference
books, the encyclopedia. But I never lifted a volume or
turned a page, just pushed buttons. Even before I
began tottering around the house in a borrowed bathrobe, I discovered the Telecom—an inseparable part
of Confederate living, as integral to a home as heating
and wiring, as common as self-repairing windows:
television, telephone, secretary, library, newspaper,
baby sitter, housekeeper, kitchen maid, bartender, catalog, and, as I had reason to appreciate, nurse.

The cast on my arm was the devil's own nuisance,
although lighter than a plaster one, and ingeniously
rigged for washing and *scratching*—in essence, merely
a rigid plastic mesh. Clarissa maintained that, along
with electronics and vitamins, it was helping me knit a
hundred times faster than I had any right to expect. I
don't know all the therapeutic details, but I'm sure the
FDA would have outlawed it.

Even one-handed, I soon got the hang of the
Telecom's tubeless picture screen and keyboard. The
portable units could be found in *any* room of the
house. I enjoyed that, recalling the catfit Evelyn had
thrown when I'd insisted on a bookshelf in the bathroom. Most rooms offered at least one wall-size screen,
usually tuned in on travelog stuff, up to and including
views hot off the beam from the Moon or Mars—
sunsets and sunrises at interesting hours.

The Telecom helped me stay out of Ed's way while
he worked on some commission he'd turned down the
day I spoiled his vacation. I tried to feel guilty but just

couldn't make it: vacations are always a chore for me
—I'd find myself hanging around the department long
before the second week was over, everybody tripping
over me and some stranger using my desk. Lucy
came over almost every evening to play cards and
straighten out all the "idiotic conclusions" my day's
reading had led me to.

A short security platoon had been stationed around
the house since the knife attack and wouldn't be gone
until the Frontenac mystery was resolved one way or
another. I looked forward to talking a little shop with
them, once I felt more like hiking around.

Mostly I hunched over the Telecom, a stranger in a
strange land, trying to figure out how we both got so
strange. What *real* differences were there between the
Encyclopedia of North America and the smattering of
history I could recall? Something vaguely bothered me
about that July 2nd Independence Day—but from
then on, things seemed jake, right up until the Whiskey Rebellion's surprise ending.

What really differed was *interpretations*.

In 1789, the unlucky year 13 A.L., the Revolution
was betrayed. Since 1776, people had been free of
kings, free of governments, free to live their own lives.
It sounded like a Propertarian's paradise. Now things
were going to be different again: America was headed
back—so Lucy and the encyclopedia said—toward
slavery.

The fiend responsible for this counter-revolutionary
nastiness was Alexander Hamilton, a name Confederates hold in about the same esteem as the word
"spittoon." He and his Federalists had shoved down
the country's throat their "Constitution," a charter for
a centralist superstate replacing the thirteen mini-
governments that had been operating under the in-
efficient but tolerable Articles of Confederation.
Adopted during an illegal and unrepresentative meeting in Philadelphia, originally authorized only to revise the Articles, this new document amounted to a
bloodless *coup d'état*.

Funny—as near as I remembered, these were the
same *events* that had happened in my own world. But

in the eyes of my new friends, historic figures like John Jay and James Madison became villainous authoritarians. Of seventy-four delegates chosen to attend the Constitutional Convention, nineteen *declined,* and sixteen of those present refused to sign. Of the thirty-nine remaining, many of whom signed only reluctantly, just six had put their names to the original Declaration of Independence. By contrast, that agreement had been *unanimous,* and most of its fifty-six signers actively opposed the Federalist Constitution.

All this seemed vaguely familiar—Patrick Henry smelling a rat at Alexander's steamroller derby—but how did it square with what I'd always known? Were there really two distinct sets of Founding Fathers, philosophically at war with one another?

Right off the bat, the newly chartered Congress okayed a number of taxes, one of them on whiskey. This upset certain western Pennsylvania farmers who were accustomed to converting their bulky and perishable crop into White Lightning. They began to wonder what the Revolution had been all about. In 1792, they got together in Pittsburgh to bitch about taxes, Hamilton and his crew, and old General Washington, a once popular hero, now Federalist President and chief enforcer of the hated tax. The farmers feared they'd traded one Tyrant George for another.

The next year saw them tarring and feathering tax collectors, a fate formerly reserved for King's minions, and seriously considering hanging a few as examples. Lucy thought highly of this practice; I remembered IRS agents I'd had to work with and grinned. The old General issued a warning proclamation, and when that didn't quiet the whiskey farmers, followed it with fifteen *thousand* troopers under command of "Light-Horse Harry" Lee. He quickly became known as "Dead-Horse Harry" when the crack-shot sodbusters blasted mount after mount from under him—it became the Whiskey Rebellion's running gag.

I'd always thought Kentucky rifles had made *the* difference against the British and so on, but rifled weapons were rare during the Revolution and for a long time afterward. Federal troops carried French smoothbores. The "ultramodern" *rifled* guns were the private property of volunteer guerillas despised by Washington, but the only kind of army Thomas Paine approved of. The encyclopedia waxed downright eloquent about civilians being traditionally better-armed than the authorities, a principal element, it claimed, in the preservation and expansion of liberty.

It made me think about my uniformed years packing a bureaucratically mandated .38 against shotguns, magnums, and autopistols. I've sometimes wished the population stripped of weapons, but I never fooled myself that it was right or even possible. Later I simply broke the regulations and carried the biggest cannon I could handle.

In 1794, a Pennsylvania gentleman stepped into the fray. A former Swiss financier, Albert Gallatin disapproved of the way Alexander Hamilton handled the nation's checkbook. He organized and led the farmers and began convincing federal soldiers they were fighting on the wrong side—a tactic that created important precedents in Confederate warfare. Eventually he even persuaded General Lee, who was tired of having to find new horses, and the punitive expedition disintegrated.

Thus "fortified," the 80-proof revolution marched on Philadelphia, Washington went to the wall, Hamilton fled to Prussia and was killed in a duel in 1804. Gallatin was proclaimed President. The Federalists evaporated, substantial numbers of them winding up neighbors of the Tories they'd driven into Canada. The Constitution was declared null and void, and with it the tax on whiskey.

Gallatin's wizardry saved the tiny nation from becoming the world's first banana republic. Economic problems that had precipitated the Constitution Conspiracy were solved with a new currency, backed by untold acres of land in the undeveloped Northwest Territories. The Articles of Confederation were duly revised, with stringent limits on the powers, not only of the central government but of the states. They could have *nothing* to do with trade—such interference, in Gallatin's view, had caused all the problems in the first place. Only private individuals could "create" money, backed by any valuable commodity, to be accepted or rejected by the marketplace on its own merit. Gold and silver were soon in competition with wheat, corn, iron, and—yes—even whiskey-based currency.

Gallatin's land certificates were redeemed, the last money ever issued by a United States government. He served five four-year terms in all, and lived long enough to see his own peculiar brand of anarchism begin spreading throughout the world.

I hadn't forgotten my conversation (only last week?) with Jon Carpenter and the Propertarians. In my own world, Gallatin had calmed the Whiskey Rebellion down, not stirred it to victory. What had made him change his mind here? Is history simply absurd? Did Gallatin revolt because he had a headache that day or hadn't been invited to one of Martha Washington's cocktail parties?

A policeman's view of life, his relationship with other human beings, is from a pretty seamy perspective. One of the things that keep me hanging in there, if only by my figurative fingernails sometimes, is a vague sort of confidence in the ultimate rationality of it all: the universe is *lawful*, and, like a Saint Christopher's medal, works even if you don't believe in it. So if history proved a meaningless jumble of fever dreams and belly rumbles, I might just contemplate resigning. Human will and reason *have* to count for something.

Confederate history after the Rebellion was a mishmash of the familiar and the fantastic. Gallatin adopted a new calendar and a system of weights and measures, both devised by Thomas Jefferson. A metric ounce, I discovered, is the weight of a cubic inch of water—a *metric* inch, that is.

Jefferson enjoyed an even more illustrious career than back at home. *Fourth* President, after Edmond Genêt, he'd almost single-handedly lectured, argued, and shamed the country into giving up slavery, freeing his own slaves in 31 A.L. On the lecture circuit,

four years later, an irate reactionary put a nine-inch
dagger into his leg, leaving Jefferson with a limp and
a cane he carried the rest of his life. They hauled the
assassin out with a faceful of pistol lead as the
inventive future President had mounted the rostrum
bearing a repeating sidearm of his own design. He
finished the speech before he'd see a doctor. Slavery
was abolished in 44 A.L., the year Jefferson ascended
to the Presidency. He never really descended, but
died in office during a second term, on July 2, 1826
—50 A.L.

History goes crazy after that. Inventions come
sooner and faster. There seems no mention of Indian
trouble—a Cherokee is elected President in 1840,
that same Sequoya, I think, who taught his people to
read and write. The N.A.C. fights a Mexican War,
but only for a few days. Mexico and Canada enthusiastically join in the "Union" half a century later. With
no slavery and no tariff, there's no Civil War.

History must have some weird elastic logic, though.
Hamilton got eighty-sixed, but his malady lingered
on, becoming vogue with dispossessed European no-
bility. Splinter groups continued to clash for years,
often violently, over who was really his "legitimate"
intellectual heir. Amusing, when you consider their
idol's bastard origin. In 1865, while Lysander Spooner
presided over a rapidly shrinking national government, a politically shady actor, John Wilkes Booth,
plodded through a backwoods tour with an English
play, *Our North American Cousin,* when out of the
audience an obscure Hamiltonian lawyer stood and
shot the thespian through the head. Confederate history writes it off as a conflict between rival Federalist
factions, but I wonder . . .

The list of Confederate Presidents is short, many
serving five or six terms without upsetting anybody.
Year after year, their steadily diminishing power was
less an object of envy or violent ambition. Nearly
everybody got a chance to play King Log: there was
another Indian President, Osceola; Harriet Beecher
was her own First Lady; in 1880, a French-Canadian

of Chinese extraction was elected—so much for the
Yellow Peril, *mes enfants!*

Here and there odd familiarities pop up: the
Chicago fire and San Francisco earthquake; Jeff
Davis and James Monroe; the *Nicaragua* canal; the
first atomic reactor in Chicago, but in 1922! Color
TV appeared in 1947, and dirigibles remained im-
portant. There's something resembling World War I,
but no trace of the Spanish-American War, World
War II, Korea, Vietnam, or New Guinea. And
nothing about Karl Marx, Socialism, or Communism;
European revolts in the 1840s are called "Gal-
latinite." Men first walked on the Moon—with women
right beside them—in 173 A.L.—1949! And North
America fought a bitter war with Russia in 1957. The
Czar was finally overthrown.

The Czar?

Tuesday, July 14, 1987

"Well," I said, over my CALIFORNIA TEN-HIGH—100
PROOF, "that's certainly not the way I heard it in
school!" We were sitting on the side terrace, my first
excursion outdoors. The afternoon sun was beaming
cheerfully, and I'd just had my first gawk at an airship, a mile-long apparition of titanium and ecto-
plasmic Mylar, on her way over the Rockies at three
hundred miles an hour. Life seemed pretty good, and
so did the company. The Telecom was filling Ed's
garden with beautiful music.

Captain Forsyth, head of the security contingent,
was an old friend of Ed's, a grizzled, wiry customer
in a gray herringbone lava-lava and long black cut-
away coat—right in style for Confederate rent-a-cops,
and not the least bit funny once you took in the wide
leather gunbelt and heavy automatic strapped around
his waist.

Not that he was without his little peculiarities. He's
a nineteen-year veteran of Professional Protectives'
on-the-spot guard service, combat pistol champion of

Greater Laporte, and "saw the elephant" during the Antarctican War. A pair of warm and twinkling brown eyes made up for the angry scar running along his left cheek. He plays gin for blood, but only off duty.

Oh yes. He's also a chimpanzee.

My first day here, I'd noticed what I took fuzzily for an unusual number of dwarfs—mutants. Now I knew better. Half of Forsyth's squad were chimps (and don't say "monkeys," for the same reason you don't say "spics" or "slopes"), complete with guns, nightsticks, and corn pads.

I remembered the discovery in my own world that simians can't talk only because their vocal apparatus isn't up to it. We'd only just begun teaching them sign language. It had started here a hundred years earlier, maybe because Darwin's opinions were more graciously received, or maybe because Confederates view innovation as a blessing instead of a threat. Or maybe because they haven't wasted so much time and effort, so many useful lives, on war and economic disaster. Anyway, science and philosophy have never been separate departments here. Any critter who can handle more than a few hundred words is human. Killing it becomes murder.

As soon as they understood the set-up, chimps, gorillas, a couple of other species waded right in and began exercising their rights. That didn't arouse hostility the way it might back home: there's too much work to do, and too few minds and hands to get it all done. Anyone's welcome who can demand a place *and* carry his own weight: freedom and independence *aren't* synonymous. The first time I mentioned "welfare rights" here, all I got was open-mouthed stares.

Lacking vocal speech, simians wear a device which translates tiny muscular movements—subliminal sign-talk—into sound. As with individual handwriting and telegraphy, each "voice" has its own personality: natural variations in bone-structure, muscular development, perhaps even character. Really accomplished Telecom entertainers employ a speech device on *each* wrist—a whole new wrinkle in ventriloquism.

Gallatin and Spooner believed it: any creature who can *think* is, Q.E.D., "people". It's calmly anticipated here that someday there'll be computers with rights —and *they'll* be welcome, too.

"Then how *did* it go in your world, Win?" Clarissa asked, "I've heard bits and pieces, but Captain Forsyth hasn't heard any of it yet." She wore a long, simple, celery-colored empire gown she thought of as casual, with a white cross in a circle on her left shoulder, the symbol of her profession.

I shrugged. "I can't say exactly. Everything seems more or less normal, right up through the Whiskey Rebellion. But in my history, George Washington went right on drawing expenses."

"So what happened to old Albert?" Lucy had a tumbler in her hand twice the size of mine, but wasn't showing a sign of it. Her monster Gabbet Fairfax hung from an ornate shoulder strap like a *bandito*'s cartridge belt. "How come he chickened out?"

"I wish I knew. Gallatin's hardly remembered at all in my world. Only reason I ever heard of him was . . . " I showed them the coin I'd taken off Meiss.

Forsyth put down my forty-one—he was fascinated —revolvers had gone out here ninety years ago—and examined the golden disk. "Nothing but an ordinary gold ounce. What's so unusual—besides the fact I never see enough of them?" He scratched idly and reached for the salted nuts.

Ed smiled wryly. "It showed up on the other side, Win's world. People there aren't *allowed* to own gold. They use paper for money!"

I grimaced. "I still don't understand you people. You're all a bunch of crackpots—like the Propertarians. Only in this society, it's the anarchocapitalists who run things!"

" 'Don't understand' is an understatement, Winnie my boy," Lucy said, "*Nobody* 'runs things' here— 'cept their own business! And folks with other cravings . . ." She patted the holster on her hip.

Forsyth wrinkled his upper lip and screeched with laughter. Ed grinned ruefully. "Lucy's the last of a vanishing breed—a revolutionary with nothing left to revolt against. Blew up half the Winter Palace getting at the Czar, to hear her tell it—but tends to embroider her adventures a little, as you've probably—"

"Embroider?" Lucy lowered her eyebrows and hunched forward. "Eddypoo, you'll be hearing from my *seconds*. And speaking of seconds, my glass is empty!"

X: Shots in the Dark

When I was a little kid, I could never get to sleep the night before Christmas. With Dad gone, Mom tried hard to make that day special for me, but she left me with a curse: I've never faced a crucial day in my life with a full night's sleep.

Tonight was going to be like that. Our cocktail party had turned into dinner, then into a few more drinks. Eventually the ladies had gone home, Captain Forsyth, outside to supervise the evening shift. Before taking off, Clarissa had given me the happy news: the cast was coming off tomorrow, and I'd get my first excursion around the city of Laporte.

To me that sounded like a visit from Saint Nick— *and* I was back in the detective business: Ed came in just as I was getting ready for bed, sorting my pocket contents on the dresser top. Even wearing a bathrobe, I'm a traveling junk collection.

"You're on your own tonight. I have to go check security for a client." He watched me disgorge my pockets with the fascination of a small boy watching seventy-three clowns get out of a Volkswagen.

"I guess I can take care of myself—with the help of Forsyth's finest occupying every foot of the property line." I pulled out *Toward a New Liberty*, dog-eared half a dozen places where I'd given up in disbelief, and tossed it on the bed. At least Mary Ross-Byrd was easier to understand than three-quarters of what was on the Telecom, and she never failed to put me to sleep.

Ed shook his head. "Don't let your guard down. They're good men, but load that blunderbuss of yours anyway, and tuck it under your pillow—or would you prefer a real gun?" He indicated his autopistol.

I reached for the Smith & Wesson lying amid the ruins of my once functional shoulder holster. "This'll do fine—it and its little brother. Wish I had some ammunition for the Browning, too."

"What for?" he asked with a fairly straight face, "—shooting mice?"

"Meiss was shot with a .380, wise guy. I was thinking more of cockroaches, the two-legged kind, and I'll have you know this fine specimen of Belgian gunsmithing develops over three hundred foot-pounds of—"

"And this"—Ed swept back his cape to uncover the .375—"develops nearly four *thousand!* Look, Win, we can find somebody to make you ammunition for these toys, but you owe it to yourself—"

"Hell—with any luck, I won't be needing more ammunition, anyway."

"We could use some luck like that." He stood, idly poking through my personal debris: badge carrier, pocket change, empty cartridge cases. I might have objected, but these artifacts must have been as curious to him as the Gallatin coin had been to me. He straightened, took a deep breath. "Well, can't stand here all night." He glanced at the bureau again and felt around in his tunic. "So *that's* where it got to! Mind if I confiscate my pen?" He held out the one I'd found in Meiss' desk drawer.

"Welcome to it, brother, but that one I brought with me from the other side. It belonged to my defunct physicist."

"What? Impossible! I— Wait a second." He slammed out of the room, was gone a few minutes, came back holding his hands like a freshly scrubbed surgeon, in each fist a felt-tip pen. "Found it. Look at *this!*" They were cheap advertising giveaways, identical right down to the commercial inscription: PARATRONICS, LTD., LAPORTE, N.A.C., TELECOM GRAY 4-3122.

Here, obviously, was a clew (as they spell it here) I shouldn't have overlooked. I'd carried this damned

pen every day without so much as twitching a gray
cell. Clarissa could take the cast off my arm and re-
apply it to my head.

But the upshot was that I'd be employing my new-
found mobility tomorrow following a sure-enough
lead—asking the Paratronics folks how come their
property was winding up in the Twilight Zone. It was
more important than it might seem: it was Paratronics, Ltd. that Ed was working for that night, investigat-
ing losses somewhat more significant than felt-tip
advertising pens. The coincidence bore examination.

I had a big day ahead of me—which, of course, was
the problem. I squirmed restlessly under the blankets,
resigned to being something of a zombie the next day,
finally drifting into that miserable state where you
can't quite tell if you're asleep, staying there about a
century and a half, sweating into the sheets, then
freezing to death, struggling with the pillow, discovering my feet weren't comfortable in *any* position . . .

"YAWWP!" went the Telecom. I jerked awake—
both feet on the floor, gun in hand—stuck a speed-
loader between my teeth, wishing for my other arm,
and dashed into the hall. "INTRUDER AT FRONT
GATE! INTRUDER AT FRONT GATE!" I fumbled with the door, found myself on the sidewalk,
then the driveway. At the gate a cluster of forms
wrestled just inside the entrance. Forsyth's men, human and otherwise, were rushing in from other posts.
I hoped this wasn't a feint.

One guard lay on the ground, blood seeping ugly
black onto the driveway, someone in charcoal-colored
coveralls standing over him. Ed was on his back, arms
outstretched and empty. A huge figure, also in gray,
was pointing a weapon at his face. I lined up on the
stranger's chest and pulled the trigger, launching a
blinding fireball in the semidarkness. The figure
leaped and crumpled. The first gray-clad tough lifted
a gun toward me, did a double take, and lowered his
hands for a moment. It cost him his life. I put two
ragged holes through him; he was dead before he hit
the ground.

The intruders started to scatter. I snapped a shot at

one, but misjudged the distance. He stumbled but kept on, hopping on one leg, until the guards piled on top of him. The rest of the bad guys, four, maybe five, were gone.

Ed sat up on the dewy rubber paving, dabbing one side of his face with the hem of his cloak. He winced a little. "Win. How nice to see you—or anything at all, for that matter. Is that a Denver police uniform you're wearing?"

I looked down and was suddenly chilly, attired in the gun in my hand and the cast on my arm. I took the speed-loader from between my teeth. "Didn't know this was a black-tie gunfight. That's a nasty bruise!"

"It'll mend." He heaved to his feet, swaying for a moment with one hand on my shoulder, then steadied and took command. "Is the captain all right? Take that other guy into the house." That other guy, the one I'd winged, clutched his thigh and whimpered. He was on his feet with a little uniformed assistance; must have had a bootful of type O by now. A guard was tying on a tourniquet. Maybe I'd missed the femur. Too bad.

Forsyth had been brained the same as Ed, but more effectively. They were carrying him into the house, but he was "talking", issuing instructions and calling for reinforcements.

He wasn't the only simian casualty. My second and third shots of the evening had bagged a gorilla, R.I.P.

At 2 A.M., Ed didn't want to bother Clarissa, even though we had three wounded bodies to take care of, plus a couple of deaders out in the driveway. He was willing to let what passes for the authorities handle things.

Lucy, jolted out of bed by the fireworks, came plunging over, frustrated at missing all the excitement. She absolutely insisted on calling my favorite M.D., who was on the way by the time Lucy got out three words and a grimace. The captain frightened us by throwing up—a bad sign with a head wound. By then

Ed was glad we'd yelled for help—he was pretty groggy himself.

That left our friend with the hole in his leg, parked sullenly in a corner, two angry chimpanzees holding him none too gently and exchanging interesting notions about what to do with him if Forsyth got any worse. That gave me an idea, so I went upstairs to put some clothes on. Draped in a bathrobe, I came back with my forty-one. Ed was on the Telecom while Lucy looked after the captain. The prisoner stiffened visibly when I caught his eye, kept looking over at Ed, then back at me, with an occasional wild glance at the S & W.

"Okay, asshole," I said in my best backroom rubber-hose voice, "You gonna come clean, or do I hafta ventilate you some more?" I aimed at his other leg, resting my thumb on the hammer. The guards got a little wide-eyed, but stood their ground.

"Barbarian!" he spat, "You don't frighten me!"

"Is that so?" I shifted the muzzle to rest between his eyebrows. "I got two more slugs left. Think the boys here'd mind if I splatter your brains all over their uniforms? I'll pay for the dry-cleaning. Or would you like it somewhere neater, fellas?" I pointed the gun at his crotch.

"Get this savage away!" he screamed. "I stand on my rights!" Every face turned toward us, even Forsyth raised his head, took in what was going on, and sank weakly back. Ed rang off and limped slowly across the room.

I turned and gave him a broad wink out of sight of the prisoner. "Win," he shook his head wearily, "that's not the way we do things here."

I knew. I'd unloaded the revolver after dressing. Now if only Ed would catch on. "What the hell do you mean? This guy and his friends rough you and Forsyth up, and now I can't even *bend* him a little? We'd know how to take care of him back home!" I began describing the Spanish Inquisition, the Iron Maiden, certain North Korean variations. I was just warming up the hot pincers when Ed worked himself in between the prisoner and me.

"Look, Win, we'll do this *my* way. I've just called Civil Liberties Association—"

"Hunh?"

"What would you prefer, a lynching? He's got *rights,* my friend, the same rights you'll want, if *you're* ever accused. The CLA or some other professionally neutral organization takes care of everything. They'll call *his* security company, his relatives, friends—"

"Or maybe his *employer,*" Lucy contributed, "*That'd* be educational!"

"And what do *they* do, send him to the country club?"

Ed looked exasperated. "He'll spend the night in custody, just as I might, under similar circumstances, wind up under Professional Protectives' supervision. No, they won't let him go—not the way they're bonded!"

"Y'gotta admit, Eddie," Lucy butted in again, "the accommodations're pretty accommodatin'. Shucks, the *guest* pays for 'em—and recovers with interest if he's proven innocent."

"*Innocent?* This son of a—"

"Lucy's only generalizing. The CLA collects evidence and testimony. There could also be some lawsuits over the bodies outside. The CLA does that, sometimes, just to make sure no one can murder some friendless wino, for instance. Or, if the accused, here that is destitute, they'll defend him. In that case, they pass official neutrality on to some other group in the business. Then we'll get together and hire a judge acceptable to all sides. Any appeals will go to a second judge—"

"*Paid for by the first!*"

"Yes, Lucy, paid for by the first. And if *that* decision doesn't stick, a third judge may be called. His vote is final. Any two judges finish the matter. The whole process could take as long as a week."

A week? Ed spelled out the rest of the procedure. There aren't any real prisons in the Confederacy. People who hurt others are expected to pay for it, *literally.* There are no "victimless crimes": shoot heroin, snort a little coke, ride your bike without a helment, do anything—*to yourself*.

The "law" only compels you to restore your victims to the state they'd be in had the crime never occurred. Fail in that, and your name and face get plastered all over, a formidable threat in a society geared to something like the Telecom. Who'll do business with somebody who refuses his *moral* debts? No place to purchase food, clothing, shelter, ammunition—any of the necessities of life.

And one *certain* way to get ostracized is to commit an *irrevocable* crime, like murder, for which restitution cannot be made.

Insanity is no excuse. The judge is only interested in how you're planning to make up for what you did. Society never takes the rap: in North America, there are only individuals.

Exiles can take their property and leave. Several countries still accept them, and a number of asteroid colonies. None very pleasant. The bright side is there's no professional criminal class, no "ex-offenders." Once you've made it good, you're square. Every day is a fresh start, and that beats hell out of sitting in a concrete box, stamping out license plates.

All of this assumes, of course, that the criminal survives his initial attempt against his well-armed victim, a *considerable* assumption, and another reason there aren't many jails and no real prisons. Now that he was safely caught, our prisoner was relying on a highly-civilized system: no *Confederate* would harm him, but he was afraid of *me*. And that was intriguing.

"Screw your goddamned CLA!" I bellowed, working up a totally artificial rage, "I'm gonna get some answers the good old-fashioned way!" I waved the gun, brushing the tip of his nose. "You wanna wind up with your friends out there, face down in the driveway?" I shoved the muzzle against his left eye and clacked the hammer backward, grinning like a demon.

He screamed and struggled. The guards had to plant their feet. "Don't hurt me! Please don't hurt me!"

"I'm not gonna hurt you—I'm gonna *kill* you!" I

made a production of slow pressure on the trigger. Sweat streamed down my purpled face.

"All right! I'll tell you!" He jerked from side to side, trying to evade the gun. A stain crept along the legs of his pants. "Anything you want to know—only *please* don't let him hurt me!"

I let Ed shove me away. "I won't let him hurt you," he soothed.

The prisoner sobbed, head forward on his chest. "It was Madison. He said it was for the Cause! Keep that savage away!" I was suddenly afraid he'd faint before he really opened up. "Madison will *get* you! He'll take care of you all! He's—he's got *something,* something from the other—" He stared at me, I think in sudden comprehension. *"He'll blast you all to radioactive slag!"*

With that he collapsed, and to judge from the rumblings in my midsection, my Method acting was about to claim a second victim, too.

When I got back from the bathroom, Clarissa was tending our unconscious prisoner. Ed was bandaged, and Forsyth asleep, breathing comfortably with an electronic contraption over his eyes. She glared. "Is this the way you treat wounded prisoners in Denver?"

"Not for a long, long time," I shook my head slowly, "Back home, he'd have more rights than honest people. I'm sorry."

"My patient in shock, and you're *sorry?* I hope you got what you wanted . . . *Lieutenant!"*

I winced. "Don't know yet. Who's this Madison, Ed? Let's see what the 'com—"

"Way ahead of you, boys!" Lucy waggled a Telecom pad. "Madisons, a regular epizootic of 'em!" Rows of names and numbers flashed across the little screen.

Clarissa conferred in whispers with the guards. "Lucy, can you take over, here?" She crossed the room to me. "They tell me it wasn't even loaded." She looked up, wanting something. I wasn't sure what.

"Didn't trust myself with the bastard."

"That doesn't excuse you," she said, "It was a hor-

rible thing you did. Immoral. I'm not sure I like you
very much, Lieutenant Win Bear!"

"I'm not sure I like myself very much," I answered,
tasting bile. "And what do you mean, 'immoral'? After
what he did? I've had about enough of this self-
righteous crap. You're all so smugly satisfied with
your Confederate status quo, you can't see the lunacy
of it flapping right in front of your silly noses!"

Lucy turned, disbelief on her face. "What's bitten
you, son?"

Suddenly they were all strangers, creatures from
another world. "The good doctor, here—for something
I already feel rotten about, thanks—while everybody
in this safe, stable, oh-so-humane society carries a
handgun, prepared to kill at the drop of a hat! What
the hell are you all afraid of? How come such well-
adjusted people cling so hysterically to their perverted
phallic symbols?"

Clarissa eyed me with cynical understanding. "I
thought you might be carrying a conflict or two around
in there! Snuggled up against that six-gun you use so
well is a regular moon-gazing pacifist—"

"Or potential dictator!"

"Let him alone, Lucy! Win, your built-in contradictions will tear you to pieces, here. I've known a few
poor devils, afraid to let others defend—even possess
the means to defend—themselves, unable to stand being alone more than minutes at a time, frightened
their own shadows will betray them, projecting their
fear onto others, interpreting every gesture as a threat.

"Or are you the other kind, who can't tolerate independence, who secretly burns to control people's
lives and suffers their desire for self-defense with
a twinge of guilty conscience?"

"You know better than that!" I spluttered, "But
look at you, berating my society, while here, women—
my god, even children—are weighted down with weapons!"

"Sonny, anybody with his gears meshed wants to
be free," said Lucy. "Don't matter what sex or age,
and freedom always calls for a little hardware,
even—maybe especially—if you're a little kid."

Clarissa went on, "Win, that first type, the poor wretch, battles every minute of his life against the temptation to bow his own unhappy brains out. He hates weapons—not because of others, but because of what *he* might do to *himself!* The second type, he's simply afraid he'll get what he deserves!

"You don't wear that gun for yourself, as an act of independence; you're *licensed*. Some bureaucrat 'gave' you a right you were already born with! A right you're paid to *deny* everyone else!" I held up my hands to stop her, but she rolled right over me. "I've heard that phallic-symbol argument before, and always from ineffectual people driven to make everybody else as helpless as they are. Who's more confused, those who think weapons are sexual organs or those who want to take everyone's sexual organs *away?*

"Win, *civilized* people go armed to say, 'I am self-sufficient. I'll never burden others.' They're also saying, 'If you need my help, here I am, *ready*'—yes, a contradiction, but a pretty noble one, I think. Independence is the source of freedom, the first essential ingredient of mental health. You're good at taking care of yourself, Lieutenant. Why can't you allow others the same right?

"Armed people are *free*. No state can control those who have the machinery and the will to resist, no mob can take their liberty and property. And no 220-pound thug can threaten the well-being or dignity of a 110-pound woman who has two pounds of iron to even things out. Is that evil? Is that wrong?

"People who object to weapons aren't abolishing violence, they're begging for rule by brute force, when the biggest, strongest animals among men were always automatically 'right.' Guns ended that, and social democracy is a hollow farce without an armed populace to make it work.

"Wear a gun to someone else's house, you're saying, 'I'll defend this home as if it were my own.' When your guests see you carry a weapon, you're telling them, 'I'll defend you as if you were my own family.' And anyone who *objects* levels the deadliest insult possible: 'I don't trust you unless you're rendered *harmless*'!

"I'll tell you something, Lieutenant. Whenever personal arms have fallen out of fashion, society has become something no sane person would consider *worth* defending. The same thing happens to individuals: they start rotting, too, becoming helpless, disdaining to lift a finger because it's 'beneath them.' They're no longer fit to live and are simply proving that they know it!"

She wiped fierce tears away. "Win, is it *wrong* to be happy with a system that works, *virtuous* to be uncertain or unsatisfied? Is it *wise* to pretend you know nothing? What moral cripple, sick at heart with himself, taught you that? I'd like to find out, before I get to know you any better!" Her eyes blazed into mine, and a strange hope stirred within me.

"Give the lady a drink!" Lucy wheeled by with an enormous glass in each hand. "Have one, too, Lieutenant—you earned it!"

"I never drink anything bigger than my head," I protested, looking again at Clarissa. "Wanna fill me up a thimble?"

Clarissa grinned, eyes still brimming and her nose red. "Sorry, Win, I guess I've been storing that up all week. Maybe I sort of overstated the case. A little."

I shifted the drink to my left hand and brushed a damp curl away from her eyes. "Yeah, and maybe 'overstated' is an understatement. A little. You were pretty wide of the mark a couple times—I never busted anyone for weapons."

She laughed. "For what it's worth, I think you're one of the few who could adjust to this culture without going off the deep end."

"Compliments!" I spread my arms helplessly. "Clarissa, someday you'll take back every syllable of that diatribe—except the bit about hosts, guests, and weapons. That makes sense." I took a long, long drink. It burned. "And Ed? You see this revolver, my identical friend? I *will* forget being a charity case. I've always felt exactly the way she put it: I'll defend your home"

—I touched Clarissa's shoulder a moment—"and those in it, as if they were my own."

He nodded and took my hand. "Perhaps you understand now how I felt about the knife attack; *you* certainly didn't fail—I've seldom seen such shooting!"

"Yeah, but now I've gone and spoiled it, haven't I?" I pointed toward our prisoner, who was really in bad shape if he could snooze through Clarissa's parade-ground lecture.

" 'Fraid so, buster," Lucy absently swirled her ice, "He'll likely sue our pants off—and you don't have that much to spare. Ain't that Eddie's robe?"

"He can't get blood out of a turnip. Does that mean Devil's Island?"

"Asteroids. No, Winnie, it just means we can't sue him: our claims'll cancel out."

Ed's sour look wasn't coming out of a glass. "It may have been worth it, if we can find out who the real brains are. *Them* we won't sue. We'll just invite them to coffee and pistols at dawn!"

"Is he serious, or is it only the head wound?"

"You bet your galoshes he's serious! Say, Eddie, I'm in on this, too. Those uninsurable worm-castings still owe me a front window!"

"You think this was the Frontenac bunch, Ed?" I asked.

"Seems reasonable. Only make it the Frontenac-Rezin bunch."

"I figured as much, too. Which is *some* excuse, I guess, for the third-degree, Clarissa. You didn't hear the big finish, did you?"

"Sonny, we all heard you barfing clear in the front room!"

"I'm not talking about that, Lucy! You know what a tactical nuke is?" Blank looks—Lucy stared deliberately into her drink. "Well, remind me to tell you when my stomach is better. Meanwhile, we've got to find this Madison character. Any ideas?"

Ed gingerly fingered the side of his head. "No, but I figure this concussion belongs to you. I—"

"Say, anybody feel like some food to mop up all this alcohol?" Lucy pointed at Ed's bandaged head.

"I'm gonna feel like you, in the morning, unless I shovel in some protein." General agreement, followed by a brief session at the keyboard. Pleasant smells began issuing from the kitchen.

"Okay," I said, "Now what were you talking about, Ed?"

"Well, you know my cars are still in the shop. That machine gun did a lot of damage."

"I know, I know!" I waved my cast under his nose.

"When I went out tonight, I caught the underground, did my security check, then I headed back. These"—he indicated the prisoner finally coming around—"were waiting for me at the front gate. They'd slugged Forsyth and one was wearing his hat. In the dark I didn't notice until—Win, they thought I was you!"

"What?"

"There was a car parked across the street, waiting—no, not the Frontenac.'"

"It wouldn't have been a white station wagon?'"

"Hmm? No, no. Just as I got under the gate light, I heard somebody say, 'That's him—that's the cop!' Somebody else said, 'Shut up, Bealls!' The next thing I heard was BONG!—then you, blasting away with your flintlock, there."

"Bealls?"

Confederates have a sensible attitude about time, having recognized long ago that, while some folks can function in the morning, others better not even *try* until 2 P.M. And people who stayed up until dawn, scrubbing bloodstains out of the carpet and trying to make up with pretty physicians who think they're uncivilized, postpone their appointments, and sleep in.

By the time I got to bed, the authorities had carted off the bodies, living and otherwise, along with depositions in living color and stereophonic sound, from every witness and participant—a lengthy process, but not without its rewards.

I wasn't going to the asteroids, after all. Our damaged guest denied being intimidated—was downright vehement about it. I wasn't looking any gift horses in the mouth, but everybody else was curious as the CLA shook him down.

"What's this?" The representative removed a medallion from the prisoner's neck. She may have been a Civil Libertarian, but she looked all police matron to me, maybe even All-American. At least Most Valuable Player.

"Private property!" he snarled. "Give it back!"

"Once you're bonded out." She handed it to Ed. "You make anything of this?"

"Eerie sort of thing. Take a look, Win." He passed it across the coffee table. Different societies use symbols different ways—there's a limited number of simple designs, and they show up over and over. The swastika, for example, has never been anything here but an Indian goodluck sign. On the other hand, our European street-sign indicating "Men Working" means "Don't open your umbrella in the subway." The medallion was bronze, an inch and a half in diameter, featureless on one side except for the number 1789. The obverse, cut deeply into the metal, was very familiar indeed.

"The *Eye-in-the-Pyramid*: It appears on paper currency back home. Never could figure why."

"*I'll* tell you!" Lucy almost upset her plate snatching for the medal. "Check those bodies out there! This is all starting to make sense!"

The prisoner thrashed his way toward Lucy. "Shut up, old lady! Shut up or we'll get you!"

"You want to open that leg again, fella?" The matron held him back. "Hey, Louie! Go out to the wagon and see if those stiffs're wearing any jewelry, willya?" She addressed Lucy, "Don't let this guy worry you, Ma'am."

"I've seen his type before"—Lucy chuckled grimly —"back in the War in Europe. Coulda collected a mess of those medals if I'd been the souvenir type."

Ed looked exasperated. "There you go again, Lucy, that was seventy years ago, and the Confederacy was neutral. The only Americans over there were volunteers in—"

"The Thousand Airship Flight! Bloody Huns shot

us to pieces, but I got my passengers down okay, and joined the fighting. That's how I met Pete!"

"Pete?" My eyebrows did a little dance at the top of my skull.

"Her late husband—some kind of Prince, to hear her tell it!"

"And a prince of a fellow he was! Started fightin' Prussians in '38—that'd be nineteen-fourteen to you, Win—an' tended the sick ones through the Flu afterward. A philosopher of no small repute, and a hell of a good shot. Sure miss the skinny little so-and-so."

"1914? Lucy, *we* had a war back then, against the Germans! And influenza, too! It's a strange universe."

"Stranger'n you know." Lucy handed the medal back. "Never thought I'd see one of these again, 'specially in this country. Kinda makes a body sick."

"It's Prussian?" I asked.

"Misfires and malfunctions, no! Belongs to the schemers *behind* those goose-steppin' sadomasochists. Thought we'd cleaned 'em all out in the *last* war— Antarctica. Last place anybody heard of 'em was the postwar coup they tried in Luna—naked through the airlock, deader'n dollars."

Ed goggled. "You mean it's really—"

"That's right, Eddie, it's *them.* And Win, I do know what an atom bomb is. I helped move Phobos into synchronous orbit over Coprates." She jerked an unkind thumb toward the prisoner. "If these crablice're plannin' t'use thermonuclear earth-movers as *weapons* . . ."

"Who the hell are you talking about?" I demanded, "Who's *them?"*

"The Hamiltonians," Ed answered quietly. "They're the ones trying to kill you, Win."

"Federalists?" Clarissa whispered with horror, "Right here in Laporte?"

XI: The Eye in the Pyramid

Wednesday, July 15, 1987

Ain't science wonderful? Through the marvel of Clarissa's electronarcosis, I zonked right into REM and awoke at noon, merely feeling like the living dead. First the cast would come off, weeks earlier than standards I was used to, but none too soon for me. Then we'd pay a call on Freeman K. Bertram, President and Chairman of the Board of Paratronics, Ltd., concerning his wandering felt-tip pen.

The day began with a small disappointment. Clarissa didn't show up to do the honors. Perhaps she was still miffed. In any event, one of her staff performed the ceremony, a young female named Briit. I hate admitting to prejudice, but a four-foot chimpanzee in hospital greens is no substitute for a cuddly blonde.

Sorry, Briit.

The plastic slithered off at the touch of an electrode. I was free! I flexed the fingers, tried a few rapid dry fires with my Smith & Wesson. Everything was working a bit stiffly, but, thanks to the meshed construction of the cast, I wouldn't be going through the usual scrubbing and peeling.

Much to my annoyance, Ed was in no particular hurry. After a leisurely brunch, Clarissa arrived with several bulky packages and an uncharacteristically sneaky smirk. Lucy drifted over, and Forsyth's bandaged-but-unbowed appearance a few minutes afterward made it official: something was going on.

Ed cleared his throat: "I want you to know, Win— we all do—that we're glad you pulled through." Ed's wounds had healed overnight, though the captain was still wearing plastic mesh under his hat.

"Thanks to you, especially *you,* dear doctor. If I had to do it all over again, it'd be worth it—I guess."

"Look, bud," Lucy interrupted, "Who's running this testimonial? Keep quiet and let the man talk." She rose and headed upstairs.

"Win," Ed grinned, "I'm not the sort to paw through someone else's belongings out of idle curiosity—last night, I mean. I was just returning your badge."

"My badge? All you had to do was ask."

"And spoil the surprise?" Clarissa broke into her sunniest smile, and I felt completely recovered.

Suddenly it really was Christmas. Lucy returned with Clarissa's stack of packages. "Just so's you won't get any exaggerated notions," she said, "we didn't order this stuff until we were pretty sure you'd live!"

I'd never had a family before; how else can I explain why Homicide Detective Lieutenant Edward William Bear needed a handful of Kleenex all of a sudden? Inside the first box were street clothes: a light, hooded, knee-length robe, blousy trousers and tunic, and a sort of cape or poncho. "You can't do all your gunfighting in the nude," Ed observed, "people will talk!"

I was hustled to the bedroom where other packages lay piled on the bed. Lucy leeringly offered to stay and show me how things worked. Clarissa stood aside and blushed. Pretty silly, since she'd spent most of one night pulling foreign objects from my naked outraged flesh. On the floor stood a tall pair of black boots, more evocative of gauchos than cowboys, embossed with swirls and scallops that were suspiciously familiar—some brilliant craftsman had duplicated the ornate engraving on my detective's shield. I sat down and wiped my eyes again, grateful for the solitude.

Another carton revealed socks, undershirts, shorts, all pretty familiar, and, to my satisfaction, not a single necktie or cufflink. I tried the satiny trousers which fastened with a toothless zipper, pants-cuffs tucked into fourteen-inch stovepipes. The formal tunic I decided to skip, as I'd seen Ed do, in favor of the robe,

which was silvery where sunlight caught the folds.
Along one seam, a sewn-in rod the diameter of a
pencil would regulate temperatures on chilly days or
when it got too hot. I put up the hood, and slipped
the tabard, black with silver trim, over my head.

Something was missing. I picked at the leather and
elastic that had been my shoulder harness, fingering
the remnants of my ammunition. Perhaps I should
take Ed's advice, and get another gun. I hefted the
forty-one fondly, hating to part with it.

"SURPRISE!"

Thank heavens for steady reflexes. They stood
crowding in the doorway again, giving me the once-
over. Ed pulled a bulky object from behind his back—
a tooled gunbelt, matching my boots, holster fitted to
the Smith & Wesson. "How'd you pull this one off,
wise guy? I'd sure as hell have missed my gun!"

"Easy—took it one night last week when you were
under electronarcosis, and had it back before you
woke up!" I strapped the rig under my poncho and
below my paunch and tried a few fast draws.

Forsyth stepped forward. "Here's something for that
toy autopistol of yours." A lightweight shoulder holster.
I thanked him, wondering what I'd do with it—and no
Browning ammunition.

Next came Lucy. "Sure hope this works better'n it
did for the last guy!" It was the Rezin—Bowie knife—
sheathed now to fit my gunbelt on the offside, where it
almost balanced the revolver. "Now you can either
shoot or carve your way outa trouble—might like some
latitude with them Federalists on your tail!"

Clarissa handed me two small boxes, familiar from
their weight. "Lucy's right. If you're going to stick with
obsolete weapons, here's some brand-new obsolete ammunition. There's more out in my car, fresh from the
fabricator. We had quite a time finding a 9m/m casing
to duplicate. Ran a metal-detector all over between
here and Tabor Boulevard. I hope we've guessed the
ballistics right.

"I don't know what to say." I tried to choke back
the tears. "I hope I prove as good a friend as you've
all been to me!"

Lucy wrinkled her nose. "Now he's gone and got maudlin on us!"

My first survey of Laporte was something of a busman's holiday. I'd seen the insurance tapes of Ed's garage: the brand-new Neova, a sleek little machine that put me in mind of a giant Instamatic camera; a steam-driven Stanley Landmaster with six powered wheels for rough country; the Baker Townmobile drawing power from induction coils beneath the grassy streets. They'd been smashed to pieces.

However we weren't thrown on the mercies of public transport: Lucy had a matched pair of elderly Thorneycroft 418s, a stately machine dating back almost to the beginnings of hovercraft production. Enameled a garish yellow paisley, they'd rolled off the assembly line sixty years ago, but, with the help of an adoring mechanic, Lucy proudly kept them in mint condition.

We crossed a hundred yards of lawn, climbed a hedge stile, and were suddenly in Lucy's heavily cultivated garden, where columbines grew in profuse, multicolored splendor. She walked with us on a crisp carpet of fallen pine needles, full of warnings and advice. "You gotta meet 'em half way—not like these FANtastics and Neovas that practically drive themselves, take all the adventure outa travel—the Thorneycrofts will drift right up the camber on the turns, and dump you on your head!"

"I know, Lucy," Ed nodded continuously, "but it's wheels-down all day for us. We won't be leaving town."

"I'd have figured wheels on a hovercraft are like, well, screen doors on a submarine!"

"Not at all, Winnie!" Lucy preempted. She'd heard me describe cars back home, now seemed compelled to explain to everyone about Fords and Chevies, Bahias and Cabrals. "Still can't believe you people ride the rubber all the time like old maids." Lucy patted one of the gaudy 418s affectionately and hiked up its flexible plastic skirt. "See? Like big inflated doughnuts." She pointed toward the drive fans, rudders high and stately behind them. "Can't handle more'n a six-degree incline unless you give 'em full power and blow out every window in town. Can't steer without headway, either, so you use the tires."

I remembered the absence of propwash on the streets, the Frontenac blasting along at full speed. "Are the wheels powered?"

"Naw, just for brakes and steering." She pulled a recessed latch and swung down a set of folding steps. Getting into a modern machine was like pouring yourself into an MG—this was like boarding a stagecoach. We climbed up behind the dual controls and pulled the canopy down behind us.

Lucy headed indoors, hollering something about "spoiling my storebought hairdo." Ed keyed the ignition, a turbine whined, rumbled, then died to a whisper. He tapped a brassbound panel gauge: "Road-bearing meter—weight on the wheels. Too little, no brakes, practically no steering. Too much and you're digging ruts in the turf!" He shifted a lever labeled DRIVE FANS and I twisted around to see the twin blades blur and disappear as we slid onto the rubbery surface of the driveway.

The Telecom chimed—an animated cutie like the one who runs the phone company: "Road Service," she chirped, "This afternoon we're showing *South by Southwest,* starring Archibald Leach and—"

Ed interrupted. "We'll be on manual this afternoon."

"Very well, good day, sir." The image faded and we curved silkily to the gate, my controls moving in synch with Ed's. I held on gently, getting the feel of the ponderous road machine.

As near as I can figure, Laporte occupies about half the area of Colorado's Larimer County. According to the ad agencies who keep track—a census-taker would be cold meat before his second nosy question—population varies between two and three million—North Americans are incredibly mobile. A lot of that is underground. We swept through timber and prairie Ed swore was high-density industrial, then the forest primeval would give way with breathtaking suddenness to skyscrapers swooping five hundred stories into the clear bright air.

Ed's place is in south-central Laporte, dominated by the university, an enormous park I was acquainted with, various retail businesses and small industries. We slid easily and quickly through the manicured streets, finding an artery that let us rev up almost to eighty, and, with cross-traffic whisking around us by landscaped viaduct and tunnel, were in the Old Town in minutes.

That expression, "Old Town" conjured up mental pictures that couldn't have been more wrong. Most Confederates do business out of their living rooms, which discourages undue formality and keeps enterprises small. Mention time clocks or commuting, they'll look at you like they *know* where you escaped from. But like many inhabitants of Laporte's older district, Freeman K. Bertram had things turned around: the high-powered executive's version of sleeping over the delicatessen.

Paratronics, Ltd., an impressive pile of Aztec Modern rock, was planted where the Poudre River canyon empties onto the plains. We slid into an underground parking lot, dismounted, and pulled three gees getting up to the 223rd floor. Bertram was a tallish, nervous type who preferred hornrims to getting his eyeballs resculpted like everybody else; he affected a sort of Italian Renaissance beard and a kilt. He swung his bony knees back and forth in a swivel chair, making steeples with his fingers while I got introduced and told him how I'd gotten here and what had happened since. He nodded and mm-hmmed at what seemed the right places, but finally interrupted. "Do not mistake us, sir, for one of the wild-eyed research boffins we are compelled to employ at the University. Do you somehow imagine that these events are germane to the warehouse thefts you were engaged to deal with? You'd led us to believe we'd heard the last of those."

Ed stiffened in his lounger, set his drink firmly on the tabletop beside him, and ground out his cigarette.

"I don't know what's germane to what, yet. But I'm going to find out! The leads in both cases point right back to your company. Only an inside man could get past your warehouse security, and this"—He slapped the pen down on Bertram's desk—"showed up on the other side. In Win's world. Maybe I *ought* to have a talk with those boffins of yours."

Bertram squinted at the evidence with distaste, slid it carefully to a far corner of his desk, and scrubbed his hands of some imaginary contamination. "Mr. Bear, we had the impression you were working exclusively for us. If we were misinformed, shouldn't we renegotiate our business arrangement?" I couldn't see anyone else in the room, and decided Bertram was being editorial. Or coming down with a bad case of royalty. "It was our hope you would apprehend those responsible for the pilferage. Such violations of propriety cannot go un—"

"Hold it!" Ed sat forward. "I told you when this started, I can protect your property in the future, discover how the thefts were carried out, but as to catching the ones who—"

"Furthermore—" Bertram insisted.

"I didn't want this case, remember? But you pleaded with me, and Win's sudden appearance made it possible to help you. Now you're complaining because I'm helping him, too?"

"Furthermore," Bertram cleared his throat, "whether you have prevented future thefts is moot. We have no means of ascertaining *that* until the thieves are caught. And understand this: we do not appreciate these feeble attempts of yours to excuse failure by means of this . . . this . . ."

Me?

"insupportable fantasy. A simple admission of incompetence would—"

"If you don't like my work, you can take your contract and—"

"Worse," Bertram waggled a disdaining finger toward the pen, "you seek, for some insidious purpose, to implicate our company—and its scientists —in your accomplice's misfortunes! Now we put it

to you, sir, we realize how profligate the liability
judges have become of late, but even the most
gullible . . ." He waved it all away.

Ed exhaled slowly. "Okay, I've tightened your
perimeter, reorganized the duty squad, and replaced
your inside night man. You'll get my bill. I assume—"

Bertram blinked. "By no means, sir! We've no
intention of arousing your indignity. On the contrary,
we're simply pointing out the distractions inherent in
engaging in more than one enterprise. Would you
really leave your job half finished? Have we not
worked together harmoniously so far? Very well, then
—*find* these miscreants. See that they receive the
harshest—"

Ed shook his head. "Bertram, I protect property.
I don't collect people!"

The Chairman of the Board smiled indulgently.
"These things will work themselves out. In the meantime, as irrelevant as it may be, I suppose I can refer
you to Dr. Thorens at the University." He brightened,
as if struck by an idea. "In fact, we shall be only too
pleased to cooperate."

Outside Bertram's apartment, I said, "Reminds me
of another guy who was 'only too pleased to cooperate'—in my funeral arrangements. You really
heard Bealls' name last night?"

Ed nodded. "I told you, the voice said, 'Shut up,
Bealls!' "

"Well, there's plenty of them in the phone book.
Could be coincidence. I know something that isn't,
though."

Ed pushed the lift button. We spent half the
descent in free fall. "What are you talking about
now?"

"About conspiracy," I said. "You know, this
country could use a few lessons in elementary sneaki-
iness." The car found us and we climbed aboard.
"Didn't you notice Bertram's hands?"

Ed looked annoyed. "Sure," he said, "expensively
manicured, moist."

"You saw the ring?"

"The ring? Oh yes—heavy bronze, matched the fastener on his sporran. Shouldn't get so angry—makes me forgetful."

"Sorry. 'We're simply pointing out the distractions inherent in engaging—' "

Ed cocked a fist back, let it drop and grinned. "Come on, tell me what you saw!" He fiddled with the ignition key.

"Well, while you were doing a slow burn up there, I was busy observing. Bertram's sporran was Aztec Modern—goes with the building. Hey—I wonder why I didn't think of *that* before!"

"*That?* You going to tell me, or aren't you? Wish Lucy would get a proper starter for this monster!"

"Clever—a giant Aztec temple. No one would ever associate the two!"

"*Draft* you, Win, the *ring!*"

"The ring? Noticed when we shook hands—you're right, by the way, they're damp. Checked it closer on the way out. Hope I wasn't too conspicuous."

"Come on, man, the ring!" The hovercraft coughed and rumbled to life.

"Oh. That. It was the Eye-in-the-Pyramid. Thought you'd like to know."

XII: Necktie Party

We skimmed up out of the parking garage. Before Road Service could offer us another old movie, I grabbed the phone. "Busy! Bertram didn't waste any time. Wonder how long he'll keep the line tied up."

"Hold your wheel, I'll find out." Ed noodled with the Telecom.

"Howdy, pard!" An animated cowboy appeared in full regalia: ten-gallon hat, boots and spurs, a pair of low-slung autopistols. He was also a gorilla. "Western Telephone and Telegraph here. I'm Slim. What can I do y'for?"

"The number I'm calling is busy," Ed told him, "Can you let me know—"

"Soon as it's clear, I'll hook y'right up!"

"Just let me know, okay? I'll get in touch myself."

"Any way y'want it, pard. At WT & T, y'pick yer own pizen!" The drugstore simian jerked a little bag from his vest and rolled himself a cigarette. Ed gave him the number. "Thanks a bundle, pard. Be seein' yuh!"

Bertram's not-so-subtle Mexican pyramid dwindled in the distance. "Tell me something, Ed. Doesn't this place seem a little silly, even to you, sometimes?"

He steered us into heavy traffic. "What makes y'say that, *pard?"*

We hadn't heard from WT&T by the time we wafted back into the heart of the city. I was driving now, beginning to feel almost a part of Lucy's paisley monstrosity. Held to a timorous eighty, it was like piloting a vacuum cleaner on ice skates, but with a siren and flashers up top, I'd have felt right at home.

114

First stop, Valentine Safe & Vault, where the thrifty shopper can get anything from a titanium can that'd hold both Thorneycrofts, to a tiny padlock smaller than a matchhead, guaranteed to withstand a full clip of .375s.

Most Confederate crooks post bond, not to assure appearance in court, but restitution to their victims. Such arrangements are seldom called for, though: Laporte feels safer than London, which made me ponder Clarissa's lecture all over again. England has very little crime; guns are strictly forbidden. But Switzerland has even less, and *by law*, everybody's armed to the teeth. Someone said it once: guns cause crime like flies cause garbage.

Valentine was in the hoosegow biz sort of by accident. Some client had ordered up a pair of cells, intended for the rare bird who wouldn't make bond, then had gone bankrupt before the goods were delivered. Valentine had tried to make up the loss by renting them out. That was a decade ago, and the damned things still hadn't been amortized.

Penology's scarcely a science here, but Valentine hadn't taken precautions any two-bit county calaboose would consider elementary. Our prisoner, subcontracted to Valentine's by his insurance company, had torn up a bedsheet and hanged himself in the night.

"And this makes money for *me?*" I asked, unsure what Ed was talking about as we bellied up to the counter.

"It better. You put that bullet in his leg, so I listed him as your prisoner." He fixed the manager with a frosty glare. "It's just as if he'd escaped."

"It's not the same at all!" the proprietor said unhappily, "You should've seen him, all purple an' bulgey-eyed. Word gets around, I'll never rent that cell again. The things some people think of!"

Ed was inclined to argue. "Jimmy, we've been friends too long for this. Look, the guy never identified himself, or gave you an address, did he?"

Valentine looked wary, seeing where Ed was leading. "Nor his insurance company, those tight-lipped, tight-fisted sons of—"

"We needed that information, Jimmy, that's what we turned over to you for safekeeping. Now where is it?"

"Oh, liver flukes! Since you put it that way, let's see . . . standard surety, minus a night's room and board . . . comes to a little over two hundred, the way I—"

"How's that again?" Ed asked quietly.

"Make it three hundred, then . . . and seventeen ounces!" He wiped his hands on his tunic and started pushing buttons. I let my gaze wander nervously over the show-room displays, out the big front window where our polychrome transportation rested idly on its deflated skirt.

"And four tenths," Ed added firmly, "gold."

"Nine-ninety-nine fine?" I squeaked.

"What else?" Valentine demanded, "You want credit, or will you eat it here?"

"Calm down, Jimmy. What about his hardware?"

The manager sighed. "You had to ask. I figured, there being no next of kin, and all . . ." He groped beneath the counter, producing a gunbelt in soft gray suede. The pistol was slimmer than Ed's, and lighter. Where the bore should have been, it was solid, glassy smooth. The trademark said Walther-Zeiss.

I looked at the lenslike muzzle. "What's this thing shoot, eight-by-ten glossies?"

"It's a hand-laser," Ed grinned, "just the thing to replace that ridiculous wheel lock you're—"

"Revolver, not 'wheel lock'! And if lasers are so great, how come you're carrying a slug-thrower?"

He laughed. "Because I grew up with titan-mongery, and I'm almost as set in my ways as you are! That laser'll do the job, though, believe me. Messy!"

"I don't know. Always figured a weapon that cauterizes as it drills would . . . hell, they'd keep right on coming, unaware they'd even been shot."

He looked at me oddly. "Who mentioned drilling? This thing converts water—ninety-odd percent of your tissue—into superheated steam. Whatever you hit blows up like the Second of July."

"Fourth," I corrected automatically, "How about stopping cars?"

"One reason I prefer the Browning. Anyway, the laser's yours, now . . ."

"Same rule as the Rezin?"

"Along with the belt and charges," Valentine replied wistfully. I shrugged. Kill somebody in self-defense back home, and they take *your* gun away. After a decent interval, it usually winds up in some policeman's hip pocket. "Say, bud, where do you want this forfeit credited?"

"Good question. Ed, where do they send *your* money?"

"Mulligan's. But hand them a second 'Bear, Edward W.', and I'll never get balanced again!"

I felt around in a pocket for the Gallatin goldpiece. "Then how about The Laporte Industrial Bank?" Congratulations all around, exit stage left.

I still haven't figured out if it's blood money.

DICK SCRAGS TWO, DEMANDS PRIVACY
Laporte (Telenews)—Unknown assailants last night attacked the Genêt Place residence of consulting detective Ed Bear, Telenews learned this morning, possibly in connection with gunshots rumored here last week. Witnesses report that Bear, despite head injuries, killed two alleged hoodlums, wounding a third who was subsequently captured.

Invoking privacy, Bear promised full details on completion of his current commission. As usual, the Civil Liberties Association refused comment, pending adjudication.

This is Ted Agnew, All-News, Telenews, Channel Seven-Ten!

WT&T's galloping gorilla rang as we hove to at Mr. Meep's Spanish Hideaway. Bertram was finally off the phone, after an hour and forty-five minutes. "Sorry, pard, that's all I can give yuh. Privacy, y'know.

"A hell of a note!" I complained as we dismounted,

"Back home that phone company'd open up in five
seconds flat. Or else."

"Great. How do you tell the freelance criminals
from the official ones?" Ed paused in the entrance.
"I wouldn't mind knowing who was on the other end
of that conversation, though. Maybe Madison—Hey
Meep! Keeping busy?"

"¡Ah, Senor Bear! ¿Que pasa? Have you seen Telenews? They're talking about you, *mi amigo!* I show
you a nice table, okay—I mean, *con permiso?*"

Meep would take explaining in anybody's universe.
A chimpanzee, he'd adjusted his wrist-talker for what
he fancied was a Spanish accent, then grafted a gig-
olo moustache to his upper lip to go with his bolero
jacket, Mexican bellbottoms, and one of those off-
duty bullfighter hats, the kind with little balls of fringe
around the brim. When he lifted it, his hair was dash-
ingly oiled, parted down the middle like Rudolph
Valentino.

Culture shock is a terrible thing. Ask the man who
has one.

He parked us beside a two-story waterfall and tore-
adored away. "Last month," Ed muttered, "it was
Herr Meep's *Gemütliche Bierhefe,* and the month before that, Col. Meep's Down-South Barbecue. Wish
he'd give the decorators a rest."

I grinned. "At least he takes a catholic interest in—"

"Kosher, too. Sometime back around December.
Best food in Laporte, but it must drive Mrs. Meep
crazy. She and the kids run the kitchen."

" 'Our Food Untouched By Human Hands'?"

"What?"

"Never mind. What's after lunch? Wanna see where
I landed in the park?"

"No—what the plague's a *tacarito?*—we'll visit the
university, look up this researcher Bertram referred
us to so reluctantly. The park's just across Confederation Boulevard from there, if you insist."

"What the hell, it isn't the detective who has to return to the scene of the crime." While I was punching up a menu, I heard a soft voice calling:

"Cigars, cigarettes, marijuana? Cigars, cigarettes—

something for you, sir? We have some excellent Khmer Rouge this week."

"Sweetheart, I used to arrest people for selling that stuff. Just a cigar, thanks. Anything, Ed?" He tapped his cigarette pocket and shook his head without looking up from the menu. I paid the little chimp, who gave me a curtsey and a complimentary lighter.

Ed took longer finishing his meal than I did—I still say chocolate turkey is a little heavy for lunch. Since I was suddenly wealthy, I decided to pay. The bill popped up on the screen and I turned to my munching messmate: "Ed, is this right, a silver quarter-ounce? That's only a buck and a half!"

"Mmphl. Probably added in your cigar by mistake. Need some money?"

"No," I observed absently, "nor does anybody else around here, apparently."

He tossed me a suspicious glance. "What are you getting at?"

"Well, it's been bothering me ever since we left Valentine's. Ever since I first got here, really. Take Lucy's car, for instance—"

"You take it. I like my Neova better, even full of bullet holes." He tore the corner off a *sopapilla* and poured the honey in.

"Her house, then. Or yours. You realize, my old apartment would fit—hell, it'd practically fit into one of Lucy's hovercraft! Everywhere I go in this town, everyone has lots of cash, and everything costs practically nothing. Where are you hiding your poor people?"

Ed peered critically into the pastry and kept on filling it. "What in epidemic's name do you think *we* are?"

I started to laugh. "Come on, now—"

"No, you come on! Lucy's a retired lady, Forsyth what you've been calling a rent-a-cop. And when did you ever know a rich detective?"

"What about Clarissa?"

He bit into the *sopapilla,* honey glopping out past his chin. "A tradesperson, just like any other. Let me ask *you* something: how long did that shoulder of yours take to heal?"

"By standards I'm used to?"

"Fractured bones are a problem we've solved, largely with substantial amounts—by standards you're used to—of scientific and economic freedom." He took the last bite of pastry and wiped off his chin. "We've also solved *hunger,* and by the same means. All you have to do is leave people alone."

"To die in the streets of old age or starvation? That's why you need government, Ed, to take care of those who can't—"

"Wrong way around, Win. Politicians *need* human misery, for their very—"

"Now wait a minute! We spend trillions, just to—"

"Spread the misery around! My friend, government's a disease masquerading as its own cure."

"We must be doing something right, the U.S. is the most prosperous—"

"*Slum* in your world."

"The poorest American's rich, compared to other countries!"

"And the poorest Confederate's rich, compared to most Americans. All your taxes and regulations freeze old wealth, and make new fortunes impossible—except for those with political pull. The rich fend off the law, while those below get picked clean by your IRA."

"IRS, though I'll concede there isn't much practical difference."

"New opportunities, Win, new ventures! That's how wealth really gets distributed. In any civilized society, the poor get richer, too. Pretty soon it's hard to tell who's who. Tell me: how long does an American work to buy a car?"

"He can't, any more. We used to spread it over a couple of years, why?"

"Win, a Confederate hoverbuggy represents about three weeks' earnings—don't look at me that way! How about a home?"

"Nowadays, forget it. Ten years ago, maybe five years' wages. Actually, you're talking a forty year mortgage, even with—"

"I paid my house off in six months. And Win, this meal you've kindly provided is an expensive one. Meep's got decorators to pay, after all. We could've eaten under the corner for the same price in copper!"

"How come everything's so fucking cheap? Don't your workers have to eat? Or is everything automated?"

"Automation doesn't help: it always takes more people to create and maintain the machinery, and a healthy economy's real problem is chronic labor shortages. Things aren't unnaturally cheap, Win, we simply don't tolerate a parasite that takes half your income and then builds more taxes into everything you buy! You people have been trying to get by on a quarter of your productive capacity—an eighth, when you count the costs of regulation—while the State eats up the rest! It's a wonder you've survived at all!"

I thought about that for a minute. Maybe we weren't surviving. "So you're saying that none of you are really poor?"

"Not the way you mean. You'll find we're 'hiding' our rich people, too, in exactly the same way. They're us!" He laughed and fished out a cigarette. I lit it for him and relit my cigar.

That complimentary lighter must have been old stock. It was embossed *Meep Feng's Oriental Palace.*

We bade farewell to our host. Lucy's image was on the screen the second we climbed into the car. "Been tryin' t'raise you half an hour, Eddie! There's a flock of newsies on your front stoop. What do I tell 'em?"

"I said all I'm going to say when they woke me up this morning!" Apparently I'd slept through that, another advantage to electronarcosis. "I'm invoking privacy—and so are my neighbors!"

"Got it, kiddo! I—" Someone peered over Lucy's shoulder. He didn't need a press card to have "reporter" written all over him.

"Which one of you clowns is—*Ow!* That's my best pair of shoes, lady!"

Lucy faced the intruder nose to nose. "Wanna be

burried in em? Get outa here!" She turned to the pick-up. "Sorry, Edward."

"That's all right, Lucy. Hold the fort. One more errand, then I'll come home and punch you up a steak."

"Nothin' doin! I'll do the programmin', something that bleeds for a change! Good luck, boys, try think-in' kindly of a senile old lady who lets smartass young whippersnappers sneak up an' get the drop on her."

"Buffalo shit, Lucy."

"I was kinda hopin' you'd say that, Eddie. Bye!"

"Half an hour?" I asked, "You ought to carry a pager, so your calls get—"

Ed looked at me sourly. "You *are* a barbarian, Win."

Laporte University, Ltd. is the local push-back-the-barriers joint where Bertram's people shared facilities. The Confederacy draws no distinction between ap-plied science and pure research. Those who can, do. They also teach. Those who can't, maybe they wind up in Congress like back home.

Dora Jayne Thorens didn't belong in Congress, un-less you prefer the delicate way they put things in Vic-torian novels. A six-foot platinum blonde with a figure that should have won her a staple through the navel, she was also chief of paratronics research. Her office reminded me of Meiss', even to the squiggles on her blackboard. "Mr. Bear?" She looked at Ed, and then at me.

"We're both Mr. Bear, Ed and Win. Did you lose this felt-tip recently?"

"I've got a deskful just like it. Is this what detec-tives do these days? It's certainly service." Her broad office windows looked across the park. I could see "my" Telecom booth, and part of the path I'd followed getting to it.

Ed smiled. "There's more to it than that, Miss— Doctor—Professor . . ."

"Deejay. Look, I hate to rush you, but I've got work in the lab before my next class. Mind walking?" We headed down a corridor that was *all* windows. The view—well, I was watching Deejay do things to a lab-coat that—

"As I was saying," Ed neatly derailed my train of thought, "it's not so much *what* you lost—"

"Yeah," I agreed, "these things are a dime a dozen."

"Copper," Ed corrected.

"Just plain fuzz, if you prefer. What's important is *where*."

She paused. "I hope this isn't anything about breaking a contract. I just don't get involved with married—"

"Neither do I. I just thought you'd like to know I found this pen in a desk drawer, too. At Colorado State University. The United States of America."

She touched my arm, then looked at Ed again, and back at me, a light dawning. Suddenly she snatched the pen and ran off screaming, "Ooloorie! Ooloorie! We've done it! We've done it!"

XIII: The Meiss Connection

Ooloorie Eckickeck P'wheet first conceived the Probability Broach in 192 A.L., when Deejay Thorens was a mere calf whose present position was occupied by another landling. Unfortunately, she'd been looking for a way to get to Alpha Centauri, and was particularly disappointed since her mathematics had seemed flawless.

At first she thought she'd simply missed by four and a half light-years. Microprobes indicated dry land, terrestrial temperatures, pressures, gravity. It was *Earth*. But how?

Swimming in faculty quarters at California's Emperor Norton University, she pondered the landlings, whom a tradition more ancient than tradition itself named "those we love and know not why." Perhaps it had been *their* clumsiness. She considered the possibility, lashing her flukes in annoyance. For all their pride in a manipulative ability to translate their childish abstractions into substance, she never really trusted their machinists and technicians. She had never seen the need to clutter philosophy—*science,* they called it, or *physics*—with apparatus.

Philosophy was a matter of cool contemplation in the quiet waters of the mind, of gentle debate through many generations, of decorous integration into the poetry and legend of her people. Why must the landlings always hurry? Let my grandchildren find the end of the migration, she thought, if only I can begin the path rightly. Why must the dry ones always *do-something* with it? Is not philosophy enough, in itself?

"I'm gratified to meet you, Mr. Bear. You and your counterpart from this continuum are a welcome though scarcely necessary confirmation of my hypotheses." This Telecom was different, a wheelchair with a table model TV on the seat, a periscope sticking out of the top. Ooloorie guided it remotely, moving her "eyes and ears" around, peering critically over the shoulders of people who were her "hands." There was no screen at her end, a tank of salt water twelve hundred miles away. The periscope cameras translated what they picked up into an auditory hologram, super-high-fidelity wave fronts that, to her, were "television."

Like the squiggles on her blackboard, Deejay's lab reminded me of Vaughn Meiss. Replacing rows of computers, Telecom pads were scattered here and there, but the rest looked unsettlingly familiar.

I told my story to the two scientists. Deejay listened with barely suppressed excitement, Ooloorie mostly in absorbed silence. "It grieves me to hear that Dr. Meiss is . . . is no longer . . ." Struggled the porpoise. "He had an unusual mind for a landling and accomplished, by himself, much of what it took dozens to do here."

"At least we know what happened to our Broach," said Deejay. "If it had failed spontaneously, I'd never hear the end of it from fish-face, there."

"If I were a pale, spiny, dessicated being, I'd insult beautiful females myself, distractable one," Ooloorie remarked.

"Why don't you tell me more about this Broach thing," I interjected. "I figured it was some kind of time machine, but—"

"It is," declared Ooloorie, "a paratronic locus, creating a permeable interface between two contiguous probability continua. Energy consumption is calcu—"

"Hold on!" I protested, "One more word and you'll lose me. Try again, with short sentences and *no* numbers. Remember, I'm a public servant."

"Perhaps you had better do that, Deejay. What is a public servant?"

"Tell you later, dear—a long, depressing story. Mr. Bear—Win, I suppose you could visualize the Probability Broach as a sort of time machine—"

"A sideways time machine?"

"Very good! But it's better to think of it as a *window*, through the wall that separates two universes . . ."

Paratronics began as a study of energy phenomena *not* related to the electromagnetic spectrum—at first, much like xenobiology before space travel, a discipline without subject matter. But as decades of mathematical deduction began to sire practical conclusions, it left the realm of computers and the minds of dolphins, to become an experimental science.

In 194 A.L., Paratronics, Ltd., attempting to reach beyond the limited range of ion-drive spaceships, stumbled upon the Probability Broach. Peering through a microscopic hole in the fabric of reality, they expected to view deep space from some vantage point other than their own solar system.

Instead, their first photograph showed:

NO PARKING

Reorienting themselves ninety degrees produced:

THE SILVER GRILL
FINE EATS SINCE 1935

This was not Alpha Centauri. Nor could it be the Confederacy, which hadn't used a Christian calendar for two centuries. In fact, in all the system, only Hamiltonians disdained the calendar devised to honor Albert Gallatin.

Investigations proceeded slowly. Boring holes through reality is expensive: the university's lights didn't *quite* dim whenever they switched on the Broach; the comptrollers just felt that way. Even thermonuclear fusion has theoretical limits, and the Probability Broach approached them.

Microprobes went into the hole: air, soil, and a few tiny insects came back for analysis. The atmosphere on the other side was filthy with hydrocarbons and other chemicals, the water similarly dirtied. One source was quickly identified as crude internal combustion vehicles. But why didn't anyone drag their owners into court?

In 198 A.L., Paratronics shelled out for a new reactor. Now a relatively stable hole could be punched through, and larger samples taken, but they told the same depressing story: an unknown, exclusively human, English-speaking people, wearing uniformly drab, tubular clothing, riding in poisonously primitive vehicles. A culture inexplicably bleak and impoverished.

The "portable" Broach head was achieved in 201 A.L. Now, from the deck of a medium-sized hoverfreighter, scientists could transport their point of view, explore beyond whatever happened to lie on the "other side" of their laboratory. They began modestly enough with something nearby called Al's Newsstand —Candy, Newspapers, Tobacco. What they found there stunned them into cautiousness:

THE WORLD ALMANAC
& BOOK OF FACTS
1977

They deposited a half-ounce silver disk on the counter one midnight, reached with carefully sterilized tongs through the newly widened Broach, remembering the wisdom of Poor Richard before he'd gone Federalist. They learned a great deal, none of it encouraging: the Revolution; the Whiskey Rebellion; *a War of 1812?* Mexico; and, horror of horrors, a *civil* war—three-quarters of a million dead. Financial crises alternated with war, and no one seemed to notice the pattern. World War I; the Great Depression; World War II and the atomic bomb; Korea; Vietnam. And towering above it all, *power politics*: a State growing larger, more demanding every year, swallowing lives, fortunes, destroying sacred honor, screaming in its bloatedness for more, capable of any deed—no matter how corrupt and repulsive, swollen, crazed— staggering toward extinction.

And yet this catalog of horror admitted one tiny spark of light and hope: eleven minor but distinct references to a group whose values and goals might gratify any decent being in the North American Confederacy—the Propertarian Party.

"You see then, gentlemen, how Vaughn Meiss became the focus of our hopes and fears. I rather imagine Fort Collins newspaper editors looked forward to the way he livened up their Op-Ed sections. We obtained such publications the same way we abstracted the almanac and other documents, including street maps distributed by your Hall of Childish Tradespersons."

"That's the Junior Chamber of Commerce, Ooloorie." I laughed. "But I like it better your way."

"Thank you, Mr. Bear. We had little trouble locating the author of these strangely familiar sentiments. His office number was available from a directory that we purchased at the campus bookstore." The police had likely never heard about this miniwave of petty thefts, accompanied as each was by an ounce or so of highly illegal but instantly negotiable silver.

"We found ourselves in a narrow channel," the porpoise said. "It was necessary that we have cooperation: power consumption would fall ten thousandfold *if* we could establish a resonant field on the other side, essential to bring larger samples—and people— through."

"It's like wireless." Deejay added. "You *can* send messages simply by beamcasting so much power that bedsprings and lighting fixtures will—"

"So I've heard. But if the other person had a radio receiver, you need a lot less power."

"I'm sorry, Win, I didn't mean to be condescending."

"Well, what was the problem in getting cooperation from the other side?" Ed asked.

Ooloorie answered. "You see, Mr. Bear—oh, dear, I believe I shall call you Ed and Win—you see, the almanac alarmed us about a number of things."

"Such as?"

"Such as the unpopularity of Propertarian anarchism, as these primitives conceive it. Most will gladly murder anyone desiring independence from a coercive state. There are worldwide organizations *dedicated* to such violence, and—"

"That's *my* world you're talking about! I don't know of any such—"

"Then what did *you* do for a living?" Ed asked. "Isn't selling marijuana acting independently of the state?"

"You know what I did, I was a cop—*am* a cop!"

"I rest my case," Ed replied smugly. "Ooloorie's, too. And a good thing—they were—"

" 'Getting pretty heavy.' " I answered. "Groucho Marx, 1932. Okay, so Meiss was as politically naïve as the rest of you. How'd you get in touch—hold a séance?"

"It's pronounced *'science,'* " Deejay smirked. "No, we'd learned so much from the almanac that we prepared a document rather like it, describing ourselves, our project, and culture—and popped it onto his desk one afternoon, when—"

"That was risky," I said, thinking of the empty notebook in Meiss's lab. "It might have fallen into the wrong hands. Why not just holler through the Broach hole? Or string a telephone line?"

"Apparently our manuscript *has* fallen into the wrong hands," said Ooloorie, "This person Bealls you mentioned worries me. Your culture is ahead of ours only in its ability to wage nuclear war. If this SecPol . . . Well, we'll just have to see."

Deejay went on. "Understand our limitations: we couldn't open a hole bigger than three inches, and not for more than a few seconds at a time. Beyond that, things would start to blow: fuses, circuit breakers, the department's budget—as for telephone lines, just imagine the field collapsing on an occlusion . . ."

"I don't understand," Ed said, a beat behind me.

"I'm sure you remember the explosion that got you here."

"Things afterward, not so well perhaps," I agreed, "but the explosion—"

"All right, now if anything protrudes through the Broach when the field collapses, well, watch this—" She extracted a breadbox-size device from under a countertop, set it on the bench, and plugged it in.

"An early experimental model?" Ed asked, conspicuously not touching.

"Goodness no! It's a classroom demonstrator. Our first mission-dedicated generators filled three rooms. It's warm now—watch closely, I'll shut it off."

POP! A blue flash at the center of the contraption reminded me of high-school tricks with hydrogen. "What you saw," Ooloorie lectured, "was a few air molecules interpenetrating the theoretical junction between two worlds. When the interface ceases to exist so do they—or try to."

"And bigger machines make bigger flashes?" I asked.

"Not particularly," Deejay answered. "In theory, the interface is two-dimensional; enlarging the area doesn't appreciably enlarge its volume. Ordinarily, the flash is about the same unless some mass extends through the Broach—then you get a *considerably* bigger flash, believe me!"

"So you can't use telephone lines. What would happen if you did?"

"And the field degenerated? It might take the roof right off this building."

"So you decided to contact Meiss by . . . by mail. A wise decision."

"We thought so. He sat there for five hours, reading the whole thing. I expected he'd write us a note back, and was ready to widen the Broach again, but he was ahead of us there—used his blackboard, which we could see and record easily."

"You sent him the pen and the coins?"

"Eventually, and, I think, a cartridge from my Deane & Adams."

"And here it is," I said, "the whole bundle, except for the manuscript. I never saw that. Three guesses who's got it!"

"Thank you, Win, though I'd rather he'd been able to keep it. Anyway, he began constructing his own Broach, but after a few preliminary tests, we stopped hearing from him. Then something wrecked our half of the mechanism, and now, here you are."

"Yeah, here I am. How come I didn't pop up here in this lab?"

"But the Broach is in the park, coextant with Vaughn's laboratory! Didn't you see our power shed? It was sitting beside the actual field locus, which was excavated to make the land contours match—blue, corrugated titanium?"

"Hell, I figured I'd been thrown hundreds or thousands of feet." I began laughing. "The damned silly thing only tossed me over a hedge!"

Deejay, however, looked concerned. "That explosion still bothers me. We'd left pilot power on, because it takes so long to run up. After Vaughn missed his appointment, I finally let the engineers go, and was in class myself when the blowup came. When we got there, the excavation had fallen in. We just pulled up what was left of our pole pieces and shut the whole thing down."

I thought back through the fuzziness of that afternoon. "Could the Broach be activated from the other side?

"Yes, the way we designed it. A trickle current acts as a carrier. and—"

"Well, that solves one mystery. I turned the bloody thing on myself, by accident."

"So I'd surmised," Deejay said, "although the exact sequence—"

"Might've been initiated already, by a little gremlin named Bealls?"

"Not unlikely," she conceded. "The real question is what turned it *off*—collapsed the field?"

"You're wrong," Ed said grimly. "The question is what or who made it explode?" My stomach lurched and I had to sit down.

"And recall, my brilliant colleague," said the fishbowl in the wheelchair, "that the effect is not symmetrical!"

Deejay paled. "Ooloorie, I hadn't thought of that at all!"

"What are you talking about?" I demanded, wondering what a man would look like after—

"Oh, Win, you were afraid your world might not still exist. Ooloorie's saying that the force of the explosion isn't symmetrical, it depends on the distribution of the interrupting mass!"

"What?"

"I mean, the little bang that tossed you over the hedge was part of a *much* bigger bang on the other side! Let's see now . . . No, we weren't the initiating side, this time, so—"

"*How* much bigger?"

"I'm trying to figure that out! Ooloorie?"

A long, uncomfortable pause. "I can't tell you. Transference was initiated on . . . I just don't know."

"Supposing the interrupting mass were a . . ." I hesitated. "There were five or six guys chasing me, and—"

Deejay's head snapped in my direction. "The field collapsed because it overloaded!"

"Okay, suppose one of them got caught. The force of the explosion would depend on—ulp—on how *much* of him was in the Broach?"

"N-no, on—er, how much was left on the other side." She looked a little green. It was nice having company.

"Suppose . . . suppose it was just his feet?"

"About the same as our explosion here, one to five microtons—about two ounces of pistol powder," Ooloorie estimated.

"And—uh—if only his *head* made it through?"

"A thousand megatons, possibly more." Perhaps her thrashing was a sign that she was upset, too. If the original explosion hadn't done the job, certainly NORAD would have interpreted it as an attack: World War III, the end of the Earth I knew.

"Only one way to find out," Ed said. I stirred from dismal contemplation.

"I concur," said Ooloorie, flukes agitating violently.

"Y-yes, you're right," Deejay said.

"What in hell's name are you people talking about?"

"Anybody got a shovel?" Ed asked, "We've got some digging to do in the park!"

XIV: Meeting with Madison

A detective learns to tolerate looking at dead bodies in the hope of finding out who made them that way. I've tried to specialize in the freshly deceased, or those kept wholesome in the city meatlocker—never been much good with *spoiled* corpses.

One of the high spots of my career—in fact, the bust that got me a detective's shield—was something I privately call the Barfbag Burglary. I was working graveyards—funny how they name these things—helping stake out an amazing second-story man. He could open any lock in twenty seconds; his time inside averaged less than three minutes. The guy was really good, and we all grudgingly admired him. But he had a nasty habit of emptying the victim's refrigerator on every job—his signature, as it were, and it saved buying groceries.

This particular evening we had four places under surveillance, all showing carefully arranged signs of vacancy—newspapers, milk bottles, lights on in the bathroom. By luck he hit mine; inside as quickly as usual, he stayed an unprecedented ten minutes. I waited, figuring to nab him on his way out.

When the burglar finally emerged, he lugged five or six sacks to his car and, just as I was about to collar him, went back for more! He returned, again and again. I couldn't take the suspense: the next time, my partner and I were crouching behind his rear bumper. I put on the cuffs and read him his rights. "Strictly off the record," I asked, "how come so many trips? You're usually more efficient."

He sat in the back of my car, irritated with himself, but genuinely pleased we knew his work. "It was the damned refrigerator. They got a walk-in, full of plastic garbage bags. I wanted to clean it out, to needle you guys. Only thing, it must've broken down a week ago! Everything high as a—but I had my gimmick, dig? I could always dump the garbage on my way home."

I was holding my nose when we undid the twist-ties on the big green trash bags. They never determined exactly how many people it had been—three heads, seven hands, five feet, six elbow joints. In Denver's miserable summer inversion, that freezer had become a sweatbox. All that remained, really, was soup and bones. I didn't ask for the recipe.

We never found the murderers. I tried regarding it not so much as losing a supper as gaining a promotion. Somehow my stomach didn't see it that way. For a week or so it wouldn't hold anything but tea and toast. The burglar pulled down three to five, then got a job with a famous lock manufacturer. Last I heard he was a vice president.

That's what I was thinking about as I watched Deejay dig: what we'd find at the bottom. I'm even game for mummies and dried-up Indian relics, but something unembalmed that's been down there a week with *things* nibbling on it? Pass the smelling salts, Mother.

I stood on the grass beside Ooloorie's whatsitmobile. Clarissa and Lucy were on the way. We'd need a doctor—possibly for me—and Lucy, of course, wouldn't be left out. Ed was digging like a sandhog, taking his fair share of the faraway porpoise's backseat shoveling. I was grateful there wasn't room enough for me down there.

It wasn't really so bad. I peeked through my fingers. From what the worms had left, we figured he'd been chopped off just below the knees. Oolorie, counting on her flippers, informed us that Bealls's entire building was now a pile of second-hand cinderblocks. At any rate, we hadn't destroyed the planet or invited it to be blown up by Strategic Air Command. I still had a place to go home to.

I was pretty proud of myself—managed to look that corpse directly in what was left of its eyes, and then hold out all the way to the bathroom in Deejay's lab. Ed was next in line. Toughness is a funny sort of thing, Clarissa didn't turn a hair. I wonder where they recruit doctors?

"Well, friend detective," I asked over hot tea and toast, fresh from a Bunsen burner, "we've saved my world. What's next on the agenda?"

Ed groaned. "Just look at these blisters! And you, standing up where it was dry and clean, giving directions!"

"That was Ooloorie. Anyway, if you'd paid attention, you wouldn't have had to dig that second hole."

"Third," Ed corrected, "and I don't care—I'm going home to bed!" Clarissa put down her cup, examined Ed's hands again. I felt a little twinge, but what the hell? Who was I, a middle-aged, overweight, balding newcomer, to be staking claims? I watched her apply some kind of salve to Ed's wounds.

"C'mon, Eddie! The night is young, and you promised me a steak!" Lucy wandered around the lab, prying into apparatus with utter disregard for her own safety or anyone else's.

"I know, Lucy, and I'll deliver, too—right through the heart! But in the morning, when I can swing a mallet with more enthusiasm."

"I've just been called an old bat!" Lucy mused, "But I still want that steak—who's for grabbing some calories?"

"Sounds good to me," I said, surprising myself, "Clarissa?"

"No thanks, Win, I had a heavy case load today. I think I'll ask Ed for a lift home."

Twinge. "Well, how about you, Deejay? I owe you. Let's go get something to eat."

"All right. Ooloorie? I'll say good-bye, now . . ." The Telecom was silent. "Shh!" Deejay whispered. She giggled and we tiptoed out of the laboratory, Deejay, Lucy, and I for a late dinner, Ed and Clarissa for . . . who knows? It was the first time I'd been out of the house, out of their way, since I'd gotten here.

The Whiskey Jar wasn't as entertaining as Mr. Meep's, simply a pleasant, unassuming place that, like all restaurants in this twenty-four hour society, offered you breakfast, lunch, or dinner at any time of the day. We ordered from the electronic menu.

"Great Albert's Ghost, Winnie, it's good to see you up and doing! Think of it: fresh outa sickbed, in as foreign a country as they come, and already you're out with a pair of good-lookin' women!" She winked at Deejay.

"Win, now that you know your world's still in one piece, will you be going back? If we can get another Broach running, I mean."

I thought about it. "Not until we've straightened this mess out. We've got to find whoever's trying to kill me, and I hate to think of this beautiful place plastered with nuclear weapons. After that? I have a career back home, and nothing much to do here except get in the way and mooch off my friends."

Lucy wiggled her eyebrows. "Nothin'?"

I looked at Deejay, thought of Clarissa, and sighed quietly. "Well, we need to find out more about these Federalists. How about it, Lucy, are they as dangerous as you all seem to think?"

"Dangerouser! No one with all his marbles'd listen to 'em, but they seem to find enough power-greedy dummies each generation to cause the rest of us a lot of trouble."

"If we find them, what can we do about it?"

"Depends on what they're up to. Gonna be hard, 'less we catch 'em settin' fuses. It's a free world: you can't shoot people for havin' stupid ideas. Otherwise we'd all go to the wall, one time or another!"

I considered some stupid ideas I'd had about Clarissa. "Well," I answered glumly, "how do we find this Madison character, put an ad in the paper?"

Deejay looked up from her steak, "That wouldn't be *John Jay* Madison?"

"Dunno, honey," Lucy replied. "All we know is he's the brains behind Hamiltonianism here in Laporte. You know a Madison?"

"Not really, but there's one giving weekly lectures in

the History and Moral Philosophy Department. My engineers were talking about it—something about the War in Europe from the Prussian point of view."

"Lucy, if this isn't our pigeon, what're the chances he'll know the guy we want? I mean, Prussians, Hamiltonians—don't they sort of go together?"

"Not necessarily, Winnie, my late husband was a Russky, but he wasn't any Czarist!"

"Sure, I'm sorry. Deejay, how do we find this John James Madison, quick?"

"John *Jay* Madison. (Certainly sounds like a Federalist, doesn't he?) The lectures will be listed on the campus information channel. Or you could call the H & MP Department."

"We will! Look, Deejay, if this pans out, we'll owe you a lot more than another steak. Is there anything I could do for you? Anything at all?"

She looked thoughtful. "No, I—wait a minute, yes. *Three* things, I believe."

"Three wishes it is! Name them!"

"All right, if you have any coins or other distinctive artifacts from your side, and can spare them, I'd like something for analysis—and," she admitted, "as a sort of trophy of the thing's having worked, know what I mean?"

"Sure. I've got coins, cartridges, a paperback book I'm not too fond of. Anything you want."

"Thank you, Win. Second, well, my father was killed at Diamond Head. You have to promise to keep me posted—let me in on it if things get rough."

"You've got it, kid. What else?"

"I—uh," she hesitated, looking shy. "You might ask Dr. Olson who programs her hair. It's really very nice, you know."

"I know."

Lucy gave me an odd look.

We dropped Deejay off and went home. "You're lookin' kinda peaked, boy." Lucy coaxed her ancient Thorneycroft into the garage. "Maybe overdoin' it your first day out. Go home and get some shut-eye, hear?"

Yeah.

Thursday, July 16, 1987

People like John Jay Madison disturb me, people who
take all my instincts and training and flush them down
the toilet with a warm smile and a firm handshake. It
was impossible to hate this man who'd probably almost killed Ed and Captain Forsyth and caused two
deaths on his own side—three, if you count the guy
who hanged himself. Nor was I overlooking the
machine-gun bullets or the fact that somebody had
tried to knife me in my sleep. Madison had a lot of
blood on his charming, well-manicured hands. That he
didn't have *more* wasn't for lack of trying.

But I had to keep reminding myself, over and over.

We'd debated that morning what to do next. I was
afraid Ed would want to be roundabout; he expected
the same from me. It took an hour and a half to
discover we both favored direct confrontation. The
History and Moral Philosophy Department provided
us with an address and Telecom number.

"Would you believe this?" I was sitting, a 'com pad
propped up on my lap "Look what I found in the
Grand Combined Directory. We needn't have bothered
with the university at all!"

ALEXANDER HAMILTON SOCIETY
J. J. Madison, Chrmn.
89 Tucker Cr. . . . . GRAy 7-2345

"Well I'll be slaved!" he said around his sixth piece
of toast. "Lucy would have a hernia if she saw that!"

"No, she'd say, *'It's a free world, sonny!'* "

"Let's find out. I had in mind to ask her along,
anyway. We may need a witness."

So it happened that we glided up to the front gate of
a mansion that made even Ed's place look seedy, a
Georgian monstrosity with a dozen sequoia-size col-
umns and twice that number of marble steps leading to
the door. We were greeted by a huge uniformed servant with close-cropped steel-gray hair and the accent

of a comic psychiatrist. "Herr Madizon vill meed you
in d'Ogtagon Hroom. Bleaze vollow me."

We were marched through a layout—dark elaborate
woodwork, highly figured carpeting, Tiffany lamps—
that'd stump a behaviorist's rat, into a sort of office
parlor, and invited to "zit." Ve zat.

The room was dominated by an ancient walnut desk
the size of a limousine, and, on the wall behind, a four-
foot bronze plaque: The Eye-in-the-Pyramid. I'd never
really noticed before what a creepy emblem it is; I was
about to compare it with a dollar bill, see whether
they'd doctored it any, when the door opened. The
butler stood at attention—I found myself rising re-
flexively—and announced, *"Herr Doktor* Chon Chay
Madizon!"

Madison breezily shook hands all around, then
relaxed behind his desk. "That'll be all, Kleingunther."
Kleingunther clicked heels, bumped his forehead on
his belt buckle, and, giving us a last suspicious once-
over, left, shutting the door. "You'll have to overlook
Hermann." Madison reached across the desk for a
cigar box. "It's embarrassing sometimes. Cigar?"

I accepted gratefully, but waited until he lit his own,
perhaps overdoing caution a bit. I had scars enough to
warrant it—would have, anyway, if it weren't for
Clarissa. He settled in his chair, taking a long drag. I
did the same and looked him over.

He was a big man, at six-two or -three, probably
dressing down in the neighborhood of 275, none of it
soft. Like Hermann Kleingunther, he had a well-
scrubbed, close-cropped, salt-and-pepper look. He wore
loose-fitting black trousers, a bright yellow blouse, and
a short, waist-length jacket allowing easy access to the
age-darkened cross-draw holster at his belt—a .354
Bolo Mauser, a hard-hitting no-frills piece of ordnance
dating from the War in Europe. A cruel seam running
from his earlobe to the corner of his mouth told me
pistols weren't the only weapon he favored. Despite
the dueling scar, he looked like some kid's favorite
sea-going uncle. Dangerous men seldom look dangerous.

"Now," he said, "what can I do for you? You were a bit vague over the Telecom, I'm afraid."

Ed started for us. "We're more interested in discussing what you've already done. Two of your people were killed attacking my house night before last, and another killed himself yesterday morning."

Madison looked exasperated. "Well, Mr. Bear, I could insist that you explain what you mean by two of *my* people—members of the Alexander Hamilton Society? I'd like to satisfy you that these men had nothing official to do with this organization or with me. We're simply an institution for the discussion and debate of political philosophy."

"First time in history that Hamiltonians limited themselves to discussion and debate!"

"My dear Judge Kropotkin. You're remembering, perhaps, our brief tenure in the Kingdom of Hawaii—brought to an untimely end by the Antarctican unpleasantness? Or the savagery with which our proposed reforms were met on the Moon, afterward?" He looked at her more closely. "Or, if I'm not being indiscreet, perhaps even the Prussian War? Your Honor, all of that was *long* ago, and your concerns now are unjustified on several counts."

"Such as?"

"I flatter myself I am an intelligent man. I take pains to associate with intelligent men. Would intelligent men fail to learn from their experiences? Even if all you imply is true, shouldn't we have learned something from direct military confrontation?"

Lucy emitted a genuine harumph.

"But even that concedes more than is just. Your Honor, at various times in history, demagogues have required scapegoats. Unfortunately, we Hamiltonians have been handy on such occasions. It's easy to condemn unworldly philosophers who have no ready means of reply. Since the Whiskey Rebellion, my fellows have been among the most unpopular in the world. What could we possibly say that would make people listen? How could we counter accusations graven in conventionally accepted history? Our views on economics and politics severely oppose the popular wisdom. Tell me: is that *proof* that we are wrong? To the contrary, it's usually the other way around, isn't it?"

"Very clever," Ed said.

"And also very true. We believe that the good of society—in fact, the good of the individual—rests with recognizing and imposing an obligation to the state. We take what measures we can to transmit our views, hence this educational organization, my guest-lectures at the university. But it goes very slowly: prejudice has such inertia."

He rose, thrust his hands in his pockets, and paced, almost talking to himself, his eyes intent on some other place, some other time. "Inevitably, your investigations will reveal that my real name isn't John Jay Madison. I was born Manfred, Landgraf von Richthofen. Quite a mouthful, isn't it? It was, at one time, a name and family of some influence in Prussia, and of not inconsiderable wealth. The War changed that, of course. So, with perhaps a false start or two, I came to America to repair my fortunes."

He spread his arms. "As you can see, I have, to a certain extent, accomplished that. I changed my name because John Jay and James Madison were, in my view, men of merit, of historical importance to both my homeland and this organization—certainly very American, something I was determined to become—and rather easier to pronounce." He grinned, and I couldn't help grinning back.

He stood at the opposite end of the room under an enormous portrait I recognized from ten-dollar Federal Reserve notes. The grim visage stared across toward the mystical symbol over Madison's desk. "I should have adopted *his* name, had I dared. I assure you it is held in the esteem it deserves, elsewhere in the System—still, I must be able to buy groceries without arousing counterproductive passions."

He went back to the desk. "Though you may disagree with what I believe, nevertheless I insist on being allowed to believe it, unmolested." He made a sudden move toward his off side where the Mauser hung—I almost went for my gun. Eyeing me with some amusement, he continued the motion and pressed a small button on the desk. "Come, let me show you around. I'd like to assure you we have nothing to hide."

"Jawohl, mein Herr!" a tinny voice said.

"Hermann, will you join us in the Washington Room?"

We followed through convoluted hallways into a larger, chair-filled chamber where Kleingunther stood rigidly at attention near a lectern flanked by flagpoles —the first I'd seen in the Confederacy. The flags, furled and covered, guarded a portrait on the front of the lectern: George Washington, wearing a canvas apron and holding drafting tools.

"Our lecture hall," Madison said proprietarily. "Here we teach Hamiltonian philosophy and hold ceremonies traditional to our organization."

"Looks like a Masonic lodge," I said. Madison started to whirl, checked, then turned slowly.

"You are astute. It is true, we derive certain rituals from that ancient and honorable order. But where have *you* heard of it? It's not a common thing to know about."

"My *brother,* here," Ed interrupted, "isn't a common man. You might say he's *an entire world* of esoteric information."

"I believe I understand." Madison smiled. "An excellent credential for a detective. Would you care to see where our directors meet?" In the smaller, more lavishly furnished place, Madison demonstrated a rear-projection device on the wall communicating with the Washington Room. "Sometimes it does indeed seem true," he mused, "that a picture is worth thousands of words."

We toured the entire mansion, at least I think we did. It was a rambling, complicated structure; we could have missed sections the size of Lucy's house and never known it. Lounges, conservatories, greenhouse. Everywhere we went, Madison preceded, a fountain of householder's pride. Kleingunther followed in ominous silence.

The Federalist chief was quite unabashed at

mementos of "early Hamiltonian history" scattered
here and there "to remind us of our impetuousity":
Prussian armor and edged weapons; Hawaiian spears
and shields; similar tokens from Uganda; gas masks
and rifles from the War in Europe. In a sort of chapel,
spread like a Bible in a helium-filled glass altar, lay
the Constitution of the United States. *"We, the People, in order to form a more perfect Union . . ."*

There wasn't any Bill of Rights.

In the basement hobby shop where, according to
Madison, members pursued electronics, sculpture,
modelmaking, there was even a little one-station press
for reloading ammunition, not too different from the
one a Denver gunsmith used to whip up my .41
Magnum. Madison was showing Lucy a spaceship in
a bottle, and didn't notice when I swiped a cartridge
from the littered bench. Then, with a chill, I remembered Kleingunther, turned, and saw with relief that
he was raptly following Madison's lecture.

We didn't quite get the full tour. Several times we
passed closed doors. "A private room. Some members
stay with us for longer or shorter periods. I cannot
violate their privacy. It doesn't look very candid, I'm
afraid, but it can't be helped." One such room was
just off the cellar hobby area. The door was ajar,
latched with a common hook and eye, and closed
against a heavy power cable originating at the fuse
box. The room beyond was dark; I thought I saw
pilot lights burning dimly through the gap.

"So you see," Madison said over brandy in his
office, "these are facilities for education and recrea-
tion—our little planetarium, our gymnasium and
steam room. But no Conspiracy Room. You would
have seen it!"

"Depends," Lucy said, looking around her, "on
what a 'conspiracy room' looks like. Glad we saw the
wine cellar, anyway. *Prost!*"

In due course we were shuffled onto the front porch
with wholesome assurances of full cooperation and an
open invitation to return for social or educational
purposes. "Something tells me," Madison winked at
me, "that you might be right at home with many of

our ideas on running a country, *right* at home . . .
Oberst?"

"*Lieutenant*," I replied, "but on pretty indefinite
leave."

As we drove away, I fished out the empty case I'd
swiped. It was far smaller than any I'd seen here—
that's what had caught my eye:

w-w .380 AUTO

A dull throb in my left shoulder: W-W stands for
Winchester-Western, and the only Winchester of note
in this world is a cathedral. .380 Automatic is equally
unknown, but it's everyday fodder for the Ingram
Model 11 submachine gun.

XV: Breaking & Entering

Monday, July 20, 1987

"Manfred von Richthofen?" Somewhere a little voice was singing, "It's only a paper moon, hanging over a cardboard sea . . ."

"The Red Knight of Prussia himself," Lucy declared. " 'Twas his Flying Circus put me afoot back in '38. Never forget it—there we were: the *Pensacola* an' the *Boise* flankin' my *Fresno Lady,* bearin' northeast outa Cologne. They—"

"But that'd make him at least—"

"Ninety-six," Ed said. "Probably turned up here for a—"

"Something else, Lucy. What's all this 'Your Honor' jazz he was handing out? You never told me—"

"Semiretired, sonny. What else would I do for a living? A little late t' try sellin' my body, don't y'think? Don't answer that, a girl hasta keep *some* illusions. Yeah, I still hear an argument now an' again. Catfood money."

We were in Lucy's parlor, surrounded by Victorian furniture and felines, both overstuffed. I'd counted eight cats so far, one sleeping in Lucy's bony lap, another making his way up the difficult north face of Ed's shoulder. I was trying to keep a kitten from perching on my head.

"Pay attention," Ed warned, "she's being *modest.* Lucy's a highly respected adjudicator and member of the Continental Congress." He pulled the cat off and placed it on the floor where it stuck its nose in his highball glass.

"A distinction," Lucy intoned, "utterly without distinction. Congress hasn't met in thirty years, and I'm hopin' like crazy it won't ever have to again. Depends on what you boys find Friday night."

We'd granted Deejay's second wish in a small way, asking her to attend Madison's next lecture, to keep the questions and answers going as long as she and a few well-chosen comrades could manage.

"Speaking of which, Your Honorship, how do you feel—in your *official* capacity—about busting into Madison's place? I thought privacy was sacred in this country?"

"Sure—along with your life, your property, and your rights," Ed offered.

"In that order?"

"No order to it," Lucy answered. "Just three ways of sayin' the same thing. And, Winnie, I *got* no official capacity. Nobody does, not even the President of the Confederacy. She only rides herd on the Continental Congress, if and when . . . What you and Ed are planning is unethical, immoral, and—"

"Fattening?"

"I was about to say, *illegal*—if we were the legislatin' kind, which we ain't. You two get shot up in there, nobody's gonna say a thing. Madison'll be within his rights. Or, he could sue you right down to your bellybutton lint."

"Well, what are we *supposed* to do while he's taking over the planet?"

"Son, we gave up preventive law enforcement *long* before we gave up law."

"We do have one chance," Ed suggested. "Find something Madison won't want made public in a lawsuit—"

"Blackmail?"

Ed plowed onward. "If we catch him in the act, prove he's planning a massive initiation of force, then we can countersue, and it might be Madison who winds up on some asteroid."

"The end justifies the means," I grunted. "A *retro-active* search warrant."

"Oh, no!" Lucy exclaimed. "Regardless of what happens to Madison, you'd still have to make restitution to him for burglary, breaking and entering, theft—"

I put my head in my hands and groaned.

"Better'n gettin' shot full of holes, ain't it?" Lucy asked. "Still don't get it, do you? Well, take that kitty-cat off your pate—Lysander, get down!—and I'll explain again. See, we make restitution to Madison, but he's making restitution to us, for—what, attempted world conquest? He winds up owing *us* a lot more money than . . ."

Friday, July 24, 1987

Stakeouts aren't remarkably different anywhere. I'd just finished my fifth cigarette in the last hour, and it didn't help that Lucy's old Thorneycroft only gave coffee—a Confederate dollop of chicory made it even worse.

We sat, biting our nails between puffs, watching the Hamiltonian mansion, doing what cops have done since they staked out the pyramids in horse-powered two-wheelers: we swapped war stories. He told me about hanging on the outside of a sports-dirigible while a triple murderer did everything to shake him loose into fifteen thousand feet of empty space. I told him about the wonderful things you find in plastic garbage bags.

Madison was off to a late start. We hunched down in our cloaks, trying to keep warm—another thing that doesn't change: you're deaf with the windows up and the heater roaring away, so you freeze your ass off, consoled only by the knowledge that being able to hear has saved the lives of countless cops.

"Look out!" Ed whispered. We slumped farther down as a pair of enormous black hovercars—the Frontenac, lately repaired, and its twin brother—came around a corner and pulled up in front of the house.

Ed offered me a set of goggles with half-inch slabs for lenses. I started to strap them on, thought better of

it, and simply held them before my eyes. "Infrared?"
I asked. The images were in color, the hues wildly
distorted. The Frontenacs were still black, but the
landscaping was sickly shades of red-violet.

"Paratronic. Convert almost anything to visible
wavelengths, with pretty strange results sometimes,
depending on the — Quiet!"

People emerged from the building, gathering briefly
on the porch. Kleingunther I could tell by his size, and
Madison, bundled up against the evening chill. Two
others were unrecognizable. I squinted over the edge
of my goggles and gasped, "Bealls!"

"I thought so," Ed whispered. "Who's the other
one?"

"Gotta be from back home." The fourth character,
ludicrous in American slouch hat, poncho, and baggy
Confederate trousers, lit a cigarette. The sudden flare
illuminated a harsh, narrow, pock-marked face: "Oscar Burgess!"

"Are you sure, Win?" They walked down to the
curb and boarded.

"Is a bear Catholic? I'd recognize that face over the
radio!" As I watched the cars pull away, I shivered,
but not from the cold.

"I'll take your word. So Madison's a charming liar,
but a liar nevertheless."

"You expected different?" The gears in my head
were grinding. I wasn't surprised that SecPol had been
on my trail, but Burgess himself? Unless they had
their own Broach working, he must have followed me
to Fort Collins, into the the lab, and out through
Meiss's machine. How many others had made it
through before the one we'd found buried in the collapsed excavation?

"Come on, partner," I said, like a hundred times before, "we got work to do." The thought of entering
without a warrant didn't make me feel any worse than
I ever have on late-night searches. Maybe some judge's
piece of paper isn't the blank check I'd always
believed—we were still invading someone's castle, and
maybe we deserved to be shot.

We parked in the nearest alley and headed for an

underground crossing. Traffic wasn't any lighter at this
hour, but speed was the main consideration: on a
thoroughfare like this, a car could be on top of you before you'd noticed. At the other side, we approached
the darkened mansion from behind. Ed produced a
device, slid out an antenna, and unfolded a sharp-
pointed ground stake.

"This is *my* defeater—like the one our burglar
used."

"I hope it works better than his did."

"Different principle: it's in contact with my Telecom
at home. We mightn't prevent the alarms from tripping, but if they do, my computer will start arguing
with theirs, delaying the lights and sirens for a while."

"How long?"

"Depending on their unit, maybe ten minutes. We'll
have longer if we're careful going in." He shoved the
defeater into the ground.

My hands shook as I accepted another gadget.
"S-sorry. I'm used to working the other side of the
burglary game!"

"Calm down! You don't hear *my* teeth chattering,
and I'm not used to it, either."

"Now he tells me. Another amateur cracksman! It's
been a swell evening, Ed. Think I'll go downtown and
see what's playing at the Rialto."

"Shut up and strap that on your wrist! As long as its
face is green, we're clear. If it turns orange, we've
tripped something and the computers are discussing it.
When it turns red, drop everything and *run*—we've
lost the argument and the house defenses are working
again. I'll check upstairs, Madison's office and so on.
You do the basement. Get a good look at that closed-
off room—Deejay'll want every detail. Almost forgot
—take this little pickup, and we'll crank it through the
'com when we get back."

"If we get back. Anything else before the massacre,
mon capitaine?"

"We may have to do the upper floors, too. We need
to know how many of your people are here."

"They're *SecPol's* people, and they've all got guns!
Great big—"

"Okay, okay! Give it ten minutes, unless your tell-tale turns orange. Meet me in the office. If it turns red, it's every being for himself."

"Right. Hope I remember my way around this pile of bricks." The back porch wasn't locked, but the floorboards were real groaners. By the time Ed was doing things to the back door with tiny tools, I was surprised my pants were still dry. He taped the latch to keep it from springing shut. We slipped past the kitchen and reached the cross-hall to Madison's office. I took the other branch, to the basement, adjusting the goggles on my nose. The place was eerie with shadows, and the weird colors didn't help.

With a couple of false turns, I found the hobby room. Through paratronic lenses, most of the light seemed to be coming from a closet door, the dull, ruddy glow of iron in a blacksmith's forge. I opened the door to find a water heater, bright as neon. Peeking over the goggles I could see nothing, although I could feel heat on my face.

Lenses back on again, I walked to the bench. I'd left the furnace room door open, but my body cast a shadow on the tabletop. Then, with inspiration, I found a soldering iron and pulled the trigger—it worked as well as a flashlight. I examined the reloading area, carefully keeping away from powder and primers, found more .380 cases, a couple of 9 m/m's that might beong to Burgess, and a matchbook from a Denver speakeasy.

Across the room was the latched door. Holding the iron in my left hand, I drew my revolver, lifted the hook with its muzzle, and opened the door carefully. Nobody home, but it seemed very familiar: same cabinets, same tangles of wire, a replica of Deejay's cluttered lab, and of the infernal machinery that had propelled me here. I crossed the room, one eye on the door, another on my wrist, trying to keep a third on what I was doing. How would the telltale look through color-distorting goggles? Just now it was a pale pink. A quick glance *sans* eyepieces returned it to a nice safe green.

Bealls didn't trust the Telecom. He was using very

conventional computer equipment. Must have raided some museum. On the console was an untidy sheaf of papers. The sight, surrounded as I was with dormant Broach machinery, made me uneasy. If I went through a hole in *this* world, where would I end up?

Print didn't carry well through goggles, so I risked a match: circuit diagrams, mathematical notations, Vaughn Meiss's name neatly typed in the corner of each sheet—the contents of that empty aluminum notebook, but with many marginal comments in a different hand.

I turned slowly, showing everything to the double lenses of Ed's miniature Telecom pickup, hoping it was equipped with some sort of light-amplifier. As I climbed upstairs with a sigh of relief, and was threading my way toward Madison's office, the telltale turned purple—orange to the naked eye.

Ed stood before the eye-and-pyramid plaque, now split down the middle to reveal a cabinet in the wall behind. "I'm afraid I've done it," he whispered, "Notice your indicator?"

"Yeah. What have you got here?"

"Nothing I know anything about." The cabinet was divided into dozens of small compartments, each holding a tiny silvery goblet no bigger than a thimble. "Ten rows of eight—eighty of these doohickeys in all."

"Close it up, and let's get out of here. Find anything else?"

"In the lecture-hall closet, carefully tucked into a pile of table linens—These . . ." Three canned reels of sixteen millimeter film lay on the desk, half concealed in a fancy napkin. I struck another match:

TF 53-9354
CLASSIFIED
MOPPING UP IN THE ATOMIC AGE
Post-Strike Tactical Deployment
PROPERTY OF U.S. GOVERNMENT
CLASSIFIED

"Training films—!"
"Put that out! Didn't I show you—" He twisted one

of my eye-pieces—a softly glowing light was visible through the lenses.

"Army indoctrination films," I repeated. "What are the others?"

"Something about 'anti-guerrilla counter-insurgency,' and . . ."

"Well?"

"How hydrogen bombs work."

"Saw that one myself, when they were trying to involve us in Civil Defense. Don't let that classified crap fool you, they show this stuff to the troops—and on TV, Sunday afternoons. But they *can't* have brought this with them the day I—"

"No, they couldn't. We'd better get out of here, back to the kitchen!" Which is where we went, my nerves screaming every inch of the way. Ed wanted to stop off for sightseeing.

"Are you out of your mind? This thing's been orange for—"

"Three minutes. Don't panic. I just want to see what Madison wouldn't show us."

Admittedly, I'd thought it peculiar that we weren't allowed into a room just off the small kitchen. I held my S & W, trying to keep the muzzle steady. He opened the door, we started in—

Ed went for his gun. "Hold it!" I whispered hoarsely. "He won't do us any harm now." Huddled on the floor between two hanging beef carcasses was a body, frozen stiff. Oddly, it didn't seem cold in the tiny room. "What is this place?"

"Paratronic freezer. Something like a microwave oven, only the other way around. Shuts down when the door opens." The body was propped in a sitting position, ice crystals glittered in the light from our goggles. "Here's the sheath to your Rezin. Want it?" Ed rotated the body onto its face. Clothing and flesh were tattered at the back, as if blasted with a shotgun —nothing fatal, just messy and painful. Some of those gleaming particles wouldn't be ice, but glass from my bedroom window. We'd found our intruder.

"Tricky Dick Milhous," Ed said, "a third-rate second-story man. He's no assassin, just a petty crook.

Nice way they paid him off. Couldn't have been pleasant, freezing in the dark."

I shuddered. "Shouldn't we get out of here, before the same thing happens to us?" Shelves full of foil-swathed packages glinted dully in the eerie half-light.

"Right. We'll make an anonymous call. The CLA can—"

Our wristlights, through the goggles, had turned bright blue. I didn't even peek—the freezer door was swinging shut. I plunged through, revolver in hand, figuring to nail whoever— "There's no one here!"

"Doors close when the alarms go off!" Ed said, hurrying past me. "Old-fashioned, but effective." Happily, someone had removed the one between kitchen and hall. Bells were clanging as we reached the back door. "This would be locked if we hadn't taped it." We did a fast sneak down the alley. "Can't cross the underground now with all this racket. We'll have to risk the Greenway."

"Let's do it!"

"Look out!" He yanked me behind a bush as a car full of uniforms whisked around the corner. We were trapped. There'd be security in all four undergrounds, a perimeter established before we could get across.

I rose, dusting off my knees. "Follow my lead and try not to look guilty." I turned the corner, strode deliberately down the sidewalk, Ed dithering along behind *me* for once, and right up to the front door of the Alexander Hamilton Society. Guards were milling in and out.

"Bear Brothers, consulting detectives," I rapped. "We're staking out a burglar. Find him yet?"

The patrol boss looked us over with a grudging smile. "Ed! Might've known you'd show up. Didn't know you had a brother. Who're we supposed to find, the ghost of Alexander Hamilton?"

Ed opened his mouth, I barged ahead with "Win Bear, Captain, just in from, uh, Tlingit. It's Tricky Dick Milhous we're looking for. Busted into a place we're . . . responsible for the other night, and damn near killed a resident."

"Uh—right!" Ed added brightly. "We'll probably

find him here somewhere. This is an old bulkhead security system."

The captain looked skeptical. "Well, you boys do your homework, anyway. If you're right, we'll all be collecting bonuses. Been after Dick for three weeks, after the job he pulled over at Wasserschranken's. Hear about that?"

"We've been on another case."

"Yeah. I heard about that. Some guys get all the publicity. Well, let's take a look around."

Ed was showing the strain. Not enough practice in deception. My own heart was pumping briskly against the film cans rolled up in their embroidered napkin and stashed inside my tunic. Hanging back a little, I whispered, "How long does it take a corpse to freeze clear through in that thing?"

"Only a few minutes—paratronics—ask Deejay about it."

"Sometimes I wish they'd stuck with home appliances. Well, Stanley, how do we get out of this gracefully?"

"Stanley?"

"To my Oliver—and this is another fine mess you've gotten us into."

Ed frowned. "I worry about you. Have to hang around until they find him. Then we'll—what was the expression?"

"Slope? Vamoose? Make like a hockey team and—"

"*Split,*" he said, watching the men reopen doors. "What'll they make of that empty sheath and the glass splinters?"

"Won't see them for the ice, at first," I answered. "Anyway, we're not responsible for the peculiarities of some small-time crook, are we?"

" 'Not our department,' right?"

I grinned. "We'll make a bureaucrat out of you yet."

It took forty-five minutes, but find that body they did, in one of the longest due courses of my life. At any moment Madison might be back, and that wouldn't be any fun. Of course, he'd learn later that we'd been here, but by then, he'd have other things on his mind, such as the body in his freezer—*"And if*

it isn't a burglar, Mr. Madison, what's he doing here?
—and three missing cans of film.

Finally congratulations were in order, cigars passed around, Tricky Dick sledded away to greener pastures, and we were off in a cloud of expelled breath. It was only midnight: if Deejay were on her toes, Madison might still be answering dopey questions.

"Tell me something, partner . . ." I'd found something better than coffee behind the driver's seat. "What about the alarm defeater we left back there? Especially when they trace it to us—I mean *you*—and maybe I'd better scratch that 'partner,' too."

He shook his head. "I hate losing valuable equipment, but considering the alternative . . . They'll assume it's Tricky Dick's. No trademarks, no serial numbers, no problem, really."

"Surely there are other ways—"

"Oh, I see what you mean. Win, you're the only person in the entire Confederacy who knows about fingerprints, I promise!"

"Okay, since I'm playing Poor Dumb Nut, answer me another: we saw Madison, Kleingunther, Bealls, and Burgess leave tonight, the place was dark. But weren't there supposed to be *other* Hamiltonians living in? How'd you figure—"

"Elementary, my dear Whatsit. Madison *lied* to keep us out of some of the rooms. We saw conservatories, a gymnasium, all kinds of lecture halls. But only one small kitchen, and no dining room large enough for more than half a dozen people. *Ergo,* nobody besides Madison, Kleingunther, and their two American guests!"

The hair started to rise on the back of my neck, and I wondered if I should let him live through the night. "Turn in your calabash, Sherlock! Didn't it occur to you that the residents *might cook in their rooms?*" I pulled a corner of Madison's napkin out of my tunic. Embroidered in satin, the Eye-in-the-Pyramid shone dully in the dashboard lights. "Or that they might simply redress their lecture halls for dinner? *What in hell do you think that linen closet was for?*"

He jammed on the brakes, slewed over to the road-side, and sat, staring blindly into space. "Great government! I never thought of that!"

"SQUAAWK!" The Telecom lit up, Lucy's worried face crammed in the focus beside Forsyth's. "Get back here quick, boys! While you were doin' it to them, *they've gone an' done it to Clarissa!"*

XVI: Balance of Madness

Saturday, July 25, 1987

"Horrible!" cried Clarissa. Ed sat paralyzed, his face a frozen mask.

"Never realized what it could mean in a populated area." Lucy wiped her eyes as if to erase the images: Hiroshima, Nagasaki, and the rest.

"They propose doing that to us?" Deejay trembled with anger as the films showed buildings, automobiles, ships resting innocently at anchor, *vaporized* beneath the mushroom cloud.

"Only if you don't knuckle under. It's pretty simple. An old game where I come from. They finish their Broach, bring in troops and weapons, and the Hamiltonians are suddenly in charge—under SecPol supervision, of course."

Lucy emitted a disgusted grunt.

"That Broach is a pretty narrow bottleneck," Captain Forsyth observed. "We could close it off with a couple ounces of Hercules' No. 6."

Ed stirred. "It isn't that simple, Cap. These people have developed mass-warfare into a science."

"To the neglect of everything else," said Lucy.

"Perhaps so. At any rate, all they need is a hole the size of—what did you estimate, Win?"

"A typewriter case—or an automotive fusion reactor."

"Yes, and they don't need it more than a few minutes. Once they have weapons like *these,* we'll have to leave them alone. They'll be holding the entire city for ransom."

"And with a secure base," I added, "there's nothing

to stop them setting up Broaches everywhere. Give them a week and they'll own this world. With the resources and the technology available here, they'll own mine, too."

"But why, Win? Would they do something like this for money?"

"Clarissa, they have all the money they need—they own the printing presses. They want power: utter control over the populations of two worlds—more, counting your colonies."

"Many more," Deejay said, "if there are other worlds the Broach can reach—we haven't begun to explore *that* possibility yet." She shuddered.

The six of us were gathered in Ed's living room. It had been time-consuming but not particularly difficult to hand-crank film from reel to reel past a recording pickup. The Telecom had done the rest, we were watching the result. The actual films were back in their cans, stashed in the deepest recesses of Mulligan's Bank and Grill.

Before we'd done anything else, Deejay had insisted on seeing my recordings of Madison's basement, and pronounced, to our tremendous if temporary relief, that Bealls was *weeks* from sustaining even a microBroach. "He's a subcompetent," she'd added, scanning his jury-rigged assemblies, "working from third-hand information. On his own, he could putter away till Doomsday without making a dent in the continuum."

Now we watched the last of the government films, this one on occupying areas that have been H-bombed into submission. It was terrifying: I kept imagining Deejay raped at bayonet-point; Ed shot for resistance; Forsyth's fur falling out; Lucy vanishing in a cloud of incandescence.

"I don't understand! These people have shot me, attacked Ed and the captain, murdered their own hitman, *and now this latest outrage on Clarissa!* Why don't we just round up some muscle and—"

Lucy sighed. "Winnie, ain't a body in this room—least of all me—wouldn't do that in a minute, 'specially after what happened to Clarissa last night, but it can't be done that way! Think, and you'll understand why."

"Go ahead, Your Judgeship, this I've got to hear."

"Well first, nobody's gonna break into that fortress of theirs twice."

"That's right," the captain said. "My dispatcher says they've ordered three squads from Brookstone's, and a weapons specialist. That means lasers—big ones." He wrinkled his upper lip and bared his teeth—definitely not an expression of good humor among his people.

"Why not get *four* squads, then, and even *bigger* lasers? Once everybody understands, every security company in Laporte will—"

"Companies don't fight each other," he shook his bandaged head, "Nobody'd last five minutes in this business—wouldn't deserve to—if all justice amounted to were 'My thugs're tougher'n yours!' We're supposed to *preserve* the peace—otherwise, we'd just go back to your arrangement, and have some *real* wars."

"What the captain isn't saying," Ed added, "is that there's simply no *profit* in smashing one another to pieces. That was settled, long ago."

Lucy nodded. "Little village off the east coast—one gang decided they'd try running things, four or five other companies objected. Before the dust settled, they'd nearly wiped each other out. Manhattan, if I recall correct. Ever since, security outfits—*and* their insurance companies—have been big supporters of adjudication."

"Well, *I* won't take what they did to Clarissa! If I have to—"

"Calm down, boy! Give an old lady a little credit—and about fifteen more minutes. I got a connection or two, and one of my best is about to pay off. Wait and see!"

Clarissa crossed the room, laid a hand on my shoulder. "Win, I'm all right—*really*. Just frightened, and they didn't do me any *lasting* harm."

I looked up, seeing unshed tears quivering in her eyes. "Sweetheart, if I believed that, I'd be a great prospect for Florida real estate. If I ever get my hands on those . . ."

She patted my shoulder again and went back over to sit by Ed. If only she'd come to me . . . Well, no point thinking about it—always a bridesmaid, etc. At least she was alive, reason enough to rejoice.

The doorbell chose that moment to ring. I loosened my forty-one in its holster. A little paranoid, perhaps, but considering last night's events—

"Ladies and gentlemen . . ." Lucy announced from the hallway, *"The President of the North American Confederacy!"*

The President entered, pausing a moment to commiserate with Forsyth, expressing pleasure at meeting Deejay, nodding grimly over the news while being introduced to Clarissa, greeting Ed like an old friend. Under the peculiar circumstances, I had to be introduced to the President, too. But no one had to introduce her to me.

I know Jenny Noble when I see her.

"I made some stupid assumptions last night," Ed told the President, "as Win tactfully pointed out later. One of them was that Burgess would attend Madison's lecture, just because he left at the same time."

"That's ridiculous," Clarissa argued. "What else could you assume?"

"That's right, dummy," I said. "I ought to know that bastard myself by now. He's haunted my worst nightmares for thirty years."

Jenny was sitting next to Ed, a truly Presidential bourbon in her pretty hand. Clarissa'd made room by sitting at his knee. I don't know what Ed's got, but logically, I should have it too, shouldn't I?

Only it wasn't Jenny *Noble* here. My counterpart shares a common name with me, we're lucky having different nicknames to avoid confusion. Jenny Noble's opposite number calls herself Jenny Smythe.

"Who's telling this story," Clarissa protested, "the person it happened to, or the Two Bears?"

"Well tell it, then, Goldilocks!" Ed answered.

"All right, I'd stayed late with a client who's having

a rough regeneration—geriotic complications to be cleared up before the limb can replace itself . . . Anyway, I went home and freshened up, intending to come over here and see what mischief these two had accomplished at Madison's. Just as I was starting out the front door, a couple of huge men smashed it in. I ran back through the house, but someone was there with a machine gun, shattering my windows."

"How many were there?" Jenny examined Clarissa's pistol, leaned over and handed it to me.

"Two in the front, and the one out by the pool, with the hideous scars—I turned around again and practically ran into them. I had my Webley out, and sort of waved it around with the trigger held back."

Lucy chuckled. "Walked right into it, the jerks." She held one of the wicked little projectiles, eleven caliber, an inch or so long. "A thousand of these a minute, ten thousand feet a second. It'd ruin your whole day, wouldn't it?" I examined the pistol with considerably more respect. Its barrel was a single massive coil, driving little steel needles by linear induction. There were *hundreds* in its magazine.

"I stepped over the bodies, ran out front, and drove away. There was a blinding flash in my rear viewscreen and a huge ball of fire"—she shook her head sadly—"pointless destruction for its own sake. They'll pour me a new house, and my professional records are transmitted every day to the insurance company, but my furniture, clothes—everything is gone."

"Least you got a couple of the bugsuckers!" Lucy said. "Bunk at my place. I got some togs might fit you—used t' carry more meat on my bones. Pete liked 'em well rounded."

"Thank you, Lucy." That girl just wouldn't cry. I handed back her pistol and patted her arm. "It won't be more than a couple of days, they—"

"Plan on staying a couple of *weeks*," Ed stated. "That wasn't just vandalism last night, Burgess was there for a purpose!"

"Second the motion," I said. "Madison couldn't get to us, so he decided to pick on you, probably as a threat to hold over our heads. As far as I'm con-

cerned, it would have worked, too—A-bombs or no
A-bombs."

"Why, Win, do you mean that?"

"Oh hell, Clarissa, I don't know what I mean any
more. Deejay, we'd better think about precautions
for you, too. They won't be long figuring out the connection."

"I'll be all right," the scientist said. "I've got a cot
in the lab, and *nobody's* going to get through Campus Security."

"Who's got the contract now?" Ed asked, with an
appraising look. "You've aroused my professional interest."

The son of a bitch. That wasn't the only thing she'd
aroused.

"Griswold's, I believe."

"Brr! Well, *that's* settled: Griswold's can take care
of Deejay—"

"*And* the Broach equipment," I added. "Bealls would
love to get his hands—"

"With all due respect for Deejay," Ed replied,
"that's half the reason I asked. I'm never going to
live down last night, am I?"

"Shit, we all learn by mistakes, Ed. If I weren't
such a hotdog, I'd be eating lunch at Colfax and York,
right now."

"That's better?" he asked. "Captain, double the
guard and throw the perimeter around Lucy's place,
too."

"Right." The captain started giving orders into the
lapel of his jacket.

"Hey! Who's paying for this? If I gotta be wet-
nursed by a bunch of uniformed babysitters, I
wanna—"

"With any luck—" the President said.

"Lucy," Ed answered, "this was my party to start
with, and it's still—"

"With any luck—" the President said.

"You stay out of this, Ed Bear!" retorted Clarissa.
"As long as I'm staying with Lucy, *I'll*—"

"*With any luck*—" the President said.

"Hold on, now! I started this whole thing by getting shot, without invitation, on Ed's front—"

"Shut up, you guys! My gosh, how does a person get listened to around here? I've been trying to tell you that, with any luck, the Confederacy's going to pay for everything!"

Lucy narrowed suspicious eyes. "How y'figure that, girl?" I was interested, too, since there didn't seem to be enough government on the whole planet to buy Forsyth a box of ammunition.

Jenny laughed. "It's really very simple. In a week or so, there'll be people standing in line to contribute You see, I've decided there's only one way to deal with the Hamiltonians. *I'm calling a session of the Continental Congress."*

Tuesday, July 28, 1987

It wouldn't have been so bad if I'd had more hair. As it was, Lysander tended to slide off my head. Add trying to balance a teacup on one knee, a plate of pie on the other, and you can see the kind of afternoon I was having.

In the three days since the confederacy's rusty political wheels had begun groaning to a start, life had achieved a kind of routine: Ed had a case to pursue for Paratronics, Ltd.; Clarissa had her patients; Deejay and Ooloorie continued their scientific efforts.

One project was a means of detecting someone else's Broach-work—to keep tabs on Bealls's progress. Another, something they called a dirigible Broach—nothing to do with airships—was simply a machine you wouldn't have to lug physically to the point in this world *coextant* with wherever in mine you want to do things.

Forsyth guarded houses, provided escorts, and kept a careful eye on Madison. In addition, Griswold's Security received a little unobtrusive supervision.

As Jenny flitted about the continent persuading balky Congresspersons into their first parley in three decades, Lucy acted as anchor, relaying messages, confirming "crazy" stories, arranging tickets and travel schedules.

So what did Lieutenant Bear do to make himself feel useful? *Zilch*. Well, I had some minor value as Exhibit A: the Barbarian from the Land of the Bomb. Wonderful.

I'd have preferred bodyguarding Clarissa. With clients to attend, she couldn't be cooped up. But as Forsyth conveyed diplomatically, I was a *greenhorn* here, needed protection myself (that *did* hurt!) and when Congress finally got its stuff together, I'd be a key witness against the Federalists.

To tell the truth, I wasn't really prepared to spend time listening to Clarissa tell me all about Ed. I didn't know exactly what they were to each other—I'd filed under "Peculiar" the datum that she was sleeping over at Lucy's—but I knew what we'd be if *I* were in Ed's shoes.

So here I was, at low point in a life that wasn't much to write home about anyway, a fifth wheel— alone and unemployed in a land right out of Freud— sipping Lucy's "tea" out of politeness. And marijuana's never done anything but get me *more* depressed.

Lucy rang off and joined me in the parlor. "Winnie, you look like the Before model in a cocaine commercial. Been watchin' you the last week, sinkin' lower'n lower. Before I get to thinking it's my company, you wanna tell me what's ailin' you?"

I put down my cup and pried Lysander off my lacerated scalp. "Lucy, I feel about as useful as a Cracker Jack prize in a box of diamonds. All I've accomplished this week is finding out that, even with fifteen hundred channels, there's still nothing decent on afternoon TV."

She sighed. "Bad as that? Well, you're helping me. That ain't useless."

"Bullshit! I'd do better if I wore green hides and stuck a bone through my nose. That's what half these delegates of yours seem to expect anyway!"

She smiled and shook her head. "I'm sorry about that, son. Rudeness is rudeness, no matter what world you're from. What would you like to be doing?—Lysander! Stay down from there, hear?"

"That's okay," I said, extracting a paw from my eye. "Lucy, that's the worst of it. I can't think of a damn thing. Captain Forsyth's right—I'm a liability. I don't have to like it, though!"

She sipped her tea, made a face, and put it down again. "You sure don't. Boils and blisters! If I'd listened to 1 percent of the people who've told me to siddown and stay outa the way, I wouldn'ta done anything with my life so far! Why not help Ed with this warehouse thing?"

"He's winding it up—identifying some of the goods. Anyway, it sounded like a one-man job." I took out a cigar and lit it without much appreciation. "You've done a lot, at that—Prussia, South America, Antarctica, Mars—a hell of a lot, judging by all the pictures of your husbands around here!"

"Oh, carbuncles! A girl has to have companionship. Do seem to pick ones who die off young—always liked 'em *adventurous*." She gazed fondly at the portrait of "Pete"—Crown Prince Piotr Kropotkin—she kept beside her favorite chair. There were other husbands in other rooms, including one poor fellow hanging over the fixture in the bathroom. She wouldn't say why, but conceded it was her second husband, "—or was it my third?"

"If I'm not getting too personal, Lucy, exactly how many husbands—"

"Not more'n six or seven. Figured out one time, I was married to each an average of seventeen-point-something years—ain't one of these gay divorcées, y'know."

I looked at her in disbelief. "No, but you'd have to be at least a serial *trigamist*, or a hell of a lot older than you look—mind you, I'm not asking . . ."

"But elevatin' your eyebrows that way is downright obscene. I *was* tryin' t'spare you the shock."

"Lucy, *you* don't think I'm a barbarian, do you?"

" 'Course not. But I'd hate for that bone in your nose t'drop out right in your lap. Son, I was born in 75 A.L. Don't count your fingers, you ain't got enough.

Besides, I already figured it out: 1851—sounds more romantical that way, don't it?"

"You're—er—a hundred and thirty-six years old? I, uh, I remember some Russians back home who claimed—"

"Them Georgians always was liars. But somethin' tells me you haven't got to what's really on your mind, Winnie."

"I'm not sure I— It makes me feel like an adolescent all over again, and I always hated—"

"Sonny, compared t'me, you *are* an adolescent. *Clarissa*—can't say you been subtle about it. Somebody mentions her name, you look like a camel with three kinds of stomachache."

"Thanks a lot, Lucy, should I take out an ad, or—"

"Touchy! You ain't been *obvious,* either. 'Cepting to someone like myself, with refined sensibilities and suchlike." She brushed a cat off her lap, went to the sideboard, poured two battery jars full of whiskey, and slapped one into my hands.

"Tell you a story: seems like when I was younger —maybe better lookin'—there was this fella. But he was a stuck-up little cockroach, seemed like, so I just sorta pined away until I forgot him. Forty years later, by odd circumstance, he married one of my sisters, and one day—I was happily married to my third, or was it fourth . . . Anyway, I braced him about it, and he told me that back then—we were workin' in the Dodge City General Merchandise, as I recall—he was painfully shy, plain frozen scared of everybody. Especially me, he said, 'cause I was the prettiest girl working there. 'Course I was the *only* girl working there, but the point's the same, I hope."

"I think I see what you mean, but where does Ed fit in?"

She laughed suddenly. "Tell me, boy, you planning to stick around? I mean after Deejay's thingamajig's back in working order?"

That caught me by surprise. "Haven't thought about it much." I'd been thinking about very little else. "I guess I just assumed—"

"All you talk about's 'back-home-this' and 'back-home-that'—what in lumbago's a girl gonna assume?"

"I just never imagined— Besides, I have obligations *back home*." I gulped my drink. Suddenly my throat felt like half a yard of fiery steel wool.

"Who says you're obligated to attend the funeral of your own civilization or get buried with it? Pretty obvious that's what's going on back there. Wanna go back where there's no cigars like that one, no fine liquor like this, no real money or clean air? *No Clarissa?*"

I squirmed in my seat. "I hadn't looked at it that—"

"Well, that tears it!" Ed broke in, slammed a stack of hard copies down where they slid and scattered on the floor, went to the sideboard, and charged a glass. "That lying, no-good anal-extrusion. Know how I spent my day? Going over those vids you made at Madison's, with a fine-tooth microscope. Know what I found?"

"Come on in, Eddie," Lucy said. "Why not pour yourself a drink?"

He stopped, looked down at the glass in his hand, and grinned sheepishly. "I'm sorry, Lucy. Anyway, that basement's got every dial and gauge, every coil, transistor, and interociter that's missing from Bertram's warehouse, that's what!"

"What?" Lucy and I both sat up.

"My friends, you're looking at the System's number one, platinum-plated, grand champion idiot! Edward William Bear, Consulting *Defective!* Win, my apologies. From now on, *you* do the deducing, I'll stay home where somebody can fasten my gunbelt for me and wipe the drool off my chin!"

I had an idea. "Now we can take Madison to court —here's the evidence!" Two of the cats were batting at the copies and rolling around in the resultant mess. "He can't plead ignorance with a basement full of stolen parts!"

"Sorry," Lucy said, "That information was obtained unethic—"

"But I thought that could be taken care of! Don't keep changing the rules!"

Ed sat on the floor with his drink, gathering papers

and finger-fencing with the cats. "More to it than that, Win. Oh, if we retrieved Bertram's property, it'd delay Madison, but he'd acquire what he needs eventually, and we'd be right back where we are now. But what really makes me mad is that, in order to sue, you need a victim, a complainant. Once I'd done the analysis, I called Bertram."

"And?" I said, not liking where this was headed.

"And he was *very* upset. I found out why later on —he'd flown the coop. Forsyth's team watched Madison greet him at the door, and they weren't exactly acting like enemies."

"So Bertram's been stealing from his own company," I said, "For the Cause, no doubt. Say—why *steal* the stuff, some insurance angle?"

"He probably wanted them kept out of it. Anyway, it's only his company in the sense that he's president and chairman. There are thousands of stockholders who aren't going to be fond of him in a few days."

"You boys want something to eat? I'm gonna punch up a few nice overstuffed chickens. Clarissa oughta be back in half an hour, hungry."

"Thanks, Lucy. Ed, were you serious about me doing some deducing? I've been going bananas around here. You know I can take care of myself, and I'm tired of being on exhibition."

Ed frowned. "Well, Captain Forsyth's a good old ape, but you're right: nobody's going to outshoot you in a fair fight, even with that archaeologist's wonder on your hip. I've been making all the mistakes, so far. Might as well have someone else to pin the blame on."

I grinned so hard it hurt.

"Don't blame Forsyth, Win. He thinks all of us nakes are a little bit helpless."

"Okay then, what do we do next, partner?"

Ed got up and shook my hand. "How about dinner with the ladies?" He looked down where Lysander had his head inside the whiskey glass, lapping happily at the hundred-proof liquor. "And we could always join the cats in another drink!"

XVII: Helium Heroics

Monday, August 3, 1987

You can travel, or you can *travel*. There's a difference between a Cadillac and a Greyhound, a Cunard liner and a copra tramp. I don't like it: they never stock my poison in hotel bars, and Mr. Gideon had limited literary tastes.

But I've been all over for the department, twice to Europe, even once to Japan. I used to favor big jets, the bigger the more comforting. Then I flew to Wichita in an ancient DC-3.

He was twenty-four, she a sweet sixteen, a honeymoon couple who'd hatchet-murdered their way across four states, jailed in Kansas on a parking violation. We won the coin-toss, and Wichita's assistant chief sportingly offered us transportation on his elderly bucket of rivets.

Seeing the damned thing squatting on the Stapleton asphalt, engines palpitating, showing every symptom of Parkinsonism, I considered walking to Kansas with the matron riding piggyback. But I clamped my jaw firmly, looked around for the parachute locker, and, as soon as we were airborne, my whole attitude was transformed. Instead of rocketing dizzily out of the smog, we floated along, just high enough for an occasional encounter with an orphaned cloudlet. The insides of the old bird had been remodeled and felt like a living room: comfortable loungers, a properly stocked bar, and great big picture windows. I forgot my white knuckles and settled back, drink in hand, to watch the prairie roll by.

The Confederacy has jet liners, thousand-passenger

fusion-powered titanium monsters that bash their way through near-space at five times the speed of sound. Ed felt I might see more of the country by dirigible. I was packing when he stepped into my room.

"Is that briefcase all you're taking?"

"Damned right. I don't care if we're in session six months, I won't be saddled with suitcases." I stuffed a pair of socks into a half-empty cigarette carton.

"Well, don't forget that little yellow ammo box. Slip it into a pocket where it'll be handy, and *hurry,* or we'll miss the shuttle!"

We began by driving into the center of town. Lucy and Clarissa met us. They'd already sent the Thorneycroft home, and I watched Ed do the same with his Neova, programming the freshly repaired machine back to Genêt Place, where it would wait faithfully until summoned again.

Entering the offices of Lilienthal Aeronautics, we punched our confirmations. I hoped the Seventh Continental Congress was up to footing the bill: I had visions of conducting government on charity back home. The aeroline was willing to go along with the joke. We were invited to repair to the roof, where a shuttle would waft us up to a dirigible passing overhead. We must go to the mountain, it seemed.

Riding the corridor to the elevators, we encountered a security setup not too different from the ones back home. Ed bellied up, drew his Browning, pulled the clip and chamber round. Lucy's horse-pistol materialized from some region of her person, and Clarissa unsheathed her Webley Electric. Following their example, I unholstered my Smith & Wesson, wondering what would happen next.

At home, the officer would lose control of her sphincters, and forty thousand federal marshals would trample in and haul us away for the next several eons. If they discovered something besides weapons—bullion, tobacco, Japanese merchandise—they'd add a snotty smirk. Whatever happened to the Fourth and Fifth amendments at U.S. airports? Or the First, for that matter?

"Excuse me, sir," the attendant said politely. "Is

your ammunition in compliance with aeroline policies?"

Ed nodded. "Frangibles, at under nine hundred feet per second."

"Thank you, sir. Please pass this way. Madame?" Clarissa showed her Webley. Its tiny stingers would never penetrate an aircraft body.

Lucy's bazooka caused a momentary logjam: the .50 Gabbet Fairfax isn't exactly common. Things got settled by reference to the Telecom—its 400-grain slugs were safe—adequate for defense, but harmless to the flying machine—as long as they showed a special air-travel headstamp.

The official took a hard look at my revolver. Naturally, she couldn't find it in any of her references. "I'm terribly sorry, sir, would you mind if we took your, er, gun, until you reach your destination?"

Ed grinned smugly. "See the trouble that museum piece causes? Use the cartridges in the yellow box."

ELMER'S CUSTOM HANDLOADS—CERTIFIED FOR
AIR TRAVEL

I reloaded cylinder, speed-loaders, and my derringer —which caused another round of dithering—with this new stuff: bright-yellow plastic bullets. They'd explode into harmless powder on aerocraft-tolerance materials. Ed poured my real ammo into his suitcase, for which I got another ribbing, and an automated dumbwaiter collected our bags for the shuttle's belly.

"Look, friends," I said, once we'd cleared security, "I know you're enthusiastic about weapons, but haven't you heard about hijacking?" I had to explain.

"Silly way to commit suicide." Ed laughed. "And if you lived, you'd be paying restitution the rest of your life!"

"*If* they caught you."

"You'd be begging for it, by the time the paying customers finished with—"

"What about capturing the crew?" I insisted.

"Like to see 'em try that on *my* ship!" Lucy, our former combat pilot, said. "One of these big balloons, they'd just switch over to auxiliary control, while the regular crew mopped your brains off the dashboard."

"Security's pretty good, these days," Ed added. "Crew-country bulkheads are titanium. No one gets in unless invited. Besides, the minute you ban handguns, criminals will take up less detectable and less discriminating weapons. Bombs, for instance."

I persisted. "But what happens if I point a gun at the passenger sitting next to me, and threaten to blow his head off if they don't take me, say, to Algeria?"

"Algeria?" Lucy asked. "Isn't that somewhere at the bottom of the Sahara Sea?"

"Come on, you're stalling! What happens if I take a hostage?"

"The hostage kills you," Clarissa said, and that seemed to be that.

"You people are just naturally crazy or maybe you're all criminals yourselves!"

Lucy's laughter echoed off the elevator doors. "From what you've said about the U.S.A., I guess we're criminals. Here's to crime!" She hoisted an imaginary glass. Suddenly we were on the roof.

I never saw the outside of the shuttlecraft. The elevator door opened, a miniskirted gorilla showed us to our seats, and we were flung into the sky. The light suddenly dimmed—we'd flown into the biggest shadow this side of a total eclipse, the silvery-transparent underside of the mile-long airship *San Francisco Palace*.

Dirigibles have a reputation they don't entirely deserve. If you added up all the people killed in *heavier-than-air* machines, from Icarus to that latest crash in Oklahoma City, the few lighter-than-air tragedies of the twenties and thirties wouldn't make a measurable percentage.

Dirigibles *do* expire spectacularly: blazing block-length torches, people pouring off the keel like doomed ants. But the *Hindenburg* was *stuck* with hydrogen— we'd cut off her only supply of helium. *Akron* and *Shenandoah* were simply overwhelmed by sudden storms in a day when twelve cylinders generated fifty horsepower.

U.S. airlines are subsidized; every one of those big tin birds can be instantly converted to some military use, blueprints on handy file at your friendly neighborhood airport. Airships have no such potential; they're vessels of peace, big, fat, and vulnerable to uniformed strangers with evil intentions. Ask Lucy, who wound up touring Europe by shanks' mare.

The *San Francisco Palace* is a universe apart from the throbbing jet-powered cigar cylinders I was used to. On long flights, you can go to bed—in your suite! Dozens of lounges, conservatories, and bars are scattered throughout the ship. Yet the *Palace* isn't as big as they come. Her route's a milk run: Isthmus of Colombia to Heinlein City at the Bering Strait, by way of the Great Plains. A mile from rudders to mooring cone, she's a flying saucer with secretary's spread—a cross between a football and a frisbee—operating on fusion, generating helium as a by-product. Helium holds her up, too, most of it from stationary reactors on the ground. If we'd had to cross the Rockies, heating coils within her ballonets would lighten us more.

Lucy left us in the lobby, an elegant vaulted chamber with translucent ceiling and Victorian trim. She was addicted to a serial that no mere Continental Congress was going to interrupt. I'd watched a couple of episodes. It was a weird mixture of Buck Rogers and *Masterpiece Theatre*. Ed made a beeline for the bar. Maybe he was a white-knuckle passenger, too.

Clarissa had been oddly quiet all day. Now, suddenly, she didn't feel "dressy," though she looked fine to me in scarlet medical tunic and slacks. "I'm almost grateful for that fire," she confided absently. "It's an excuse to pick out a whole new wardrobe. Think I'll find a hairdresser and do a little shopping." She gave herself a critical eye in the mirror on a nearby marble column. "Win," she asked, laying a gentle hand on my arm, "if I get pretty enough, do you suppose we can persuade Lucy and Ed to switch accommodations in Gallatinopolis?" She wasn't provocative about it; her eyes were big, filled with questions.

My heart was pounding. I'd planned to share a room with Ed. "Er—uh, um . . ." I explained.

"Me, too." A blush, then she reached up, kissed me lightly on the earlobe. "I'll see if I can catch Lucy now. See you in a couple of hours!"

I staggered to the bar, dimly aware that ordinarily you do that going *out,* not in. Out of the fog, Ed gave me an ambiguous look and shoved a glass in my hand. We circled around the gambling tables, plunking ourselves down where we could look outside. Half the *Palace,* more or less, is a tough, transparent skin stretched over titanium bones. These great windows ran from floor to ceiling, twelve feet. Scenery unrolled beneath us as we plowed northward: "Wyoming" now, a barren cattle-dotted plain in my world, a lushly irrigated breadbasket here.

I stared at other passengers while they stared at us. The place bustled pleasantly but wasn't crowded. Many must have been curious about me—I'd helped Lucy round 'em up, via Telecom, but no one disturbed our privacy.

Naturally not all of them were human. Nuclear blackmail concerned every being on the continent—the entire planet, to judge from languages I heard around me. Some felt more threatened than others: Hamiltonians hold that animals have no place in society except as slaves and breakfast. A quarter of the Congress would be chimpanzees. There were gorillas, too—one group passed in peculiar robes and headgear that marked them, according to Ed, as academics from Mexico City.

At another suggestion from Ed, we negotiated a complicated series of diagonal and horizontal escalators that carried us forward half a mile to the cetaceans, traveling in luxury equivalent to our own. Through transparencies we viewed water-filled passageways in which they swam, intent on errands or simple touring the ship. Along *our* hallways, double-lensed cameras translated images into audio wave fronts, giving finny observers a view of the landlocked world.

Now and again through the glass, I saw scuba-equipped land-dwellers mingling directly in marine society. Occasional killer whales made that an un-

attractive proposition as far as I was concerned. Not
that I feared their razor-sharp teeth (*orca*'s just as
civilized as anybody else): those critters really fill up a
corridor! Porpoises and whales seemed to suffer no
similar qualms: dozens of self-propelled "iron lungs"
rolled along our passageways, and in several areas,
land and sea folk visited in big overcrowded swimming
pools.

Scattered through the ship like potted palms, Tele-
coms posted announcements, public and private. I'd
started keeping an eye out for Clarissa or Lucy trying
to find us, so I wasn't altogether surprised to see my
name on a screen:

LT. WIN BEAR: MR. VON RICHTHOFEN REQUESTS
CONFERENCE, SUITE 1919, WITH YOU & YOUR
COMPANIONS. KINDLY RING FIRST. MESSAGE ENDS.

"Madison!" I snarled.

"I know," Ed said. "I was hoping to enjoy this trip."

"We might, yet." I fingered the handle of my knife.
"Why his real name? What's he trying to tell us?" I
remembered Lucy's tales of the murderous Red Knight
of Prussia.

"Perhaps he's reluctant to announce himself publicly, considering where most of us are going. And
why." He stepped back and began checking his pistol.

"So you think we oughta accept the invitation," I
observed.

"No harm in being ready." He let the slide down and
holstered the .375. "Let's find Lucy and Clarissa, and
see what they think."

"Why don't we leave them out of this, especially if
there's going to be shooting? We can deal with Lucy
afterward."

"You deal with her." He inserted a copper, punch-
ing 1919. The screen rearranged itself into John Jay
Madison, reclining in his smoking jacket, Oscar
Burgess glowering in the background. I pushed past
Ed.

"Ah," breathed the Hamiltonian, "I wasn't expecting so prompt a reply."

"Can it, Madison. What do you want—before you're shipped out to Pluto, that is? And leave your trained pit-viper there out of this!"

Burgess charged the pickup, veins standing out on his cratered forehead. "Save it, asshole! You won't be so glib when I get you back to the—"

"You and whose—"

"*Gentlemen!*" Madison said. "Oscar, the world loves a gracious winner." He levered Burgess away and leaned back again. "I'd like to offer you fellows a truce, an essentially friendly meeting to discuss exchanging certain 'valuable considerations.' As you might surmise, I'm attending the Continental Congress to speak for my society. However, there's no reason we can't do business along the way, and it might render this whole Gallatinopolis affair unnecessary."

Ed barged in. "That's why you're importing thermonuclear weapons—for purposes of a truce? We've *seen* your films!"

"Ah. Direct to the heart of the situation. I know you've seen the films: a small gift from Mr. Burgess to our organization, before the lieutenant's entry disrupted communications. There, you see? A token of good faith: free information. At Oscar's urgings, Dr. Bealls contacted us, not long after Paratronics recruited Dr. Meiss, and in not too dissimilar a manner. Unfortunately, you had an equally disruptive effect on Dr. Bealls's apparatus. A matter of harmonics, I'm informed. He followed you here with Oscar, or would be dead long since.

"Permit me to add that *I* argued strenuously against prosecuting you for your unexpected visit? There were others among us who—"

"Yeah," I said, "right after you ordered a hit on Clarissa Olson!"

"I thought I'd made that clear, Lieutenant. I *won't* be held responsible for what our less self-disciplined members may do—especially by those who willfully misunderstand our motivations. It's *your* assumption that we intend importing these weapons, for example. I am *deeply* interested in studying the plight of your world, and are not such weapons an element in its tragic history?"

"They're never gonna be a part of history here, Madison! Stop kidding around. What do you really want?"

He looked squarely into the camera. "Very well, to begin with, the films, immediately—and I want this Congress nonsense called off. Also, you will cease harassing me, either by further intrusions or by means of the thugs you have placed around my property."

"Anything else—while we're *talking* about it?"

"Since you ask, I want Paratronics to turn over its technology in full and at once. I confess to growing impatience with Dr. Bealls's flounderings. Both of you will permanently absent yourselves from North America—that's quite a concession, considering the desires of Mr. Burgess."

Ed shrugged. I looked at Madison again. "Don't want much, do you? What's in it for us?"

Madison searched for the proper euphemism. "This is rather delicate. I'd rather not discuss it over the—"

"Spill it!"

"As you will: wouldn't even a pair of perfectly capable ladies be found at some disadvantage, *under a hair-dryer or in a darkened theater?* I leave you to draw your own inferences and to consider my generous offer while you have time. Good day, gentlemen." His image vanished.

"Ed, go find Lucy! Meet you back in the bar!" I ran, skidding at the corners, until I collided with an attendant. "Look—if I wanted my hair done, where would I go?"

"Sir?" he wriggled his wristvoder.

"I got a sudden urge for an emergency fingerwave!" I displayed a silver coin.

"Up nine floors, forward to frame eighty-two. The Bower of Pulchritude." He put his hand out.

"That's the only pulchritude joint on this ship?"

"By no means, sir. But it's the only one we're paid to—I mean, it's—"

"Up eight floors and forward to ninety-two." I gave him the money.

"Nine floors, sir, eighty-two. Will there be any—"

"Yeah—call the cops. Tell 'em to meet me, *fast!"* I charged up an escalator, shoving riders aside. Eight, nine, down corridors in a wake of angry shouts and cursing, past tennis courts, bowling alley, and shooting range, out into the mall. *There* was the Bower of Pulchritude. It *looked* like a bower of pulchritude.

Clarissa wasn't there. I made a mess demanding to know where she'd gone. When I explained, and ladies' guns were back in their holsters all around the shop, someone said she'd mentioned buying shoes. They'd recommended the place next door. It was the only one they were paid to—

She wasn't there. At the next place over, *I found her medikit on a chair* outside the try-on booths. I considered shoving curtains back at random, but remembered the girls in the beauty shop, the ones with the artillery. Instead, I grabbed a clerk. "Where's the lady who belongs to this bag?"

"Bag? Oh—she left her bag."

"You mean she's gone?"

"Afraid so, sir. Should I be telling you this? I mean, are you—?"

"I'm a lost little boy, and she's my mommy—I'm old for my age. What happened?"

"Well, she came in, tried on a few things. Then, while she was changing, her husband—"

"Her husband?"

"Yes, a very tall man with an accent and almost no hair. He came in to wait. Next thing I knew, the lady had collapsed. Fainted. He said it was her "condition." Practically had to carry her out. She was quite a sight. Her eyes . . ." Suddenly I was very, very afraid. I asked where they'd gone.

"Their suite. Said she'd be fine if she could just lie down and— Are you sure this is any of your—"

"You bet it is, honey. Whenever the cops finally get here, tell 'em I got a sudden yen to watch *Galactic Horizons*—get that? Now where would I do that on this levitating subdivision?"

"One of the Telecom lounges, I suppose. Number seventeen is the closest. I watch it myself when—" I headed back into the mall. Lounge seventeen would be about right, assuming Clarissa'd caught up with Lucy. If it wasn't, I'd try paging her.

Lucy *was* there, but I can't say the same for the two thugs they'd hauled out of the theater. A small crowd had gathered around the cashier's booth, along with a medic, two security attendants, and Lucy, arms folded, gun dangling from one finger. "Miserable flea-bitten— You know I'm missing my program while you're fiddle-farting around!"

"Now Madame," one of the official contingent pleaded, "if you'd put that away, and tell us what happened here. We must have an explanation. It's a company rule."

"*Stuff* your company! If two punks wanna get hurt— I'm practically an innocent bystander!" She gestured sharply with a toe at the figures on the floor.

The medic looked up and scowled. "Come on, lady —you've already fractured his skull! Trying for some ribs, now?"

"Lucy!" I elbowed my way through the crowd. "Kleingunther's got Clarissa! Where's Ed? He's supposed to—"

"Ed ain't here. These," She kicked at the bleeding form again, "were lounging around when I— notice how this one matches Clarissa's description? Anyway, they came in, sat either side of me, and—" She aimed a kick at the other unconscious thug, but was restrained. "He had a hypo. *They were gonna stick me!* So I bopped 'em—couldn't fire in a crowded theater. *Taxation!* They bent my front sight!" She peered along the barrel, the crowd in front melted discreetly away.

"Lucy, put that wherever you carry it, and listen! We've got to find Ed!" I lapelled an attendant. "We're Congressional witnesses. One of our people has been kidnapped, and this was another attempt. Can we shake loose of here *fast?*"

I fidgeted as they blotted up the assassins and wheeled them away. "If the *lady,*" the girl said, "will leave her name and address. There were witnesses, so we can get depositions." A few remaining bystanders

mumbled assent, one frosty-haired chimp in a leisure
suit shook his fist at the departing miscreants.

Lucy got stubborn, so I butted in. "Lucy Kropotkin,
628 Genêt Place, Laporte! Sorry, Lucy, no time to
stand on your dignity." To the attendant: " 'Com
ahead and check with the President if there's any
doubt."

"The president of what?—oh, yes, the Continental
Congress."

"With any luck," Lucy added, "There'll be *more*
violence! Where's Madison?"

"Suite 1919. If somebody who looks like me shows
up, tell him where we went—and send troops!"

"I'll tell my assistant. I'm coming, too!" She herded
us to a metal door marked EMPLOYEES ONLY and
opened it with an odd-looking key. "Hold on tight!"
she ordered, pushing buttons as the stainless-steel
capsule shot down, sideways, down again, and way,
way up, coming to a screeching three-G halt. We
tumbled out into four inches of carpet, a door across
the hallway said 1932. "This way!" she whispered. I
unlimbered my Smith & Wesson, wishing for something
better than plastic bullets.

1919's door was shut. I raised my foot level with
the lock plate and *kicked*. And kicked again. While
I was rubbing my toes, she opened the door with her
passkey. We found the note lying propped on the telecom:

> Lieutenant:
> We enjoyed more success with Dr. Olson and
> Mr. Bear. Instead of wasting time—and—possi-
> bly lives—attempting to follow, reconsider my of-
> fer before Congress convenes.
>
> M.v.R.

At that moment a mechanical maid entered, followed by a senior flight attendant and a pair of obvious newlyweds. "What's going on here?" I demanded
as the same words left the glorified room clerk's mouth.

"If it's any business of yours," he answered both
me and himself, "I'm making this suite available to

Mr. and Mrs. Snedigar, here. Who are you, if I may—"

The security officer flagged him down. "And the previous occupants?"

"Why, Mr. Richthofen and his party took a groundward shuttle not more than five minutes ago. I arranged it myself."

XVIII: Congress Shall Make No Law

Gallatinopolis, geographic and political center of North America, is a crusty little patch of buildings surrounded by an entire planet of wheat fields. A lone highway stretches from the south: Greenway 200, an emerald ribbon in a sea of gold departing northward until it's covered with a springy mutated moss.

Our ship found mooring east of the little part-time capital. I wasn't in a mood to enjoy the scenery— Clarissa and Ed were gone. Everything else seemed pointless. Visiting the *Palace*'s dungeon, a hastily padlocked tool crib, had proven useless. One prisoner was dead. The other was beyond saving, and beyond telling us anything. Hadn't anyone here heard of poison in a hollow tooth? He had several week-old bullet wounds, though. Eleven-caliber Webley. I watched the son of a bitch die.

Now, Lucy chattered as the great ship made fast. "They'll wheel a derrick in behind us and lower the whole shebang to the ground."

I tried to help: "Why not just fly off, the same way we got on?"

"We would," she answered, "but most of these passengers are delegates. Simpler to get rid of us all at the same time, doncha think?"

"Maybe not. If there's any of Madison's people still aboard, I'll kill the bastards with my bare hands!"

"Might be more effective than that little gun of yours. Look, Winnie, prudence don't suit me, either— Pete was the deliberate one in the family—but we gotta sit tight and see what develops first."

"You call that a plan?"

"It's all we got. Maybe if we beat 'em in Congress.

They're only holding Ed and Clarissa to keep us from sayin' our piece . . ."

"You're kidding one of us, Lucy. Madison'll waste them just for spite."

"Hmm. We'll think of something, son. My old cerebrum's on autopilot right this second. By the way," she pointed out the window, "if any of those folks down there look like ants, it's 'cause they *are*—we're down!"

Vast sections of wall swung outward, daylight crashed into the cool Victorian lobby, people began filing out. Minutes later, standing at a luggage carousel lowered from the ship's belly, I replaced the plastic-tipped cartridges with 240-grainers from Ed's bags, now piled around my feet with Clarissa's things. I waited for Lucy to hire a taxi, but with thousands of humans, simians, and cetaceans deblimping all at once . . .

During the Whiskey Rebellion, it says here, government in the Old United States meant Philadelphia—convenient for rebellious farmers, less so for George Washington—but as the country expanded over the next century, it was subject to increasing pressure to move west. Many cities declined the honor vehemently, and, as suits the national style, nothing official was done. In the freewheeling post-Revision days, the capital tended to be wherever the President lived, wandering to Charlottesville, Albany, Boston, back to Philadelphia again, until it was "dumped" as Lucy is fond of saying, in the Dakota Territories, near Balta.

"*Sorry, Winnie!*" I jumped. "No cabs. Did manage to snag this wheelie frammis for the luggage." I loaded the thing while Lucy held it upright.

"*This* is progressive, modern, space-age Gallatinopolis?" I snorted.

"This is miserable, backward, *rustic* Gallatinopolis. Ain't it swell?"

I eventually learned not to look down at my feet: the city is preserved exactly as it was eighty-seven years ago—its chief and only industry the much-to-be-despised operation of occasional government. The

place looks like a mining boom town: tarpaper shacks
ready to burn given thirty seconds of warm weather
and a mild breeze, streets narrow runnels of churned
mud—but *frozen*, under two inches of transparent plastic. Walking on polymerized "air" is downright un-
nerving. The boardwalks and rough buildings are concrete under carefully maintained exteriors.

"Y'see, Winnie—that's right, don't look down—we
didn't locate this place to make it more accessible—
Whoops! Almost got *me* that time!" She laughed,
and seemed, despite the circumstances, younger than
I'd ever seen her.

"Oh?" I asked. "How come it's in the precise center of the continent then?"

"To make it just as inconvenient as possible to
everyone! If Tucker'd had his way, the poxy thing'd
be in Siberia! Government *needs* to be tiresome. Folks
think twice before they agree to come up here. We've
met only six times since the capital was moved. That's
six times too many, but anarchy takes practice. Now
where's that hotel? These streets were planned by a
committee, all right!"

In 138 A.L., Prussia decided to emulate North
America by confederating Europe—even if it didn't
want to be confederated. In brief campaigns, the other
German states, France, Benelux, and the Italies were
gobbled up. Spain and Portugal fell to fifth chan-
nelists, and England, as usual, was in trouble.

An agitated Congress assembled, the first since 1900,
a disheartening sight to Europeans who'd come begging for assistance: even the assembly hall was
roughed out of pine planks. The Old World was mys-
tified at the vital barbarity of the new, but they had
good reason to ask for help: Scandinavia was threatened by a Czar emboldened by the Prussian distrac-
tion, the Finns fighting a gallant but futile guerrilla
war against the Cossacks; two great barge fleets stood
ready to invade England—under Hamiltonian leader-
ship, the Irish were preparing a final revenge.

By a substantial margin, Congress voted strict neutrality. There was ample precedent: this nation had

avoided wars in 1812, 1860, 1898, and ended its
1845 engagement with Mexico in four virtually bloodless weeks. Yet it surprised no one—except, again,
the Europeans—when a volunteer force gathered to
make the fabled Thousand Airship Flight, and many
a delegate who'd demanded official neutrality boarded
those dirigibles, some never to return.

The war lasted one hundred days. The exhausted
Hamiltonians, already being nibbled to death by native Thomas Paine. Brigades, couldn't comprehend the
fresh, disorderly, leaderless Americans, unwilling to
surrender—unable, even if they'd wanted to. The
aerolift volunteers were better-clothed, better-fed than
peasant-conscriptees, who'd only recently traded their
pitchforks for clumsy Prussian bolt-actions, and fell
before the machine pistols Confederates had lived
with all their lives. A German officer complained, in
an unfinished letter, that these American devils only
shot their enemies between the eyes. He was found
shot, perhaps by coincidence, between the eyes.

Wherever they went, Confederates left anarchy behind. Gallatin's ideas carried them fully as far as the
force of their arms; enemy and friendly nationals alike
learned quickly. Many a nobleman returned home
to find his castle turned into a resort hotel by some
local enterpriser. The Germanies and Italies remained
fragmented. Spain fractured into a dozen polities.
Brittany seceded from France. Armed at Prussian expense, Eire returned to her ancient tribal anarchy.
The Balkans subsubdivided until every village was a
nation.

England held on. Scotland, Wales, the Isles of Wight
and Man departed. Skye and Mull promptly seceded
from Scotland, and Oxford University erected customs
barriers. The formerly United Kingdom began to re-
semble a badly done jigsaw until it established a
Gallatinist Parliament, and the perplexed King was
persuaded to add "Anarch of the Commonwealth"
to his titles. Ireland was gone, but Normandy was
petitioning for annexation.

In 1918, amid the aftershocks, a worldwide influenza epidemic struck. Nearly four hundred Confeder-

ate airships had somehow survived the war. Stocked, again at private expense, they flew around the globe dispensing a new and powerful medication to the disease-ridden planet.

We finally found our lodgings, across the street from Liberty Hall, and were graciously ensconced in the third-floor "penthouse." It was a good thing our accommodations had been reserved. All over the tiny capital lobby floors were being rented by the square foot, and people were sleeping in hovercars. I looked at the large, inviting bed and thought of Clarissa. For a man of my age, I was doing a lot of crying these days.

Gallatinopolis was never intended to be large. Except for the Quadrennial, a sort of political skeleton crew meeting every four years to select a President, the city had remained quiet after the War in Europe, stirring again briefly in 1933 with the ascension of President Chodorov, who filled the vacancy created when President Mencken shot his own Vice President in a duel, only to be gunned down by the Veep's irate mother.

Accommodations disposed of, Lucy and I crossed over to the assembly hall, passing through its doors beneath the foot-high letters:

THIS IS LIBERTY HALL
YOU CAN SPIT ON THE MAT AND CALL THE CAT A
BASTARD
—Fleet Admiral His Grace A. B. Chandler

We paused at a sign in the rough-paneled hallway promising THE JEFFERSONBURGER—IT'LL SET YOU FREE and, with understandable trepidation, elbowed our way into the crowded snack bar.

"Third time Congress met," Lucy said around the greasy fringes of her lunch, "I only just made it. Always liked politics. Just perverse, I guess. After the war, Pete and me tried ranching the Matto Grosso, but between Jivaros and the soldier ants . . . Finally got ourselves a little stretch behind the Admiralty range, settled down carving out uranium. Antarctica's downright homey, compared to Brazil—no poison darts! Damn sight better off than those first Moon-steaders in '73!"

1949?

"There we were, rich as Croesus, an' getting richer, when the Czar up and claim-jumped the whole bloody continent! Kinda stupid, seein' as Russian nationals didn't amount to a full 1 percent of the population—refugees, at that. Troops came about three weeks later. Pete got kinda shot up, so I herded our old hover-buggy clear to Tierra del Fuego—dodgin' Russky war subs, Pete all feverishlike beside me, and all we had left in the world piled on the back seat."

Piotr Kropotkin, bloodsoaked bandages and all, addressed the Congress. Antarctica was a bonanza of coal, oil, other minerals. Its colonies were popular. America outfitted another volunteer expedition.

The Czar declared war, attacking Alaska, occupied the Kingdom of Hawaii, and invaded Japan, shattering her centuries-old isolation. The Confederate Hoverfleet, a small-but-deadly 250-mile-per-hour navy, won decisively at the Bering Strait. Their Imperial dynasty murdered by the Czarists, the Japanese adopted a strange quasi-Gallatinism, with feudal undertones that still confuse political scientists. Another political mystery is the precise nature of Hamiltonian involvement with the Czar—why were they allowed to maintain their regime in Hawaii, finally overthrown when massive numbers of occupying Russian troops were reassigned south.

On the ice, attrition had had its way with the first Siberian waves. Now troops came from the warmer Motherland, lacking the preparation and technology for an environment that made the Steppes seem tropical. North Americans in heated spacesuits simply led them where they could die most efficiently.

By 1958, the real war was being waged by advertising people. Broadcasts into the Russian homeland told serfs that their lives were their own, and disputed the fatherly intentions of a ruler who'd let them perish by millions. Fusion-powered spaceplanes rained propa-

ganda into the streets of Saint Petersburg. In the
meantime, Lunar colonists constructed Sequoyah I,
history's most powerful wireless transmitter. Fusion-
potent, it modulated Russian bedsprings, lightbulb fil-
aments, and tooth fillings, singing the praises of
well-ordered anarchy, and hissing the vile Czar from
moonrise to moonset.

Angrily brandished agricultural implements and
machine tools leavened by aerodropped Confederate
weapons overwhelmed the Russian government. Czar
Rasputin IV vanished; rumor often places him in Ar-
gentina or some other remote corner of the System.
Today, the hoe and spanner symbolize the birth of
Russian liberty.

The war was over, the last significant nation-state
on Earth destroyed.

The rough-hewn corridor was filled with milling
people. Elaborate wrought-iron sconces illuminated
portraits between the gift shops and storefronts.

The first, G. Washington, that hated tyrant, hung in
a frame no less distinguished than any other. Beneath
it a cuspidor was bolted to the floor. Gallatin, Genêt,
Jefferson, Monroe, Calhoun—Sequoyah and Osceola
in their turbans. Jeff Davis, Gifford Swansea, Arthur
Downing, Harriet Beecher, massive bearded Lysander
Spooner. Jean-Baptiste Huang, Frederick Douglass,
—Benjamin Tucker, his face benign as we passed.
Nock, Mencken, Chodorov, Lane, Rand, LeFevre—
and suddenly an empty frame with a small brass
plate:

NONE OF THE ABOVE IS ACCEPTABLE
A.L. 192–196

"Lucy, what's *this?*"

She paused, grinning broadly. *"That,* my boy, may
just represent our finest hour—and the sole legacy of
the Fifth Continental Congress. Wouldn'ta missed it
for buckets of rubies!" She fondly patted the frame.
"Back in '91, it was. The Quadrennial couldn't stom-

ach any of the candidates, an' the ballot always carries this other choice, so . . ."

"That's what they elected?"

"Well, who'd really *die* without a President for four years? Been thinkin' of suggesting it again, sometime."

None-of-the-Above gave way to someone named Hospers, then, appropriately enough, to a Portrait of Jenny—twenty-fifth President (if you count old George and None-of-the-Above)—of the North American Confederacy.

We jostled into the delegates' chamber. I don't know what I'd been expecting—the U.N. General Assembly or Flash Gordon's Bathroom—it was a *barn*: weathered pine, rough beams, dominated by a huge Telecom screen up front. Somewhere a vendor was crying *"Peanuts! Piñons! Fried Grasshoppers!"* My belly rumbled and I tasted greasy hamburger. Two walls were stepped into tiers of upholstered benches. Thousands of desks cluttered the football-field-size floor. I started toward the spectator seats.

"Hey, whatcha doin', youngster?"

"Sorry, Lucy. Is this reserved or something?"

"Shucks no! Just thought you'd like to see the mayhem up close."

"From the floor, you mean?"

"Sure, as a delegate's guest. I got connections. Have a grasshopper?"

"God, *no!*" We threaded out way along: medium-size consoles for humans and chimps, great-big daddy-size ones for gorillas.

Lucy pointed at the untiered wall. "Those cylinders over there are for cetaceans. Mostly don't give a hoot in hot water, but occasionally they want something done bad enough to take being cooped up. Usually prefer staying in a hotel pool, managing by Telecom."

"Their delegates can vote by Telecom?"

"Hives and heatrash, no! This place is supposed to be inconvenient! *You wanna encourage more government?* What a thought!" She shuddered dramatically, then winked and sat down abruptly at a console, keying the terminal. Her name appeared at the front of the room, among a few others already present, fol-

lowed by a number: 6076. "My constituency, such as
it is, six-thousand-odd people—odd enough t'let me
stand for 'em at this quiltin' bee, anyway. *Sure* y'won't
have a grasshopper?"

"Ulp!" I shook my head, taking the extra seat.
"Lucy, you continue to amaze me. You represent
some district in Laporte?"

"No *district* to it, son. We're all "at large" here,
though there's some as shouldn't be. Anybody can
represent anybody else—or nobody but themselves.
Not *even* themselves, if they just wanna sit in the gallery and be entertained."

"Well, who *do* you represent?"

She punched up a couple of drinks, which arrived
a moment later through a slot. "European war vets,
mostly. Colleagues, friends from the old days in Antarctica, some of Pete's chums. You want that lemon
slice?"

"Trade you for the maraschino cherry. Is that the
usual way to select representatives?"

"Ain't no usual way, Winnie. Learn that, you'll get
along fine. Most folks just show up representing
friends, neighbors, people in the same trade. Maybe
half a dozen are professionals, with a million proxies
each."

"That many?"

"Don't get sarcastical! Votes don't amount to much,
anyway. It's what gets *said* here. Though nothing guar-
antees anyone'll listen." The screen changed again,
more delegates arriving, vote-strengths shifting as
viewers all over the continent punched in proxies and
cancellations. Totals were revised moment by moment; many a politico with thousands of supporters
might suddenly discover that, through the miracle of
electronics, he was representing no one but himself.

"Interesting," I said finally, "but not very democratic."

Lucy laughed. "The object's getting things done
without violating anybody's rights. Hardly a traditional
democratic concern. But this is probably the *most*
democracy ever to park its brains on a bench. Anybody's welcome, anybody can vote, an' you can change

your mind any time. Whole thing's telecast so you can see how your rep's treatin' you—maybe shift to somebody else if you want. Representative Participatory Democracy—Gallatin's contribution to creative political instability. Don't take it too seriously—ain't good for you." She flagged the seedy-looking peanut vendor. I buried my nose in my glass, refusing to watch.

"But it *should* be taken seriously," I finally protested. "It's only the seventh Continental Congress in—"

"Even so, I'll bet more folks're watching that Mike Morrison western on channel 962 tonight. Everybody's got a right to ignore the state and be safe doin' it. Makes up for fanatics, like me."

"Hmm. What would President Jackson say about *that?* By the way, you haven't told me about the *Sixth* Continental Congress, yet."

"Nothin' t'tell. Buncha waste motion, huzzahing the two-hundredth year since Independence. Slept through most of it." She crunched another grasshopper.

"I see. Lucy, we had a Bicentennial, but it all seemed kind of flat."

She looked at me closely. "What was left to celebrate?"

Time ground slowly onward. New names blinked onto the screen, the room gradually filled. Important-looking people stopped by to greet Lucy like a long-lost friend. Apparently I'd underestimated this batty little old lady. We ordered a meal. More nothing happened. Finally: "When does this show get on the road anyway?"

She glanced up at the screen, shading her eyes. "Can't tell, exactly. You bored or something?"

"Or something," I admitted.

"Ain't no certified regulation starting time. How could there be?"

"God damn it, Lucy! Clarissa and Ed are prisoners! Maybe *dead* already." I cringed inwardly at the words. "And we're sitting here on our—"

"I know. But whatever happens—even to them—

is gonna happen right here, and not until at least nine-tenths of North America's represented. Oops!— forgot t'tell you. Take a gander at the tote screen. See that number?"

I looked: 0.83901256. "Eighty-three percent?"

"Closer t'eighty-four, and no Congress till it hits ninety." As she spoke, the figure jumped to eighty-six. "Y'see, this place is never really empty. Always somebody wheelin' an' dealin'. But that number's only gone over oh-nine-hundred six times in history, and nothin' else counts."

"Even if enough wheelers and dealers showed up just by coincidence?"

"Ever try organizin' 90 percent of *anything?* Highest it's been the last thirty years is seven-hundredths of a percent—I *know!*"

"So it takes something really big to get them all together. But Lucy, this could take *weeks!*"

"Give Jenny and me a little credit—an' one of those seegars, too. I might's well *look* the part." She lit up from a hot spot on the console.

"Lucy, I just can't get my bearings. You all keep changing the rules on me, then I turn around and there *aren't* any rules! How can you live like that?"

She puffed professionally. "Only stability this side of the grave, I always say, is in the funeral parlor. Hey—looky there!" The screen was filled with names, the percentage 0.90000002 and still climbing.

The Seventh Continental Congress had convened.

Jenny entered without fanfare, punching in at her terminal. Her image appeared overhead as she said softly, "The Seventh Continental Congress of the North American Confederacy is now in session. Mr. Parliamentarian, may I have the protocols?" Conversation, briefly abated during this opening "ceremony," mounted again as a chimp to Jenny's left began typing furiously:

SEVENTH CONTINENTAL CONGRESS:
PROTOCOLS
FRANKLINITES: CONTIGUOUS SESSIONS
DISSOLUTIONISTS: ABOLITION

TELECOMMUNICANTS: YIELD TO FRANKLINITES
PROSIMIANS: YIELD TO SAPIENT MACHINES
SAPIENT MACHINES: PETITION, ORANGUTANS
NEOIMPERIALISTS: YIELD TO ANNEXIANS
ANNEXIANS: PETITION, GREENLAND
GALLATINISTS: DECLARATION OF EMERGENCY
DISSOLUTIONISTS: REBUTTAL TO NEOIMPERIALISTS
HAMILTONIANS: GALLATINIST CRIMINAL PRACTICES
ADJOURNMENT

"What the hell is *this?*" . .

"Shh!" Lucy whispered. "Let's see how it's gonna go."

Jenny again: "Mr. Williams, we have a proposed emergency before us. Will you yield?" The screen cut to an unkempt, toothy individual with apparent adenoid problems: BUCKLEY F. WILLIAMS, FRANKLINITE FACTION.

"Erh, Madame President," Williams answered in a bored tone, "insofar as the responsibility were mine alone, I would be deliriously gratified to accede to your charming request. However—" The audience booed enthusiastically, and someone shouted, *"Cut the crap!"*

"I take it you won't yield, Mr. Williams?" Jenny said patiently. "Very well, you have ten minutes."

"Erh, thank you very much, Madame President. Fellow delegates, as you all are consummately aware, we who deem ourselves Friends of Benjamin Franklin have long advocated an unequivocal terminus to the irresponsible and apathetic governance of this polity. There are grave and consequential matters being heinously defaulted to irrational, whimsical, and venally individualistic instrumentalities." He tapped his prominent teeth with a stylus and sniffed. "Such nugacity is insupportable. Accordingly, and with full assent of my associates, I urge adoption of the following resolution, to wit: that the Seventh Continental Congress hereby decree an *Eighth* Congress, one year hence, and in each successive year thereafter, hencforward and forever." Nose toward the rooftree, he rolled his eyes like a dying horse, sniffed again, and sat down.

Jenny waited for the boos and hisses to fade. "Thank you, Mr. Williams, do I hear a second?" Someone near Williams bobbed up and seconded before the camera could catch him. "It's been moved and seconded that—Mr. Williams, will you kindly transmit your motion to the secretary?—that a permanent legislature be reestablished. Discussion?"

A thousand lights were blinking on the board, wrangling for recognition. Lucy cut her volume and chuckled. "Now maybe I can answer your question."

"What did I—oh, yeah— *What the hell's going on here?* What about the Federalists? Who's this Williams, and what's he up to?"

"Calm down, son. We're here: 'Gallatinists: Declaration of Emergency.' "

"Okay, but what's all this other shit?"

"At least you understand its nature. But we gotta wade through it, anyway."

"I thought we called this Congress to warn—"

"That's where you're wrong. This is just us good ol' folks, whose number 'happens' to be 90 percent, remember?"

"But you said it was all carefully arranged!"

"And so it was. But everyone's entitled to speak, and in practice, they reserve space on Jenny's agenda, in case we ever have a Congress. Some been waiting for decades, carried over from her predecessors' lists. Offering 'em this rare shot helped us put it together. Lucky there ain't ten times as many. Managed to convince a few we got a real emergency. Williams and the rest are holdouts, then we'll get down to *real* business."

"This isn't any different from my own state legislature! Who are these Franklinites, anyway?"

"They just want a permanent government—been around since Lysander was a pup. Looks t'me, though"—she squinted at the screen—"like they're still dwindlin'. Never stood much chance. What they want, under the rhetoric, is a nice coercive system of franchise monopolies, government contracts—"

"Rotarian Socialism," I mumbled, quoting Mary Ross-Byrd. "That's what Propertarians call it: 'Free Enterprise—*and keep those subsidies coming!*'"..

"You got the point. Listen—they're about through." The Franklinites had lost, 99.99 percent to 0.01; on to the next order of the day.

"The Chair recognizes Sandy Silvers of the Dissolutionist Faction."

"Madame President," said a pretty, honey-haired girl with a wry smile, "I move that Congress *adjourn*—"..

Catcalls and curses filled the room.

Shouting over the tumult, Jenny exclaimed, "I'll remind the delegates that a motion to adjourn is always in order! Second?"

"Madame President! May I be allowed to *finish* my motion?" She was still on her feet, others around her standing in their chairs. The noise died down—what can you add to a motion to adjourn? "Madame President, delegates assembled, I move that this body adjourn—*permanently!*"..

Her cohorts jumped and cheered, answered by yells around the room, some friendly, some not. The Franklinites shot a unanimous raspberry at them. Sandy answered, lowering her voice seductively in the pickup, "We love you, too, Buckie."

Lucy had leaped up, shouting, "Second, Second!" Now she came back to herself, grinned sheepishly, and sat down. "Always did have a radical streak, I guess." She relit her cigar. The Dissolutionists lost, three to one, but for some reason they cheered again, and Lucy beamed. "Highest total yet! Hope Pete's restin' happy tonight. He's got good reason."

The Telecommunicants, who simply wanted voting allowed remotely, yielded to Buckley F. Williams. Amid hisses and boos, he moved that Congress be conducted by Telecom—*on a regular basis*. This time the ayes were too small for the big screen to express accurately. The Franklinites got up and walked out.

"Tryin' t'sabotage us," Lucy explained. "Below 90 percent, we're outa business, remember?" She didn't seem perturbed. "They hope the Dissolutionists will

join 'em, but Sandy's too smart for that." She waved
at the young anarchist leader who grinned and waved
back.

"I don't know, Lucy, all this petty maneuver-
ing . . ."

She pounded my shoulder. "What else you expect?
Politics brings out the worst in people every time.
Maybe I'll join the Dissolutionists' after all." I glanced
around later that evening. Most of the Franklinites
had sneaked back in, not wanting to miss the real
action.

The big board went on shifting as more viewers
tuned in. Next up, the Prosimians, contending that
orangutans and gibbons should be admitted to the
Confederacy. All of their delegates were human.
Forsyth had mentioned these worthies in disgust: do-
gooders and ward-heelers looking to benefit from the
proxy-power of others. The captain had curled his
lip, "Orangs and gibbons may be the most intelligent
folks on the planet—won't have anything to do with
politics!" But the Prosimians were yielding to the
Alliance of Sapient Machines.

"Lucy, are there really any sapient machines you
know of?"

"Well, some sure have their own personalities. My
two old Thornies have consecutive numbers, but each
one handles differently. You've probably noticed the
same thing with guns. The day a machine walks in
here and— Come to think of it, some prankster tried
that, back in—"

"But there's some seriousness in all this?"

She considered. "Probably not now, but y'never
know about tomorrow . . ."

I nodded emphatically, looking around idly for an
exit and a bathroom.

The Alliance—as human as the Prosimians—
moved to admit orangutans, and any "other in-
telligences" (their definition), automatically hence-
forward. Their definition would have included canta-
loupes, elephant's-foot umbrella stands, and at least
half that FBI agents I've encountered. The proposition
failed.

The Neoimperialists, after a brief, Cato-esque commercial demanding destruction of any remnants of government left anywhere in the world, yielded to the Annexians. "Nothin' new," Lucy explained. "The Neos, mostly war vets, start with a good enough idea. Government's morally repugnant to any decent person. But how'd they avoid killing a lot of the very folks they're liberating? Just won't *wash*."

A slight twinge in my bladder. "What about these Annexians?"

"They just want Antarctica and some other places admitted. I dunno—we generally encourage other continents t'do things on their own. On the other hand, Greenland"—she indicated the agenda—"that might not be a bad idea."

The Annexians took the floor. By Telecom, the current speakers for Greenland were testifying. Independent more than a century, the island had a Gallatinist assembly. In a recent 90-percent-or-better session, they'd decided to petition for admission.

The vote was affirmative. The North American Confederacy, a culture which routinely handled English, Spanish, and Quebecois, now would add another language. Well, if they could handle Cetacean, why not Danish?

And now, just as I was desperate to leave the room, I found I couldn't.

It was our turn.

XIX: State of Emergency

"Y'all enjoy them goobers now, y'heah?" The vendor smiled nervously at Lucy as she handed him a few small coins.

"Thanks a bunch, Jimmy-Earl, I sure will." She offered me a handful. "Can't help it, Win," she whispered, "that little guy gives me the creeps. Well, looks like they got Greenland seated. Told you it wouldn't take long."

Scratch another chance to leave the room.

Jenny rose and cleared her throat. The roar of random conversation faded. "The Chair now yields to Dr. Olongo Featherstone-Haugh"—she pronounced it "Fanshaw," but the read-out told a different tale—"Vice President of the North American Confederacy." From her right, nine hundred pounds of *Gorilla gorilla* ascended to the rostrum. Jenny stepped down. I'd been warned about this gambit: people might take our case more seriously, presented by the leader of the Gallatinist Party, a pretty, well-liked lady who just happened to be President.

"Mr. Vice President!" Jenny shouted from the floor. The background murmur died in anticipation. We were coming to the main event.

The mountainous Vice President held his wristvoder near the mike. "The Chair recognizes Jennifer Smythe of the Gallatinist Party."

"Thank you, Mr. Vice President. Assembled delegates," she addressed the cameras, "people of North America and the System. Twice in the last century, our culture has embraced new peoples—peoples we had long known, but failed properly to understand. I refer, of course, to simian beings and to the people of the seas, the cetaceans. Today, we anticipate a time when new life is discovered on a distant world, life that shares with us that sum of values we call Civilization."

The assembly buzzed again, but shut up as Jenny caught her breath. "Fate has chosen me to bring you that news—with two shocking qualifications: the new world is called *Earth,* its location, *anywhere you look around you,* for it shares *space* with our own, existing at a different point along one of the several dimensions of *time.*"

The audience began to stir. "Ladies and gentlemen! We shall be *at war* with this new Earth within days— weeks at the most—a terrible new kind of war, ending only when all life on both our planets *is utterly extinguished!*"

The stirring became a jumbled buzz. "Therefore . . ." It was useless. The noise crested: shocked reactions, fervent denials, even an isolated catcall. *"Therefore,* ladies and gentlemen . . ." In the roaring chaos she went unheard. This was affirmation of weeks of circulating rumor. Faces stretched around to stare at me. Others tried to hush the noise, adding their own to the uproar. Jenny climbed back onto the dais, tiny beside the Vice President's furry bulk. *"THEREFORE!"* she shouted into the pickup.

"Thank you. Therefore, I move that Congress declare a state of emergency to deal with this situation before civilization itself is destroyed."

A tidal wave of noise swept over the crowded room. Lucy grabbed her mike, punching for recognition. This too was prearranged. "Mr. Vice President!—Shuddup, you varmints!—Mr. Vice President!" In exasperation, she drew her enormous pistol, triggering three devastating blasts into the timbered ceiling. Sawdust fell, and with it, silence.

"The Chair recognizes Lucille Kropotkin."

"About bloody time, too, Fanshaw, old ape. Okay, I second Jenny's motion, so's we can explain to all these yahoos here exactly what's been going on!" She holstered her pistol and sat down.

"It has been moved," Olongo said, "and rather vigorously seconded, that we declare a state of emergency. Discussion? Mr. Madison, of the Fed—er, Hamiltonian Society." At the far edge of the room, Madison rose. I stiffened, but Lucy reached out quickly, pinning my gun hand to the console.

"Mr. Vice President, we have just witnessed the introductory maneuvers of an unprecedented criminal conspiracy. I—"

"Oh, yeah?" someone shouted. *"What about Hawaii?"* There were echos to this, stomping and whistling.

Madison waded on. "I myself have been accosted by these lunatics, and have some acquaintance with what they're trying to sell. In the interests of decency, I demand that their fantasies be dismissed immediately, so that we may all go home." Boos, hisses, interspersed with a cheer or two. One of his henchmen rose and shouted, "Second!"

"Out of order, Dr. Skinner. There's a motion already on the floor. Captain Couper, you have a comment?"

Couper was a beefy Neoimperialist wearing double shoulder holsters. "If Miss Smythe would accept a friendly amendment . . ."

"That depends, Captain," Jenny answered.

"Would you consider reconvening in committee-of-the-whole, delaying the vote until we fully understand the nature of this emergency of yours?"

She hesitated. "I'm not sure I could accept that right now."

"Good going, Jenny!" whispered Lucy.

"Then," Couper replied evenly, "I offer it as a formal amendment."

"Second!" cried Sandy Silvers.

"There's a precedent." Lucy giggled. "Dissolutionists seconding a Neoimperialist motion!"

"Thank you," Olongo said. "Any discussion on the amended motion?"

"Mr. Vice President!" A Franklinite chimpanzee was recognized. "As I understand it, Captain Couper merely wants more discussion before we commit ourselves." For some reason, Lucy tensed. "You're not proposing any long-term study, are you, Geoff?"

"You know I'm not, Fred."

"Captain Couper, Mr. Muggs, will you gentlemen *kindly* address the Chair?"

"Herr Doktor Vize Prezidendt!"

Olongo sighed resignedly. "Mr . . . um . . . Kleingunther?"

"If Herr Oberst Couper did not zo intendt," Madison's butler said, *"I* vould ligh zuch a ztudy formally to propoze." He bowed stiffly and sat down.

"Second!" Skinner shouted.

Olongo sagged. "We now have," he spread his huge hands helplessly, "an amendment to the amendment to the original motion." He hunched over the lectern, lowering threatening eyebrows. *"Any discussion?* I didn't think so."

"QUESTION!" a hundred voices cried, Lucy's foremost. "Ain't politics fun?" she whispered gleefully.

"The question's been called. We will now vote on the—"

"Point of information?" A plumpish lady stood up, waving her arm.

"What is it, Mrs. Grundy?"

"Olongo, dear, I don't understand. Are we voting on a declaration of emergency, or a *discussion* of a declaration of emergency?"

"Neither. We're voting to . . . Mr. Kleingunther, please reiterate for Mrs. Grundy, and anyone else who's confused."

"Oh for blither's sake!" Lucy muttered. Kleingunther started to speak, looked confused himself, read over his notes, and consulted with Madison. Finally, he restated the motion.

"Now if everybody understands what's going on, we'll proceed. All in favor of Mr. Kleingunther's amendment to Captain Couper's amendment, please signify by entering 'aye.' " In a mass-flurry of keyboard activity, many of the names on the screen turned from white to green. I began counting, but lost track when—

"All opposed, type 'nay.' "

Lucy's name and others changed to red. A few remained white—the delegate beside us was snoring softly. He didn't have my aching bladder to keep him awake.

But we were outnumbered, sabotaged before we'd even gotten started! Would Madison be allowed to take over two worlds without a fight? Would we ever see Clarissa and Ed again? Would I ever get to the bathroom?

"Mr. Secretary, please assess the proportions!" Suddenly, everything reversed. I'd forgotten that each delegate carried a different voting weight, from those representing only themselves, to the tiny professional minority with millions of proxies. The motion had failed, twenty to one!

The next order of business was Captain Couper's amendment by itself. All in favor? Furious typing. All opposed? More of the same. The board looked hopelessly green, but this time I waited for the proportions. Slam! went the gavel. "The amendment passes by a majority of 99.44 percent. This body is recessed and reconstituted as a committee-of-the-whole!"

I groaned. Had we lost?

"Great goiters, no!" said Lucy. "We were hoping for something like this, but couldn't figure a way to swing it ourselves. Those Hamiltonians did it for us, bless their cruddy little hides."

I rested my head in my hands. "I give up. What's going on this time?"

"You'll learn," she laughed. "Look. Anybody wants to speak at this bellywhop's limited to ten minutes, right?"

I remembered something like that. "But what's all this other junk?"

"Well, now we're a committee-of-the-whole, just asittin' around the potbelly stove. No time limit, no question to be called. Trouble was figurin' how t'get it done. Never woulda passed if *we'd* suggested it."

"I see," I said. "So you got Captain Couper to—"

"Like pox we did! Neoimperialists don't do favors for Gallatinists, and everybody knows it. It was just dumb luck. The Federalists finished the job, annoying everybody with their amendment to the amendment!"

I shook my head. "More smoke-filled-room chican-ery."

"Winnie, it's the same game, wherever it's played. Only difference is, *this* Congress can't force anyone to do anything. Hell, you people can raise taxes, steal land, deny justice and the laws of nature, all before noon recess! Ain't a soul in this room—'cept maybe the Hamiltonians and Franklinites—doesn't want to get rid of politics altogether, someday. Got something better back home?"

"Hmm. You may have a point in there among the land mines."

"Well, try doin' a little thinking sometime. Might get to like it after a while."

"They always said it'd make us go blind. Speaking of that, are the whites of my eyes turning yellow? I need to—"

"Hush, boy! They're startin' again!"

"Marvelous." I crossed my legs and bit down hard on my cigar.

Resuming the Chair, Jenny called on Deejay Thorens, via Telecom, to describe the Probability Broach. A second circuit, to Emperor Norton University, allowed Ooloorie to chip in by split-screen. It was the first I'd seen of Deejay's recordings of my world. They were depressing. The United States now looked dingy and threadbare to me. I'd forgotten already what grime, noxious fumes, and poverty in the soul of a society can do to the people who have to live there.

"Madame President!"

"The Chair recognizes Mr. F. K. Bertram."

"Madame President, we demand this demonstration cease! Those recordings are private property, which these two individuals"—he pointed to the inset images of Deejay and Ooloorie—"are using without authoriza-tion!"

The main screen went white. Everybody blinked. "Is this true, Dr. Thorens?" asked Jenny, knowing per-fectly well it was.

"I'm afraid so," Deejay admitted ruefully.

Bertram shook his fist at the 'com. "Thorens, you

and your, your—specimen, are discharged! Turn those recordings over this very minute!"

"That, sir," Ooloorie answered coolly, "is a logical impossibility. They're *already* in your custody, being run from a telecomputer in Laporte."

"I don't care! I—we want it stopped, right now! *Right of private property!*" It was growing harder for me to follow the action. My bladder was demanding full attention.

"Wait a minute!" It was Olongo, our of order and towering above the rostrum. "What do you mean, private property? I'm one of your stockholders, and *I* want to see those recordings!"

"Mr. Vice President, with due respect, *we* are obligated to make decisions in the best interests of the company as a whole."

I glanced over at Lucy, typing frantically into her console. She'd established a datalink with a Chicago stock exchange, summoning up a list of stockholders and cross-referencing it with the roster of delegates. "Oh horsehockey! There's only four of any significance here, and one of 'em's Madison. He's in for five percent! Couldn't raise a majority if our lives depended on it—which they might!"

I shifted painfully. "Lucy, may I make a suggestion?"

She looked at me, mildly surprised. "Say on, Mac-Duff!"

"Well, didn't you say these delegates represent nine-tenths of the country?"

"Quit fidgeting, boy. You feel all right?"

"*No!* What percentage, do you suppose, is watching this clambake?" Now she had me doing it.

A predatory gleam dawned in her eyes. "It just might work! But it'll take time. Hold on a second."

"What do you think I've *been* doing?"

"Shush now!" She punched more buttons. "Running a cross-check: individuals *represented* at this palaver, versus stockholders." The Telecom burped:

ESTIMATED RUN-TIME:
FOUR MINUTES, THIRTY-TWO SECONDS

"You dash down to Jenny and Olongo. Tell 'em what we're up to." It felt more like sloshing than dashing. I crossed the great floor self-consciously, but I needn't have worried: as the wrangling continued down front, I noticed delegates napping, several reading books or their electronic counterparts, and at least two poker games along my route to the rostrum. Someone was working a complicated 3-D crossword in his display, others were walking around, chatting, eating dinner. And I was heading down front, instead of out back where I needed to go.

I reached Jenny. "Lucy's onto something." She punched Lucy's combo, the screen read PRIVACY and faded out. "She needs about five minutes." I explained the idea.

Jenny snapped her fingers. "Didn't think of that!" She leaned over to whisper briefly in Olongo's furry ear.

"Madame President!"

"Yes, Mr. Vice President?"

"I move a five-minute recess. I have to go to the john."

"SECOND!!" I found myself running wildly for the door.

Jenny didn't wait for an assenting vote. Slam! "This committee stands recessed for—" She must have seen my rapidly receding back. "—make that . . . make that *ten* minutes. Personal privilege of the Vice-President!"

And Win Bear, too.

Jenny gaveled Congress back to order. "The Chair recognizes Lucy Kropotkin, of the Gallatinist Party!"

"Madame President, we strenuously protest!"

"That's nice, Mr. Bertram, but the Chair still recognizes Mrs. Kropotkin."

Lucy stood. "Madame President, as a *stockholder* in Paratronics, Ltd."—I looked at the certificate on her desk: one share, purchased from a Dr. Featherstone-Haugh, still warm from the facsimile printer—"I'd like a straw-poll of my fellow stockholders, concerning disposition of these records, which, after all, are *our* private property." Bertram and Madison were frantic at their keyboards. I smiled and shot them a bird.

Jenny asked, "Is a majority of stockholders present?"

"No, Madame President, but there's a majority represented by *delegates* here. If the Secretary will display the data I've just transferred to him." A number of delegates' names turned blue, numbers trailing behind them indicating shares held by their constituents.

Jenny handed over to Olongo, stepped down, and was recognized. "Mr. Bertram, I'm prepared to move adjournment, just long enough for an impromptu stockholders' meeting here and now. I believe all that's required is a majority of stockholders who—"

"Woman!" Bertram rose, face flushed, trembling with fury. "You can't pull this quasilegal nonsense on me—us!"

Jenny smiled sweetly. "Oh yes I can, and afterward, your stockholders will likely want a new chairman of the board, won't they?"

"All right, all right!" Bertram collapsed into himself like a worn-out concertina, burying his face in hands. Madison caught Kleingunther's eye. The butler nodded, patting a bulge under his left armpit. Bertram was about to discover that politics wasn't fun anymore.

The room darkened once again. Crude internal combustion engines, pushing rubber tires along grease-stained asphalt, carried rigid stick-figures, naked of human dignity or the means of self-defense. I'd been adjusted out of my own culture. Would I ever be able to return? There was Vaughn Meiss, alive, unaware of being observed through a keyhole in time. Deejay and Ooloorie described the first contact as we watched it being made, then covered Meiss's decision to construct his own half of an improved Broach.

"But apparently," Deejay reported, "his work was being duplicated. These United States have a long, brutal history of internal and international warfare, often employing weapons only a Prussian might consider wholesome."

"Meiss had once developed such weaponry,"

Ooloorie continued. "It's difficult conveying to a free people how this involved him with an absolute authority of which he came to live in mortal terror, even after he'd resigned. His work had been in secret, in a ferment of paranoia, and failure to perceive that not letting one's real defensive capabilities be known, is a principal cause of war." In the flickering screen-light, I could just see someone joining Madison and his cohorts, someone I thought I knew.

"There are many secret police forces," Deejay, explained, "responsible for ferreting out enemy secrets, preventing their own from being discovered. One such, covertly keeping watch on Meiss, began duplicating his Broach. At the time Meiss was murdered, they'd gotten far enough to pass small objects into this world . . . and contact certain people here." I was sure now who'd joined Madison. I didn't like the implications of his sudden availability.

"The secret agency," Jenny took up the narrative, "established liaison with the only advocate of tyranny left in North America." She pointed an accusing finger. "John Jay Madison of the Alexander Hamilton Society, formerly know as the Federalist Party!"

Madison leaped to his feet. "I reject this calumny! These fanatics have distorted their personal antipathies —which might better be satisfied decently in the courts or upon the field of honor—into a ludicrous fairy tale! These Gallatinist monsters have waged their war of lies upon my inoffensive compatriots for two centuries!" He slapped his weapon. "By Almighty God, I swear I'll end it now!"

I unsnapped my safety strap. Jenny faced Madison unflinchingly. "Sir, you'll have ample opportunity to reply in due course. But I am telling the truth, and no threat, *on this Earth or any other,* can frighten me into doing less. Do you understand me?"

"Be warned, then, young woman. You are gambling with your life!"

"Up yours, Manfred, with a prickly pear!" Lucy shouted. Madison jerked his head in our direction, the entire room burst into laughter.

"The Chair," Olongo said, blowing his nose, "will

now examine . . ." He peered at a slip of paper,
". . . Captain Edward William Bear, late of the United
States Police Force."

A bit nervous, I got up and walked slowly to the
dais, detouring to approach the Hamiltonians. Sure
enough, there was Oscar Burgess, sneering at me. I
glanced at the SecPol agent. "Stay out of this, slime!
Madison, I want my friends back, quick, in good
condition—Hold it, Kleingunther, or you won't leave
this room attached to your nuts!" I shoved Burgess
back, gave Kleingunther an elbow in the eye, and
snatched their leader's lower lip, digging in with my
thumb. "And Madison," I warned, watching blood
seep up around my thumbnail, "I've got no more
scruples about initiated force than you do. So think
about it, while you've got a chance!"

I let go, wiped my hand on Burgess' shirt, and
pointedly turned my back on them (not without a
nervous qualm or two), continuing on in a widening
circle of shocked silence.

Someone brought me a chair. I sat on its edge, letting my holster dangle within easy reach. "Captain
Bear," Olongo asked, brown eyes twinkling down at
me, "you're from this other Earth we've been discussing, an important police official there?"

"Well, yes and no," I answered, thinking about
Perry Mason. "I'm from the other Earth, all right, but
as for being important, I'm afraid you've been mis-
led. It's lieutenant, not captain. (Why does everybody
here seem to be Captain something-or-other?) And I
work for the *city* government—don't look so shocked!
—of Denver, sort of similar to Laporte, only farther
south."

"Mr. Vice President!" Madison again, his diction
a little worse for wear. "I demand the right to cross-
examine this psychopath! Or have we Hamiltonians
lost every vestige of our—"

"Ask anything you wish, Mr. Madison. But you're
out of order and will have to wait your turn. Please
carry on, Jenny."

"Thank you, Mr. Vice President. Lieutenant . . .

Win?—is it true that you, and others, were physically attacked in an attempt to keep the Probability Broach under government control?"

"Well, I can't exactly testify to their motives—"

"And these attacks continued in our world?"

"Yes. Two good friends of mine, who tended my wounds, took my risks, helped me orient—they're *gone!* For all I know, they're—*You're gonna get yours, you scummy bastards! Do you hear me? Are you listening, you—*"

Olongo rested a kindly paw on my shoulder. "Please calm yourself, Lieutenant. You're making reference to someone in this room. Mr. John Jay Madison. Isn't one of his companions from your own world?"

I breathed deeply, wiping my eyes with a corner of my poncho. "Yes, Oscar Burgess, over there with Madison. He's Denver Chief of Station for the Federal Security Police. They kidnapped my friends, to keep me from testifying."

Olongo addressed the assembly. "Any more questions, before we move on?"

Madison came charging down the aisle. "Isn't it true you're a charlatan? An ordinary, third-rate commercial peeper, covering up thefts from a client whose trust you've also rewarded by implicating him in this fantasy of yours? Speak up! The nation must understand the *depths* of your depravity!"

I sat it out while Olongo hammered down the crowd. The gavel suddenly snapped, its head bounced across the floor, landing at Madison's feet. The gorilla drew his sidearm and went right on pounding. "Order! Order! There'll be *quiet* in this room, or I'll start awarding extra navels!" He turned the weapon in his fist, but kept it pointed aloft. "Who's first?" Someone tittered, Olongo cracked a hideously fanged grin, and holstered the piece. "Lieutenant, would you care to answer this *gentleman?*"

I struggled not to get angrier. "Mr. Vice President, in the place I come from—in my history, George Washington defeated the Whiskey Rebellion. Just as there were two George Washingtons, in your world where he was executed, and in mine where he died in bed,

there are two Edward William Bears—*and Madison's
perfectly aware of it.* The Edward Bear in your world,
a man I've come to regard as a brother, is a detective
in Laporte. I met him—"

"Just a moment," Madison interrupted, "if there
are two of you, why not simply *produce* this superflu-
ous Edward Bear for us?"

"Because, you son of a bitch, he's one of the people
you kidnapped aboard the *San Francisco Palace!*
There were also two Manfred von Richthofens, you
know. The only in my world got what he deserved!"

Madison affected an exaggerated gesture of tolerant
amusement. "Honestly, ladies and gentlemen, is there
no length to which these lunatics will spin their fantasies? I have no more questions, Mr. Bear, or whoever you are. Try to get some professional help, soon."
He waltzed back to his desk before I could plant my
boot where it might do the most good.

Other delegates wanted answers, too. Bit by bit, I
managed to tell the whole story, then Lucy was called
for corroboration. I sat, clenching and unclenching
my fists, as she told of Clarissa's disappearance. Whatever else happened, I was deciding to kill Madison
before this was all over, or be killed myself. I didn't
really care which.

Past midnight, when I was beyond feeling tired,
they showed more film—sixteen millimeter, this time.
Before Madison could finish screaming protestations,
the Seventh Continental Congress sat, stricken by a
horror they'd never imagined possible.

The old films were grainy, scratched with age and
many reproductions: over a large industrial city, a
single B-29, a steel cylinder dropping from its belly.
A flash, smoke billowing 50,000 feet, forming the
poisonous mushroom of death. Then Nagasaki.

Then bigger, better bombs, fission giving way to
fusion, kilotons to megadeaths. Years passed: Japanese
cities, Pacific islands, Nevada, the Sahara, the Negev.
Finally that hideous night in 1983 when the Soviets
delivered their ultimatum to China, a last "humane"
demonstration: a searing flash in the dark that left a

jagged crack from pole to pole, visible across the surface of the Moon. The Chinese surrendered the next morning.

Freeman K. Bertram rose in something like terrified dignity, pale as the screen the films had finished running on. He sidled carefully from behind the Hamiltonians, avoiding contact as if they were contagious, and crossed the floor to Jenny and Olongo.

"Madame President, if it's not too late . . . if there's still some hope, I'd very much appreciate your permission to join, in whatever capacity you'll have me, the Gallatinist Party."

XX: A Matter of Honor

Liberty Hall emptied in stunned silence, leaving Lucy and me behind. I'd lived all my life with a nuclear sword dangling over my head; it's something else to be informed suddenly, to be *shown,* that your whole world's slated for flaming destruction. That, or abject surrender, and Confederates didn't strike me as the kind to lie down and spread their legs, even threatened with holocaust.

Gallatinopolis would be a quieter, more thoughtful city tonight. I'd like to report that I spent the night swashbuckling over the rooftops, wrenching the whereabouts of my friends from the villains, but I won't. It was past three in the morning, Congress would reconvene at nine. I'd had a long day: the *Palace* kidnapping, eleven hours of parliamentary games, the sudden ominous appearance of Burgess—

As we staggered out of the assembly hall through the portrait gallery, there were a dozen blinding flashes. I was suddenly showered with difficult questions: "Mr. Bear! Are you from another planet?" "Mr. Bear! Isn't this whole thing an elaborate hoax?" "Mr. Bear! Is your planet radioactive?" "Mr. Bear! How do you like Confederate women?" "Mr. Bear, is that an atomic-powered gun?"

"What can I do, Lucy? I want to go to bed!" I squinted against the glare. Didn't they realize it *hurts?*

"Son, these vermin used to juggle, paint their faces up, and stand on their heads a few centuries ago. Treat 'em like any other morons—ignore 'em when you can, humor 'em when you can't. You *could* holler 'Privacy,' but—"

"Great! I'll—"

"It won't help our side much. Lemme handle this." She waved her hands, hollering, "All right! All right! Lieutenant Bear'll answer all reasonable and intelligent questions, but let's make this an *orderly* stampede!" We found an unoccupied caucus room off the hall; I sat up front, Lucy riding shotgun, and did my best, while my sack-time evaporated. Toward the end, I don't even remember what I said. Anyway, that's my story, and I'm sticking to it.

"Sam Hayakawa, *Interplanet News*. With me is 'Win' Bear, focus of the Seventh Continental Congress. Lieutenant Bear, may I call you Win? Would it be accurate to say you're from another dimension?"

"I haven't figured it out myself. I come from a place—a time, really—where *history's* different, where—"

"I'm sure that'll interest our technical-minded viewers, heh, heh. For us laymen, what's it like to escape from a Federalist dictatorship, and win free to—"

"Now wait a minute! In the first place, I didn't *escape,* I was *pushed.* In the second place the United States isn't a dictatorship, it's—"

"Win, since arriving here, you've left a wake of shootings behind you. We ordinarily expect perhaps a dozen murders per decade. You've killed that many in a month, and—"

"Friend, I'm going to explain this *once:* I didn't ask to be here; I didn't ask *your* Hamiltonians to—"

"Well, how many people have you killed, then?"

"Nobody who didn't have a weapon out and pointed. Until now. I'm thinking of making an exception in your—"

"Umnh, one more question, Win . . ."

"Call me Lieutenant Bear."

"Erh . . . since your nation-state—is that correct?—has a long history of atomic warfare, do the ruins of your once-great cities really glow in the—"

"How'd your viewers like it if I took that mike and shoved it right up your—"

"This—this is S-sam Hayakawa, Inner—Interplanet News. G-goodnight!"

Tuesday, August 4, 1987

I tried to get up. The 'com buzzer was wrecking my hearing. I found a thousand places where it hurt just to exist. Slipping a leg off the bed, I fell to the floor, gun butt digging painfully in my ribs. Even through the drapes, daylight was drilling straight into my skull. I reached up, groping along the edge of the keyboard, and must have hit the right button. The 'com suddenly squawked. "Win! Where are you, boy? What's wrong?"

"Why nothing, Lucy. I was just admiring the carpet. Such color, such texture, such—You ever been hung over without drinking anything?"

"Politics, son, hazard of the profession. It's ten-forty-five. Ready for another round? We got 'em on the ropes already!"

"At least," I groaned, "they have ropes to hold them up. What—"

"One thing at a time. I just talked to Forsyth, back at Madison's place. When Burgess took off yesterday, they loaded a lot of stuff onto a freighter and—"

"Burgess is here. Where did the freighter go?"

"South along the Greenway. They were gone before Forsyth could get a team on 'em, worse luck."

I got up painfully, sat on the edge of the bed. "What's Madison up to?"

"Nothing. Maybe a dozen guns around his rooming house, and we've got people watching them. Haven't even used the Telecom since they got here."

"Lucy!" I said, "Surveillance? Wiretapping? Next you'll tell me you've been out all morning collecting taxes!"

"Don't talk dirty, boy. Sure, we been watching those snakes. They can *sue* me. I'll forfeit everything, even

take a nice long asteroid vacation if I have to. What damages you suppose Ed and Clarissa could collect from *Madison?*"

"Not a cent, I hope!"

"See your point, son. Change your socks'n get over here. Things're about t'pop!"

I took longer than that, but even after I met Lucy in Liberty Hall, things still weren't about to 'pop.' A few were eating Telecom breakfast. The guy to our left was napping again. If I hadn't seen his chair empty last night, I could have sworn he hadn't moved. I ordered another glass of milk and waited, thinking about "Anarchist Standard Time." Shortly after noon, Olongo used a brand-new gavel to hammer things back into shape. Jenny looked fresher than the day before. Politics agrees with some people. "In the light of what we witnessed yesterday, I move a state of extreme emergency!"

"Point of information, Olongo, dear."

"What this time, Mrs. Grundy?"

"What does Jenny mean *emergency?* Are we declaring *war* on this United State?"

"*States,* Mrs. Grundy, plural. A point well taken, I confess. Jenny?"

Jenny took the microphone again. "Oh dear. I guess we mainly intended to warn everyone. I certainly don't want to declare—"

"Wait a minute!" I surprised myself by jogging forward.

"Lieutenant Bear." Olongo recognized me, perhaps a bit gratefully.

"Thanks," I said, climbing up beside the shaggy Vice President. "Listen, folks, I have friends in trouble. This whole world's in trouble!" Scattered approval, and one or two boos. "I'm not a delegate or anything, but back home, the lowliest ward-heeler would have everything doped out by now, from appropriations and troop movements to a little graft for himself." General amusement, and a purplish scowl from Buckley F. Williams. "Maybe I can tell you what would happen, and whatever you don't like, you can throw out—including me, if necessary. Whatever you do like, one of you could propose formally, and we can get on with it."

"That might be permissable, if there are no objections. Do I hear—"

"Objections?" shouted Madison. He and his entourage were just coming in. "If this *person* is who he claims, he has no right to address this body, not being a citizen of the Confederacy! Or, he's a criminal impostor, to be ejected immediately! In either event—"

"Sez who, Madison?" Lucy hollered. "Call *me* a citizen, you'll get a Dakota pine cone planted where it'll germinate quick!"

"Order! Lucy, deplore as I might the way you express it, I must say I agree. We will *not* have guards at our borders, nor papers to establish who belongs. There are no *citizens* here, Mr. Madison, nor subjects, nor serfs. Lieutenant Bear, do you live and work upon this continent?"

"I guess I do now, Mr. Vice President. Say, I have a bank account in Laporte. Does that help?"

The great anthropoid smiled. "I've no better qualification, myself. I don't believe anyone would challenge my right to speak in this assembly. Would you, Mr. Madison? *Good.* Please continue, Lieutenant."

"Okay. First, go ahead, declare your emergency. It'll get people off the pot. Back home, we'd raise a lot of money, get working on the Broach so it can be used militarily, or prevented from being used. I know you can't collect taxes, but . . . Second—third, I mean, because first you should arrest Madison—I don't know about declaring war. The United States has enough problems already, and SecPol is one of them. There are a few people over there who see things your way, too. You used propaganda in the Mexican War, and the war with the Czar. With Propertarian help, you can probably do it this time, too. The main thing's to arrest *this* gang, and bend them until they tell us where my friends are. Will that do for a start?"

"So moved!" shouted Captain Couper.

"Out of order, I'm afraid," Olongo said. "Jenny, will you accept Lieutenant Bear's, and Captain Couper's, amendment?"

"I don't know. It doesn't sound very principled."

"Well then," I said, "I'll make it a formal amendment."

"*SECOND!*" The Neoimperialist delegation rose in unison.

"Mr. Vice President," Madison said, "if we're to be imprisoned, I'd like to hear the charges . . . and who the damaged parties are."

"He's got a point," Jenny admitted. "Name the crime, name the victim—the basis for all adjudication." Lucy was halfway down the aisle, and moving fast.

. ."What about Clarissa and Ed?" I shouted.

"Did we *see* these people snatch 'em?" Lucy asked, joining us up front. "Any witnesses to Madison's threats?"

"What about Kleingunther? That shopgirl saw him take Clarissa!"

"Win, Madison'll just disavow him, same as before."

"Madame President! Mr. Vice President! Are these proceedings to be conducted among your cronies, in secret?" Madison stood, flanked by Burgess and the others. I began to get an idea.

"We are attempting," Olongo enunciated icily, "to answer your question. Will you permit us to continue?"

Madison smiled nastily. "As you will, sir. Permit me to make a number of salient points, though. First, accepting *only for the sake of discussion* that all these accusations are correct, I'm afraid there is still nothing you could do about them."

Jenny looked startled. "Why do you say that? You saw the films!"

He nodded, grinning even more. "Which, *in theory,* were criminally removed from my possession. However, forget that. If I intended to import foreign soldiers, by your own arguments I've done nothing wrong: *you* are attempting to restrict immigration!" He laughed while the rest of the room buzzed in confusion.

"*Order!*" Olongo bared his fangs. "Is there more of this?"

Madison affected a sweeping bow. "I am getting to

the meat, sir, but another illustration first: suppose I do intend to use atomic bombs. Who in this room will be the first to move against importation or possession of arms? I remind you that, pistols or nuclear weapons, the principle involved is precisely the same!"

There was even greater commotion, it took longer for Olongo to quiet them down. "Your point, Mr. Madison?"

The Hamiltonian was beaming. "Ah. I simply want you all to remember, over the coming weeks, that this highly-principled anarchism you're so proud of renders you *helpless* to deter even threats of the most desperate nature. A more rational social order will have no such problems. *That* is why, in the end, we will triumph. I wish to thank you for an extremely entertaining two days, and bid each and every one a fond *and anticipatory* good—"

"Just a mind-forsaken minute, Madison!" Lucy ran toward the Hamiltonians. "I move a recess—sixty seconds!"

What was she up to? "Second!" I yelled determined not to let her horn in on my action. She could even have Burgess. Madison was *mine!*

"Oh, very well," Jenny said. "It's been moved and seconded—I don't have any idea why—that we recess for one minute. All in favor?"

Lucy gestured, there was a spatter of hesitant "ayes". Without waiting for the gavel, she took the few remaining steps. "John Jay Madison, also known as Manfred von Richthofen, I accuse you of kidnapping and attempted murder. The victims: Edward William Bear of Laporte; Clarissa MacDougall Olson of same; and Edward William Bear of the United States of America. Also, Lucille Gallegos Kropotkin of Laporte, Lesser Coprates, and Ceres Central. Select a neutral adjudicator and post bond in the amount of five thousand gold ounces per complaint. Failure to do so will be proclaimed throughout the land, and you may be ostracized and banished from Civilization. What say you, John Jay Madison?"

"Nice try." He punched out a bank transfer and tossed it at her. "There's more where that came from,

Your Honor. I'll see you in court . . . in thirty days! Somehow, I suspect you won't be able to make it." He continued in a whisper, "I *guarantee* your cocomplainants won't."

Congress died with a whimper. There was nothing else it could do. Weeping openly, Jenny declared, "Individual rights are sacred. We can't touch you, John Jay Madison, without destroying everything we believe. Perhaps, in the end, you will destroy us, but let it be said that we refrained from murdering the Confederacy ourselves . . . I will hear a motion to adjourn."

"Quick, Lucy," I said, "do you have some gloves?"

"What?—oh, I see. You *are* a romantic. Wish I'd thought of it myself. Y'don't need gloves, dear, just go to it!"

"So moved," said a dispirited voice.

I hurried, trying to remember the appropriate customs.

"Is there a second to the motion?"

I began running, tripping over feet in the process, some of them mine. Others were heading the same way, probably with the same idea. Captain Couper, for one. I stopped to untangle my cloak from someone's terminal, finally ripped it from my shoulders and left it, running as fast as I could.

"Second," came the halfhearted reply.

"It's been moved and seconded that Congress adjourn. All in favor, say 'aye.'"

I fixed my gaze on Madison and half a dozen others converging on him. Leaping the row of consoles, I strode along the table, not caring whose fingers I stomped. I leaned on Couper's shoulder, braced myself, and raised a hand. Suddenly Madison was pushed aside. I struck the upraised arm of Oscar Burgess, who grinned. "Say your piece, so we can get it on, Bear!"

I ignored him. *"Madison, my quarrel's with you!"*

Madison looked innocent. "Then why did you challenge Mr. Burgess?"

"What?"

"There are a thousand witnesses around us who saw it. Correct, Captain?"

Couper looked daggers at Madison, then: "Hope you shoot straighter than you punch, kid."

"Madison, when I'm through with this *dirt,* you're next. Or are you afraid?"

"Lieutenant, when you burglarized my home, you encountered a cabinet in which there are eighty silver goblets, one for each of my solo air victories during the War in Europe. All told, I have killed one hundred ninety-three men in single combat, just as Mr. Burgess is about to kill you. Whatever happens, no one will ever be able to say—"

"Enough talk," Burgess spat. "Let's do it." He rubbed his palms on his thighs, leaving grimy creases.

"This Congress stands adjourned." *Slam!* went the gavel. So did my stomach.

Confederate custom requires a cooling-off period between a challenge and its "execution." As far as I was concerned, etiquette could take a flying leap, and a barbaric disregard for protocol seemed to suit Burgess as well. I remembered him so well from CLETA. How many times had he insinuated that killing is the same as, possibly better than, intercourse? How many times had we heard his sickening war stories—from Vietnam and the streets of America— always with a twisted sexual ending?

But to get at Madison, I had to go through Burgess. I was short on sleep, felt like something the Salvation Army would turn down, and I'd never been able to beat Burgess before. I was a dead man. Well, it had been an interesting life, if not a very edifying one.

The crowd began drifting back in, we were soon ringed with spectators, and technicians zeroing in their cameras. At least I'd go out in living color, on a nationwide hookup.

I tried to remember more. Burgess favored a Luger with a modified safety. My .41 Magnum gave me the edge in everything but speed. I was getting scared. My old instructor had a psychological advantage, and

knowing it didn't seem to help. My little engrams—
not to mention my knees—weren't listening.

They cleared the center of the hall. Once the dueling ground was oriented, people began making room
at each end. We stood in clumps, Burgess with his
friends, I with mine. Captain Couper offered to serve
as referee. He called us to the middle, to examine our
weapons. "You're going to fight with these little
things?" he asked. "If you want to hurt each other, I
can scare you up some real guns." We both refused.
There's something to be said for sticking with what
you're used to—I don't know what, but something.
"All right, we'll do this by the book." I scarcely heard
him. My legs felt weak, I couldn't see very well, and
a dull ache was beginning where Clarissa had put the
cast on my shoulder. Burgess grinned, flushed and
excited. From his warped point of view, we were about
to make love. I wanted to throw up.

"Each of you will take his position, preparing his
weapon at my command. You will observe the handkerchief I hold out. When I drop it, draw from the
leather and fire. Shoot again *after* your opponent has
fallen, and I'll personally splash your brains all over
this auditorium." He drew an Antarctic War-vintage
.476. "After the drop, you may move in any way—
duck, even charge and kill your opponent point-blank,
if he doesn't kill you first. But I will remind you once
again, you are barred from shooting at a fallen man.
Clear?"

Dianetically.

"Take your positions." I walked to one end,
Burgess to the other, perhaps twenty yards between us.
"Turn your backs and check your weapons." I wondered if Burgess would risk back-shooting me. Not
with tough old Couper watching. I rolled out the
cylinder. The 240-grain semiwadcutters glinted dully
in my hand. I reloaded, closed, and holstered my
weapon, leaving the safety strap unsnapped.

"Gentlemen, resume your places!" I pivoted, facing
Burgess—a ghastly skeletal leer on his face—and began having an idea (the last had landed me in this
mess, I reminded myself). If you could move after the

flag, then I knew what Burgess would do. He'd
taught a variation on FBI tactics: draw, shift a fast
yard to the right, and snap your shots. I'd trained under him, but now preferred to stand and slug it out,
holding the revolver in both hands. It was riskier, but
a hell of a lot more accurate. Works swell against paper silhouettes, anyway.

Burgess would assume I'd dodge, and fire to my
right. I'd nail him, I hoped, before he got in a second
shot. Lugers don't have a lot of stopping power. If he
didn't miss, and I could stay on my feet after being
hit, I might still be able to nail him.

I kept telling myself.

Couper raised the handkerchief. Everything became
very still and clear. The cloth fluttered to the ground. I
went for the forty-one, watching Burgess draw and
shift. I brought my gun to bear, too late. Over my
front sight, Burgess's muzzle blossomed brightly. A
sharp bite in my right forearm, and I knew I was hit.
He'd corrected faster than I'd counted on. I pulled the
trigger once, twice, hoping to connect before he fired a
second shot. I pulled the trigger once again.

The Smith & Wesson bucked and roared, spewing
fire at Burgess. Two fist-size crimson gouts splashed
his shirt-front, and his head exploded in a hazy red
mist. His feet left the floor, he slammed against a desk
and sank, blood obscenely pumping from his wounds,
head smoking hideously where the upper half had
vanished, mocked by the smoking Luger in his hand.

I swayed, still holding my weapon extended, aware
of the peppery powder odor hanging in the air. I
looked along my arm for brittle ends of shattered
bone, and was astonished. My sleeve was torn from
wrist to elbow—a round brass button from my cuff
was imbedded in the fleshy part of my forearm,
smeary dent in its top. I plucked the button out and
a smeary dent in its top. I plucked the button out and
stuck it in my pocket.

Fuck you, Burgess—another rattlesnake extermi-
nated.

I pried the empties out and replaced them, holster-
ing the S & W. "Okay," I rubbed my slightly damaged

arm. "What now, Captain?" I glanced around, trying
to locate Madison.

Couper shook his head. "You go on living for a
while. Who's going to clean up this mess?"

Slap! Slap! I wheeled around, unconscious that I'd
drawn my still-warm revolver until its sights rose
before my eyes. Above them, Freeman K. Bertram, an
automatic in his outstretched hand, pointed not at me
but at the crumpled ruin of Hermann Kleingunther's
face. I looked again for Madison. He was gone!

Bertram's pistol thumped to the floor. "I couldn't
let him—" He collapsed. I covered the distance in
three steps.

"Bertram!" I'd never seen a belly would like that,
the insides churned like goulash, the outer edges
charred. Kleingunther had been a laser man.

"Win Bear!" Bertram whispered. I put an ear down
to his face. Lucy and Couper were behind me, trying
not to look away. "Never shot a man before. Your
friends . . . Ham-Hamilton House. It's so cold! Cold!"
He stopped talking and gurgled. I knew that sound. I
closed his eyes, holding them until they'd stay shut for
themselves.

"Win, what the plague are you doing?"

"Can't you see, Lucy? He saved my life. Now he's
dead!"

"We've got to get him into stasis," Captain Couper
said, lifting me away. "The ambulance is already here
because of the duel."

I looked at Lucy in disbelief. "He'll be okay?"

"Will be if y'don't put his eyes out."

"You mean I'm going to have to kill Burgess all
over again?"

"Are you kidding? Boy, you blew *his head* clean in
half! Let me be the first to congrat—"

I didn't hear the rest. I was busy puking in living
color on a nationwide hookup.

XXI: Escape Velocity

We jumped into the hovercraft to find Olongo Featherstone-Haugh at the wheel. "Hold onto your hat, Lieutenant!" Before he'd finished the sentence, we surged toward the end of the alley behind Liberty Hall. Leaning on the horn, he swerved right, and was doing three hundred before we hit the next intersection.

"I called the dispatcher," the gorilla said. "Your transport should be hot by now. How's the arm?"

"Only a scratch," I mumbled, cringing as we whipped through another turn. "Did I really say that? Feels more like an amputation!" Another corner whirled sickeningly around the car.

"Don't forget Captain Forsyth," Lucy reminded. Don't wanna rush into a fracas without backup!"

"I'll call as soon as you're off," Olongo promised. At the edge of town, the road curved around the mooring area, but he cut straight across, flashing beneath leviathan shadows, leaning on the horn as simians and humans scattered like fruit flies on a melon rind. We did a sudden nose dive as he killed the lift. "Here we are! Wish there were room for three in that cannonball! Keep me posted, and cheerio!"

There wasn't time to answer. Attendants hustled us out of the hoverbuggy toward a stubby metal cylinder the size of a Volkswagen bus. The nose was sandblasted and missing paint, the stern scorched and blistered. Between them was an oval hatch, and the legend *Columbiad*. Then we were through the six-inch hull, being belted into deeply cushioned seats. The machine's interior was almost featureless: two couches in tandem facing a Telecom screen, no windows, and, when the door slammed shut like a coffin lid, dimly lit by a few instrument pilots. "It itches!" Lucy complained. "Every time I get strapped down for acceleration, my uninsurable nose itches!"

As the vehicle began moving ponderously, a man appeared in the screen, head and shoulders, wearing coveralls like the attendants who'd sealed us in. *"Columbiad,* Traffic Control. We'll have you chambered in a moment. Please don't touch any controls, keep your arms and legs within the couches. You'll be pulling close to six G's. Questions?"

The vehicle slanted downward ominously, rocking from side to side. "Where will this frammis dump us out?" Lucy asked unperturbed.

The controller glanced down at his keyboard. "Right now you're simply routed for LAP. You have a specific destination in mind?"

"How about 89 Tucker Circle?" I asked sarcastically, trying to ignore my heartbeat. He punched his console, paused, punched some more, then looked up.

"We'll shunt you into the underground system, to the southeast corner of that block. Be prepared to exit quickly—I could only get a thirteen-second window between two scheduled trains. Your restraints will release when you drop below five mph, door-releases to your left will be illuminated. Good luck. Keep your hands and feet inside the couches."

The view cut to a circular metal tunnel-mouth in the center of a familiar-looking hill, the median crest of Greenway 200 seen in cross-section. Now I knew what a rifle shell feels like. We entered with a loud *thump* as they slammed the breech behind us. "Acceleration, five seconds . . . four, three, two, one, *fire in the hole!"*

An invisible hippopotamus suddenly draped its full weight the length of my body. I tried screaming, but couldn't even breathe. My bruised arm began burning; I couldn't move to see whether it hung over the edge of the couch. Too late anyway, I figured. I found myself wishing I'd taken time to arrange certain private parts a little more carefully. I was going to have bruises in some strange places.

Almost as an afterthought, I noticed the noise, the loudest thundering I've ever heard. More than noise, really, a bellow that excluded anything else, made it impossible to tell which was crushing me, the acceleration or the roar. And suddenly, it was gone. The screen glowed softly, the tunnel walls rushed toward us faster than anything has a right to be traveling. Blessed silence, and the weight had gone away.

"Lucy?"

"Mmph?"

"*Lucy!*"

"Aw c'mon, Pete, roll over! I can't breathe!"

"Lucy!"

"What? Oh, sorry. What is it, Winnie?"

"What the hell is this thing?"

"Hunh? Oh—Express. Fastest transport on the planet, whatever needs hurried: rattler antitoxin, bodies in stasis, but mostly *talent.*"

"Talent?" I squirmed around in my seat, trying to get a look at her.

"Only irreplaceable commodity. You need a surgeon *fast,* you need the genius puts out oilwell fires, you need Express. Knew a virtuoso banjoist did it once too. Expensive, but he was in time for the concert."

"Talent," I muttered. "Well, what is it—a rocket? Olongo called it a cannonball."

"Sorta halfway between," she said. "Up front it's vacuum, maybe twenty miles ahead—big metal doors like a camera iris. During the squishy part of the trip, they were pouring on liquid hydrogen and oxygen behind us and torching 'em off. If we weren't down in this titanium wormhole, we'd just shoot off the horizon and wind up in orbit. Planes goin' this fast spend delta V just to stay *down!*"

"Are you serious? Wouldn't we burn up or something?"

"If that vacuum fails ahead of us, you'll see some fireworks! Rode one of these contraptions with Pete once, all the way from Tierra del Fuego. They haven't made 'em any more comfortable since. I feel like a sack of broken— Whoops! Here comes turnaround!"

"Deceleration, five seconds . . ." A red light flashed above the view screen. I braced myself, but never heard the count. The chair slewed wildly, my insides going the opposite way. That hippopotamus hiccupped and sat down again. Another sudden lurch and the deceleration eased off. Suddenly we were in an ordinary subway tunnel. We rocked, gasping and screeching, to a halt. I let the belts fall from me, saw Lucy hit the door, and followed her into the coolness of a shopping center, up the escalator as fast as our elbows could push us, and out, blinking in the sunlight.

I'd left my coat in North Dakota. I wondered who was paying for the ride.

I spent an exhausted moment leaning on the wrought-iron fence outside Madison's front yard. A hovercraft on full fans skated up to the curb. Pistols drawn, Forsyth and two of his men jumped out.

I straightened. *"Let's hit the door!"* I charged up the steps, bounded onto the porch, drawing my forty-one, and blasted the lock panel with three quick shots. The door creaked open. No one was there to greet us.

"Search the place!" I ran wildly through deserted corridors, nearly shooting several man-size pieces of covered furniture. The entire house seemed empty. I could hear the Captain's men rummaging around in other rooms. "Anybody find anything?" I hollered.

"Nary a sign," Lucy said quietly. *"Watch* where you're pointing that antique, will you son?"

"I'm sorry, Lucy. Where the hell do you suppose they are?"

"Vamoosed. Forsyth's checking upstairs. Wanna try the basement?"

"I've seen it, thanks. I'll bet it's empty, too. That was Bealls's equipment they shipped out in the freighter, had to be. Question is, did they take Clarissa and Ed too?" I sat down, scratching a vagrant itch with the front sight of my revolver.

Suddenly Lucy looked old and close to tears. "Might's well face it—they only got shipped outa here one way. They're no use to Madison, now we've testified. Ed and Clarissa are—"

"Here! According to Bertram, they are. You sure he won't be conscious for—"

"At least a month." She shook her head. "He was shot up something awful, Win. They'll keep him quick-frozen and—"

"I know. Ed was right about lasers. Bertram tried to tell me they were here, but— Cold! He *wasn't* talking about himself! Come on! We might still be in time! *Forsyth!"* I raced down the hallway, skidding on the turns. An eternity later, we finally reached the kitchen —and the freezer door.

"Help me!" I clawed the fastenings, about to shoot them loose, when they gave. Clarissa stumbled into my arms. We both fell sprawled on the floor in a hysterical heap. Ed hopped up and down, slapping his arms, while Lucy pounded on his back, laughing and cursing, great round tears rolling down her face.

"Clarissa! Clarissa! I thought you were dead!" I wiped my own face with a sleeve.

"N-no, you great big beautiful detective—just c-cold!"

Forsyth slammed the freezer door and reholstered his weapon. Mine was still in my hand. I sat back a little.

"What's all this stuff?" I asked. They were both swaddled in aluminum.

"Clarissa's idea," Ed noted, stripping tattered foil from his arms and chest. "It's how we stayed alive. Okay, doctor, what do we do now?"

"We could boil some water," Clarissa suggested.

"Makes sense," Lucy declared. "They always do it in the movies." She rummaged for a pan in the cupboards. Forsyth looked us over carefully and signaled his way out the door.

"For tea," Clarissa explained. "Or coffee, chocolate. There wasn't enough of that foil to cover *everything."* I brushed frost out of her eyebrows.

"The whole place is empty," I told Ed. "Any idea where they've all cleared out to?" For once, he looked nearly as old as I did.

"No, an hour ago, I didn't even know Clarissa was still alive."

"That's right," she chipped in. "They kept us locked up separately, me in a closet, and—"

"Me in the boiler room downstairs, trussed up to the water heater. Funny—I *thought* I was going to roast to death. Brr!"

"We weren't watched," Clarissa said, "we weren't spoken to, or even fed. I didn't want you to see me like this, but I was so glad when you—" I put my arm around her. She pressed an ice-cold nose into my collarbone.

"A little while ago," Ed said, "they brought me up and shoved me into that . . . thing. Clarissa a few minutes later. The one they called Mikva and a couple more I didn't recognize."

Lucy turned around, a pair of steaming mugs in her outstretched hands. "How come they left you two untied?"

"Great Albert, that tastes good!" Ed said, spilling as much as he drank. "I don't know. They didn't exactly let us in on their plans."

"Maybe so it'd look like you'd wandered in there and died." Clarissa's frozen hands inside my tunic were giving me frostbitten armpits. "Like T-tricky D-dick M-m-milhous. Nice folks we're dealing with. But I still don't get the tinfoil bit."

"Paratronic radiation," Clarissa explained, "the kind used to keep patients in stasis. It damps molecular motion, but metallic objects interfere, slow the process down. It doesn't matter with something like frozen food, but with patients you have to be very careful. That's why you didn't get stasis, Win. Too many bullet fragments. Anyway, we peeled foil off a lot of food in there, and wrapped it around ourselves." She'd finished her hot drink. Lucy shoved another into her hand. "It wouldn't have bought us much time, but—"

"Enough to save our lives!" said Ed. "Now we have to figure out Madison's next move. How did the Congress go?"

"Lousy!" Lucy answered. "Except for Dead-Eye, here. He managed to—"

"Later, Lucy! We got here about five minutes after

adjournment, Ed. Madison's people carted off a lot of stuff yesterday. What'll you bet Bealls is setting up somewhere else right now?"

"Agreed, but where?" He finished his second drink, looked around unsuccessfully for a chair, and sat down on the floor with Clarissa and me.

"You're the great detectives around here," Lucy said, piling food on a tray. "Start detecting . . . or does that Bear Brothers, *Limited* refer to intelligence! Wanna sandwich?"

"Sure, Delegate Kropotkin, Your Honor." I took a sandwich and a cup of chocolate. "And what have *you* in the way of ideas to contribute?" Clarissa ate while I rubbed her cold-numbed arms and shoulders.

Lucy stood munching absently on one of her own creations. "Dunno, exactly. For starters, despite appearances, they didn't really take it on the lam. They had us stopped in Gallatinopolis, and they knew it."

"How did they stop you in Gallatinopolis?" Ed asked.

Together, with many interruptions and not a few contradictions we recounted our North Dakota adventures: Madison confounding Congress; Burgess's demise and Bertram's part in it; the wild ride back to Laporte. Clarissa insisted on looking professionally at my arm. "Ouch! It's only a bruise! Say, you're still cold. I'd offer my cape, but as far as I know, it's still jammed in a teleprinter back at Liberty Hall. Want my tunic?"

"Why, Win, the very shirt off your back? I guess that means we're going steady." Her eyes crinkled appealingly.

"Not until I get a straight answer from *somebody* around here! I've been trying for *weeks* to find out whether you and Ed . . . I mean, nobody will tell me . . ." I spluttered to a finish, more confused and embarrassed than ever. Lucy began laughing, and Clarissa actually blushed this time, eyes carefully on the floor.

Ed put up a hand. "We're not laughing at you, Win. It's just that—"

Clarissa whirled on him. "You let *me* tell it, Edward William Bear! Win, Ed and I practically grew up together. I guess everybody assumed we'd eventually —everybody but *us,* I mean. Anyway, you came along, and I—well . . ."

"There we were," mused Ed, "freezing our asses off in there, and all she could do was blubber about never seeing you again, and how worried you must be. That's why she thought of the alminum foil—said it'd give you a little more time to rescue us! Never stopped hoping, right up to when we heard you blow the hinges off the front door. About half an hour after *I'd* given us up for dead."

"I hate to break this up, folks." Forsyth stood in the doorway, his arms full of clothing. "But the boys and I have to get back. Thought you could use these." He passed the bundle to Clarissa. I looked up at the captain, all four and a half furry feet of him. Relieved of his burden, he automatically assumed the time-honored position, hands behind, rocking back and forward on his heels—all veteran beat-cop.

"Thanks," I said. "You guys were a welcome sight. I assume that stuff's from upstairs. Any clues to where they've gone?

"Like tourist brochures from Ganymede?" He paused. "You might take a look at the basement. Lots of stuff moved out, very recently. Heavy stuff: scratches in the floor, torn-up wiring. Took off in a hurry, I'd say." I looked at Lucy the Theorist. She stuck out her tongue.

"Thanks, Cap." Ed rose stiffly to his feet. "Send me your bill—a *big* one."

"Part of the service." He touched his cap and turned. "C'mon, you monkeys, we got work!" He paused again, looking back over his shoulder. "I saw your little set-to on the 'com. Pretty fair pistol work, especially the head shot. If we're going to have a war with these . . . people—well, look for me in the front lines. I'll be there." He turned again and left.

"So will I," I muttered, watching Clarissa shiver. "So will I."

XXII: Surprise Party

I don't think I've ever been more depressed. While waiting for Ed's car to wend its electronic way to us, we examined what the Federalists had left behind: their furnishings, trophies, clothes in the closets— everything except Madison's tiny silver cups. Yet there were no signs of hasty retreat, no unfinished meals on the table, not even a dirty dish.

Every scrap of paper in the building lay in the wastebaskets, reduced to a fine white ash. They'd been through this before, in a dozen countries, and were good at it. Downstairs was a different story: tangled broken wiring, scarred woodwork, splintered crates— as if they'd made the decision to move at leisure, then gotten hurried halfway through.

"They've rabbitted, all right." I told Ed as we surveyed Bealls's empty workroom. "As soon as he's set up again, they'll have their weapons and manpower."

"The question is, where's he setting up?"

"Lucy, even if we knew," I answered bitterly, "how could we do anything about it? You people and your goddamned principles!"

She kicked at an empty carton. "I dunno. Guess I'd rather have my principles shot from under me than finish 'em off myself. We do have two real live witnesses now. We could make kidnapping charges stick this time."

Clarissa shook her head. "I'm afraid not, Lucy. We never saw any of the real leaders, just Mikva and his two henchmen. Madison was in Gallatinopolis at the time, with several thousand reputable witnesses."

Swell, I thought. They could set up, pull whole armies through, and no one could stop them until they started initiating force—and by then . . . "Wait! Madison took off before I finished with Burgess. He still owes me a duel!"

"So what?" Lucy asked. "Nobody *has* to fight a duel."

"Yeah, but how would that look to his followers?"

Ed clapped his hands. "By Spooner, that'd throw a spanner into their plans, either way you figure it!"

"It sure would." I mused for a long time, trying to imagine where I'd be if I were a Federalist. Suddenly I stood up. "Hey—how come I came through that hole in the park?"

"Because," Ed said patiently, "that was the . . . the *coextant* point. The Confederate equivalent of Meiss's laboratory. I thought you—"

"I do. Now, where are A-bombs going to come from in my world, the middle of Elitch's Gardens—or U.S. government property of some kind?" I tried sitting on a packing crate, picking up splinters.

"Well, that narrows it down, Winnie, old sleuth. Your government owns only about a third of the United States, after all."

"Three-quarters of Colorado, Lucy, mostly national parks and such. But it'd have to be somewhere with security, somewhere they normally store the weapons or could hold them safely."

Ed's forehead furrowed. "How about the militia?"

I laughed. "SecPol gets along with the Pentagon about as well as it does with local cops! Nice try, though. There's even a couple of National Guard units in Fort Collins, as I recall."

Lucy shook her head. "Fort Collins can't be right. That freighter was heading south, out along the Greenway."

"Which is why I think Madison's here in Laporte! If someone's following you, do you lead them right to your hideout? Look at this. I picked it up trying to find my way around Fort Collins." The map was grimy and blood-stained. I unfolded it gingerly. In these late, great days of the Republic, you never know when you might want to turn Uncle Irving in for operating an unregistered Xerox machine. One advantage to a police state is that it's easy to find the police: all maps printed in the Land of the Formerly Free are required to indicate local SecPol offices with a brand new little map symbol, a mailed fist grasping an unsheathed dagger. Yech.

"Here it is, in the center of town. The Post Office, and in the same building, SecPol. All the easier to censor your mail, m'dear. Anyway, find the coextant spot in Laporte, and we'll find Madison and blow him full of nice juicy holes."

Ed examined the map. "This won't do us any good. Where's Confederation Boulevard? Or Laporte University?"

"I can't tell you that, Ed," Clarissa said, over my shoulder. Her breath was warm on my cheek. I liked it a lot. "But I'll show you the park. Where's Meiss's lab, Win?"

"Well, here's CSU—see the oval drive here? That's the Sciences Building, and—got a pencil?—right here, I'd say, is the lab."

"Which tells us where Deejay set up the Broach!" said Clarissa.

"Yeah," Lucy added, "And that river, that Cache La Poudre, why that's nothing but piddling little old Slade Creek! Had a plague of a time with the water table when they started building the—"

Ed stood up abruptly. "Okay, folks, we've got some computing to do, and I don't want to be caught here in case Madison comes back for his toothbrush. Besides, I want a bath and out of these filthy clothes!"

"Me, too!" shuddered Clarissa. "Lucy, I'm claiming your hottest tub for the next sixteen hours!"

Lucy grinned. "You've got it. Gentlemen, shall we take our leave of this House of Ill Philosophy?"

It was fine with me. I was running short of ammunition.

Even if the end of the world's tapping you on the shoulder, sometimes you have to stop and say, "Screw everything—I'm going to bed." Two days' self-abuse—pardon the expression—were catching up with me, six G's twice in one afternoon and a thrilling duel to the death had finished the job.

Back at Genêt Place, Clarissa disappeared next door, Ed fell asleep in the bathtub over brandy and cigars, and his frail, elderly neighbor sat, map in hand, punching hell out of the Telecom. I tried to stay awake cleaning my revolver.

It didn't work. Next thing I knew, it was my shoulder Lucy was punching hell out of. I peered dimly at the 'com pad she shoved under my nose.

". . . this display here? Wake up, youngster, it's important! The little pulsing dots are Meiss's lab and the SecPol office, orange and green, respectiv—"

"On a yellow background? Lucy, I've been sick already once today!"

"Fooey! Now here's your Cache La Poudre 'river,' and Presto!—Laporte, but with the cursors still showing, everything lined up so the creek still matches, give or take, and it's 95 percent that this here's the present lurkabouts of Madison's crew!" She fingered the map where it showed a residential area.

"That's only four blocks from here! I'll wake Ed. You get Clarissa! On second thought, leave her out of this. Might be dangerous. Boy I'm glad I cleaned my gun. I—"

"Hold your horsepower, sonny! You'll wake Ed, all right, and point him toward the sack. Boy's probably wrinkled up like a prune by now. We ain't goin' anywhere without some sleep!"

"But Lucy, Madison will—"

"Fooey squared! Uprooting Bealls's equipment's gonna slow 'em down plenty. Son, at 136, a girl *really* needs her beauty sleep. Do as I say. We'll meet at dawn, loaded for revenooers!"

I didn't put up much of a fight. Just getting Ed transferred seemed a major effort. By the time I got to my own room, the whole damn world could have blown up for all I cared.

Darkness.

The door opened softly and closed. I reached for the forty-one in a pile of clothing beside the bed.

"Win?" Her gown whispered and I felt weight on the bed.

"Hmm?"

"I'm still cold, Win." Before I could think of anything clever to say, she was cuddling close beside me. I sighed and laced trembling arms around her, praying I wouldn't wake up. Together, we breathed a long time in the silence.

Win, don't men *ever* take the initiative where you come from?"

After a while I said, "Most of the time, Clarissa. I just sort of gave up, a long while ago."

"That's sad. Why did you do that? Give up, I mean —don't stop what you're doing now!"

I didn't. "Well, you know I was married once. She left, and others, they didn't stay. Just as well."

"How—how many others, Win?"

"None of your business, nosy!"

"You're right. I'm sorry—and that feels *good!*"

So did she. "Two."

"Mm?"

"Only two others, Clarissa."

"And then you gave up trying? At all?"

"You were lying to me—your *hands* aren't a bit cold."

She giggled. "It appears you didn't give up altogether. All those years—my, what a waste!"

"You exaggerate, dear thing, but thanks for doing it." Then she was everything at once, firm, soft, heavy, but light in my arms. I began to roll over, but she pushed me back gently.

"Wait a minute—first time never lasts long enough . . . though I'd say you're plenty long enough—second time is better."

The bed jostled. I pulled the covers down so she could breathe. "Clarissa," I said, blushing in the dark, "you won't get any warmer down there."

"You'll make up for it later. Now hush. I won't be able to answer for a while." Waves of shocked pleasure coursed through me; tears in the corners of my eyes. I ran my fingers through her lovely hair, cradled her face in my hands as her head bobbed up and down.

"Great Mer-ci-ful *HEAVENS!*" The bed bounced briefly again and she laid her cheek on my shoulder. I held her close, trembling once again, tears rolling down my face. A long while later, after I had *more* than made it up to her, she sat up, kneeling beside me in the dawn light. Her enormous hazel eyes held mine, her strong slender hands were on my shoulders.

"Win, you've got to promise me something—"

"I'll respect you in the morning, honest I will. God, I respect the hell out of you right now!"

"Be serious, idiot!"

"Okay, okay."

"Win, *please* never give up again, okay?"

"Never. Not as long as you're right here to keep me from it."

"Right here? Don't be silly. We'll have to get our *own* bed, sooner or later."

"*That* I can afford," I laughed, "It'll have to be a pretty sturdy one."

"I suppose so. Now I know what they mean by 'police brutality'!"

"Yeah, but what I mean," I said, nervous all over again, "it'll have to last a long time—won't it?"

"Dearest cuddly Bear, it'll have to last until our great-great-grandchildren roll us out and bury us! Don't you realize that yet?"

Thank you. Whoever it is up there, even if you're not really there, thank you. "I just had to make sure, darling Doctor. It's a deal, partner. From now on, I'll blast 'em, and you sew 'em back together. Okay?"

"What about Ed, your other partner?"

"Let him get his own girl!" I sat up and hugged her till she squeaked. "What do y'know—the Hero gets the Girl! Now if we can manage to survive through the last thrilling—"

"Oomph! You got any of that energy left for an-other? . . . " She flopped back onto the pillow and I settled beside her, happier, I believe, than I've ever been in my entire life.

"Ain't a matter of energy, lady," I told her, "It's

a matter, at this point anyway, of inspiration—make that respiration: think you can breathe through your nose for a little while again? I'll hold the blankets up."

It wasn't quite a raid at dawn. Two people forgot to set their alarms: Lucy the indefatigable and efficient, and Win the enormously pleased and exhausted. The 'com started wailing at noon—Lucy'd finally managed to wake up. We ate hastily and girded for battle. Considering everything we'd been through, we were doing great to leave the house at two.

I strapped on my Smith & Wesson, tucked the derringer into what passes for hip pockets, and added the Browning for good measure. I thought about it for a while and added the Bowie knife to my belt.

Lucy had arrived with the mate to her Gabbet Fairfax. One was bad enough, two were even worse. The huge pistols were wearing her instead of the other way around. Still, if SecPol had issued cannons like those to its agents, I'd be looking around for a new arm this morning. Or a new incarnation.

Ed had a spare .375 as I expected, but that wasn't what caught my eye. He was holding the first two-handed piece I'd seen here, a very, very large-bore Coltomatic, firing clusters of evil-looking fléchettes that could fill an alley full of whistling death at a touch of the trigger. The drum magazine looked a bit cumbersome, but I kept my own counsel. No veteran cop's going to sneer at a nice, comforting scattergun when there's rough work to be done.

Clarissa, of course, would not be left behind, and it had been dumb of me to expect otherwise. She stuck sensibly with her everyday Webley, a couple of spare magazines, and, somewhat ominously I felt, a hefty emergency medical kit.

Almost without speaking, Lucy clutching a hard-copied map, our little Doomsday squad went downstairs. Ed climbed into the Neova and fired up the engines. I got in beside him, and the women, occupying somewhat less volume than the pair of us,

wedged themselves into what Ed optimistically considered a back seat. We were out of the garage before
the Neova's gull-wing doors were down and locked.

"Let's see that map, Lucy." Ed looked back over
his shoulder. He was running full fans, and I kept
watching for road-company traffic cops. Hate to get
busted doing 175 in a 90 zone. He glanced at the
print-out and took a corner that would have been on
two wheels if we'd been using any.

We swayed to a halt across from the target address,
leaped out and started up the walk to a single-family
dwelling, half the size of my Denver apartment block,
painted a pleasant beige over brick. A finely manicured lawn wrapped itself around the usual hedges
and shade trees.

Ed motioned silently: Lucy should circle around
back. He went for a side entrance, Clarissa and I
took the front. Halfway up the curving walk, we
dropped into a canter. I gained the doorstep, flattened
beside the door, and tried the knob. Open. Clarissa
covered a window. I bashed my shoulder against the
door, drawing the Smith, snatching the Browning
from my armpit. We ducked down a short corridor
and to the left, weaving, jumping at shadows. I heard
Lucy shout something, Ed crashing the side door, just
as we exploded into the living room.

"*ALL RIGHT,*" I screamed, "*FREEZE, YOU—*"

"*Happy Birthday to you, Happy Birthday to you.
Happy Birthday, dear . . .*"

"—bastards?" I finished lamely, both pistols pointed
from a crouch, Clarissa leveling hers over my shoulder. Ed stared grimly down the barrel of his fléchette
gun. Lucy looked like Clint Eastwood in drag. We
had 'em covered, dead to rights: about sixteen five-
year-olds and their mothers, sitting around a table,
birthday cake in the center blazing idiotically away.

I draw a discreet curtain over the ensuing recrim-
inations. To this day, I'm grateful we weren't a year
or two later. Around age six or seven, little Confederates begin acquiring handguns the same way I got
my first bike. Let it be said, only, that little Junior
Higginbotham, the tyke-of-honor, enjoyed a rather

more remunerative birthday than he ever had before. Or was ever likely to again.

In brief, we settled out of court.

At the curb, Ed glowered. "You gonna let me see that map of yours again, or not, Lucy?"

"Don't look at me!" she replied. "I only did the programming!"

"Yeah," he grunted, "garbage in, garbage—"

"Now wait a minute, you two! Blame the Fort Collins Chamber of Commerce—that's where I got the original map. And put that gun away, Lucy, I'm rattled enough already!"

"Chamber of Commerce, my— Oh, pshaw!" She holstered her pistol. "Anybody got any ideas before we all become reluctant Hamiltonians?"

"Or radioactive vapor," Ed reminded, leaning dispiritedly against the hull of his car. "I guess it isn't Fort Collins SecPol they're trying to contact, is it?"

"Unless we've just been routed by a force of invading midgets. How about it, dear?" Clarissa grinned ruefully. "Any midgets in SecPol?"

"Only mentally, my dear Watkins, only mentally— and we're giving them stiff competition for the title!"

XXIII: Deadly Window

"DENVER!"

"What?"

"Denver, that's where they are!" I slapped my forehead, disgusted I hadn't thought of it sooner. "The regional SecPol headquarters."

Ed nodded grimly. "Saint Charles Town. It makes sense."

"All this is very interesting," Lucy said, "but are we gonna stand out in the street all day, burning daylight?"

"Wait!" Something else clicked in my head. "I've just had another thought."

"Did it hurt?" Lucy and Ed asked simultaneously. Clarissa grimaced and put a hand delicately over her mouth. I like loyalty in a woman.

"Okay, wise-asses. Burgess was regional head of the most important federal agency in the country. There were a couple thousand flunkies available to get their hands dirty for him on field operations. So why his *personal* involvement in this whole thing? Why did he return to the Meiss murder scene? Why did he follow me to Fort Collins? Why did he kill everyone who interfered with him: Meiss, MacDonald, all the attempts on me?"

Lucy nodded impatiently.

"He was up to something on his own," I finished. "Something he didn't want others—especially his bosses—horning in on. He had a plausible excuse to keep Meiss under surveillance, but some Federal lab in Denver or Washington should have been duplicating Meiss's work, not a second-rater like Bealls."

"Now wait a minute," Ed said, "are you implying

that your 'benevolent' government would never have gone along with—"

"No, Ed, I'm not. Burgess just didn't want to share the pie. I think Bealls will be contacting SecPol *cold*. They may not even know that the Confederacy *exists*."

"That's pretty iffy, Winnie."

Clarissa had caught on. "But if Win's right, Bealls will have to send a great deal of information through to SecPol, something like Deejay sent to Meiss. That's going to take time, isn't it?"

"Yes," I said, "and perhaps a bigger Broach than Bealls is capable of generating. It also means bureaucratic delays of all kinds, passwords, countersigns—"

"So we're not gonna get nuked day after tomorrow," said Lucy. "That's good news."

Ed was shaking his head. "Based on a tenuous string of unsupported suppositions. Win, you're making up fast for all *my* fumbling. Suppose you're wrong and the whole agency knows about the Broach. Suppose they simply assigned their top man because it's important. Suppose—"

"Okay! Okay!" I said. "I'm still betting they're in Saint Charles, and I'm going down there to get Madison. You coming?"

"I am, Win," Clarissa said. I put my arm around her, wanting to refuse, knowing she'd never understand or allow it. This was a different culture, and Confederate womanhood is quite capable of loading hell in its own holster.

"Oh, very well. But no more birthday surprises, okay?" Ed scowled hard at Lucy and me, creasing his face into a reddened, fleshy X. We all burst out laughing.

"So how do we find Bealls?" Lucy asked, blowing her nose. "Saint Charles Town ain't exactly the big time, but—"

"I've got an idea." I lifted the Neova's door panel, punched the combo for Deejay's laboratory. Presently the screen displayed a terrific view of another Telecom screen.

"Please identify yourself," requested Ooloorie's twice-relayed image.

"It's me, Ooloorie. Is Deejay there?"

"Greetings, Win Bear. I witnessed your combat yesterday, gallantly against sharks. If you'll wait a moment, I'll—"

"No need, dear." Deejay squeezed in beside the robot. "Win, I was just about to try your number again. I wanted—"

"We've been otherwise occupied," I grimaced, outlining our recent humiliation and such conclusions as we'd reached. "You mentioned building a device to detect someone else's use of a Broach?"

"But that's why I've— We finished it this morning. A simple matter of harmonics. We could have saved you all the trouble you got into!"

"Oh my aching bank account! Any idea where Bealls might be by now?"

"I'm afraid so. Somebody's firing up a Broach a hundred miles or less to the south. But Win, my small-scale *dirigible* Broach could—"

"Swell. Can you pinpoint that other Broach—point it out on a map, even narrow it down to a street address?"

"Oh, much better than that! I can name the square foot within a room! But once you know where it is, what are you planning to do about it?" She gave Ooloorie a concerned glance.

"Do about it? Why, we'll just smash in there and—"

"*Landling,*" observed the porpoise, "you leave too much to random factors. Had it not occurred to you that they will have taken security precautions?"

"Well sure, I—"

"Have you not also reasoned that you will be violating their rights, as fully as they plan to violate ours? Would you—"

"Fuck all this philosophy jazz!" I shouted. "This is a matter of survival!"

"And importing unprincipled behavior is an aid to that end? My poor ignorant—"

"I agree, Win," Deejay interrupted diplomatically. "It's not only suicidal, but morally wrong, as well."

"And unnecessary," the principled porpoise added.

"Nothing encourages ethical practices so well as a practical alternative to evil."

"Didn't Gallatin say that?" Deejay asked.

"No, I did," Ooloorie replied.

"What are you two driving at?" I demanded. Clarissa, Lucy, and Ed crowded behind me, following the debate.

"We've discovered *an interference factor!*" Deejay said excitedly.

"A who?"

"Stated very simply," Ooloorie condescended, "one Broach mechanism can interfere with another, an effect, ordinarily, of little or no practical benefit. However—"

"Who's telling this, Ooloorie, you or me?"

"Why, I was, naturally, Deejay."

"Well, I'm telling it, now. Ordinarily, it wouldn't mean a thing. You'd have to line up two generators, practically touching, before you'd notice any effect. But a *dirigible* Broach, one that projects over distance—"

"I get it! If Bealls turns his machine on, all you have to do is send your . . . your . . ."

"Field interface?"

"Field interface close enough to interfere with his! That's great! We can hold 'em off forever!"

"It isn't quite as simple as that, Win," Deejay said. "There are some qualifications. Alignment is critical; the two fields can't be more than a tenth-inch apart. They must also be non-concentric. It's like the inverse-square law for electromagnetics, only in this case, the exponent is—"

"Exponential. What happens if the fields *are* concentric?"

"Well, I . . . hmm. It's just like building one window in front of another: whatever goes into Broach A comes out Broach B, instead of winding up in the other universe."

I thought about that. "Sounds like you've invented matter-transmission. But seriously, can you interfere with Bealls, way down in Saint Charles?"

"If that's where he is, no, Win. That's another quali-

fication. Range. It's less a consideration of power than
of accuracy, but—"

"How far *can* you do it from?"

"Detection or interference?"

"Well, both."

"Oh, detection is easy. I'm picking up intermittent
signals now. I think Bealls is tuning up his machine.
Interference—not more than a couple of miles, I'd
say."

I looked at Ed, then back at the Telecom. "How
difficult would it be to set your machinery up somewhere else?"

She considered. "Providing we had sufficient power?
All we'd need is a pinhole, and detection hardly requires—"

"Great! We're all going on a little trip!"

We dropped Clarissa and Lucy off to get another
car, and headed for the university, where Deejay read-
ied several bulky packages. We filled Ed's luggage
boot and waited for the Thornycroft to take the rest.
A few minutes later, a little red Sunrider swept up
into the lot. Clarissa at the wheel, Lucy beside her
looking unhappy.

"I told you this was a mistake!" she complained.
"That junk'll never fit in this wind-up toy of yours!"

"Lucy, your car just isn't fast enough to keep up.
Isn't that right, Ed?"

"I abstain," he equivocated, "on grounds of long
friendship—and continued survival."

"Not to mention the Chinese ideogram for 'trouble,' " I added.

"Besides,"—Clarissa shuddered—"I've ridden with
you behind the wheel before."

"No sportin' blood to this generation," Lucy muttered. "All right. Let's get this show on the road!"

Riding within the city limits hadn't prepared me
for Greenway 200. Draw two ocean waves, adjacent
curves, joined in the middle, a round-bottomed W.
That's a cross-section of the Greenway—parallel
troughs covered with mutated crabgrass, that titanium
rocket-tunnel buried under the median. Drift too far

from the center of your lane, and the upslope gently pours you back where you belong. The outside edge works the same, except for an occasional off-ramp or feeder advertised miles in advance.

Don't let the simple construction fool you: within and underneath the roadbed, sophisticated systems provide power for induction vehicles, guidance, information and entertainment, arrangements for eliminating ice and snow.

We entered a landscaped cloverleaf, accelerating until the upcurved roadbed was a greenish blur. Deejay and her equipment were crammed into the scanty back seat. The Sunrider followed, "bumper-to-bumper," about a mile behind.

I glanced over at Ed's instrument panel—my own controls were folded away, making room for an extra box resting uncomfortably on my lap—and read our ground speed: 355.

"Say, Ed, I thought you said this thing would fly. Wouldn't that get us down to Saint Charles quicker?"

Ed snapped a final switch, and, to my horror, folded his steering wheel into the dash, turning his seat around to face me! "You look a little pale, Win. What's that you were saying?"

"I s-said how come we don't fly down to Saint Charles?"

"Relax, we're on autoguidance. The Greenway's practically a straight line south anyhow; we wouldn't gain that much. Besides, we're overloaded—with Deejay's bulk in the back seat."

"I *beg* your pardon!"

"All your equipment, I mean. We can make better speed down here. Convertible or not, this is still primarily a ground vehicle. We'll be in Saint Charles in another ten minutes."

I shook my head. "Not even time for a good cigar. Do you realize this trip used to take me nearly two hours and without an automatic pilot? I had to—"

"Walk to school every day through six feet of snow?" Deejay asked.

"Split rails for a living, too. What can I say?" I

craned back over my shoulder, trying to see through the sloping rear canopy. A tiny bright-red hovercar trailed behind us.

Abruptly the dashboard Telecom bleeped. Clarissa's face appeared, Lucy squished into the display beside her. "Hello, darling! Ed, radar says we've got company about ten miles back. Altitude, three hundred feet. See it?"

He cleared the display. "Got him now. Making about four-fifty." I twisted my neck again, trying to see what was coming. "I'm going back on manual. May be nothing at all, but—"

"There he is!" Deejay screamed. "Look out!"

A long slender shape flew beside us, paralleling the right-hand road crest, perhaps twenty-five feet off the ground, and dropping to our speed.

"I was an idiot!" Ed growled. "So busy watching Madison it never occurred to me he'd be watching us! Hold on!"

The aircraft pulled ahead, suddenly veered to the left, plopping clumsily into the roadbed. It wobbled a little on its rapidly inflating skirt and rode the camber down ahead of us.

"Another bloody convertible!" Ed wrangled with the wheel as we buffeted in the other's wake—extremely dangerous proximity at these speeds. It was slowing gradually. Ed warned Clarissa to drop back. Still the other vehicle closed until less than ten yards separated us.

A rear section of the intruder gaped open—the turbulence inside must have been unbearable—the ugly nozzle of a weapon pointed at us. Ed slammed on the brakes, fishtailed wildly, while the barrel ahead spouted flames. Our windshield starred; a deafening whistle shrieked through the car. "Any way we can shoot back?" I yelled.

Ed jerked the wheel through evasive maneuvers, skidding up the right bank, then slowly back to the center. "No! If he keeps slowing, we won't have enough momentum to climb the bank. He'll have us trapped!" He charged up the left bank this time; we didn't get as far, and came down sooner, describing a diminishing sine-wave on the road. When the curves finally, fatally flattened out . . .

I sat there, chewing the inside of my mouth. "See if you can pass. Will your rear hatch open so I can get off a couple of shots?"

"I'll try. Get in back!"

I swiveled, squashing Deejay aside amid a tangle of equipment. She pushed into the front seat. I fumbled with the canopy toggle. Bullet holes screaming in the windshield were drowned suddenly in a roar. I was nearly sucked out the back with the ashtray contents.

"You okay, Win? Hold on!" We swerved to the right, gaining speed, and had pulled almost even with the enemy when he veered, forcing Ed to drop back. He tried again, on the right. Suddenly the car snapped back to center.

"Sorry—junction back there! We'd have smashed into a tunnel mouth!" He played the wheel side to side, avoiding shots from ahead. "We'll try something else. Hold on tight! Really tight!"

Engines bellowed above the hurricane inside the car. We surged forward, *upward,* yanking my ears down to my bellybutton, and left the ground with a lurch. The other car passed *beneath* us, then we were down with a bump, the Neova groaning in protest. I climbed off the floor and rested my gun on the seat-back, sighting as the hatch flopped wildly in the wind.

BLAM! BLAM! Their front window whitened in the center. Aiming more to the right, I smashed the windshield there with two more quick shots. Their car skidded up the center, slid down crabwise, and straightened—someone at the spare wheel now. Two more shots, badly placed. I didn't relish trying to re-load in this confusion.

"Try mine!" Ed passed his .375 back. I thumbed the cocking lever, peered along the top, and took up the trigger-slack. To my surprise, a brilliant spot of light appeared on the car behind as the laser sight caught it. They took evasive action, just as we had, swinging from bank to bank.

"No good!" I shouted. "Get back even with them!"

"I can try!" He nosed us up the left bank, almost flipping her with the brakes. The others rode beside us as we whipped past a sign: SAINT CHARLES TOWN 5. I laid the glowing dot on a shadowy figure at the controls, pumping the trigger as fast as I could. *Slapslapslap!* My own side window disintegrated, glass and chrome spouted from the other car, smoke began to pour out. They slowed, spilling dense black clouds, swerving desperately for an off-ramp.

They didn't make it. The car glanced off a concrete pillar and came apart, smearing itself down the right embankment. Burning shards and a wall of smoke dashed across the road.

Ed twitched the wheel, dodging bigger chunks that bounced ahead tearing ugly swaths in the grass. Then we were through. I watched nervously for Clarissa's car. The road behind us was a sheet of flame.

A mile. Two miles. Smoke billowed a thousand feet or more. Then, through the flames, her little red machine emerged unscathed. I turned and sat back in the seat, one leg up on a carton, breathing easier, and lowered the .375's hammer as gently as I could. Buildings began flashing by. Ed slowed the Neova, turned adroitly into a curving tunnel and out into the streets of Saint Charles Town.

We left Saint Charles as quickly as we'd entered it, at Deejay's direction crossing a ford, gliding through Auraria to a sliding stop beside the local outlet for Paratronics, Ltd. We hustled Deejay's cargo into the office. On my second trip to the car, Clarissa's little red machine skated up gracefully beside ours. This close, its plastic skirt looked scorched, the canopy cracked in several places. Clarissa was fine, though, Lucy energetic and noisy.

"C'mon, c'mon—plenty of time for kissy-face later, you two! Let's get this crap inside!" She shifted one shoulder-slung holster around and grabbed the largest box in the car. I let Clarissa go and followed suit.

Deejay was inside, doing ghastly things to the in-

nards of the office Telecom. "After I pick up their
field, we'll do a little microBroach reconnaissance."
Flipped from her iron, a surplus drop of solder sizzled
its way into the carpet. "We'll hook an optical fiber
system into the 'com, here, and see what's what!" She
buried herself in the circuitry, groping along the counter
for scattered tools without looking up.

Ed rooted around in the office, found coffee and a
bulb of Coke for me. I tried handing tools to Deejay for
a while, but couldn't seem to give her what she
wanted. I finally turned the job over to Lucy. All we
could do was wait.

It was dark by the time Deejay sat back, turning
knobs and watching the Telecom. Abruptly, the screen
blossomed into an intricate moiré pattern. She began
making frantic adjustments. "I think I've got something here! Wait—yes, here it is! He's just warming up
again! Okay, I've got him. Hand me that meter,
Lucy . . . we'll know more in a few minutes." She
fiddled with the equipment, unable to resist lecturing.
"You may notice that the heart of this rig is that little
classroom demonstrator I showed you."

"I remember too well. Pop!"

She grinned, nodding. "Well, now I can steer the
field locus anywhere I want—up to a couple of miles,
anyway." She inserted a slender filament into the guts
of the machine, plugged the other end into the
Telecom, pushing buttons. I jumped three feet as the
screen bulged with the proximity-distorted image of
John Jay Madison.

"Whoops!" Lucy cried. "Another inch, and we'd be
staring right up his nostrils!"

"Shh!" I whispered, a beat behind Clarissa.

"No need for that," Deejay explained. The only
thing coming across that interface is light, and that,
only one way."

I nodded, relieved. "What's it look like from the
other side?"

"Like a dust mote. We're magnifying what the fiber
picks up at the interface. Want a look around?" The
picture backed off and swooped around the room in

Saint Charles, panning 360 degrees to catch Madison's associates: Skinner, others I recognized from the Continental Congress, finally resting on Bealls himself, up to his armpits in haywired paratronics. An animated conversation was in progress, but we couldn't hear a word.

"That was our friend Mikva!" Ed exclaimed. Clarissa clutched my hand.

"So what happens now?" Lucy asked.

Deejay started turning knobs again, the viewpoint whirled dizzily. "Forward a bit," she muttered. "A little more . . . There! Now I'll punch up a short program, and— Good! Bealls is still calibrating. When he goes on full power, we'll match him, foul up his field symmetry, maybe give him some feedback to play with. The best part is, he'll never figure out what's going on. He doesn't know enough field theory yet."

Clarissa crossed over to the 'com, dragging me along. We watched Bealls's distorted, sweaty face as he concentrated. "One thing I don't understand, Deejay," she said. "Do we have to watch him every minute, from now on, just to prevent him communicating with the other side?"

"That's the cockroach in the hollandaise, all right!" Lucy muttered grimly. "Say, y'don't suppose we could put a couple dozen slugs through this contraption of yours and . . ."

"Perhaps he'll just get discouraged after a while," Deejay offered, "and give up."

Clarissa looked closely at her. "Would *you?*"

She frowned a little and then grinned. "No."

"Deejay," Ed asked, "I've been thinking. Remember what you said about the two fields becoming concentric? Well, what would happen if we did it deliberately? Bealls passed his first message over and we just grab it from him!"

"Better yet," I suggested, "we can pretend we're SecPol and string the bastard along for weeks!"

"Sorry, boys. It's a great idea, but we simply don't have the power. On regular wall current, this Broach is good for about three-tenths-of-an-inch diameter. I can louse up Bealls's operations, but that'll have to satisfy us until we think of something else."

"Nuts!" Lucy complained. "Can't get a fifty-caliber bullet through a thirty-caliber hole!"

I scowled at the Telecom. Looking pleased with himself, Bealls backed out of the field of view.

"Here it comes!" Deejay warned. "I've got to be careful now. It tends to drift. Don't jog my elbow!" She sat tensed at the controls, making minute adjustments. The screen blurred, then sprang into a mindtwisting kaleidoscopic display. *"Shit!"* Deejay startled all of us, ripping the fiber-optic tube out of the interface. "It's gone concentric!"

A tiny silvery button popped out of the Broach and sprouted toward us on a slender supporting rod. When the second joint passed the interface, I recognized it. "Not a manuscript!" I whispered hoarsely. "Not even a note! That's an antenna, an ordinary walkie-talkie antenna!" On impulse I snatched a pair if vise-grips from the bench and clamped them onto the chromeplated shaft. "Let the son of a bitch figure *that* one out!"

The antenna stopped sliding into the room, backed up suddenly until the pliers banged against the Broach chassis, lurched forward, and retreated again, trapped. "Reminds me of that old Vice detail joke," I laughed. "You know, the one about the public restroom where—"

"Out!" Deejay screamed in horror, pointing at her instruments. "Get out of here before he shuts the field down!" She scrambled for the exit, dragging Lucy by the gunbelt. I shoved Clarissa through the door behind Ed, just making it to the sidewalk outside, when—

The world erupted in fire and thunder. Windows bulged and splashed, twin balls of fire either side of the door. We tobogganed along the walkway, fetching up beside the little Sunrider. I shoved Clarissa's face against my shoulder for fear of raining glass. My hair and eyebrows crisped and singed. The world was hell, a raging, incoherent furious roar.

Yet, even above the explosion we'd escaped, I could hear a distant rumble, see the smoke and flame of a vastly greater cataclysm, a mile across the river in Saint Charles.

XXIV: The Second of July

Monday, September 28, 211 A.L.

The Saint Charles Town explosion left a crater a hundred yards across. Of Madison and his people, we never found so much as a shirt button. Their hideout was an isolated building in the middle of an abandoned buffalo feedlot. I was grateful for that, although neighbors who had to shovel themselves out from under several kilotons of bison-flops weren't quite so happy.

It could have been worse. The coextant point in Denver is a densely populated area, the four-hundred block of East Eighth Avenue. Thousands might have died, even some who didn't deserve to.

The explosion in Auraria was a mild summer breeze compared to what had happened across the river. Clarissa and I were last out of the building, and escaped with mostly minor scrapes and flash burns. She lost the back half of her coveralls, and, sadly, a lot of her beautiful hair. Protecting her eyes, I got a little careless about my own, so I am now sporting a rakish eyepatch until they clone me a transplant.

At least Lucy says it's rakish.

Freeman K. Bertram won't be up and around quite as soon. He's regenerating a whole new set of internal organs. They've got him wedged into a complicated machine that reaches from his throat to his knees, like an iron lung he's somehow outgrown. He offered to show me—the upper section hinges off, and you can see all the clockworks and half-formed organs whirling around under glass. I politely turned him down.

Naturally, he's sorry as hell about his part in the

Hamiltonian conspiracy. I don't know whether his
stockholders and other outraged Confederates are
going to accept that, but I can't hold much of a grudge
while he lies there with the laser burn intended for me.
Like lots of people in politics, he'd thought it was all a
game, and found out too late that Madison was playing
dirty and for keeps.

But the really important development concerns what
happened at the Seventh Continental Congress after
Lucy and I blasted out of there via underground
cannonball.

I don't know why I expected that stubborn con-
gregation to sit on their hands with the world collapsing around their ears. Too used to the U.S. Congress, I
guess. Jenny, Olongo, and Captain Couper conducted
a rump session that was still hotly arguing pragmatics
while I was being wheeled into intensive care. The
explosions in Saint Charles and Auraria didn't really
change anything—maybe relaxed the timetable a little
—because the Confederacy has decided to strike back.
Not against the Hamiltonians, who were never regarded as a significant threat, but against SecPol and
the culture that allows such an abomination to exist.
And not with Confederate A-bombs or troops, but in
the same way that Sequoyah won the Mexican War:
with ideas.

There's a lot of fundraising and enlistment going on
in the Confederacy now. We're preparing to change a
world, an entire universe, and drag the United States
of America, kicking and screaming, through two centuries of peace and freedom it managed to miss by
letting Alexander Hamilton screw things up back in
1789.

You can't draft anybody or raise war taxes here,
but you can ask folks to chip in, and try to explain
why it's important. And you can try to explain to the
Propertarian Party why the first copy of this manuscript and an initial seventy-five pounds of 999 fine
have suddenly materialized in the middle of their
conference table. I hope it makes up in some small
way for Vaughn Meiss's death. This is what he was

trying to accomplish: contact with a free, clean, new world.

And it's only the beginning.

Propertarians won't be the only ones to get help, simply the first to know why and where it's coming from. Denmark's Progress Party, the oddly named Workers' Party of Australia, lots of poets, painters, and scientists behind the Iron Curtain, are slated for mysterious shipments, too.

The simians are preparing a small army of volunteers to travel across the Broach. They have a tough job ahead of them, taking their borrowed culture to relatives who have, as yet, no culture at all. I'd love to see the first CIA reports of well-dressed, heavily armed "infrahumans" roaming the African countryside.

Ooloorie haughtily assures me that her own people will have no such difficulties. Cetacean civilization, she claims, was already ancient when *H. sapiens* was discovering the useful properties of obsidian. I've spent a lot of Telecom time with her while I'm recovering, listening to fascinating stories: how porpoises first discovered the forgotten world above the sea; how they decided to observe and protect man until he was fit company for civilized beings; how the finny folk met in a roving, decades-long convention, deciding at last to let the Confederacy join *them.*

So watch out, tuna fishermen! As I've had reason to learn, lasers are *nasty* weapons.

While Congress lays plans for the long run, always the first priority in this back-assward place, they're trusting Deejay Thorens to guard the short run, which, by itself, may help Freeman K. Bertram keep his job and reputation. Paratronics, Ltd.'s Broach-detector is being miniaturized, mass-produced, and marketed all over the System, because we still don't know for sure how much SecPol knows. Should they or anyone else try poking their interfaces into this world uninvited, an interfering field will make their Broaches impassable.

I suppose Jenny has the toughest job of all. The second shipment to Denver won't be manuscripts or gold, but the President of the North American Confederacy. Naturally, the first person she'll see there will be Jenny—of the "Party of Principle." I had some advance warning and a nice cushion of delirium the first time I met Ed Bear. I hope it's not too harrowing for them. They've got a lot of planning to do!

As for me, politics and world-mending were never my forte. I stumbled into this mess, and just sort of dithered my way out of it. Clarissa and I will have a nice long vacation, as soon as her flash burns have healed. Ed's reservations, a pretty thoughtful "wedding" gift, are still good up on the Leadville slopes. I may try some one-eyed skiing. Then it's back to doctoring for her and detecting for me. By the time we get back from the mountains, they'll have finished restoring her house, which, I am happy to say, we'll be sharing for the next couple of centuries.

It'll be nice working for live people for a change. My only regret is that I won't be working with Ed.

It's strange. When you first move to a new place, you unconsciously assume that everyone you meet has always been exactly as you first found them. I don't know why I didn't notice that Lucy was the only gray-haired little old lady in Laporte. Busy at the time, I guess, and after all, she's 136 years old, isn't she?

The better part of the last thirty, she's spent on Mars and in the asteroids as an engineer, jockeying rocks like Ceres and the Martian moons into locations and shapes that people prefer. Being Her Honor, it seems, was just a hobby.

Until 205 A.L., that is. In that year, Lucy had an accident, picking up enough radiation to fry a dozen ordinary people her size. If it hadn't been for paratronic stasis, a fast spaceship, and the skills of Confederate medicine, this universe would have been deprived of one of its most interesting—and irritating —inhabitants.

Lucy recovered just fine, except that she had to sit out her fourth—or was it fifth?—regeneration. Almost alone in this country, Lucy had been growing old. It took several years for her cellular metabolism to settle down before she could have her youth reinstalled.

During that time, she retired, moving back to Laporte. She met Ed, got to know him. He got to know her.

I might have realized she'd be a cradle-robber, too. Once Lucy's a pretty young thing again, she and my erstwhile partner will be heading back into space, toward a million ice-cold rocks just waiting to be turned into gold mines by aggressive pioneers like Lucille Gallegos Kropotkin and Edward William Bear.

I hope they remember to write. I'll miss Ed; I never had a brother before. And I'll miss Lucy, for all her ridiculous advice and uncalled-for opinions. Just this afternoon, she was at it again.

"But Lucy," I said, exasperated as usual, "you can't call Americans warlike, exactly. We went to all kinds of trouble to avoid war, more, sometimes, than we should have."

"And still managed ten or eleven real good ones!" she snorted. "That, plus all your rules and regulations, put you a hundred years behind us and at about 3 percent of our standard of living." She rolled a cigar in her fingers, listening to the tobacco. "Anyway, I never said your *people* are warlike, Winnie. People don't cause wars, governments do. Eliminate governments—hell, just eliminate conscription and taxation —and you eliminate war. Simple as that!"

"Bullshit!" She had a disconcerting habit, pacing toward my blind side, and I was tired of craning my neck. "You anarchists managed plenty of wars on your own. Look at the War in Europe, or the one with the Czar."

"Whoa there, boy! The last war we fought *as a nation* was in Mexico, and we were still the old United States, then. The Confederacy ain't a nation, and it doesn't fight wars."

"Oh? Well, who does, then?"

"*Governments,* son, like I said. 'Twas a Prussian government decided to gobble up Europe. Same with the Czar in Antarctica. Every fight we've stumbled into has been that way, from the Revolution to this silly thing with the Hamiltonians: individuals tryin' to stop what some damn fool government started. Look at the Whiskey Rebellion. But all that's done, now. We're never likely to see a war again. Every time some over-organized gang of highway robbers decided to push people around, us raggedy and disorganized anarchists smashed 'em good and proper!"

"Lucy, you've got an answer handy for everything. I can't argue with you."

"Sure y'can, Winnie, it's a free world, ain't it?"

Wednesday, October 7, 211 A.L.

Lucy still thinks we've seen the last of the Hamiltonians, although there's no guarantee that we killed them all in that explosion.

But even if Madison had gotten everything he wanted from SecPol, I now think he would have lost anyway. Most Confederates would have taken to the hills, fought for centuries if necessary, rather than surrender to tyranny. And nobody in this crazy quilt of a country has the authority to surrender. Nobody. Eventually that would have driven Madison or his successors nuts. As it is, the few hypothetical surviving Federalists have other problems: their leaders are dead. People like Federalists *need* leaders. Confederates don't. That's why they'll always win.

Lucy says it's the next evolutionary step. We carried government with us from the trees, and later we hunted in packs, like dogs. We don't require that kind of social organization any more. True, without any official sanction, we fumbled Madison to a standstill. But does natural selection favor anarchy? Go ask Lucy. She's got plenty of opinions.

I'm satisfied: I finally found out where the two worlds split, though, damn it, I'm no closer to understanding *why*.

Clarissa and I were recuperating at ten thousand feet, but hadn't done much skiing. It's difficult with one eye—you wind up intimately acquainted with a lot of trees. Going over the Telecom's version of history and Deejay's almanac had cleared up one mystery, though: July second is the correct date, *in both worlds!*—Confederate historians are just a little more accurate. That's when Independence was really de-

clared, at the instigation of Richard Henry Lee and
John Adams. The document *explaining* what they'd
done was adopted on the fourth.

"Win? . . . Honey? Look here. I wonder if this
means anything."

"Zzzzz!— What? What's that?" I rubbed my good
eye and sat up beside her. It's nice having a lady who
reads in bed till 4 A.M., too.

"This almanac and the Telecom don't agree."

"Neither do we, sometimes, but there are compen-
sations." I leaned over and bit her on the ear. "Anything to eat around here—besides each other?"

"I'm serious, you one-track, single-minded . . ."

"Flatfoot?"

"Thank heavens it's only your feet, darling. Now
where was I? Oh, yes: 'Drafting the Declaration was
assigned to Thomas Jefferson . . . Congress suggested
a number of changes, which Jefferson called deplor-
able . . . eighty-six changes, eliminating 480 words,
and leaving 1,337.' "

"Yeah, I remember that. Nit-pickers bitching that
there's no such word as 'unalienable'."

"Yes, but look at the Telecom. I've retrieved a similar entry, essentially the same information, except for
the *numbers.*

"How's that?" I fished my cloak off the end of the
bed, looking for a cigar.

"Well, they both agree that Congress eliminated
480 words, but the 'com says that left 1,338. There's
an extra word somewhere in our Declaration—one
that's not in yours."

"Or someone miscounted. Lemme see that thing.
How the hell do you get it to—goddamned buttons!"

"*Those* are my pajama buttons, lecher!" She giggled and took the pad, made a few adjustments, and
there it was.

"Swell. How do we find a surplus 'and' or 'etc.' in
all that mess?"

"*Et cetera* is *two* words, illiterate one. But no need
to hunt—" She passed the scanner over the almanac,
punched out COMPARE/SEARCH on the keyboard. The
screen dimmed and the word OPERATING appeared. I

took this opportunity for some *applied* lechery, marveling all over again at the miracle that had brought Clarissa into my life. Ooloorie talks blithely about going off to fight, but as for me . . .

The screen split, showing nearly identical documents side by side, the handwriting far too small to read, one tiny, illegible word blinking on and off. Clarissa punched ZOOM. The vital paragraphs leaped into visibility, the U.S.A.'s on the right, the Confederacy's on the left:

> . . . *Life, Liberty, and the Purſuit of Happineſs* —*That to secure these rights, Governments are inſtituted among Men, deriving their juſt powers from the* . . .

"There it is!" I paused. "But what the hell does it mean? Is this what I've been searching for, what made all the difference?"

She shrugged. "Well, the sentences do have rather different implications, don't they?"

I thought about that. Yes, if each were followed to the letter. I read "my" version aloud: ". . . deriving their Just Powers from the—"

"—*Unanimous!*—" Clarissa supplied from hers.

"—Consent of the Governed," I finished. "'The *unanimous* consent of the governed.' Back home, consent usually means the result of an election. One side wins, the other loses."

"And a lot of other sides," Clarissa added, "don't get any hearing at all. Of the minority eligible, only a few actually vote, especially the way they would if they had a completely free choice of candidates or issues—things that never get on the ballot, somehow. And of those few, only slightly over half will win. The *real* majority always loses. Consent of the governed? Confederate delegates represent themselves and only those others who publicly and explicitly give them permission to do so."

"The unanimous consent of the governed," I repeated.

"Win, why do you suppose Jefferson added that one extra word?"

"I don't know. It would explain Gallatin's supporting the Whiskey Rebellion. Unanimous consent? Ask those Pennsylvania farmers! Try getting *any* bunch of people," I paraphrased Lucy, "to agree unanimously on anything! No wonder your government is so harmless and impotent!"

"Unlike somebody *I* know. But they all agreed on the Declaration, didn't they?"

"That's what it says at the top, anyway: 'A Unanimous Declaration.' But *why?* Why that one word?"

Philosophers have debated the causes of human behavior: heredity or environment? Are heroes and villains made or born? Confederate school children know that nature and nurture are only part of the answer, two-thirds, to be exact. The remaining third, taken as axiomatic here, is *individual free will*. They don't dismiss it as an illusion, or a whimsical choice between trivial alternatives.

There's only one act of free will, they say here, a decision which determines everything else: *to think or not to think*. Precisely, to engage in the formulation and manipulation of concepts: abstractions, generalizations. Mentation. Cognition. Remember how you had to force yourself to do that algebra homework? It was an effort of *will*. You can feel it operating if you give yourself half a chance.

To think or not to think: if you decide upon the latter, then it's back to good old heredity and environment again, by default. They'll call the tune if you don't call it for yourself. Everybody is motivated by some constantly shifting mixture of the three, different for each of us, at each minute in our lives. In human terms, this is the basis for all causation, for all reality—the one I'm living in now, or the one I was born into.

History isn't determined by some mysterious impersonal machinery, but by people *deciding* whether to use their minds or slough it off. In this world, Jefferson *decided* to insert that one little word. Win Bear and Ed Bear don't exist in twinned realities because they're both Indians, but because they—their ancestors—*decided* they would, history be damned. That's why there are two Jennies, two Marion Morrisons, two Mark Twains. A Smith & Wesson beats four aces; human will beats random chance. The mystical forces of history are so much buffalo dung, a fact both encouraging and a little scary. The old alibis won't wash any more: we're responsible, and nothing's ever written indelibly on that wall.

Death and taxes? Forget it. Gallatin took care of taxes, and Clarissa and her colleagues are taking care of death. Average life span in this crazy place is up around three hundred, but no one's taking any bets, because by the time you've made three hundred, what will they have invented to see you through a thousand, or ten thousand?

What'll they think of next?

I'm growing a new eyeball, but it's even more exciting to look at the mirror each morning and see the wrinkles and the bald spot fading. And Clarissa tells me the ulcer's gone.

Having choices makes a difference. People with options fare better than people with "discipline." That's why I add the following, at the specific, and unanimous, request of the Seventh Continental Congress:

You Propertarians have a choice. You can stand and fight, and we'll help you. But if you're like me, and you'd rather go fish, Deejay's Broach is a two-way proposition. The Confederacy lacks a lot of American "necessities": border guards, customs inspectors, naturalization. *Strangers are welcome here.*

We'll see you around—unless Clarissa and I *decide* to follow our friends out to the stars. We've got *centuries* to make up our minds.

And so do you. Maybe more.

What'll they think of next? In a society where no one is afraid to try *thinking* for a change, you never can tell.

But there's plenty of time to wait and see for yourself.

Appendix: A Brief Historical Outline*

In 1796 C.E., with Revision of the Articles of Confederation underway again, Thomas Jefferson proposed a new calendar to mark Albert Gallatin's ascension to the Presidency. Gallatin protested that the *real* Revolution was in 1776, that the Federalist period should be regarded as an aberration, and that commemorating, even by implication, the execution of George Washington might set a hideous precedent.

In its final form, the Jefferson-Gallatin compromise tilizes 1776 as its "Year Zero." Dates prior to the Declaration of Independence continue numbered as they were before, sometimes followed by C.E. for "Christian Era."

A.L.	C.E.	EVENTS
0	1776	Declaration of Independence (July 2); Revolution begins.
7	1783	Treaty of Paris (Sept. 3); Revolution ends.
11	1787	Federalists under Hamilton, Jay, Madison meet in Philadelphia, illegally adopt new "Constitution" creating strong central government.
12	1788	Ratification by ninth and last necessary state (New Hampshire).
13	1789	Constitution in force; Hamilton Secretary of Treasury to George Washington.

* Compiled from the *Encyclopedia of North America*, TerraNovaCom Channel 485-A, by Edward William Bear of Denver, with the kind permission of the editors.

15 1791 Hamilton's Excise Tax passes; angry Pennsylvania farmers rally at Brownsville for beginning of countercoup.

16 1792 Pittsburgh Convention of antitax forces; Washington issues warning proclamation; farmers tarring and feathering tax collectors.

18 1794 15,000 federal troops ordered against farmers; Albert Gallatin joins rebellion; Washington shot in Philadelphia; Constitution declared null and void; Gallatin proclaimed President; Hamilton disappears.

19 1795 Caretaker government organized; Gallatin declares general amnesty; all taxes repealed; property and rights restored to Federalists, Tories.

20 1796 Gallatin confirmed by Congress; calls for neutral stance between England and France, humane Indian policies, and revision of Articles.

21 1797 New Articles ratified with emphasis on civil and economic rights; Northwest Territory "land certificates" liquidate war debts; governments otherwise forbidden to coin or print money.

24 1800 Gallatin re-elected (second term); Jeffersonian weights and measures.

27 1803 Gallatin and Monroe arrange Louisiana Purchase, borrowing from private sources against value of land.

28 1804 Gallatin re-elected (third term); Hamilton killed in Prussian duel; Stevens invents steamboat.

30 1806 England attempts to restrict shipping; Gallatin commissions privateers to defend American vessels.

31 1807 French uphold American sea rights; *Chesapeake* drives off British war vessels; Forsyth invents percussion system for firearms; English outlaw slave trade; Jefferson begins antislavery crusade.

32 1808 Hundreds of British ships captured or sunk by American private navies, thousands of English seamen desert; first ocean-going steamship, *Confederation* (Stevens), sinks British warship; Gallatin re-elected (fourth term).

35 1811 Jefferson wounded in assassination attempt, kills assailant.

36 1812 Gallatin announces retirement; Edmond Genêt elected President.

37 1813 Privateers' League lawsuit overthrows Doctrine of Sovereign Immunity.

38 1814 Gallatin publishes *Principles of Liberty,* systematic expansion on philosophies of Paine, Jefferson.

39 1815 Privateer Admiral Jean LaFitte publicly denounces slavery.

40 1816 Genêt re-elected (second term), proposes abolition of slavery, reparatory landgrants to slaves in West.

41 1817 Slavery abolished for children born after A.L. 44.

42 1818 Gallatin publishes *Rule of Reason,* advocating nonbinding voluntarist legislature; in England, Guy Fawkes Day explosion of Parliament believed precipitated by Gallatin's works; British government falls.

43 1819 Collier-Shaw percussion revolver; patent system breaks down under Gallatin's criticism of government enforcement of monopolies.

44 1820 Jefferson elected President; all slavery abolished; Jefferson publicly rejects offers of Presidency for life, threatens resignation.

45 1821 Mexico grants land to American settlers in Texas.

47 1823 Monroe drafts "Jefferson Doctrine": political isolationism, elimination of trade barriers, moral support for colonies asserting "fundamental right to secede."

48 1824 Jefferson re-elected (second term) inter-

nal combustion engine; mechanical calcu-
lators.

50   1826 Jefferson dies in office; Monroe assumes
          Presidency.

52   1828 Monroe elected.

54   1830 First steam railroad (Philadelphia).

55   1831 Monroe dies in office; John C. Calhoun
          assumes Presidency.

56   1832 Calhoun elected; Nathan Turner first Ne-
          gro Congressman; Britain experiments
          with Gallatinist legislative system; Cal-
          houn's new Indian policies denounced by
          Gallatin.

57   1833 Britain abolishes slavery, exempts Ire-
          land; British government falls.

59   1835 Colt's double-action revolver; Gold dis-
          covered in Georgia.

60   1836 Gallatin comeback defeats Calhoun; Tex-
          icans declare independence; Santa Anna
          defeated and killed at San Antonio.

64   1840 Gallatin retires again; Sequoyah Guess
          elected President.

65   1841 Mexico declares war on Old United
          States, Republic of Texas.

66   1842 U.S. forces in Mexico; Sequoyah's "Read-
          ing" of Gallatin at Buena Vista causes
          massive Mexican desertions; Mexico City
          surrenders itself; Sequoyah felled by
          sniper; Osceola assumes Presidency.

68   1844 Osceola elected.

69   1845 Jonathan Browning Arms Company es-
          tablished, Nauvoo, Illinois.

70   1846 Revolution in California; Hamiltonian
          "republic" declared under "Emperor"
          Joshua Norton.

71   1847 Self-contained cartriges for revolvers.

72   1848 Gold discovered in California; Gallatinite
          uprisings throughout Europe; Jefferson
          Davis elected President.

73   1849 Gallatinite revolution in Canada.

74   1850 Gallatinite revolutions in Mexico, China.

75   1851 News of pogroms against Gallatinists in

California; air conditioning; Lucille Gallegos born, San Antonio.

76 1852 Albert Gallatin dies; mourning observed throughout world; rumors of celebrations in Prussia, California; Gifford Swansea elected President.

79 1855 First all-steel steamship crosses Atlantic.

80 1856 Arthur Downing elected President.

81 1857 Gallatinite revolt suppressed in India; British government falls.

82 1858 Joint paper on evolution by Darwin, Wallace.

83 1859 Downing dies in office; President Harriet Beecher advocates banning alcohol.

84 1860 Lysander Spooner elected President; Gallatinite revolts in Italian states; Chinese Gallatinists overthrow Hamiltonians in California.

85 1861 Great Northern Pacific railroad begins transcontinental operations, opens extension into Republic of California.

88 1864 Spooner re-elected (second term); Moray automatic pistol.

89 1865 Actor John Wilkes Booth murdered by obscure Illinois lawyer.

90 1866 Mexico, U.S. negotiate Confederation.

91 1867 Elisha Gray invents telephone; smokeless powder; Alaska purchased by Texas consortium.

92 1868 Spooner re-elected (third term), proposes Gallatinist legislature in U.S.; telephone service established, Atlanta to Philadelphia.

93 1869 Litigation establishes women's vote; Gallatinist legislature adopted, Articles revised.

95 1871 Great Chicago Fire: official explanation ridiculed in press.

96 1872 Spooner re-elected (fourth term).

99 1875 Electric Street Railway (Chicago).

100 1876 Centennial; Giant "Statue of Gallatin"

erected in Lake Michigan; Spooner re-elected (fifth term).

101 1877 Hovercraft; A. G. Bell invents mechanical larynx for chimpanzees.

102 1878 Manhattan "war" between private security companies.

104 1880 Spooner retires; Jean-Baptiste Huang elected President.

108 1884 "Moving pictures" popular, Chicago; Huang re-elected (second term).

109 1885 Canada joins U.S.–Mexico negotiations.

110 1886 Geronimo, a Mexican national, becomes first congressman to represent others, *but not himself;* wireless telephony; simian suffrage.

112 1888 Great Eastern Blizzard; first electrically heated streets (Edison); Frederick Douglass elected President.

115 1891 First transatlantic wireless relays betting on American horseraces; Manfred von Richthofen born, Silesia.

116 1892 Benjamin Tucker elected President.

117 1893 North American Confederacy includes Alaska, California, Canada, Cuba, Mexico, Newfoundland, Old United States, and Texas; first heavier-than-air powered flight (Lillienthal); British Gallatinists propose Confederation with North America; British government falls.

120 1896 Tucker re-elected (second term); dirigible invented.

124 1900 Capital moved to center of continent; Tucker re-elected (third term).

125 1901 First transcontinental aeroplane flight.

127 1903 Dirigible *City of Akron* flies nonstop, length of continent and return; first all-talking movie (*Ragtime Dance*) premiers, New Orleans.

128 1904 Nicaragua Canal; Tucker re-elected (fourth term).

130 1906 San Francisco Earthquake, Fire, and Barbecue.

132 1908 Tucker re-elected (fifth term).

133 1909 First transatlantic aeroplane flight; first transpacific dirigible flight; "Sydney Tea Party": all government officials thrown in harbor.

136 1912 Albert Jay Nock elected President.

138 1914 Prussia attacks bordering countries; Continental Congress declares neutrality; Confederate volunteers launch Thousand Airship Flight.

140 1916 Nock re-elected (second term).

141 1917 Goddard rockets decimate Prussian air squadrons; revolt sparked by heavy broadcasting of Gallatin's works.

142 1918 Influenza epidemic; round-the-world dirigible flotilla dispenses experimental vaccine.

144 1920 Nock re-elected (third term).

146 1922 Nuclear pile demonstrated (Chicago).

148 1924 Nock re-elected (fourth term).

151 1927 Television; dolphin communications; fission power plant (Chicago).

152 1928 Cancer linked to malnutrition; H. L. Mencken elected President; lasers.

153 1929 Fusion power plant (Detroit); Ooloorie Eckickeck P'wheet born, somewhere in Pacific; heart-lung machine.

156 1932 Jet aeroplane; fusion-powered dirigibles; Mencken re-elected (second term).

157 1933 Mencken assassinated; Continental Congress chooses F. Chodorov successor; cetaceans join Confederacy; heart transplants.

160 1936 Gallatinite revolution in Spain; Chodorov elected.

161 1937 Artificial satellite launched, southern Mexico.

163 1939 Edward William Bear born, Saint Charles Town, N.A.C, and Denver, U.S.A.

164 1940 Rose Wilder elected President.

165 1941 First simian in orbit reads works of Gallatin, plays chess with porpoises at

Emperor Norton University (loses); Hamiltonian coup in Hawaii; 3-D television.

168   1944   Wilder re-elected (second term); F. K. Bertram born, Boston.

170   1946   Clarissa MacDougall Olson born, Laporte.

172   1948   Wilder re-elected (third term); limb-regeneration demonstrated.

173   1949   Lunar expedition establishes colony; laser pistol sights.

176   1952   A. Rand elected, becomes first President to travel to Moon.

177   1953   Gallatinist and Hamiltonian revolutions rock Africa.

178   1954   Jennifer Ann Smythe born (stasis delay).

179   1955   Eugene Guccione invents power cell.

180   1956   Russians fire on Antarctican colonists; Continental Congress issues warning; Czar declares war; Rand re-elected (second term.

181   1957   Russians attack Alaska, aid Hamiltonians in Hawaii, invade Japan; Admiral Heinlein wins decisively at Bering Straits; Russians suffer huge losses in Antarctica, Japan, Hawaii.

182   1958   "Operation Sequoyah": heavy wireless and television, tons of written propaganda employed against Russian homeland.

183   1959   Lunar colonists beam continuous transmissions into Russia; government collapses; Czar disappears.

184   1960   Hamiltonians attempt Lunar coup, survivors are "spaced"; Robert LeFevre elected President.

188   1964   LeFevre re-elected (second term); Dora Jayne Thorens born, San Francisco.

192   1968   Mars colony, Coprates Canyon; "None of the Above" wins election.

194   1970   Probability Broach discovered in search for faster-than-light drive.

196   1972   John Hospers elected President; asteroid colonies established.
197   1973   First stable Broach.
200   1976   Bicentennial; Dissolutionist Faction; Hospers re-elected (second term).
201   1977   First "large-sample" Broach.
202   1978   John Jay Madison founds Hamilton Society, Laporte.
203   1979   Hamiltonians lose final foothold in Uganda.
204   1980   Hospers re-elected (third term); Extrasolar radio signals detected.
208   1984   Jennifer A. Smythe elected President.
210   1986   First contact with human (V. Meiss) on other side of Broach.
211   1987   First human travels through Broach (E. W. Bear, Denver); Hamiltonian conspiracy; Seventh Continental Congress convened.